JARITA STEWARD

YAMANU

CREATOR SERIES BOOK 1

YAMANU
The Creator Series Book 1

ISBN: 978-1-943342-25-9

Dr. JaRita R. Steward
Jaritasteward@gmail.com

Published by: Destined To Publish | Flossmoor, Illinois
www.DestinedToPublish.com

PROLOGUE

Have you ever imagined something so vivid, so real you automatically tucked it into the category of a dream? It seemed to run away with itself until you were no longer guiding your own imagination, but it was guiding you. The nuances and details so clear and unforgettable that imagined things transform themselves from dreams to a memory of a time long gone by? A time you will never forget because it is as real as any memory you have ever held dear. Then you wonder, on occasion, was it real? Were you truly here? Are these bits and pieces of places you can see so vividly in your mind really places you have journeyed in body as well as mind? How could you ever really know the truth of it? To that dream turned into a memory, I owe thanks. Thank you for sharing Amani with me.

DEDICATION

To the creator for all the creative power he has invested in me, I owe thanks. For placing me in the womb of a woman who has encouraged, motivated, and uplifted me since birth, I am all the more grateful. This book is dedicated first to God, secondly to my Mother, who fell in love with Amani as I did, and lastly to my Aunt Barbara, who excitedly embarked on the journey and encouraged its growth.

TABLE OF CONTENTS

CHAPTER 1

Once upon a time, there was a super, normal, boring girl...no seriously that's how it starts.

Sitting at my desk, attempting to multi-task, I realized that I'd made a grave error. The plan was to walk to my classroom, grab my purse, walk right through the side door a few steps from my room, hop in the car with Aseema, and head to lunch. Instead, I'd walked to my room, grabbed my purse, sat down at my desk, and began looking over a lesson plan on one screen while watching music videos on a second screen and randomly marking reminders in my calendar as they came to me.

My aunt tells me that this isn't a sign of ADD but rather that I'm creative. So, the chaos of my mind is attributed to the fact that it is consistently attempting to create something new. I didn't think this would fly with my hungry best friend once she caught up with me. She did, on the other hand, carry a great deal of respect for my auntie, who had practically taken her in as a young girl.

Personally, I believed my aunt was incapable of any human vices. She was superhuman in her own way. That's why when she asked me to move back home, I acquiesced without much of a fight. I missed her, and although she looked no older than 40, I knew she was beginning to age. It was in her walk, her gradual decrease in pace. If she needed me, I wanted to be there for her. Staring out the window, I contemplated this recent move. Fresh out of college, I went straight to a work-study in Africa, where I taught the brightest, most eager students. I learned just as much from them as they learned from me. After two years there, I convinced Aseema that South Korea needed us for the next year. Then Spain called out to me for a year. Four years abroad had been the most amazing adventure of my life. Had Auntie not summoned me back home when she did, I might have taken off again.

I had to admit it felt nice to be back home on the south side of Illinois, teaching an amazing group of third graders. This was, of course, the least exotic place I'd ever taught, but it was home. It was mostly home because here is where Auntie Rami lived and had raised me. I would have liked to have traveled more, but family came first, especially having one that consisted of three people, including me.

My parents, after being married for 15 years, had given up hope of ever having a child. Inexplicably, no matter how or what they tried, they couldn't conceive. Friends and church members were on their third or fourth child while my parents simply prayed for one. It was my mother's fortieth birthday when her prayers were answered. On the day of her birthday, she woke up vomiting. Surprise, surprise, Mrs. Nichols, you're two months pregnant! Though they were shocked and amazed, they rejoiced in the fact that their prayers had been answered. They hadn't even been trying anymore. Having given up on the painful fertility treatments and disappointment, my parents were considering adoption when I came along.

Aunt Ramla says that I was a joyful baby, even in my mother's womb. I was always on the go, kicking and dancing around, ready to get out and see the world. The story she tells is that when I was born, I came out with one soft cry and immediately opened my eyes to observe my surroundings. I'm told that I came out looking around imperiously, ready to take over things and run the world!

"You looked quite queenly, even then Mali," Auntie would say solemnly. Crazy how we read into such arbitrary things. So, they named me Malika, which means "Queen," saying that someday I would rule. Cute, right? Well, I'll be 25 in two weeks, and the only thing I rule is a third-grade classroom. I wonder what my parents would think of their little Malika? A car accident took them when I was four years old, so all my memories of them are a bit faded and blurry now. Auntie took me right in since Mommy was her big sister and only family. Daddy had other family members, but they lived mostly in Jamaica. I think they'd like my little third-grade kingdom. It's a good little kingdom, but while my subjects are very loving, it is certainly far from a world domination gig.

With a sigh, I wrote in my personal planner under tomorrow's date, "*March 11th, try to take over the world.*" Tapping my pen on my lip in thought, I tried to come up with how many hours that might take; was it a 9-5 type planning process? I might have to take some days off work. Just when I decided it may take me more than 24 hours, my best friend Aseema walked into the room. She looked amazing, built like one of the Dora Milaje: slender, gently muscled, and graceful. Walking up behind me, she peeked over my shoulder at the calendar, where I was drawing hearts around my world domination reminder.

"Gee Brain, what are we going to do tonight?" she asked, her usually lovely alto voice taking on a squeaky yet dopey tone.

Holding in a giggle, I sighed loudly in exasperation and offered the expected response. "The same thing we do every night, Pinky: try to take over the world!" With my fingers curled up dramatically, grasping at the air like it was the world I was searching for, I laughed manically while Aseema chuckled.

"Growing weary of teaching third grade, sis?"

"Not at all, but a girl has got to plan ahead. Big picture here!"

"Well, my big picture at 11:30 on a Tuesday is lunch. We have an hour and a half…no wait," she checked her watch. "Now we have an hour and 20 minutes to go out and grab a bite to eat before the next PD session starts. You wasted ten of your minutes plotting world domination."

With a half glare, I said sullenly, "I used five of those minutes to lesson plan and watch videos, three to reflect on life, and only two minutes went towards world domination." She glanced at my computer screen from whence Justin Timberlake was bringing sexy back and gave me a look that clearly said she wasn't impressed. Sticking my tongue out at her, I grabbed my purse off my desk, turned Justin off, and walked toward the door singing softly, "I'm bringing sexy back, yeah."

My mouth watered as the server brought out a plate of tacos with a side of Elote and guacamole. Yum! We both dug in with gusto, and I had a mouth full of delicious, loaded chicken taco when I noticed a rather attractive man staring at me from across the room. I paused mid-chew to ask Aseema, "Is there something on my face?" Her jaw dropped, and her eyes widened in horror. I chewed and swallowed quickly before patting my face down with a napkin. That's when I noticed her shoulders shaking with laughter. I balled up the napkin and threw it at her with a look of reproach. She caught it easily. That girl and her reflexes. While I was super clumsy, the world seemed to make way for her every movement. Furniture and other inanimate objects tended to jump in my path while moving out of her way in deference. Talk about irritating.

Once her laughter subsided, she said, "There is nothing on your face. Why do you ask?"

"Don't look now, but there is an attractive man behind you who was just staring at me." I peeked up from beneath my lashes, and he was looking at me again. This time he flashed a smile of appreciation. I looked down quickly, unsure of how to respond. My interactions with men were limited, and my flirting skills were nonexistent. Aseema pushed her knife towards the floor in a casual, "accidentally on purpose" motion, then leaned down to pick it up, glancing up at the stranger who had started talking to the waitress. She stiffened slightly before sitting up quickly and digging back into her food. After chewing thoughtfully, she said, "Are you ovulating? He's a nice-looking guy. Maybe you're looking at him because you need a little loving. Wink at him, see if he'll come over."

Without thinking, I glanced over at the handsome stranger again. He looked to be about 6'2. He had startlingly white teeth against smooth brown skin. Something was enticing yet disturbing about his eyes; I couldn't quite decide which was the most prominent when looking at him. They were mesmerizing, a warm brown that sparkled with mischief. The sun was hitting him just so that the light seemed to seep from him and around his chair. It looked quite odd and was casting a greenish glow. But he wasn't wearing green; I wondered where the green was coming from? Then it dawned on me that I was staring, and I looked down quickly when he tossed me another saucy grin. When was my cycle due? Maybe Aseema was right. What was going on with me?

"Mali, it is a perfectly normal occurrence for a woman to find a man attractive. You're not dead, for goodness sake. It is past time for you to let go of the past."

I so didn't want to go there. "I have to go to the bathroom," I said, moving that way.

"You can't run from your hunger Rita," she teased, quoting an old Eddie Murphy film. I ignored her and headed toward the bathroom quickly. From the corner of my eye, I saw her ease out of the booth and walk towards the man's table. Oh God, please don't let her embarrass me, I thought, speeding up so I could at least hide while she meddled.

Quickly using the facilities, I found myself standing in front of the mirror, looking myself over. I had shoulder-length brown hair that I'd had my beautician straighten and add blonde highlights to. High cheekbones and almond-shaped eyes in a deep gold with green flecks were framed by my hair. Depending on the season, my eyes would be either more gold or more green.

My aunt called me fair-skinned because I was the lightest one in my family with what L'Oréal foundation told me was a "warm honey" colored complexion. I liked to think of myself as Beyoncé brown since it boosted my fragile ego. At 5'5, I wasn't exactly tall, but I wasn't particularly petite either at a size ten with a curvy figure that included double-D breasts, a small waist, and round hips. I was a cute girl if I did say so myself, with full lips and straight teeth. Not regal and supermodel fine like my bestie, but a cutie; and these breasts were a gift!

Smiling in the mirror, I gave them a saucy fluff to make sure they were sitting up just right. I'd never had self-esteem problems, but my track record with men was so bad. Like Michael Jackson bad. One day, Auntie had looked me in the eye and told me I had terrible taste in men. She wasn't wrong. The fact that I noticed the guy in the restaurant was a good indication he was bad news. Aseema was right, though. It had been quite some time since I'd had any attention of the male kind. Most of the time, I felt like I was invisible in that regard. Shaking myself out of that downward spiral, I smoothed my soft coral A-line dress down over my hips, did a little twirl and point in my snakeskin pumps, then sashayed out of the bathroom.

"You done with your 'woe is me, relationships never work out for me' pity party?" Aseema asked as soon as I sat down.

With my chin up higher, I responded maturely, "Whatever, turd breath." She laughed, commenting under her breath that the third graders were rubbing off on me as I looked around for my staring buddy. A jolt of shock went through me when I realized he was gone. As if reading my thoughts, my best friend said quietly, "He left, must not have been the one."

"What did you say to him?" I countered dryly.

She looked startled before grinning sheepishly and saying, "I paid the bill." I rolled my eyes and dug back into my taco and Elote, trying not to feel the disappointment starting to descend on me. We always fought over who would pay, so that was no big deal, but for the guy to leave when I was strongly considering…

Aseema cut off my thoughts. Laying a hand over mine as I reached for my bottle of Pineapple Jarritos, she said, "You are special, my lady. More than you know. The Father-Man," she corrected, "of your dreams will be more than a pretty face who winks at you the right way. He will see your light and cherish it. He will be your flame."

I turned my palm over and squeezed her hand briefly before picking up my drink and taking a sip. "You and your little romance novel fantasies. That's all fine and good, friend, but I'm just looking to get laid. Where is my king for the night?" I winked at her before giving a sassy shimmy. Aseema rolled her eyes, not taking me seriously at all. She knew me way better than that, but it was fun to joke. I'd only been with one guy technically and that had ended in such a life-changing way that I still hadn't quite recovered. Oh, to be young and dumb again. Wait…no, I was still pretty young and dumb, I thought sullenly.

Before I could journey too far into those depressing thoughts, Aseema fisted a hand in her short curls and tossed her head back in a classic "I'm too full to go on" pose. She looked like a high-end model with her close-cropped, coiled hair, which set off her beautiful bone structure. On top of that, she wore a daring neon green that made her chocolate dream skin glow. I quickly snapped a picture, but she caught me, so I snapped off a few more as she switched poses dramatically.

Sitting around eating one day, which was one of our favorite pastimes (yes, eating…we work out to make up for it), we had agreed I was the color of honey almond peanut butter (her favorite), and she was the color of the dark chocolate dream, which was my favorite. Reading my thoughts, or so it seemed, she looked at me and said, "Stop looking at me like I'm your favorite flavor of peanut butter, perv. It's time for us to get back to work. Send me those pics before you post them. They need to be approved."

With an over-the-top leer, I replied, "One day you'll stop spurning my advances and realize you want me just as much as I want you." Rolling her eyes, she motioned the waitress over for to-go containers while I sent her the pictures before digging out money for a tip.

I swear I'm going to start meal prepping next week…I know I told myself that last week, but I have the best intentions.

I was trying not to nod off during our afternoon professional development session. There was nothing like a heavy lunch to take the excitement clean out of School Institute Day activities. I totally blame the tacos. As my head was slowly starting to meet my chest, I jerked awake. Looking down at the floor, I was trying to shake off the heaviness of sleep when I noticed something on Aseema's shoe that looked odd. My bestie is meticulous about her appearance. Had I not known her all her life, I'd think she served in the military because she is just that regimented. Not a hair or article of clothing out of place. Uncharacteristically, there was some type of goo on her shoe. I nudged her as she unabashedly dozed next to me.

"Hunh?" she asked blearily.

"Sis, there is something green on your shoe."

Half-interestedly she looked down, but as her eyes landed on her shoe, her reaction threw me completely off guard. Without another word, she jumped up and high-tailed it out of the room. It was still her same graceful movements but with an urgency I didn't quite get. As I said, she's super careful about her appearance, but we both taught in Africa, living and teaching in hot, dusty lodgings. She didn't usually trip out about a little mud or whatever that green stuff was. Maybe it was guacamole. I hope I hadn't dropped it on her…dang it.

I looked down at the floor, and a smudge of it was still by her chair. It shimmered like a dull glow, almost like…I stopped mid-thought. No, that was crazy. But it had the same greenish glow as the sunlight hitting that guy's chair earlier. The one who had left the restaurant before I came out of the bathroom to get my mac on. He hadn't even eaten. I'd have to ask Aseema about how he ended up leaving. Maybe he had an emergency call. I looked down again. Maybe I was imagining things, but I couldn't see the smudge of green anymore, just grains of what looked like greenish sand? Something tugged at my memory. Blinking rapidly, I tried to jar the elusive thought to the forefront, but nothing happened. It was like the memory I was reaching for was obscured by a fog.

People around me started moving and I realized the session had ended. We were on a five-minute break, but Aseema still hadn't returned so I went to search for her. I always kept baby wipes in my purse; perhaps that would help with her stain. I babysat for a friend once and have been hooked on baby wipes since. Who knew those things work for everything? Just as I was nearing the bathroom door, my archenemy (yes, teachers can have those) came out of the bathroom, shoving into me rudely. She was the group leader who would equate to the teacher's version of the movie *Mean Girls'* Regina George – all grown up and still a complete troll.

"I'm sorry Regina, I seem to have accidentally bumped your broad shoulder with my chest cavity. Are you ok? I truly hope I didn't injure you." My smile was full of mock sweetness, and her features formed into an acidic smirk. In true mean girl fashion, two of our colleagues took positions on each side of her, arms crossed, looking like the worst cliché. Really? We are all grown women. In fact, these grown women had a good 15 plus years on me. Yet Regina had been on a personal mission to defame and aggravate me since the principal named me third-grade team lead at the start of the school year. We were well into March, and her antics over the past months had grown increasingly asinine for a woman who walked around repeatedly declaring, "I'm a professional." Yeah? Well, act like it, cretin, I thought sourly.

"Stop calling me Regina, team leader. I'd hate to have to report your juvenile behavior to the union. Then you just might lose your little team lead title. God forbid someone with more than two years of teaching experience take on the position. That would be too much, like, right?"

Oops! Had I called her Regina out loud again? I had to watch that. Assessing her, I hated to admit it, but Regina was a pretty lady – nicely dressed, tall, long legs, a sassy bob. Her friends Karen and Gretchen were basic. I could see why she kept them around as they added to her appeal. But right now, with her round features screwed up into a condescending sneer, she looked like the mistress of evil that she was. OOOOH, nice! New title! We could call her Maleficent. No, no, no...I liked Maleficent too much. Regina could be Queen Ingris. I'm Maleficent, I'm the freaking dragon...but in my version, Conall lives, and we have little dark Fae babies. Yeah...

Regina, or Queen Ingris, whose actual name is Barbara Eisner was staring at me expectantly. I had gotten lost in my head again. I do that a lot. Maybe Aseema was right, I was spending way too much time with my kingdom of third graders.

"No problem, Barbara. Enjoy the rest of the Institute Day activities," I said dismissively and began to walk past her, continuing my journey to the lady's room. Out of the corner of my eye, I saw her reach out a hand as though to stop me when she was intercepted by elegant fingers that banded around her wrist like steel. Aseema and Barbara stood eye to eye, both about 5'10, towering over my 5'5 frame – well, 5'8 in my pumps, but they were in heels as well, so there was that.

Barbara practically snarled at Aseema, snatching her wrist out of her hand. I knew from experience she was only able to wrestle that arm free because Aseema had allowed it. I'd made the mistake of playfully grappling with my bestie in the past. Sis was strong. Glancing around, I realized we'd developed a small crowd of curious onlookers. The other grade-level teams knew of the drama going on with the third-grade teachers. We are a nice-sized school catering to grades K-5. Each grade level has its own team and Principal-appointed team leader. Our group of teachers is the largest and most troublesome because we had the veterans who tended to want to stick to their old faithful habits. I think that was Principal Owens' reasoning for choosing me as the team lead.

With only four years in the game, this year making five, I'd taught abroad in Africa, Spain, and South Korea; he figured my varied experiences and youth would make me a good fit. Unfortunately, coming into the district year one and taking on this coveted position didn't sit well with those ladies, most of whom had been in the district for 15 to 20 plus years. Especially when they had discovered I refused to be a "yes man" and acquiesce to their every whim. I'm an Aries, so it's just not in me. So, out of our team of six 3rd grade teachers (seven including me), I had the support of four...two of which were Aseema, and well, me. I strongly support myself. It's a matter of principle.

"Don't touch me, little pit bull. Let your know-it-all friend fight her own battles. She thinks she has it in her to run things, let her prove it." My hackles rose at Regina "Queen Ingris" George (no more calling her by her real name, she was being a real pill) when she called my bestie a pit bull. Aseema didn't play when it came to me and vice versa. Not that she ever really let me battle. She usually swung first and let me ask the questions later. I was more than capable of handling myself, but she was an orphan. She saw Rami and I as her only family, and she didn't take risks to us lightly.

Before I could step in to defend her, Aseema stepped further into Regina/Ingris' space bubble; they were nose-to-nose, so when she spoke quietly, only those of us right up on them could hear. Meaning, Karen (her name is seriously Karen, go figure) and Gretchen whose real name is unfortunately not Gretchen, but Lara Jones, and I were the only others who could hear her soft words.

"Have you ever been locked in a pit bull's jaws?" Aseema let her gaze rove over Barbara's neck menacingly. "Once they have you, the only way out is death or missing a serious chunk of your throat. Don't test me, Barb. This pit bull's bite is deadly." Aseema bared her teeth in a savage gesture that even caused a shiver of fear to go through me. Barbara's hand flew to her throat as her cronies gasped in surprise. Before realizing what she was doing, Barbara took a step back, which caused whispers all around. No one else heard what was said. Aseema's wicked smile remained, and she held the same threatening stance as Barb who was attempting to save face.

Barbara squared her shoulders and said, "I'll make sure those exact words are reported to administration. Brush off your resume bi-." The bell rang, cutting off her words and signaling it was time for the final professional development session. Turning on her heel, Queen Ingris stalked away with her compatriots in tow.

I really needed to get on top of this Maleficent gig; she'd make a magnificent goat. As people began to disperse, I leaned into Aseema, attempting to lighten the mood. "Darn it! What was she about to say? Now I'm going to be left hanging. Bidet? Bibliographer? Bibliophile? Huh, bigot! I bet that's what it was. I got to know; I'm going to go ask."

Aseema finally broke her aggressive stance and grabbed my arm. "Stop being a butt, come on." She tugged me towards the classrooms. I guess we were ditching the afternoon sessions. Sweet.

Around 2:30, Aseema and I had finished a full bag of Hi-Chews and two bags of Boom Chika Pop Popcorn. Don't judge us; ditching afternoon workshops was tiring. I was quite proud of the fact we hadn't broken out the peanut butter yet. *Frozen* was playing on my projector because, well, *Frozen* is far superior to *Frozen II*. As we were singing along to "Let It Go" (I was being a little more dramatic with it than my BFF), the Assistant Principal walked in whistling with the song and plopped down in one of the student desks near the door. The school AP, Kimberly, was one of our few allies in the building. This year was year two of her time as an administrator in District 55, and she suffered many of the same struggles Aseema and I did. She'd worked her way up through the ranks from a fourth-grade teacher to a team lead and now an assistant principal. She was a bit older than us, but her former colleagues still didn't appreciate her impressive climb from colleague to superior over her ten years in the district.

Kim was usually poised, but now she was slumped down in the chair with her suit jacket bunched up to her chin. She kicked off her high heels and bunched frustrated fists in her neat shoulder-length locs. "The cold never bothered me anyway," I sang out, then twirled in my seat dramatically until I was facing Kim. "What's wrong, Assistant Principal Fondren? Wait, are we in trouble?"

I lifted an eyebrow at Aseema, but before I could get the words out, she said quickly, "It was Mali's fault. She's going through some type of mid-twenty life crisis, and I had to get her together." Dang it, I wanted to blame her first. I glared at her as she gave me a knowing stare, fighting to hold back her laughter.

"Institute Days are supposed to be fairly chill, especially when we go through the trouble of hiring an outside presenter," Kim started. "Unfortunately, I just left a meeting with the mean girls Barbara, Karen, and Lara."

"Excuse me," I said, putting up a finger. "I've renamed Barbara 'Queen Ingris' and I'm Maleficent. I am working on the whole turning her into a goat thing, as well as being able to turn myself into a dragon. But it has to be done after my world domination plan is finished. It's already on my calendar for Friday, going into Saturday if necessary. I may need to take the day off."

Kim gave me a caustic look before tilting her head in thought. She was probably imagining Barbara as a goat. "Let me know how that goes," she said with a small smile. "Anyhoo, I had to sit down for the past half hour, listening to the mean girls complain about the two of you. Speaking of which, I'd say that Aseema is

Maleficent in this scenario." Aseema crossed her arms and gave me an evil yet triumphant grin.

"That's not fair! I was totally about to dragon up when Aseema stepped in."

"Nevertheless," Kim said before I could protest further. "They were unable to do much but complain and have their union reps talk about 'how unprofessional' this administration is before letting it go. All we could see on the cameras was you two staring each other down, so it's your word versus theirs because no one else could hear. In the meantime, because you are both union members, it's for them to figure out, and we, as administration, will not be interfering. Either way, it was an irritating waste of my time. So, you both owe me a lunch on a day and at a place of my choosing."

Aseema and I looked at one another and shrugged. Giving Aseema a bullish look, I said, "If you get to be Maleficent, then you've got to buy the lunch. Period." Side-eyeing me, she shrugged again and opened another bag of Hi-Chews. I'm glad she did it, I didn't want to be the one to look greedy. So, I reached over and grabbed another handful before passing the bag to Kim.

"I am sorry you had to endure that, Kim. It was that or go on a covert mission after work and kill her in her sleep. I figured that was the lesser of two evils." Aseema completed her statement by popping another candy into her mouth and chewing angrily.

"She saved you from having to hire three new teachers," I said solemnly. "Cause I'd have been her accomplice; besties stick together and all. So, in the end, she did you a solid."

Kimberly shook her head and pushed herself out of her seat, straightening her clothes and smoothing down her hair. "Ladies, you know I'm not tripping about it. I know how the mean girls operate, but it wouldn't be right if I didn't get a free lunch or two after having to hear her mouth. The sessions ended a bit early; everyone is dismissed to go home." She hadn't completed her sentence before I had the projector turned off while Aseema started collecting her things. Laughing at us, she wished us a good night before heading back to her office. Nothing like an extra 30 minutes to…well, not to be at work.

CHAPTER 2

Dreams, reality, and the parts in between.

His eyes bore into mine. The gaze was so intense, I wilted under it, yet I wasn't afraid. Strangely I felt a sense of safety and homecoming in those eyes. He reached out to me, and without hesitation, I walked right into his arms. Though he had to be all of 6'5-6'6, my head tucked right under his chin. Absently I wondered if I was wearing a pair of five-inch heels... I wouldn't put it past me. I can't pass up a good heel; it does wonders for the legs and butt. His hands, caressing my back, brought my eyes back to his. He was beautiful. Not in the traditional sense, but there was something regal about him. Broad shoulders stretched above me, which led to lightly muscled arms that could become deeply muscled if flexed. His skin was a chocolate mocha color, smooth and creamy like my favorite Starbucks coffee. But I was most mesmerized by his strong, full lips; I hesitated on them entirely too long before allowing my gaze to travel up to eyes that looked like an endless swirl of warm caramel.

"We don't have much time," he said, breaking me out of the drowning sensation I felt looking into his eyes. I frowned up at him in confusion. Time? We should have loads of time. If I was going to dream about a tall, dark, and handsome man then the last thing I wanted to do was rush!

"Who are you?" I asked, slightly startled at my voice's breathy quality. It was as though standing in his arms was sucking all the air out of the room. My breathing was coming out in short pants that were honestly starting to embarrass me. He hesitated before giving me a sad smile and tucking a rope-like strand of hair behind my ear. I froze. When did I get locs? Beautiful, long sister locs hung past my waist in a balayage of red tones. I'd always wanted sister locs but never had the courage to commit. What else was different about me in this dream?

"I knew you would forget me."

I was startled at the sadness in his voice and reached up to cup his cheek in a gesture I shouldn't have been as comfortable with as I was. This man was a stranger to me…yet…I'd been dreaming about him my whole life. How could this be? He was so familiar, and there was a sense of peace wrapping around me like an old blanket. It was my dream, I thought absently, and if I dreamed somebody like this up, my imagination was on point!

Removing my palm from his face, he kissed it gently before saying, "It's time to come home, moto wangu. We don't have long. We need you." He leaned down and kissed me lightly on the forehead. From the barest brush of his lips, shivers coursed down my spine. "I need you, Malika." The way he said my name with a hint of an accent I couldn't quite place but sounded oh-so-familiar sent those shivers places they shouldn't go. Not to mention the forehead kiss! Why did men do that? It was such a turn-on. I tried not to melt into a puddle in front of him and instead focused on what he was saying. Auntie Ramla always said dreams were messages from God that we were too busy to hear from him in the daytime. So, I tried to focus. I'm sure God wasn't telling me to jump this fine man's bones, though. No Mali, no…that's not the message, I chastised my wayward mind.

The handsome stranger tapped my temple. "Still unable to slow that chaotic mind of yours down. It is good to know some things never change." He leaned in to kiss me again, this time aiming for my lips. I thought maybe I was right; God wants me to-

"Mali! You're going to be late, my love. You've hit the snooze button three times. I'll put on the coffee, rise and shine!"

I sat up in my bed, legs tangled in my sheets, wondering if the great prophetess Ramla knew she had just interrupted the most action I'd had in… well, never mind. What I really wanted to do was curl back up and finish talking to Mr. Sexy. But I dared a peek at the clock and groaned. Ugh, you'd think my body would be used to the time change by now. But I'd been jumping time zones so much in the past few years; it was as though my body was rebelling against this recent one.

Attempting to get my bearings together, I dissected my dream as my aunt shuffled around, no doubt not only turning on my Keurig but also making breakfast. There were some perks that accompanied moving back in with my kooky aunt. The hunk in my dreams had called me "moto wangu," which translates to "my flame." Weird. That wasn't a common saying or something I'd even dreamed up. He said, "we need you." Then he said "he" needed me; my body reacted at that thought…and the forehead kiss, then the almost lip lock. After pondering another few minutes, I scrambled out of bed to check the app on my iPhone; Aseema was right, my cycle was on its way. I usually became a bit of a tramp around this time. Well, in my thoughts that is.

I washed and dressed quickly, all the while recapping my dream, which was a record for me because my focus is not so good. Surprisingly that little quirk works well when you teach rambunctious third graders. I went into the kitchen to have a quick breakfast with my aunt, having decided during my morning routine to share my dream with the hood prophetess.

"Must've been some dream," Aunt Ramla said with a knowing smile. I cut her a quick look before digging into my plate of scrambled eggs, sausage, and homemade biscuits. "What do you know Shangazi?" Her eyes widened, and a strange smile touched her lips. I'd grown fluent in Spanish, Swahili, and French, and my Korean was so-so. I was like a sponge when it came to languages, soaking them up quickly. Occasionally foreign words slid out, and my aunt bore it well.

"You moaned aloud, is all." Her back was to me as she grabbed my cup from the Keurig, so I couldn't see her face to know whether or not she was joking. Surely a forehead kiss did NOT make me moan. I couldn't be that hard up. I was ovulating.

"That's not funny," I said as I continued to savor the homemade biscuits and strawberry jam. God, it was good to be home, if for this alone.

"Yes, it is, but I am curious as to who you were dreaming about. If I need to prepare for a new terrible boyfriend to come around." She sat my coffee in front me with all the right trimmings: cream, Splenda, and a dollop of whip cream. I licked my lips, reached for my cup, took a sip (lest she take it back), and gave her an evil look. She only smiled wider.

"Why don't you tell me? You are the clairvoyant in the family. You are the one who can see what others cannot." Since I was a little girl, people would gravitate toward my aunt. She'd have dreams or see visions and then give people warnings about them. After a lost little girl was found, one of our neighbors inherited half a million dollars. Countless other instances where her "visions" had come to pass helped her develop a name for herself in our little corner of Illinois. Everyone knew the prophetess that lived on 172nd St. That's what she called herself anyway, a prophetess. She said she only knew what God chose to show her, nothing more, nothing less. It didn't help her save my parents, though. Not only had Auntie predicted the day they'd die, but the very hour.

My dad was never a believer, or so I was told. But my mother believed and set her affairs in order to prepare. So, I had a nice amount of savings tucked away that helped me get through college without any loans as well as assist in my travels abroad. I'd barely put a dent in it. My only lavish expense had been my beautiful Tesla. I couldn't resist; I'd had a hard-on for that car forever. So, I splurged on that and occasionally a few nice pairs of boots. I'd lived simply overseas, and now I lived with Rami in a house that was already paid off. But I'd still rather that her vision, prophecy, or whatever it was, had been able to prevent my parent's death. I'd rather have them here with me than the money they'd left. Auntie Ramla always just shook her head and said, "It's not ours to question what God allows."

Auntie looked at me strangely. "You've been thinking about your parents a lot lately. It's hard to continue to go on when your past seems unresolved. Take cheer; everything will be revealed to you in time." I nodded, unwilling to go into it further. Sensing that the subject was closed, Auntie went back to my dream. "Tell me," she said. Without hesitation, I gave her the rundown of my dream, even the odd way the mystery man had called me his flame and said "we," then "he" needed me. The entire time I spoke, she sat quietly, sipping her coffee, nodding here and there. When I finally finished, she asked one question, "What did he look like?"

I tilted my head to the side, trying to figure out how to describe the sexiest man I'd ever seen. Finally, I said, "You know what, I shouldn't have binge-watched that show this weekend. He kind of looked like Cal, but more," I waggled my fingers back and forth. "Celestial. Perfect even. Flawless."

"That good looking, huh?"

"Yes, well, no. Yes, but he looked like he wasn't from this planet. His eyes were surreal, like the colors were swirling. His ears had a point…he may have had wings. I felt something brushing at my fingertips as they rested on his waist….and I… I had long beautiful sister locs. Plus, I was taller or had on five-inch heels. I don't know, but he was huge and muscled and…"

I paused mid-stream of consciousness. I thought she'd be laughing at me, but instead, she was watching me intently as if waiting for something. "Auntie, is everything ok?" Slowly she nodded at me, still nursing her cup. "Come on, prophet woman, spill!" Sitting her cup down and leaning back in her chair, my aunt focused on me intently. She was still a beautiful woman with smooth skin, long ebony hair that flowed to the middle of her back, and a lovely figure she hid in flowing garments of monochromatic colors. Today's ensemble was in shades of green, the colors making it look as though seafoam flowed around her body. At 62 years old, my mother's sister could pass for *my* sister. When I'd asked her why she never married or had children, she told me her calling was not to a husband and children but to something higher. Whatever that was. I'd only ever known her to sell her various preserves, healing ointments, and other assorted brews. Other than that, she worked at the local library and spent a great deal of time reading as well as meditating.

At the moment, she seemed to be taking her time to carefully choose her words. Finally, she said, "Everything will be revealed. Time is irrelevant. You have more of that than most, so live in the moment."

I raised an eyebrow at her. I hated it when she got all "mystical" on me. "Please expound. In English, this time." Standing up, she grabbed my plate and cup from the table. I waited patiently as she placed my flatware and utensils in the sink and then made me a to-go cup of coffee. She knew me so well.

"Your season of terrible men is soon to end. You will be reunited with your true flame. Then it will be time for you to walk into your destiny…together." Handing me my cup, she shooed me out of the door, mulling over her words. I lived 20 minutes from work and somehow always found a way to be late. My leadership skills are awesome! It wasn't until I'd pulled into the school parking lot that I got over the whole true flame and destiny part to realize Auntie hadn't said I'd soon meet this so-called flame of mine but rather I'd be reunited with him. That would indicate I'd already met him…or been with him. But that was impossible; all I'd ever had was terrible.

Surprisingly, I was on time for work. I hadn't meant to do that. Usually, I saved gifts like that for Bosses Day or Kwanzaa, whichever was more convenient. Either way, it worked out and gave me time to get things in order for my little kingdom of third graders. Promptly at eight, I headed down to the lunchroom to lead my group to the classroom. It was a happy moment; we all did our morning group hugs and fist bumps, then we sang cheerfully as we walked in our single file line down the hallway.

As we ventured to our learning station singing quite vociferously Imagine Dragons, we rounded the corner and bumped into Miss Sunshine herself. "Lightning and the thunder…" I trailed off. Queen Ingris, Mrs. Eisner to the children (it was mind boggling that someone married this evil woman), was standing with hands on her hips a few steps from my classroom door. Halting the line with a hand up, sadly cutting off the kids in the middle of their song, I said cheerfully, "Good morning Mrs. Eisner," to show her I wasn't holding a grudge.

"Keep your antics down Malika. Other classes are attempting to learn." Her words were dripping with malice, and I hated the way she said my name. It was in direct opposition to the way my dream man's whispers had sent sexy shivers down my spine. The way she said it felt like razors in the anus. Keeping my smile intact and deciding that yes, I did hold grudges (I'd make an exception for present company only), I responded just as cheerfully. "Learning begins promptly at 8:15. We have 15 minutes to get our students from the cafeteria and settled into the classroom. I find that starting our day off with hugs and songs sets the tone for a positive classroom environment. Please forgive us if our exuberant song disturbed you and your students' morning routines." With my last words, I looked pointedly at her classroom. She hadn't picked up her students from the cafeteria yet. While I rushed down to get my subjects right at eight (or as soon as I entered the building), she tended to wait until about 8:14 before picking them up, spending her time gossiping and spreading her personal brand of evil.

"Unlike certain other brand new, unlearned teachers, I have been working in this district teaching for the past 15 years. I don't need someone with mothers' milk still on their breath telling me how to run my classroom. Keep it down before you get reported to administration again." Her tirade was interspersed with lots of eye rolls and sassy head movements that made me want to simultaneously vomit and punch her in the face. Or, I could vomit on her and *then* punch her in the face. No, no…that wouldn't work. I'd get vomit on my hand. Switch that.

Before I could put my plan into action, one of my most loyal and intelligent subjects stepped out of the third-grade line. She had tiny braids with colorful beads all over her head and was missing about three teeth in front. So, her words came out super cute and with a lisp.

"Mrs. E, you not 'pose to call my teacher by her number-one name in front of us. Why don't you like our song? If you sang with your kids, they might like you too. But my brother says he hated your class cuz you was mean and boring." I stifled my laugh as the rest of my students nodded in agreement. I was about to correct my brave little third grader on how to speak respectfully to adults when, quick as a snake, Mrs. Eisner grabbed Amber by the arm and leaned down right in her face.

Sometimes, you have to grab a third grader gently by the arm to get their attention, but the wince that overcame Amber's face was just too much for me. Regina was hurting my baby. Then she proceeded to whisper harshly in Amber's face, "Your brother was a funky smelling, ill-behaved little boy and didn't know how to mind his manners, just like you." She shook the arm in her grasp with each word and Amber's jaw dropped as her eyes welled up with tears. Without thinking, I grabbed Mrs. Eisner by the shoulder and yanked her away from the trembling child with much more force than I had intended, if the spin of her body was any indication. Our eyes met; shocked, she looked down at me, which I hated. I should've worn a higher heel today. In my sensible wedges, she still towered over me, but I held her gaze stubbornly.

Anger seemed to hum through my veins. I was starting to feel shaky and at odds in my own skin as Barbara spurted in my face, attempting to disentangle my grip on her upper arm. I hadn't realized I was still holding her until she started to struggle. The more she tried to free herself, the more my vision clouded with red. Dimly, I noticed the students were chattering around me. But my eyes were on Barbara's angry expression as it slowly began to morph into one of shock and horror. We were both illuminated by an ever-increasing light. Perhaps someone had pulled a car up outside, but I was too angry to care about anything but the witch in front of me. A tingling sensation started in my hands as my anger simmered. Barbara's eyes were filling with dread when I felt Aseema at my back.

No clue how I knew it was her, she didn't say anything; she just rested a hand on my shoulder for a moment -- the same shoulder connected to the arm keeping Barbara in a death grip with fingertips that were almost burning as they dug into her. I felt no remorse, only a cold focus as energy washed through me in waves. Aseema's grip tightened on my shoulder, "Mwanamke Wangu, Amani," she whispered in my ear.

As if some spell had been broken, slowly my fingertips began to loosen until Barbara was able to pull herself away. She scrambled back quite comically in her four-inch heels. No wonder she had been towering over me like that. Well, that, and she's seriously tall. Suddenly, I felt a pressure in my chest that I couldn't shake. The tingling in my hands was starting to dissipate, but I felt like I was swimming through mud trying to get past the anger still flowing through my veins.

Then Aseema was leading me into the nearby teachers' lounge. Before we could get through the door, Amber called out, "Why was Ms. Nichols glowing?" I looked back stunned. Glowing?

My entire class stood with eyes as large as saucers, staring at me as Aseema half-dragged me to a chair.

Finally, I got out, "Aseema, who is going to watch my subjects? I mean, my-my kids. My students, they're just standing there." I pointed towards the door distractedly as she studied my face; her forehead was furrowed. I wanted to tell her to stop doing that, as it would give her wrinkles, but I was having a hard time just dealing with the sensations flowing through my body. "Mali, Kim was out there. She'll take care of the kids. I'm going to take you home."

"She was? Take me home? Why?" I asked, all in one gust of air; I was surprised she heard me clearly.

"You aren't acting like yourself. Or, rather, you're acting too much like yourself," she muttered. "I think it's best we leave."

"Wait! No!" I yelped, jumping up out of the chair she'd forced me into. The tingling sensation was zinging through my body again. "We're going to play multiplication baseball today and our African folklore unit is supposed to start." There was a traffic jam going on inside my brain as thoughts began to collide, all trying to get out at once. My voice gained strength as they poured out. "Why did Amber say I was glowing? How did I get away without Barbara-Regina George-Queen Ingris bopping me in the head? I had a good grip on her. I guess the extra cardio is working. Wait, oh my God! I need to go check on Amber, is she ok? Eisner really hurt her arm." I started towards the door, but Aseema was in front of me so fast that I halted in my tracks, blinking in astonishment. How had she done that? She moved so quickly. God, I felt dizzy.

"Mwanamke Wangu, Amani."

It was the same thing she'd said in the hallway. "My lady, peace." Why did she keep saying that right now? Since we'd met in third grade, she'd been calling me "my lady." She laughingly said it's because my name means Queen and that's how you addressed royalty. I figured it was just because she heard Auntie Rami say it occasionally. But I let it go and told her instead, "Just don't start calling me your majesty or people will have questions." It had become a running joke between us. But there was something about the way she was saying it. Almost like a balm, it was easing the knot that was still resting in my stomach.

The sunlight was shining on her smooth skin as she stood tall and regal in front of me. Then the oddest thing happened. It was still Aseema in front of me, only taller and more graceful if that were possible. There were even greater differences though -- her ears were pointed and behind her toned shoulders were beautiful… well, wings. What was up with me and seeing people with wings? Was I losing it? They spanned the colors of the rainbow in assorted feathers tucked neatly behind her back. But the most amazing thing was, she glowed! An effusive light seemed to shine from her center and cover her body. My gorgeous best friend looked stunning. But when I met her eyes, they'd hardened into granite.

"Mali," she said, roughly shaking me. "We must go." My eyes were still adjusting. She was flickering in between her normal form and the other unfamiliar, yet also familiar, form. So, I let her lead me towards my car without argument. Somehow, she had my purse and all my things as she rushed me out of the building. Two of the mean girl's trio, Karen and Lara, gave me hard puzzled glares as I was bustled out of the door. From somewhere I could hear mean girl number one, Barbara-Regina George, loudly demanding the police be called on me as Principal Owens tried to calm her. Something was being said about reviewing the cameras, at which point Barbara started to stutter incoherently.

Aseema smirked at me. "She doesn't want them to see her grabbing that poor baby. I bet the parents won't like that one bit. You can't be blamed for trying to protect your students."

I was still too shocked to speak. For some reason, my brain had stalled on the vision of Aseema with wings. My dream man also had them. Come to think of it, I was seeing a lot of winged people lately. Oh God! I'm having a nervous breakdown.

We entered the staff parking lot and headed for my Tesla. It was a used Model 3. On a teacher's salary, that was about as high as I wanted to go without seriously putting a dent in my savings. But I loved my baby. She was a beautiful royal blue, and I called her Tessy. Unfortunately, she hadn't come standard with the sexy man straight out of my dreams who was leaning against her trunk. When his eyes settled on us, he rushed over to grab hold of my right arm as Aseema supported my left.

"Kimoni. What has happened? Why are you here? It's five years early. Mali is struggling to contain her glamour. Something is wrong."

The man nodded, giving Aseema a cryptic look. I was shuffled into the front seat as Aseema let the man take the wheel of Tessy. I didn't know how to feel about letting this stranger drive my baby; I wasn't done paying her off yet. Not to mention, she wasn't used to strangers getting to second base with her. He was touching her gears and revving her engine like he'd known her forever. We peeled out of the parking lot and onto the street pushing 60 in a 30. I wanted to tell tall, dark, and handsome to slow down before he got us a ticket. What was the hurry? But then I really looked at him and my warnings to slow down got caught in my throat. It really was him, the man from my dream. What had Aseema called him? Kimoni? As in 'great man'? Auntie Ramla would get a kick out of that. Look Auntie, remember how all my exes were terrible? This guy's name literally means 'great man'! Can't go wrong there, right? She was the one who always said names carried great weight and meaning to how a person's life would play out.

Finally clueing into the conversation swirling around me, I found myself confused. Aseema and Kimoni were talking about a war? About someone having found me and my father being sick? My Father is dead. What are they talking about?

"What are you two talking about?"

They both gave me bleak looks that were laced with sympathy or…pity? I wasn't sure which, but, either way, I didn't like it. "I don't know what's going on or what happened back there, but I had a dream about you last night Mr. Sexy Stranger who is molesting my Tessy." I gave him a hard look of admonition, as he turned wary eyes on me. "And you," I continued pointing at Aseema. "You had wings! You had pointy ears and wings. And wait," I exclaimed, pointing at Kimoni. "You had wings in my dream as well. Side note, can I call you Ki?" I don't know why that seemed right to me, but it fit the handsome man who seemed to be sucking the air out of my car with his very presence. Then his hypnotic eyes focused on me, and I really could not breathe. Without breaking eye contact, I cracked the window, hoping to gulp in some air.

"It's what you've always called me Mali," he said gently. Still I jumped, startled. He knew my name? He knew my name! Wait, that's what I'd always called him? How? When? Had we met anywhere outside of my dreams, I would have remembered. There was nothing forgettable about this man. Before I could respond, he threw the car into a smooth U-turn and dipped off down an alley between houses. "What are you doing?" I asked. With a grim set to his lips, he said, "We're being followed."

I turned to look at my bestie in disbelief and was further stunned when I saw her pulling two throwing knives from her clothing, which was impossible given the snug fit of her pantsuit. What the Deuce Bigalow, Male Jigalow is going on here? "I will keep you safe, Mwanamke wangu. On my honor and with my life." Ki met her eyes in the rear-view mirror, and they gave each other the barest of nods. Then she opened the door and leaped out of the car. We'd sped up coming out of the alley, so we were going much faster than I'd thought. I gazed out the back window stunned as Aseema landed on her feet, somehow the door had closed behind her. A black Audi drove into the alley and four men hopped out, effusing green light. Quickly they surrounded my best friend. My heart was beating triple time with fear, but she only smiled, dropping into a crouch and holding her knives at the ready. There was a blur of movement and then Ki turned so I could no longer track the fight. How I'd been able to track it from this distance, going this fast stalled my brain for a moment.

My vision was good, but not that good! Suddenly I was feeling lightheaded. Snapping out of my shocked state, I grabbed Ki's forearm and pleaded for my friend. "Please, please, we have to go back and save her. Aseema is my sister, she's all I have next to Auntie Ramla, we must go back and help her!"

Those eyes focused on me again and my breath caught. Who was this man? He was causing some respiratory symptoms that I'd never had before he arrived on the scene. "Don't fear for her, she'll dispatch them quickly." His slight accent struck me again. How did he walk out of my dreams and into my life like this? Breathe girl, I reminded myself, breathe girl, breathe! The day's events came crashing through my mind. It was only 8:45, what was happening to my life? How did this day go from sexy dreams, delicious breakfast with Auntie, and singing with my kids to this? Fights with co-workers, wings, pointy ears, car chase with the Zaddy behind the wheel and my bestie fighting bad guys (I assume they were bad guys and not closing in for a five-some) in an alley? Quickly I leaned down and put my head between my knees, breathing in and out.

"What are you doing down there?" Ki asked, confusion coloring his tone.

"I'm trying not to pass out."

He was quiet for another moment. Finally, he asked, "Breathing into your feminine parts prevents you from…passing out?" If this whole situation weren't so wild, I might have laughed. It was like some crazy dream. Wait! I sat up quickly and paid for it when the blood rushed to my head. Fighting the light headedness I said, "This is a dream. God I am such an idiot!" I giggled in relief and started trying to pinch myself so I could wake up. Ki looked at me warily. Of course, I'd finally meet a good man and then quickly show him I was a psycho. Then again, this was a dream, and I could always imagine us doing more entertaining things in the next go round.

For some reason the pinching wasn't working, I was not waking up. I finally looked up at the hottie in my driver's seat and asked, "Will you pinch me? I'm trying to wake up." He looked at me in confusion before saying, "You've never asked me to do that before." I felt my expression transform into one of shock as without preamble he reached over and pinched my cheek of all places, like a grandma would. I slapped his hand away and flopped back in my seat confused as to why that didn't work. He looked as though he were fighting a grin and part of me was hoping he lost so I could see what his face would look like turned up into a smile. We were still traveling at high speeds, surprisingly unmolested by the po-po (go figure) and since I couldn't wake up, I decided to study the driver. I probably should have been more worried about where exactly we were going, but he was much more fascinating than our current destination.

In my dream he didn't have any facial hair, but I found I liked the neatly cropped beard he sported now. It framed his mouth just so, and what a beautiful mouth it was. I hadn't noticed his hair in my dreams, but it was cut short and sported waves that the average brother had to brush non-stop to achieve. Somehow, I couldn't imagine him going through all that work. Everything about him seemed, effortless. He had on a simple black V-neck t-shirt and distressed jeans that hugged without being too tight.

I hated when it looked like a man had to jump and wiggle to get into his pants. It was an unappealing thought.

"Are you done?" he asked with a raised brow, startling me out of my perusal of his person.

"Umm, what do you mean?" I asked. Caught! My brain screamed. The way his lips slipped upward into a small smile made my liver quiver, if you know what I mean.

"You were studying me, Malika Alika." He said my first and middle name. How did he know my middle name? Furthermore, the way he said it was like some type of magic spell and it made more than my liver quiver. Steeling my spine, I gave myself the pep talk. He's fine, just admit you were checking him, you're grown girl.

"Where are we going?" I asked quietly. Chicken, I chastised myself with a roll of my eyes. As if he knew what I was thinking that soft grin on his face increased in wattage and I wondered if he'd ever worn braces, because those teeth were so white and straight, they were giving the sunshine competition! The first two things I noticed on a man were eyes and smile. He had both of those things going for him. Oh, oh! And third, I noticed smell. I was a sucker for a good-smelling man. Without thinking I leaned into him across the gear shift, and I don't know if it was my imagination or if he shifted and leaned into me as well. Sniffing delicately, I took his scent in. Almost immediately I fell back into my seat, sighing in ecstasy. My senses had been assaulted in the best way. Closing my eyes, I let the scents tantalize my nose. He smelled like a mixture of patchouli and jojoba oil, with a hint of cocoa? Where do you even find a cologne like that? I was about to ask when I realized he was studying me intently. We'd stopped in front of a townhome in the city. Dang, he had to be really driving fast for us to make it to the city in, I looked at my watch, 15 freaking minutes!

I looked around Tessy to make sure she was ok. I'd have to check for damage when we got out. Wait no, I probably shouldn't get out of the car with this man. Especially not to enter that really dope looking townhome we were parked outside of. He might try to take advantage of me...and I might let him. Stop it, Malika! I chastised myself for thinking slutty thoughts. But he was studying me with such intensity, I was about certain I wouldn't put up too much of a fight.

"Will you please come inside with me Mali?"

I tried to stifle a shiver. This really wasn't going to work if every time he said my name all my thoughts and body parts went haywire.

"I don't know you," I said.

He pinned me with an even harder stare. "You know me better than anyone. You just don't know you do." There was that sad smile again. The one from my dream. I hated to keep disappointing him, but I truly didn't know him or what the heck was going on. After we studied each other for what felt like hours, his head snapped up and he glanced around quickly in alarm before relaxing just as suddenly. "This will help. It's really not safe in the open and I would not choose to force you inside." Before I could ask him what he was talking about a hand shot through the window and rapped me on the noggin. "Get in the house silly girl, there's not much time." I looked up at my Aunt Ramla, rubbing my head in surprise.

Ki had already gotten out of the car. After a quick bow of respect to Auntie, in response to which she touched her forehead to his. He leaned down obligingly, and they rested their foreheads together a moment before she said quietly, "Amani, Kimoni Fayola. I am glad you are here. Even if it brings sad tidings. She needs you." He nodded in understanding as my confusion only grew and opened my door. In a daze I allowed him to help me out of the car and towards the house with one arm linked through Auntie's and the other held so gently by such a large man, in Ki's. I kept glancing up at him as we walked towards the house, but he was too busy sweeping the area with his eyes. Or so I thought, when he squeezed my arm gently as if to say, I see you.

CHAPTER 3

Follow the rabbit...If the rabbit were tall, dark, and handsome that is...

We walked up five steps and into a beautiful townhome that I thought fit this dark, handsome stranger perfectly. It was a wide-open space, very minimalist, with clean lines and lots of sunlight through large full-length windows all around. The space was decorated in masculine earth tones, lots of browns and black with subtle splashes of deep burgundy and burnt orange here and there. They led me to a couch, and as soon as I was seated, Ki raced around checking the place in what seemed like hyper speed. Seriously, he was racing around the room so quickly it was hard to keep up. My eyes must have been as wide as saucers when he came flying back down the beautiful staircase.

"Kimoni Fayola," my Auntie called out sharply. He stopped in his tracks immediately, then rushed over to my aunt's side just as quickly. Touching his face with a tender look she said, "I doubled your protections with my own before you two arrived. I knew this was coming. She is safe for now."

"But Mama Ramla," Ki said hurriedly before he was cut off by an arrogant arch of her brows.

"Do you think my time here on this Earth has lessened my light, mwanangu?" He addressed her as Mother, and she addressed him as son. During my time in Africa these were simply titles of honor, not a testament to kinship. I truly hoped Auntie hadn't been hiding a son, because I'd have to have a serious talk with the good Lord during my nightly prayers about the lusty thoughts I'd had about my possible cousin.

A crash at the door caused all of us to spring into action. All except Auntie that is. She sat serenely with her hands in her lap as I jumped to my feet and Ki raced to the door. I looked expectantly toward the entryway as Ki came back with my best friend leaning on him heavily. She was covered in the same green gook that was on her shoe yesterday, only it was looking less guacamole like and more putrid. Rushing over, I knelt beside her as Ki assisted her to a seat at the kitchen table. Glancing back at the couch, I realized he probably didn't want to sully the supple leather I'd just been sitting on. I'd have to ask him where he'd gotten it. It was the most comfortable couch ever and the burgundy and gold pillows he had scattered on it were the perfect touch. Being distracted by mundane details is my coping mechanism. I was worried.

"Aseema! Are you hurt?" I asked, placing my hands gently on her goo spattered knees. Her head had been down as she breathed heavily with hands on her thighs. At my words, her head jerked up and then she raised her arms, letting the knives she'd still been clutching fall gently on the table. I was startled to see a ferocious, yet exhilarated smile lighting her face.

"Mwanamke wangu, that was the most fun I've had since we arrived here!"

My mouth automatically formed into a pout. "More fun than that night in Spain?" Her smile widened and she started chuckling. "I know not how to compare the two, my lady." I smiled, feeling better, she wasn't hurt, and she hadn't diminished the awesomeness of that crazy night in Spain at the flamenco show in Barcelona when we danced the night away with some sexy hombres. Ki had disappeared upstairs sometime during our little moment and was back with items for Aseema to clean herself off with. He was looking at me strangely as he sat them down. "What happened in Spain?" Those intense eyes focused on me again, and I felt like I just might be in trouble.

Aseema rolled her eyes and looked up at Ki. "You aren't allowed to be mad. Remember your rebellious phase." She gave him a hard look of reprimand; Ki stiffened, flushing ever so lightly. It was the cutest thing. Why did everything he did cause a physical reaction?

"We aren't cousins are we?" I asked him quietly. He looked at me, shock spreading across his face. Aseema burst out laughing. "You two work that out. I'm going to go and take a shower." Grabbing the cleaning items he'd provided, Aseema headed up the stairs as though she were completely at home in his place. I peeked up at him again, he was still looking at me like I had two heads. So, it was no on the cousin thing, might as well continue

. . . .

to rule out the possibilities. "Are you and Aseema, like, a thing? If so, we should probably stop sharing these intense gazes." His expression transformed into one of horror and a small part of me was enjoying this myriad of emotions. Up until now his range of facial expressions had been limited.

Auntie Ramla walked over and started putting together the necessities for tea and something else I couldn't quite see. As she moved through the kitchen with ease, I thought my next question should be, was Auntie playing hide the rainbow role with this handsome stranger? She was still fresh and young enough to pull him. I wouldn't put a little cougar activity past her. Glancing at him I figured he could be anywhere between 25-35; he had such smooth and beautiful skin, it was hard to tell.

As if reading my thoughts Auntie said, "Ki is a friend who is here to help. We are safe with him. Neither you nor I are his relative and neither Aseema nor I have any romantic feelings for him. Though I do love him as though he were my own kin." She stopped to give Ki a smile, then continued moving about his kitchen adeptly. He gave her a humble, almost grateful bow of his head before taking a seat at the table with me. As he settled into his seat and I watched his movements discreetly or perhaps not, he raised his brow at me in question and I tore my eyes away. But I could still feel his gaze on me as I watched Auntie work.

"I know you are confused, Malika my dear," she continued. "But we are limited in what we can reveal. You will have to try very hard to remember, for we are a bit…early. Ki will help you." I glanced over at him sharply. He'd still been looking at me. When my gaze met his, he said, "I will," and those words seemed to catch on something in my memories.

Without thinking I said aloud, "Until my star returns to the Creator or to the dust from whence it was formed." His eyes widened and he moved as if to reach for me, but then checked himself. Why did I say that? There was a memory there, but it felt as though it were covered in a thick fog. I broke away from his gaze nervously. There was something close to…love there. But that couldn't be right, I barely knew this man. I looked quickly at my aunt and she smiled. "It's already working. But we will need to move much faster so you can act before it is too late." With that, Auntie sat tea and sandwiches down at the table. How she managed to whip that up so fast I'll never know, but Ki dug in immediately while I reached for the calming cup of tea Auntie placed in front of me. I love coffee, but it keys me up. Tea is perfect for relaxation and reflective thinking. We sat quietly for a while. I had so many questions I didn't know where to start and the seer woman next to me seemed content to continue talking in riddles. As if she knew what I was thinking she smiled at me over her tea.

"Tell me about your dream again, niece."

I gave her a quizzical look and she only nodded in encouragement. This was embarrassing. Ki had been in the dream. He was the guy. The lack of a beard in the dream didn't change the fact it was him who'd held me in his arms, called me his flame in Swahili and kissed me on the forehead, then almost kissed me-kissed me. I dropped my head down, wondering how to proceed when Aseema came back downstairs dressed in clean clothes with her close-cropped curls still wet. Plopping in a chair between Auntie and I, she reached over to the sandwich plate, took a bite, and closed her eyes, letting out a groan of bliss. Were the sandwiches orgasmic? Sign me up! I reached over and grabbed one as well. My eyes closed and I groaned, echoing Aseema's sentiments. Yep, it was an orgasm sandwich. My Aunt laughed softly, arrogant old broad that she was. Ki had already eaten two or three and grabbed another as we girls worked through our first one. It was a bagel with tomatoes, nova lox, capers, and some type of smear that was divine. The sandwich went perfectly with my English Breakfast tea. Not a lot of people drank this tea, I was surprised Ki had it. I glanced over at him, and he gave me an adorable grin before going back to his bagel.

After Aseema recovered from the aftereffects of her orgasm sandwich, she looked over at me and said, "So, what was this dream y'all were talking about?" I cringed and she reached over to steal my tea. I recovered quickly shielding my cup. Auntie knew it was about to turn into a girl fight and slid a cup over to her. She smiled gratefully and took a sip. I still hadn't spoken, so she nudged me gently and said, "Spill." With a deep breath for courage I recounted my dream, leaving out the parts about my gooey feelings towards Ki as well as how tasty he looked and the kissing. When I said the part about him calling me moto wangu, or 'my flame,' his eyes started that swirling thing they did in my dream. I rushed through it and finished the story quickly.

"That's strange, you two..." Aseema seemed to choke on her words. She fell mute for several moments. "That hasn't happened in a while. I know it to be uncomfortable. Our vows hold, so your tongue you must continue to watch. She will have to come into this without your guidance. The key will reveal all." I groaned, "Auntie you're making my brain hurt. What does that dream have to do with this, I waved my hand around us, or the morning I've had for that matter?" She reached over a still silent Aseema and squeezed my hand gently.

"It takes quite a strong connection to break into a dream. Whoever the man in your dream was is of importance. Apparently, you are needed my heart, but to what end?" Auntie cast a knowing look at Ki as though she knew it was him in the dream and he put his head down again. "Aseema, will you take Mali upstairs to get cleaned up?" I looked down at my clothes. I'd gotten the green goo that covered Aseema all over my favorite pencil skirt. My shoulders sagged in silent resignation. It was probably ruined. "It will turn to dust soon," my aunt said, giving me a reassuring smile. My best friend jumped up with another sandwich in hand and tugged on my arm to get me to follow her up the steps.

This was the most spacious townhouse I'd ever scene, and the paintings sprinkled throughout were colorful and beautiful. I followed Aseema down the hallway to what I assumed was a spare bedroom. Studying the spacious layout, I decided I was impressed with Ki's decorating skills. Finally, I sat down at a small writing desk in the corner, slumping in the chair. "Do you want me to find you some toiletries so you can take a shower?" Aseema was polishing off her sandwich and checking out a painting on the wall that looked like an endless swirl of rainbow colors. She tilted her head to the side when my words caused her to turn quickly.

"Seema, I need to know what is going on." I looked at her, pleading with my eyes for an explanation of the day's events. I felt as though I were losing my mind. The two people I trusted most in the world were talking in circles, rushing me into hiding with a man I'd never met, but had dreamed of and I was being prompted to remember...something? My brain was going to explode. The one person who usually helped me navigate the world wasn't being very helpful.

We'd met in the third grade; she'd been orphaned after her mother's untimely death (she'd never known her dad) and came to live at a girl's home near the school I attended. Both orphans, we became fast friends, and she often stayed with Auntie and I for the weekends. When I decided to do an accelerated work study program in college, she followed without hesitation. I majored in history, and she majored in science, both with a minor in elementary education. Every step I took, Aseema had been my roll dog. When I said, let's go to Africa, she said let's go! Spain, I'm there! South Korea, girl you're crazy but I'm game. Now on the most confusing day of my life, she had nothing to say, no support to give. If I was being honest with myself, and I'm always honest with myself. Well, except when I'm not. I was hurt.

Wiping her hands on her leggings, Aseema walked over to me and sat on my lap. "You can't distract me with the booty woman. I'm not that easy." Wrapping her arms around my neck she nestled her head into my shoulder. I sat, unwilling to forgive her for not shining some light on this ridiculous situation. After a few moments she spoke softly, "I wish I could tell you everything my friend, my sister. You have honored me with your love, and

I honor you even now when I want so badly to unburden my soul, with my silence. Though I know this is hard to understand, I cannot explain that which you must find on your own." Great I thought sullenly, now she was talking like Auntie Ramla. But I grudgingly linked my arms around her waist. I couldn't stay mad at her. If she was choosing to allow me to continue to wander around in confusion, it was with good reason. I trusted her with my life. "So, are you, like, a ninja assassin or what?" I finally asked.

She chuckled. "Not quite." Sitting up Aseema gave me a quick kiss on the cheek and went to rifle through the dresser.

Looking over at her in thought I realized what I thought were leggings was some type of supple leather pants she had on, but it was in a reddish-brown color. The top was a corset in the same color with burnt orange laces. Absently I realized it matched Ki's home décor. The back of the top had a place for her to store what I assumed were various knives, though they were currently empty and there were thigh sheaths on her legs.

"Curiouser and curiouser," I said quietly.

Aseema smiled at me. "Would that make you almost Alice?"

I shook my head. "If anyone is going to kill the jabberwocky with a snicker snack, I'd imagine it would be you."

With clothes in hand that slightly resembled hers, Aseema walked back over. "You'd be surprised at what you are capable of, mwanamke wangu. But if it means you'll futterwacken, I'll gladly kill the jabberwocky." I laughed. We were such nerds, quoting *Alice in Wonderland,* quite casually after I'd assaulted a teacher, went on a mad chase through Chicago, where my best friend jumped out of the car and apparently dispatched four men.

Now we were at my dream man's house, hiding out from God knows who. Taking the pile of clothes before my brain turned to mush with this overload, I headed into the bathroom to wash up and change.

I found a vast assortment of expensive toiletries, mostly brand new and unopened. It surprised me to find my favorite body wash, a sweet-smelling honey and shea butter shower gel from Pink. Once I dried off and oiled up my skin, I slid into the softest, most supple leather pants I'd ever worn. Wait. I'd never worn leather pants, but these were flexible and light. While Aseema's were in a deep burgundy with orange accents, my ensemble was a purple so deep it could be mistaken for black. Where her top was a strapless corset, mine had capped sleeves and an enticing V-neck that showed just a hint of my ample cleavage. It still laced delicately up the back with violet strings.

Glancing over at the mirror, I caught my reflection with a start of surprise. I looked fierce, curvy, and 'shiny.' Was Amber right? There seemed to be a glow emanating from my mid-section suffusing my face. Something clicked inside of me, and my fingertips started to tingle again, I held them up and they were shining as well. Suddenly, I saw the girl from my dream in the mirror. Long sister locs flowing behind me in shades of balayage red, iridescent wings spread from my back, more beautiful than any fictional angel as they shimmered with colors of every hue. My eyes took on a glow, the honey and green seeming to shift and move as I looked on. Somehow, I was closer to the ceiling... was I taller? Raising my hands in the most fluid motion I'd ever made; I caressed a fingertip over my left wing. Their sensitivity startled me, and the wings as though an entity of their own, flared out, filling the large en suite bathroom with their span. The movement jarred the shelf of hygiene products on the shelf. A bottle of powder tumbled to the marble floors in a cloud of white, shattering the glass bottle into tiny pieces. I heard rapid footsteps and suddenly the door flew open. Jerking my head towards it, my eyes met Ki's as he burst into the room, holding a towel at his waist and a small blade in his hand. Was everyone around her packing sharp objects?

I stared at him as his eyes rapidly searched the bathroom for threats. In a movement that was as natural as breathing I tucked my wings in to accommodate his entry into the room. Once he was sure there was no threat, he walked over slowly. I just stood frozen, fascinated as droplets of water slid over broad shoulders down a nicely muscled chest and over a toned, 1-2-3-4-5-6! A six pack! I bet he had those little indents at his hips to, but I couldn't tell with the way he held the towel around his waist, speaking of which. Oh whoa, look away, look away! I averted my eyes quickly. Yep…yep, that towel wasn't concealing much. Sweet baby Jesus, that was one well-crafted man. When I finally tore my eyes from the heavens, Ki was standing right in front of me. He seemed oblivious to how his water slick body was causing me to have thoughts I hadn't had in a while. Running his hand over my hair gently (not helping my quivering liver AT ALL), stopping at my neck, resting his fingers gently at my nape. He didn't have as far to look down now, my head hit his chin and as I met his eyes the bathroom that felt so spacious moments ago seemed to close in around me. It was suddenly hard to take in a breath. I felt my chest rising and falling rapidly as his eyes traveled over me lingeringly before returning to my eyes. "Malika," he said on a soft exhale of breath that brushed across my lips in the most sensual manner. As if realizing what he'd done, he rubbed his thumb across my bottom lip. Feeling completely exposed by the depth of his eyes, I looked down and again connected with that darn towel, the one only hanging on due to his loose grip on it. Absently, I wondered where the blade he'd been holding had disappeared too.

"Malika." He said my name like a caress. "Do you know me?"

I met his eyes; confusion furrowed my brow and suddenly things seemed to snap back into place. I felt it like a balloon popping. Before my eyes met the mirror, I knew I'd returned to normal. Whatever dream state had me fitted with wings, sister locs and pointy ears had vanished. I was back to normal. 5'5 again, no more wings, no more pointy ears, and definitely no more shiny body parts. Kimoni dropped his head and slowly removed his hand from my face. That's when I realized we had an audience. Two sighs drifted from the doorway in near unison. Out of the corner of my eye, I could see Auntie Ramla and Aseema hovering. I took another quick glance at Ki's smooth chest…and that dang towel at his waist, before averting my eyes again. Without another word, he turned on his heel and moved smoothly, yet swiftly out of the room. All three of them seemed to be waiting for me to remember something, I had no idea what.

Looking at my only family, I asked both ladies, meeting each of their eyes, "What am I? Can you at least tell me that?" They looked at each other and then back at me sadly. Ki had paused on his way out of the bedroom door, blade in hand again. Aseema shook her head slowly and Auntie asked, "What do you believe yourself to be Malika?"

I put my head down for a moment, trying to make a fast decision. Either they were going to think I was crazy, or I was going to finally gain some clarity. I met each of their eyes again. Ki was still at the door, but he'd gotten a robe from somewhere. I was half grateful and half disappointed…ok like 10% grateful because it made it easier to think, but like 90% disappointed because him in a towel was an experience!

"I am a 24-year-old third-grade teacher who is the most normal person you will ever meet. I'm a pluviophile who loves to read with a cup of tea in hand. You both know that! But I am quite sure that I am having a nervous break. You both are apparently a part of my mind's desire to make me comfortable with my near insane state. I've been having crazy dreams for a few weeks now. In all of them a man with a kind face was reaching out to me, asking me to come back home. I didn't know what to think, so I didn't say anything. It was just weird." At that point I started pacing the bathroom, talking rapidly.

"I had the feeling he needed my help, that something was wrong. But come home where? Then I would see my abdomen glowing, like-like-like I'd swallowed a star. Every time after that dream I'd wake up and think my stomach is freaking glowing! But I thought it was all part of the dream, that it couldn't be real. Yet there are parts of my memory that seem enshrouded in a thick fog I-I just can't get through. And then there's you." I pointed agitatedly at Ki but kept pacing. It was helping me to get this off my chest. "I know you, but I don't know you." I stopped momentarily to meet his eyes. "It's as though my soul knows you, but my mind can't find the memory."

I didn't know if it was some trick of the light or if his eyes had started to water. Unable to stop, I broke his gaze and started pacing again. "Things aren't what they seem lately. I thought I saw a man with-with backwards feet and-and there was a guy who seemed to glow, like-like from his armpits. What the hell is going on? I don't know! Who am I? I don't know. But I have wings and you have wings" I pointed at Aseema. "They're beautiful by the way." She gave me a modest shrug and motioned with her hands for me to keep going. "You," I said pointing at Ki. "You have wings, but I've never seen them expanded and you glow, and both of your ears are pointed, like, like some type of elf." They all watched me intently as I paced manically. "Auntie do you have wings?" I asked incredulously. She just gave me a small smile.

After a few moments, she said, "You say you've been having these dreams for weeks, but my dear, that is not true." I gave her a look. "Auntie I would know if I'm having weird dreams."

"You mistake my meaning, Malika. I only mean to say that you have been having strange dreams longer than that, yes?" I nodded in the affirmative. "It is only that they have grown more intense of late. Why do you think that is daughter?" Again, I grew silent, chewing that over, remembering my dreams. It was obvious what was needed of me, but it had never been so real before. A million butterflies were on a rampage inside my stomach, but I couldn't let that stop me. I'd ventured to different distant places to teach and study abroad. I was brave. I could do what was needed of me. Even if this was a dream, the best thing for me to do was to see how far down the rabbit hole goes. Where was Morpheus when you needed him?

Steeling my resolve; I stopped my manic pacing, looked at my family and then the mystery man, and said with more confidence than I truly felt, "Take me there." All three of them looked at me hopefully. Well, Auntie had more of a knowing look on her face (Miss-know-it-all, that was her). "Take me to where my memories are," I said in a firmer tone.

"Mama Ramla, will that work?" Aseema asked with an edge of excitement to her tone. Auntie nodded gravely. "Yes, it will. That is why Kimoni was sent. But it will not be easy. Now is not the appointed time, so we will have to journey through dangerous places to return her where she wishes and needs to be." Then she turned to Ki with a smile. "We must give thanks to the Creator that Ki has made this journey and will be able to lead us back."

Kimoni looked at Auntie solemnly. "It will be dangerous for her traveling through the Ardhi Iliyotengwa. She is growing. It will be hard to hide." The deserted land, I thought in alarm. But then he looked at me, with eyes full of concern and it occurred to me I could fall in love with Kimoni Fayola. A great man who walks with honor. That was the meaning of his first and middle name. I'd become obsessed with native African names in my history studies and for whatever reason that name, his name, had stuck out to me. I was thinking crazy thoughts. I didn't know this man. How could I imagine falling in love with him? Tucking the thought away lest it develop any further, I pulled my eyes from him, looked at the strongest woman I know, and asked, "When do we leave?"

CHAPTER 4

Dancing, danger, and kisses...in no particular order.

The decision was made, mostly by the three of them, that we were safe under the wards for the day and that we should wait until the morning to journey through the deserted lands. What was a ward? How did one create or strengthen a ward? I thought that was something that only witches did. When I asked these things, I was met with strange looks and decided that it must fall under that list of things they "couldn't tell me." Should I ever happen upon the person responsible for this gag order, I'd have to give them a piece of my mind. I said as much to my aunt who chuckled and said, "That would be an interesting sight to see."

I was sitting on the floor, while Auntie sat on the edge of the Queen-sized bed in the spare room I'd claimed for the night. She had decided to braid my hair into two French braids. It had become a bit of a mess during the day's activities. Shortly after we'd decided on when to leave, Ki had gone to finish the shower my clumsy wings had interrupted, and Aseema went to take a nap in another one of the spare rooms. Apparently, this place was more than the simple townhome I thought it was. There was an additional level above us where the master bedroom was, and the level we were currently on had 3 bedrooms all with their own bathrooms. How did he accomplish that?

Suddenly, Auntie Ramla stopped her braiding and grabbed my left hand. I hadn't realized it, but I'd been rubbing at my shoulder blade where the wings had sprouted earlier. Turning to face her, I looked up into the most comforting face I'd ever known. Looking into Auntie's hazel eyes felt like home, family, love, and acceptance. She was all that for me and more, but now there was this huge secret that for the past 20 plus years she'd been keeping from me. It was mind boggling that the woman I told everything, from my first kiss to my deepest darkest fears would withhold so much from me. After my first heartbreak, I'd laid in her lap crying for hours before she told me to clean myself up. "We don't cry but for a moment over boy children who are not worthy of us? It's time to pamper ourselves and move on to the next one."

It wasn't until Auntie reached over and brushed the tears away from my cheeks that I realized I was crying. "I feel your heart aching my niece. For that I am truly sorry. But you must understand that though I agreed to be bound by these secrets, it was not of my choosing, what was to be kept hidden and what to reveal. That much I can tell you. Soon though, my special daughter and mwanamke wangu; all will be revealed." She leaned in then and kissed me on the forehead, whispering what sounded like the Swahili word for 'see,' tazama. Just as I thought, her forehead kiss was comforting, but nowhere near as titillating as when Kimoni did it in my dream, I saw him again. Not Kimoni, but the kind, ageless man who'd been haunting my dreams, always on the periphery, as far back as I could remember.

"I am sorry binti yangu," he said, his voice weak. Was he ill? He didn't look it. In fact, he stood before me tall, regal, and strong. His hands rested in front of him on a what looked to be a wooden staff, but it ebbed and flowed with light, mingling in with the brilliant, pure white rays beaming from his core. Though his face was smooth and unlined, he had an ancient feel to him. Don't ask me how ancient feels, but I could sense his long years in this world and the power thrumming through him as though it were reaching towards me, begging me to come closer. This being, ("man" was too mundane a word for him) was timeless. Ageless. I took a few steps forward before catching myself. He wore loose linen pants, and an open robe that swirled around him, the white so bright it seemed to catch the rainbow of colored lights coalescing around him. The brightness of that light prevented me from making out many defining factors aside from long loc's that hung over his shoulders, an impressive wingspan, those same gently pointed ears, and mesmerizing eyes…eyes that looked, like mine.

"Who are you and why do you call me daughter?" I asked, looking up at him in wonder.

"War is coming. You must come home."

"War? Home? Where?" I was so confused. I knew my father, he did not look like this, but somehow this creature's words drew me, made me want to help him. To do something to stop the pain that was emanating from him. He was injured in some way I couldn't pinpoint.

I started towards him, but suddenly it was as though we were talking across a great expanse. Finally, I dragged my eyes from his and looked up in astonishment, then down in horror. I wasn't walking on the ground. We were hovering in the sky, surrounded by countless stars, our bodies suspended in the vast expanse of the constellation.

"Take it," he said, jerking my attention back to him. He was extending his staff to me, I moved forward, mesmerized by the power that hummed through it, but before I could get close enough to take it out of his hands, I was jerked back. Slamming back into the room, back into my body as though yanked through time and space. How was that possible? What was happening to me? I looked up at my aunt, filled with confusion and frustration.

Pushing her face so close to mine that my eyes crossed, she whispered fiercely, "Not yet!" I jerked back. What was she talking about? Straightening her spine to sit up straighter on the bed, Auntie said in a milder tone, "We still have time."

After several moments of silence, where I was sure that my face was scrunched up in the bewilderment that had been my constant companion for several hours, I opened my mouth to ask her, time for what? But soft strums of reggae rhythms began to filter up the stairs, dividing my attention. Someone, no doubt, my best friend, had found the sound system and was making good use of the bass in those speakers. So much for her going to take a nap. I suppose I could understand her restlessness. Auntie Ramla smiled at me, patting my face with soft manicured fingertips. "Go. Dance with your sister. Let off some steam. Tomorrow will prove to be a strenuous journey. We must enjoy the moments of joy this life offers. If nothing else, being here has proven that much."

Before I could ask any further questions, she turned my head, put a rubber band at the end of my braid and shoved at my back encouraging me to go. The farthest thing from my mind was dancing, but I knew she wasn't going to give me any more answer than what she'd already given. Getting to my feet slowly, I made my way toward the stairs. It would be relaxing to watch Aseema dance; nothing showcased her beauty and grace more than when she got lost in music. Maybe there was some tea left downstairs to further calm my nerves. Absently, I wondered if Kimoni had a library, a good book would relax me even more. The chaos of my world was so overwhelming right now, that it would be soothing to get lost in someone else's world for a while.

Heading downstairs, I noticed the large windows that started at the first floor and flowed all the way up to the third, presented us with a lovely view of the city. There was a tint on them I assume prevented passersby from seeing inside. Ki had spent a pretty penny upgrading this place and it was spectacular.

Aseema was deep into her dance party, hands in the air, eyes closed, hips moving boneless and fluid. I stood on the bottom step watching for a moment as she utilized the open space in front of the windows. Bare foot and in her zone, I wondered if she knew anyone was there. That's when I felt him. Ki gave off energy like a live wire, a constant humming seemed to come from his body. I found it strangely comforting. I'd overlooked him, because he was sitting in the dark of the living room, blending into the shadows. He seemed so relaxed, his body slumped low on the couch, long legs splayed in front of him and strong fingers gripping a glass.

As my eyes traveled up his defined torso to his face, I realized he was watching me from beneath hooded lids. Part of me realized that his eyes had been trained on me the entire time. It was sensual. It was hot. His gaze pulled me in like some sort of gravitational force. Before my body could obey and walk to him Aseema had danced over and tugged me off the step and into her dance space.

Reluctantly, matching my movements to hers in a more subdued fashion, we began dancing together. She danced harder, smiling at me fiercely as one of her favorites filtered through the speaker. I laughed, keeping step with her, but not completely letting loose, much too aware of the audience we currently had.

Fifteen minutes later, I'd loosened up a bit more and we were glistening with a light sheen of sweat, giggling like schoolgirls. Auntie was puttering around the kitchen again. She was serious about people never being hungry in her presence. We'd morphed from reggae into African rhythms when I noticed Auntie Ramla coaxing Ki to dance with us. He gave a subtle shake of his head that oddly filled me with disappointment. He'd been watching me the whole time, only moving to drink from his glass, never once glancing at Aseema. His singular focus had been on me. It was a mixture of intimidating and incredibly enticing. After years of zero male attention, well, none I cared to entertain anyway, his intense regard was flattering. Basking in the influence of that appreciative male gaze, my movements strayed towards a more sensual bent than I'd usually gravitate to.

Aseema was low to the ground circling her hips rhythmically when Auntie called her. Their eyes met for a moment, before Aseema went, took Ki's glass, and pulled his arm to get him to join in. He resisted briefly, before she leaned down and whispered something I couldn't hear over the bass line pumping through the sound system. Stiffening momentarily, he finally got up and fell easily into step with her. I faltered, mesmerized. For a large man, his movements were so graceful. Not in the same fluid, limber way that Aseema was, but he had the type of grace you saw in large jungle cats. Movements that were deliberate and sinuous, while coming off extremely gentle for a creature of their size. I watched his hips for a moment before realizing how hard I was staring. Out of the corner of my eye I saw Auntie smiling slightly, before walking over to the iPod on the sound dock and fiddling around a bit.

The mid-tempo song that we'd been dancing to, transitioned abruptly into a slow jam, which made Aseema roll her eyes dramatically, spinning away from Ki and into a slow dance of her own. Stepping back until I was pressed against the window behind me, I let my eyes drift shut just as the beat dropped. This was my kind of music, dope lyrics and a mellow beat. As Nao crooned about her love releasing her into orbit, I swayed against the window, careful not to let my fingertips stain the glass.

Humming along, eyes still closed, letting the music wash over me, I was startled into immobility when I felt Ki's electric heat right in front of me. My eyes were suddenly heavy, for some reason, I couldn't get them to open. Instead, I just stood there; not moving, not even breathing, just feeling the intensity of his nearness seep into me. A strong, gentle hand grazed my upper arm before sliding down to my wrist, leaving spikes of heat in the wake of his tender touch. Clasping my fingers, he pulled me into step with him. I fell in, eyes still glued shut, savoring the barest touch of his body to mine. We swayed for several beats before I was able to force my eyes open to look up at him. Immediately I was captured in the snare of his gaze, completely powerless to break the hold of those caramel irises. There was that pull again, tugging at something deep inside me. My spirit? My soul?

The lyrics of the song filtered through the haze in my brain and absently I thought, in this scenario, he'd be the one to release me into orbit and leave me trying to navigate back to him. Except his eyes told a different story. There was an underlying sadness that lingered there. But it was tinged with something else, something I couldn't quite place. Was it expectancy? Hope? Where did he fit into this equation? Aseema and Ramla made sense in all this, but who or what was he to me?

Without thinking (I seemed to be doing that a lot lately) I reached up and touched his hard jaw with my fingertips. He closed his eyes as my hand connected with his skin, leaning into my palm as we continued to sway. "Niko Hapa," I said softly. His eyes flew open, startled. I began to withdraw my hand, but he caught it in his, that hopeful look transforming his expression.

Guiding my hand in his slowly to his chest, resting it right over the steady thrum of his heartbeat, Kimoni brought our slow dance to a halt.

"Moto wangu?" My flame, he said it again. Except this time, it wasn't a dream, he asked as though it were a question. I stilled in his arms. Why did he call me that? I tried to claw through the fog in my brain to find the answer, but I couldn't seem to grasp it. I'd told him "I'm here," and he'd called me his flame. What did that mean? Noticing the confused expression on my face, he seemed to deflate, and I felt like a complete idiot. Why couldn't I remember? Trying to change the subject, I pulled from his grasp, and he let go reluctantly.

"This place is beautiful, how'd you find it?" He cocked his head at me as if his brain was attempting to process the shift in my mood. The music had picked up, somewhere during the time I was locked in Ki's embrace and our current separation. Aseema danced over to us and said, "He did not find it, mwanamke wangu did." Auntie looked up at her in surprise. "Ha!" Aseema yelled triumphantly. "She did not block that part; yes, we can speak of the house, because it was for after…"

Her words cut off abruptly and Aseema wrapped her hands around her throat, then kicked her foot in apparent frustration. Ki and Auntie gave each other a cryptic look before Auntie returned to her work in the kitchen. "Stupid gag order," I said, giving her a sympathetic look. She only glared at me. Before I could ask why I was getting the stink eye, Ki turned, ignoring Aseema.

He looked at me thoughtfully. "Would you like a tour of our…" He stopped to clear his throat. "I mean *the* house? Would you like a tour of the house?" I nodded excitedly. Architecture and home design were fascinating to me. One of my favorite things about being back home was sitting up and watching home renovation shows with Auntie Rami. As if picking thoughts out of my head, he said softly, "I know that you like to…create." What an odd way to put it though.

Aseema declined to go with us, still pissed about the gag order no doubt. I wondered how long it rendered them speechless. Auntie was still puttering about the kitchen and fanned us on our way, so it ended up just being the two of us. I soon realized that we were journeying through no ordinary townhouse; this was a mini mansion. We started on the first floor. I hadn't known that there was an office and theater room past the kitchen. At first, we didn't speak much as I took in the masculine opulence that was his home. He studied me as I studied my surroundings. Finally working up the courage I turned to him and to my surprise he was looking at me expectantly. I halted mid-thought and teetered for balance. I shouldn't have made such an abrupt turn on the back staircase we'd been coming up. Without taking his gaze from my face, Ki steadied me with a firm grasp, letting his hands linger at my waist. Looking at him, almost eye-to-eye now that I was a step above him, in a rush of words I asked, "What were we to each other?"

"Everything," he said. Though he didn't grab his throat in the way Aseema did, I knew the gag order had caught him by the narrowing of his eyes and the tightening of his mouth. Curious, I stepped into him and touched his throat. Hisexpression relaxed but his hands tightened around me. Still touching the base of his throat, I asked quietly, "Does it hurt?"

"Not anymore," I heard him say. But for some odd reason, I didn't see his lips move with the words. Taking his left hand from my waist, he covered my right where it rested on his neck. I gazed up into those melted caramel eyes, deep, mesmerizing, and full of secrets. Secrets I believe he truly wanted to tell me.

"I want to remember...so badly," I said.

He smiled. A full genuine smile that reached his eyes and transformed his face. My lips parted in shock. He wasn't conventionally handsome, but at that moment, he was otherworldly beautiful to me. There was a light that came from him, that warmed me down to my toes. Slowly he leaned into me, I inhaled, lips parting, preparing for his mouth to meet mine. But instead of kissing me, he leaned down resting his forehead gently against mine. "So, do I," he said, so gently that if it weren't for his breath caressing my lips as he spoke, I'd have thought I'd imagined it.

After a moment he lifted his head to look at me, searching my eyes, he finally heaved a sigh and stepped down a step, releasing me from his grasp. "Should we finish the tour?" I felt suddenly cold, where his large, warm hands had vacated their place. It seemed so natural for those hands to be there, they fit so perfectly and if I was being honest, it made me feel delicate and cherished. Absently, I realized he'd asked me a question. I was wondering if this was the vibe on the steps, what would happen when we got to the bedrooms? I almost laughed aloud but caught it just in time. This was out of character for me to be so fascinated with a man I'd just met.

Ki lifted an eyebrow at me, and I wondered if I'd said some of that aloud. Wait a minute! "Can you read minds?" He froze for a moment, then laughed softly. "Um… how to explain this? Only certain ones of us under certain circumstances. Sorry, that is so convoluted, but it's a complicated question. If you are wondering whether I was reading your thoughts just now, the answer is no, but your usually contemplative facial expressions were very… expressive at that moment. You almost laughed but stopped yourself. Otherwise…I cannot read your thoughts without your permission, mwanamke wangu." First, I was distracted because his accent had thickened on that last bit, and it was super sexy. Then I went from relieved to confused to horrified…I'm sure my face showed it all. Was I giving off Prince's "Do Me Baby" vibes on these steps? How embarrassing. I turned to continue the climb, when it felt as though a bolt of electricity struck me right through the center of my forehead. Distantly, I heard Ki call my name as I fell backwards and into his arms, then everything went black.

This time it wasn't as much of a shock to my system that I was in the sky. The fact I'd been transported here so aggressively this time, instead of the smooth transition this journey usually was, had me a bit miffed. Looking around at the constellation in wonder, I realized I was floating quite comfortably in the vast night sky. Then I looked across the distance for the kind, ancient gentlemen who always came to me. I jolted when my eyes met another face. He felt younger, but still powerful, pinpricks stung all over my skin as our eyes met. The depth of his gaze startled me; it was like a mirror copy of the night sky we were suspended in. Black swirling eyes with what seemed like tiny pinpricks of grayish light emanating from them.

"We don't have long," he said in a rich baritone.

"I'm hearing that a lot lately," I said wryly. This was getting old. Let's get to the point already. I hoped that my eyes conveyed that as I assessed the new intruder into my thoughts. My dreams? Visions? Or would these be more adequately described as blackouts? It would be nice if whatever these things were would provide more freaking clarity!

At my words he'd smirked in answer, folding his wings in behind his broad shoulders. They were gray and flecked with sparks of light like his eyes. He was handsome, but he had an edge to him. Though he was tall, he was lean and wiry. The opposite of the solid, coiled muscle that was Ki. He folded long fingers at his waist and waited as I finished assessing him. He was wearing a deep purple Mao suit in a silky fabric, with gold embroidery around the collar and buttons. It was quite distinguished. The way he inclined his head gave me the feeling he was royalty of some kind. I fought the sudden urge to curtsy as I met his eyes. The burst fade Mohawk he was sporting, combined with the suit was throwing off pretty, rich boy vibes.

"Are you done?" he asked succinctly.

"Quite," I replied in just as short of a tone. Then I decided I wasn't and pulled a comment out of my handy dandy pocket of sarcasm. "You know what, no, I'm not. Do you sing? You've got a nice baritone voice. Not quite an Avi, but definitely a Matt. It has potential."

He let out a derisive snort, which came off quite inelegant on his regal form. "Still haven't changed, have you? Too much to hope for I suppose." As if waving away my silly comment, he fanned a well-manicured hand in front of him and said, "Do not take the staff from the ancient one, it will kill you. Trust no one. You are not safe here, you must hide. Protect yourself at all costs. I will handle things here, stay hidden. War is coming."

I frowned in concern before asking, "What? What are you talking about? Who are you?"

He smirked slightly, "Heed my words, it is better this way. Nenda kwa Amani."

At his words, "go in peace," I felt consciousness start to tug at me. "Later gator," I got out as he faded away. What an arrogant prick, just throw a gang of meaningless words at me and disappear. Wait, had he been speaking to me in Swahili the whole time? That has been happening a lot lately as well. Heed my words? Who was this arrogant guy? Somehow, I thought he was right. I needed to be careful, things weren't right around here. Way too many secrets, someone had gone out of their way to keep me in the dark. Just because I didn't like the messenger, didn't mean the message was faulty.

When I came to, I felt as though I'd been hit by a truck. Why did everything hurt? That had never happened before. My visions were usually so gentle. Like being lulled to sleep and gently kissed awake. No exaggeration, that's how it felt, and this was the opposite. This was like being yanked forcefully out and then being shoved off a building back into the here and now. Did they have control over the way I felt during this? If so, this guy was a bigger jerk than I formerly thought. Blinking rapidly until my eyes focused, I was suddenly glad they'd turned the lights down, so the room was only dimly illuminated. Glancing up from beneath my lids, I noticed I was back in the bedroom I'd been in earlier and under the blankets of the comfortable queen-sized bed. After this was all over, I'd have to ask where he bought this mattress, was it a pillow top? I snuggled into it a bit more and noticed movement to my right. Auntie Ramla was asleep in a rocking chair next to my bed and there in the corner, blending into the shadows across the room was Ki. He was casually leaning into the wall with one shoulder, arms crossed over his chest and one leg slung over the ankle of the other.

Before I could ask why he was doing a batman in the corner of my borrowed room, Auntie reached over to lay a hand on my head. "What did you see, mwanamke wangu?" I tried to sit up and groaned before slumping back down. Auntie looked at Ki sharply, then leaned in to whisper in my ear as she brushed a hand over my head and down my shoulders. She continued to whisper as she brushed a hand over my torso and down both legs. Brow furrowed in confusion, attempting to figure out what she was saying, it was a few minutes before I realized how much better I was feeling. Looking over at her in wonder, I asked, "What did you do?"

She just smiled at me a moment before repeating her previous query, "What did you see?" I glanced over at Ki again; I don't know why I felt unease at telling her about the dream in front of him. Was it because there was another man in my vision? As if sensing my hesitancy, Auntie Ramla looked over at Ki. "Kimoni, will you go and get her some tea and a bit of the food I made for everyone? Also, let Aseema know that Mali is awake." Without hesitation, Ki pushed off the wall, gave me a knowing look and headed to do as Auntie asked. Once he was gone, she rose from her rocker and closed the door quietly. Settling back into her chair, she looked at me expectantly.

With a deep breath, I told her about my vision, what was said and the aggressive way I was pulled in and ejected from it. Surely the mysterious stranger couldn't have meant not to trust Auntie Rami. Throughout my telling of the vision, she kept stopping to ask me questions. She was especially interested in what the young man looked like, and I felt her unease growing as I recited the details of the vision a third time. We'd both decided that it would be best described as that.

Once she was satisfied that she'd gotten all the details, Auntie sat back and began to rock in her chair again. "Usually only an amateur causes pain for those they pull into a vision, it is unconscious. This does not sound like an amateur. Perhaps carelessness on their part, not knowing that you aren't able to navigate the ascent and descent on your own. How did you feel throughout this encounter?" I thought that was an odd question. "That's an odd question Auntie Rami." She smiled at the childhood nickname. When my teachers asked me as a child about my mommy, I'd tell them I didn't have a mommy, I had a Rami; thus, she'd been given the nickname Rami.

"You are an intuitive woman. Tell me, did you feel you could trust this stranger when he spoke to you?" I sat up higher on the pillows I'd been propped up on, this time with no pain. Giving her a grateful smile for that, I mulled over her question. "That's difficult. I trusted his words, but I can't say I trusted him. Like everyone around me," I looked at her pointedly, "I feel as though he had secrets or hidden motives that I could not pinpoint." Rami nodded sadly. "Yes, I would imagine so. Anything else?" she asked. I shook my head slowly. "I'll sleep on it. This has been a lot to take in."

Getting up from her chair slowly, Auntie nodded. "I'll let you rest then. The house is guarded, you are safe. Teaching you how to guard your own mind is something else we will have to work on when there is time. But they cannot harm you, only speak for now. Call out if you need anything. I am in the bedroom next to this one and Aseema is in the one across the hall. Though I am sure that Ki will be close by." She smiled as she said that and then leaned down to kiss me on the forehead before walking out.

Right on her heels, Aseema and Ki walked into the room. My best friend looked me over carefully and once she seemed sure I was ok, she walked around the bed and got in beside me. When we were kids and I'd have one of my weird dreams, she always seemed to know. There she would be at my window as soon as I woke up. I'd let her in, and she'd just lay beside me and let me tell her about it, until I was comfortable enough to fall asleep again. It warmed my heart that I still had her here with me through this. Kimoni gave her an odd look but didn't say anything. Setting down the tray he'd been holding in his hands across my lap, he gave me a small smile, before placing a book on the tray, then turning and leaving. I felt my cheeks redden as I looked down at the treats on my lap. It had tomato soup, grilled cheese, a cup of tea and the book he'd placed there. This was literally my idea of comfort on a platter.

"He is jealous I get to sleep next to you," she laughed. "Eat up and go to sleep sister, he'll be here in the morning for you to continue to ogle." For once I didn't argue with Aseema. As she snuggled in to go to sleep, I dug into my food, while flipping through the well-worn copy of my favorite book.

CHAPTER 5

Darling? Light of my life. I'm not going to hurt ya. I'm
just going to bash your brains in."
- Jack (Stephen King)

The room I was in faced the side of the house with the floor to ceiling windows, so I woke up to a sliver of sun shining into my eyes. I laid, unmoving for a moment, attempting to orient myself. I wasn't in Kansas anymore. Yesterday my normal life had taken a drastic change.

For the past six months I'd fallen into a steady routine. Dinner and home renovation shows or movies with Auntie in the evening, unless she had to work at the library or help some random neighbor. Then I'd snuggle up with a book or a stack of papers that needed grading for the night. In the morning, I'd wake up and go spend the day with the brightest third graders on the planet. I missed my students. What time was it anyway? Who would be their sub today? Whoever it was they'd complain that it wasn't me. Well, all except Juwan and Carlos, I hadn't quite won those two over yet. They'd decided that as nice as I am, getting into mischief is much more fun. No argument there. I generally kept their shenanigans in check, but they were going to give the sub hell today.

Searching for my phone, I thought about calling Assistant Principal Fondren, well Kim to me. But then it hit me, I might not have a job anymore. Yesterday I grabbed a colleague and then started glowing. I threw my hands over my head with a groan. What was happening to me? Fisting a hand over my eyes I started knocking on my brain, hoping that those lost memories of mine would answer. Nope, I was way too chicken to call into work; I'd enter my absence online in hopes I'd have a job when I came back. Picking up the phone to put the absence in, I saw I had a missed call from Kim herself. Immediately I clicked on the voicemail.

"Malika," her smooth voice flowed through the speaker, "Everything is taken care of here. Do not worry about your classes or your position, the children will be fine. I have taken care of things on your behalf, mwanamke wangu. It is a pleasure to be of service to you. Nenda kwa Amani."

The phone clicked, signaling the end of the call. Go in peace? My lady? Since when did Kimberly Fondren speak in Swahili? What in God's name was going on here? When Aseema walked out of the bathroom, I was sitting dejectedly on the bed. "Sis, what are you *over*thinking about right now?"

"How many people know, Aseema?"

"Know what Mali?" she asked, mimicking my tone.

"I'm not kidding. I just got a message from Kim."

"Oh."

"Yes Oh! She called me 'my lady.' She spoke in Swahili! Kim literally said 'go in peace'! Since when, Aseema? How many people in my life know about this-this-this dream world?" Unmoved by my outburst, she made her way over to the chair that had been pulled next to the bed last night. She was dressed in another pair of those supple leathers that we'd both been wearing yesterday. As always, she looked amazing. I really hated her sometimes and I was afraid to look in the mirror, quite certain I didn't look as sensual, fierce, and glowing the way she did. She threw a bag on my bed, interrupting my jealous thoughts, which gave me the opportunity to shake myself out of it. Must be PMS, I'm not usually this down on myself. Though dating, flirting and the opposite sex and I tended to struggle to connect, I did not have a low self-esteem. I'm a stone-cold fox, so take that, hormones! Back to the matter at hand, I needed answers.

Before I could prod Aseema again, she held up a finger as she seemed to carefully think something through. "Sister, I love you. I will always be here for you and have been so long before…" She paused. "There is not much I am permitted to say, but you are protected. I would lay down my life for you and so would others."

I was torn between being touched by her utter support and the fact that what she'd just said not only offered zero answers, but it was cryptic at best! Why would people need to "lay down their lives" for a history teacher? "I'd take a bullet for you as well sis, but why are the bullets coming? Who are they coming from?

Can we talk it out? Pay somebody off? You know we ride or die. Mostly ride. But all of this is driving me bonkers!"

Aseema only shook her head sadly. "You are different. This is different. I don't know how to explain further without repercussions, please forgive my silence in this matter. If it were up to me, there is nothing I'd ever withhold from you, mwanamke wangu."

Shaking my head in part frustration, part defeat, I hopped out of the bed and looked at Aseema. "What's on the torture schedule today? Oh wait, does that fall under the gag order?" I was rifling through the bag of my personal belongings as I spoke, but I paused when she didn't answer for several moments. Looking up at her inquisitively I caught the sad expression on her face and tilted my head in question. Still no answer. Putting an arm around her, pulling her in tight to my side, I said gently, "Seema, talk to me." Shaking her head angrily as tears filled her eyes, she turned to me and pulled me into a tight hug. "Never think that our friendship is not true. In this I have followed your every wish. Understand that it has been the hardest thing I've ever had to do. With the way I have lived my years, that is truly saying a lot. I need you to remember Mali Ali." Squeezing me tightly, she pulled back and looked me over with unshed tears in her eyes. "Now, go brush your teeth, your breath is ripe!" I swatted at her with a hand, and she backed away laughing mildly. Indicating I should put another pair of the leathers on, she walked out of the room and closed the door.

It had been unseasonably warm in Illinois, but the leathers came with a long, hooded duster, and boots. If the unpredictable weather switched up as it was prone to do, I'd be good. Once I was dressed, grateful that the bag had my own fresh undergarments, I gave myself a once over in the mirror. My hair had come undone during the night, no bonnets in this well stocked house, I guess. So, I put it in a ponytail at the nape of my neck. My cheekbones stood out with my hair pulled back. The brown and deep red long sleeve top with matching brown pants that were more like leggings complimented my curvy figure. I twirled; my waist was snatched, butt had a nice curve, and my breasts were sitting up just so. Posing, I felt like a character out of the Matrix. Well, if I was going to die in this deserted place, I'd die looking like a snack. Laughing at myself, I grabbed the duster and bag, then headed down the steps. It smelled like Auntie was cooking breakfast.

Yep! I thought with satisfaction. I was looking good, Ki's eyes widened slightly, as he gave me a once over before quickly returning to his food, studying it with an undue amount of attention. Trying not to laugh aloud again, I upgraded my former assessment of looking like a snack to looking like an entire dang meal! Men only did the LL Cool J lip lick when you were looking especially scrumptious. With a little extra oomph in my step, I tossed my things on an armchair and went to join everyone at the table. Aseema said with a loud smack of her lips, "Ok, friend!"

Auntie Rami hid her smile behind her cup, taking a small sip of tea. "It's good to see you like this again."

I looked at Auntie sharply. Again? "Auntie, when did you see me like this? How long ago?" She pursed her lips, probably trying to figure out how to answer me without being gagged by that stupid gag order. Finally, almost too quiet for me to hear, she said, "Long ago." Searching her face quickly, I looked for the effects of the gag order, but saw none. She continued sipping her tea, unbothered. "Rami, you were able to answer that without hindrance, why is that?"

"It gave away nothing of import. One must know how to navigate this thing. I've had much practice in what to and what not to say."

Staring at her for a few minutes, I thought about how I could work this to my advantage. What else could I find out? I mean, long ago is not the most informational answer, but it was an answer in a world of questions! Contemplating the possibilities, I just sat for a while thinking over what else I could ask, that may at least get me a piece of an answer. At least a tiny clue as to what was going on would be of assistance. Perhaps I'd been asking the wrong things.

"Eat," Rami commanded, interrupting my train of thought.

Absently, I began putting bacon, eggs, and pancakes on my plate. I took a few bites, chewing thoughtfully, before asking my first question, "Why is the deserted place, deserted? What happened there?"

Aseema stopped mid-bite to say, "War." She took another bite and then realized she was able to get something out and whooped in excitement, "Yes!"

"Were the three of you in this war?" Auntie nodded, but Ki and Aseema shook their heads in unison.

"If I could venture a guess, the war destroyed these lands. Otherwise, why would it be deserted?"

Auntie Ramla nodded in approval. Great, I was on the right track. "So, I continued, if this place is deserted, why is it dangerous for us to travel through?"

They all glanced at each other, finally Ki said, "The name is perhaps deceptive in that way. It is not completely deserted. There are those who linger to prevent…trespassers."

"I'm guessing that they are aggressive in their attempts to stop trespassers."

Ki eyed me warily. Maybe he was worried about the gag order stopping him again, it seemed to be painful. Taking a bite of bacon, he nodded in the affirmative.

"How did you get through unscathed?"

Kimoni put his fork down and gave me his full attention. "I am very stealthy. I only encountered two on my journey and they were dispatched easily. My entry was timed just right with some assistance, but I fear with your difficulties of late, you will be unable to hide effectively enough for us to complete our journey. Those we will be up against, will be drawn to you."

Blinking rapidly in confusion, I asked, "To me? Why? What do you mean dispatched? Did-did you kill them?" My brain went into overdrive, then another thought popped into my head. "Aseema what happened to those guys in the alley?" Continuing to chew happily, she looked up at me, drew a finger across her throat and then took a sip of her coffee. I'm sure my jaw was sick of hitting the floor, but what the heck? My best friend just admitted to killing…wait? "Seema, you killed all *four* of them?"

She just smiled as she aggressively jabbed a fork into her pancakes and then took another bite. Sitting back in my chair,

I felt the numbness of shock creep over me for the umpteenth time in the last 24 hours or so. Auntie reached over and laid a hand over mine. "Think, go back in your mind." I met Auntie Rami's eyes and after a moment of hesitancy, did just that. The strange light coming from the man in the restaurant. It hadn't been the first time I'd seen it, more than once I'd encountered that strange light. Then I thought about the green on Aseema's shoe and how she freaked out about it, the same green she was covered in when she returned from her battle with the four men. These things weren't human, but what? What were they?

As the realization came to me, Auntie nodded and gave me a small smile of encouragement. There was some sort of supernatural or alien war that turned a part of Illinois to a deserted place with things who would attack to protect it, men with green blood were following me, one flirted with me in a restaurant. Then I was quite sure that there were at least three occasions I'd seen Aseema with green on her, not to mention on Rami. How long had they been protecting me? What had I done in this other life that had made me such a target?

"Don't think that way Mali. None of this started with you, it is not your fault," Auntie reassured me.

My eyes bulged out of my head, but instead of looking at Auntie sideways, I looked at Ki. "You said you all couldn't read minds!"

Putting his cup down gently he said, "I told you that it was complicated." Glaring at him a moment longer, which to my aggravation he took with good humor, I turned my gaze back on my aunt. Holding up a hand before I could start, she said, "I got a glimmer of your thought, that is all. It is not something consistent, be at peace." That made me go still, the man last night said the same, be at peace. What was that all about? Then another thought occurred to me (there goes my ADD again). "Do I need a weapon? I need a weapon. How will I defend myself? Oh, Ki do you have a desert eagle? I always wanted one. Oh, or a Heckler and Koch P30L, so I can go all *John Wick* on these fools." I mimed lifting a man's arm and shooting him in the rib cage, right through the heart just like Bobo Yaga, when I realized that everyone at the table was looking at me with an assortment of facial expressions. Ki looked mildly horrified, Auntie was giving me a quizzical look (she's never seen the *John Wick* movies; if we got out of this, I'd have to remedy that), and Aseema looked downright proud.

"Would it be contrary to orders to give it to her?" Aseema asked, breaking the silence first.

"I think not," Auntie Ramla replied.

"Do you have it, Kimoni?" Aseema asked.

He nodded, then took one last swig of coffee and went to go find whatever the mystery item was (hopefully my Heckler and Koch). Praying I was getting my gun (probably not something one should pray for), I watched him exit the room moving at a leisurely, predatory pace. Ok, maybe I wasn't watching because of the desire for the gun, but his backside in those pants was a thing of beauty. There was a muscled definition in his glutes that flexed with each step. Leaning over the table, Aseema wiped the corners of my mouth. Batting her hand away I gave her an evil look. "Just trying to help you with the drool, it was starting to puddle on the table." Before I could deliver my scathing retort, she grabbed her plate and headed to start the dishes.

Auntie Rami laughed at our banter and poured me another cup of coffee. Taking it and doctoring with two creams and five packets of Splenda (don't judge me) I took a sip, smiling happily. If this was a bribe, I had no shame in taking it. I was even forgiving enough to let Aseema live…for now. Ki came back carrying something wrapped in black. It was unnerving how his booted feet made absolutely no sound on the hardwood floors. If I hadn't been facing the direction he was walking in, I'd have missed his entry. How a man that tall and muscled could move so stealthily was beyond me. No wonder he was able to get through the deserted place undetected. How was he doing that?

I was about to ask when he sat the silk wrapped item in front of me. The wrapping was gorgeous, so much so that I didn't really want to touch it. I tilted my head to the side, this way and that, the silk seemed to swirl and move with traces of silvery light flecking the deep black fabric. "It looks like," I started before trailing off, gathering my thoughts. Suddenly I was transported back into an endless night sky I had only ever seen in my dreams and visions. The difference this time was that I was being led toward the brightest of lights. Then, I was pushing through the light, only to appear in a gorgeous city, or rather on the outskirts of it, standing on beautiful iridescent mountain tops unlike any I'd ever seen, they glowed with light, the whole place did.

Surveying the city, it was all bright and beautiful, no dark spots or shadows to be found. The very houses were built in creams, silvers, pinks, and yellows. It was glorious. Then I realized someone new had entered the room, or the mountaintop, wherever I was. Turning towards the new arrival, I found the ancient man standing next to me. He smiled; he'd been looking at me the whole time. "Beautiful, yes?" I nodded in awe, turning my eyes back to the city. "Where are we?" I asked hesitantly, suddenly feeling shy. The man smiled, causing lines to form at the corners of his eyes, indicating that was an expression that often graced his handsome face. "We are home, Malika Alika," he said in a soothing tenor. "You must return to this place. No one else can restore the balance." What was he talking about? Return and restore? He had the wrong girl.

As if knowing my thoughts, he simply smiled again and pointed to the parcel in my hand. "Open it." Somehow the vision had transported the silk, night sky cloth. Whatever was inside, was extremely lightweight. I hefted it in my left hand and began uncovering it with my right. Looking down at what I'd uncovered, I simply stared at it in awe and wonder. When he spoke, I startled, gripping the item so as not to drop it. "I can no longer give you my staff. I no longer have the strength," he said sadly. It made me want to hug him. "But you were sent this to aid you. When the time comes you will know what to do. Be careful my love, come back to us quickly." He ran a hand gently over my hair and I could have sworn I saw a tear fall from his eye as I was lightly pushed from the vision, returning to Ki's home. Puzzled again, by why the return from my visitor last night was so aggressive and my visits with this ancient man were so gentle on the return, I just sat quietly, lost in my own tumultuous thoughts.

Gazing blankly through the windows, into the sunlit day, for God knew how long. I felt Auntie Rami put a hand on my shoulder. Jolting out of my reverie, I gave her an encouraging smile before looking down at the chakram in my hands. It glowed with a bluish light, which seemed to brighten ever so slightly as I reached my hand towards it. Carefully, I picked it up by the middle handhold and noticed a catching mechanism at its center. As the glow intensified, I wrapped my hand around it, in awe at the craftsmanship. The outer edges were a sharp silver blade all around, but the inner portion was lined in gold and onyx, shimmering in the light. Pressing the catching mechanism, the blade instantly fell into the shape of an s, turning into a double-sided scythe of some sort. It was super lightweight, and I had the feeling it would be easy to throw.

Enchanted by the light it emitted, I was startled to find two smaller chakrams? What would these be called? I turned to ask Rami and she leaned in immediately. "These are Chakri, you wear them at each wrist." As she spoke, she clipped one on each arm. The inner edges were onyx, smooth against my skin, but the outer edges were a sharp, bolder mixture of onyx and gold. They glowed ever so lightly, a perfect match to its larger sister, though not as deadly.

I had a sudden vision of falling and accidently slicing my own wrists. This may not have been the best gift for someone clumsy like me. I'd just snapped the chakram carefully back into its original circular shape when I felt air whooshing towards me. Without thinking I whipped the rounded blade towards the same direction as the Shotel slicing through the air, knocking the Mambele knife headed for my face, to the ground. My head whipped around between Ki and Aseema who were now nose to nose, faces angry and unyielding. Quickly I replayed what had just happened, faster than I thought my mind could catch. Aseema had thrown a Mambele knife at me (a throwing knife) and Kimoni had pulled out a sword blocking it. The most surprising part is my reflex. I'd really thrown the Chakram at her. Why had she done that? What in the blue blazes was she thinking? And where did Kimoni get a freaking curved sword from? Who walks around with a Shotel on hand?

"Aseema! Kimoni! Ramla called sharply, we do not have time for this." Neither one of them backed down, and while I had faith in my bestie, Ki was still much taller and much more dangerous looking.

"You could have killed her," Ki said succinctly.

"We needed to know," Aseema said, looking at him with mutiny in her eyes.

Ki's eyes flared with anger, and he emitted a glow from his mid-section that momentarily blinded me. Jumping up from the table I started to cry out when I saw Aseema pinned to the wall so quickly, I don't know that I quite saw the action as much as just registered the result. Ki leaned in with his Shotel across her throat and his free hand braced against the wall.

"You will not," he said between clenched teeth, "Risk her life unduly. We have enough concern, without your childish tests. You know your duty."

Aseema glared past the Shotel blade and into Kimoni's eyes.

"Please, let her go," I said pleadingly.

Ki didn't even acknowledge my comment. Instead, he leaned further down into Aseema's face, until they had to be taking in one another's breath.

"I cannot further risk her binamu." At that, Aseema's shoulders dropped in shame. It was then that I noticed my Chakram was embedded in the wall just above her head. A little lower and I may have killed my friend. I brought my hand to my mouth in surprise. Had I really done that? Looking down briefly at my hands, I wondered again what or who I'd been? Since when was my first response to anything to throw a deadly weapon at it? Then again, the heifer had thrown a knife at me. Maybe I should ask Kimoni to choke her out a little bit.

Wait a minute, binamu, Swahili for cousin…Cousin? Were they cousins?

I looked over at them again, there was a slight resemblance. They'd ceased their aggressive posture and were collecting their various weapons. Kimoni removed my haphazardly thrown weapon from the wall. I winced, it had wedged halfway in and left an impressive gash. Thank God, she hadn't been standing by the windows. "I'll pay for that," I said quietly, as he picked up the silk cloth from the floor and put it, along with the weapon on the table. Before he could respond, Aseema rushed over and pulled me into her arms. "Mwanamke wangu. Please forgive me." She dropped to a knee, and I looked down at my best friend, appalled. "I was so eager to see you restored, I'd hoped that would activate your reflexes and-and…"

I dropped to the floor with her and clapped a hand over her mouth. She looked up at me startled and I gave her a gentle smile.

"Remember in eighth grade when you were literally fighting three girls at the same time? They thought they were going to jump you and they got their ends handed to them! So, I knew from the start I was befriending a stone-cold psycho. It's one of the best things about you. Besides, Ki has the reflexes of a cat. Thanks for that by the way." I glanced over at him, and he nodded, crossing his arms over that broad chest, watching our powwow on the floor.

Gently removing my hand from her mouth, Aseema looked at me sadly, grasping both my hands. "If only you knew my friend. It is so much more than that. So much…" She stopped, struggling for words. Dang gag order. After floundering for a minute, she met my eyes with determination. "There is no excuse for it, you are not some recruit. You are more than just my friend; this time has made me too casual, and I will not forget myself again. I will protect you." Letting go of her hands, I grasped her shoulders and shook her. "Seema, I have no idea what is going on and I know you all can't tell me, but I will protect you with my life. It may be clumsily executed, but you have my word. You aren't just my friend; you are my sister, and I will protect you." Aseema shook her head, and I gave her a hard look to quell any protests. She only gave me a tender look, before turning to her cousin. "You are right cousin, please forgive me for endangering your flame, I would never purposefully cause you such anguish." Before he could answer, I decided it was time to lighten the mood. Besides, the whole 'flame' thing kind of freaked me out.

"So, you and Ki are cousins hunh?"

They both looked at me surprised. Good, teary moment averted.

"They are," Auntie said, seated comfortably, unbothered, at the table with her teacup still in hand. Leaning into Aseema, I whispered, "All this time and you never thought to introduce me to your fine cousin? I thought we were better than that." Auntie and Aseema laughed, while Ki coughed gently to my left. Dang it, I needed to work on my whisper; apparently it was faulty. I hung my head as my cheeks reddened. Aseema stood up and helped me off the floor, when an alarm went off, startling me. Everyone else seemed to know it was coming. "It's 8AM, time to go."

Ki immediately started grabbing bags and headed for the car. I hoped that my trunk was cleaned out. I tended to drive around with a lot of miscellaneous stuff in there, bowling ball, roller skates, a speaker, a few changes of clothes…What? You never know what could happen. As everyone scrambled around, preparing to leave I ventured over to the living room sofa, and took out my book figuring I'd get a few pages in while they finished loading up. I'd already been told I wasn't needed to assist with the loading. That's how I heard them talking quietly near the front door.

"Kimoni, you must try. We need her to remember. It is you; you are the key to unlocking her memories." There was a long pause after Auntie Rami's words. "I am afraid that she will not remember me. But I am also afraid that she will remember things about me that should remain forgotten."

"That is not of import right now," Auntie said fiercely. "There is something wrong with the Second Father. Why else would he try to give her his staff of light? We cannot let this happen. You know what will occur if she unknowingly accepts it."

"Yes. But the mother sent me here with instructions and I must follow her order first prophetess."

"This I know, my dear. We must tread carefully. Our journey is a perilous one. Stay close to her, be vigilant and work on awakening her memories. You must stop being so timid."

"I am not timid, Mother Prophetess," Kimoni said hotly. "I simply want her to make up her own mind. If the Creator will grant her memory of me, I will be grateful; if not it is because I am unworthy, and I pray someone who is worthy finds her."

A gentle roaring began building in my ears. Suddenly I felt shaky and stunned at the conversation. I couldn't hear what Auntie was saying momentarily as my brain attempted to adjust once again. He said we'd been everything to each other, but if I couldn't remember him, he was man enough to let me go. Wow... never have I even fantasized about a man giving me that type of deference. I was blown away. Just as I was about to quietly exit my spot on the sofa, I heard something that made me freeze.

"We all love her Ki, but if she can't snap out of this, we will have to let her go into the arms of our creator. You cannot stop us from ending her if it leads to that."

I didn't wait for Ki's answer, I jumped up from the couch quietly fleeing to the first-floor bathroom. Plopping down on the toilet, I tried to regulate my breathing, I couldn't have heard that correctly. Shoving my head between my knees quickly, I wondered absently what had happened to my life, that in the span of two days I'd found myself on the verge of fainting twice!

Auntie.

My only family.

How could she so casually plot my…death?

Why?

What would lead to them having to kill me?

What had I done?

Who was I?

The edges of my vision started to blur and darken. No, no, I chided myself. Now is not the time to lose consciousness, sis. Strange, sexy man, best friend throwing a dagger at me. Secrets on top of secrets, my aunt saying she may have to "end me"? Did that mean something different than what I thought? It sounded like a death sentence to me!

The arrogant man in my vision was correct. If I could not trust Auntie Rami, I could trust no one. I wiped at the tears running down my face. I had to be losing my mind, this couldn't be happening, this was entirely too much for one person to handle. Despite Ki's words, would he kill me as well? If Auntie could, he could, so now I was down to one ally. Aseema. The man in the vision told me not to take the staff, he told me to hide. Perhaps that's what I needed to do now, to get away from this band of misfits and go somewhere safe. But where?

I left the bathroom an eternity later with a plan in mind. Before coming out, I'd washed my face and tried not to allow the devastation of what I'd just heard show in my eyes. Though my reflection in the mirror still showed me looking shell shocked, I figured that was acceptable given what I'd been through since yesterday. The bathroom was right next to the back staircase, so without hesitation I turned towards it, shot upstairs to where I'd spotted keys yesterday on the bedside table. Carefully, I traversed the steps, heading down and out through the back door. It was a little too easy, but none of them imagined I'd leave. They thought I still trusted them. Briefly, during my bathroom musings, I'd considered letting Aseema come with. But bestie or not, she'd thrown a knife at me. If Ki wouldn't pull the trigger for Auntie, she just might.

It was perfect because Auntie had parked her Volvo SUV in the back. As my steps neared it, I turned on the remote start, so that my getaway car was running as soon as I hopped in. Hopefully, none of them would see me through the side window. Locking the doors quickly I pulled out and sped down the alley. If my luck held, they wouldn't notice the missing car, and would instead waste time looking for me in the house before venturing out to locate me. I was going the last place Auntie or Aseema would look for me.

Once I put a few miles distance between us, I slowed down. There was no time to find my purse and I was out here driving dirty, so this would be a bad time to get pulled over by the boys in blue. No papers and driving through downtown Chicago weren't the best idea, but I had to take my chances. It wasn't until I finally crossed the border into Indiana that my tense shoulders finally fell from their stiff position at my ears. I never drove in complete silence, clear indicator of my stress levels. Reaching over I turned on the radio, mellow jazz filtered through the speakers. I tried to let it soothe my tired soul, but it wasn't working, so I started fiddling with the dial, trying to find something more suitable to my present mood. Eventually, I turned it off in frustration. My thoughts were racing. I couldn't pin one down, my brain was a hurricane of images: Auntie Ramla holding my hand, spoon feeding me when I was home from school with the flu, her hugs, kisses, and love. Then, her plotting my death, you cannot stop us from ending her if it leads to that. "You cannot stop us from ending her if it leads to that. Send her into the arms of her creator." The words were spinning through my head and my heart was pounding so fast. Swiftly, I pulled over in front of a cluster of houses in the residential neighborhood I was driving through. I'd get back on the road when my head stopped spinning if it stopped spinning. Resting my head on the steering wheel, I concentrated on my breathing. My Apple watch vibrated on my wrist, encouraging me to take deep, steady breathes. Yep, already on that, thanks for the support.

Looking down at the streets around me, I realized I was only a couple blocks from my destination. Taking one last deep breath, I tried the radio one more time, settled on Jill Scott telling me that slowly surely, she'd walk away from love. "I feel you, Ms. Jill," I said, pulling away from the house I'd parked in front of.

CHAPTER 6

Out of the frying pan and into the fire.
- Everybody's grandma

When I pulled up to his house, I was relieved to find the driveway empty. Checking my watch, I thought maybe he'd finally learned how to get to work on time. That or he was with his wife at their other house, which made the most sense. This was where he usually went to rest and relax, not suitable for the workweek. Whatever the case may be, I could squat here until I figured things out. To be abundantly cautious, I parked Auntie's car at the beach parking lot within walking distance from his place. Walking with confidence so as not to rouse the neighbor's attention, I went around to the back, removed the key from its hidden compartment in a trick panel beneath the bell, and entered through the back door. It was apparent by the stale smell of the place that it had been vacant for a while. Maybe they were on vacation; he did like to travel.

Walking through the kitchen and into the living room, I spotted something he'd never have allowed in the past. A picture of him, his wife, and oh, they had a baby girl on the mantle. I picked up the picture and gazed at if for a moment; they looked happy. Good for them.

Compared to most of my friends, I'd developed an interest in men later in life. I didn't go on my first date until senior year of high school, and it had been a huge disaster. My whole life, I've been on the go, curious about the world. I was always exploring, trying new things. From being in drama club, choir, volleyball, tennis and presiding over the student council to taking swim classes outside of school along with a short stint in tap dance that didn't last long. So, when I graduated at the top of my class and was offered a chance to go into an accelerated program to attain my teaching license, I did so without hesitation, finishing up by the time I was 20. I was a history major and education minor, so I was excited to see the world, taking a special interest in African studies. When I was offered a chance to teach in Africa, I was ecstatic. It was there that I met him. He was exceptionally charming, educated, and sexy. Though he was 10 years my senior, and the director of the school there, we fell into an easy romance. Aseema told me he was oily from the get-go and was dead set against our dating, but I wouldn't be swayed.

In retrospect, I couldn't understand why I was so drawn to him. Looking at the picture now, I could see the snake oil sliding from his slick smile. He had what people usually termed "good hair." In the picture I held it was cut close to his scalp in small tight curls, but when I'd met him, he'd grown it out into longer curls that brushed over his neck. He had beautiful grey eyes and fair skin. At about 5'10, he was still much taller than me, stocky but lightly muscled. I think it was the way in which he focused all his attention on me as though I were the only woman in the world that completely pulled me in. To ensure that we didn't offend those we were there to serve, we kept our relationship a secret, which should have been strike one. We had late night assignations where we talked, laughed, and made love all night, then in the morning, it was back to boss and employee. It stayed that way for about eight, what to me then, were blissful months. Then we were all going on leave, back to the states to visit family, before returning to continue schooling our wonderful pupils.

To me that meant that we'd be able to finally be together out in the open. Go on dates, hold hands and just be a regular couple. No more late-night rendezvous. He'd seemed just as excited as I, talking about this house, what we would do, all of that. His place in Whiting, Indiana, near the beach where we could just relax and enjoy each other for hours on end. I was excited, I was ready for our one month of leave to be together. When we got back, he encouraged me to stay at his place, which saddened Auntie, but I was just excited to be with him. He told me that at first, he'd be gone a lot to visit family and friends that had been missing him. It didn't occur to me to even ask, why I wasn't invited to meet his family and friends if I were so special to him? I was naive and stupid, blocking out the obvious signs. Those first few weeks I was in the house alone, walking the beach with Aseema when she came to visit, going to be with Auntie for lunch, but making sure I returned Home just in case he came there for dinner. Two weeks went by like this and I grew restless. I confronted him. He was repentant, everyone was pulling on him, he'd meant for us to be together more, so he promised to stay the weekend with me. That's when it happened. She came by. She'd been waiting for him to leave that Monday, curious about why he'd come home to visit only to disappear for a weekend. On a hunch, she popped by the house, waited for him to leave, and walked into the bedroom where I laid spent after our morning of lovemaking. She showed me the engagement ring. They were planning to marry next year. He'd promised to cut his time in Africa short so they could start a family.

I remembered that day so vividly. There was no malice in her tone, she was just matter of fact. He is mine; you are a fling and now it's over. Numbly I got up to dress and gather my things, holding back the impending tears. Very kindly, she told me to take my time. She'd handle him. No need to call or come back. He wouldn't be returning to Africa at months end, she'd make sure of that. I should go find someone my own age, someone in my league, she said.

At the time I was 21. It had been almost four years and I'd not bothered to date anyone else since. High School had been full of meaningless flirtations, but nothing serious. My studies were always my focus. Aside from a little fun in Spain, I never cared to try to love again. How does one recover from that type of betrayal? My first love, my first everything was a fraud. Sitting the picture down, I turned to go and explore the rest of the house but was stopped short. The front door burst inward, splintering wood flying everywhere and causing me to quickly duck down behind the couches, cowering and covering my head with my arms. Then, faster than I could blink a hand grabbed me by my hair, forcing me up off the floor.

I blinked up at him, struggling to get his hands off me before I was inadvertently scalped. Black woman no-no, you do not grab our hair. Fury raced through me as my eyes registered the sickly green glow emitting from him, making his features difficult to discern. One thing I could see was his malicious smile. He was thoroughly enjoying my angry struggles as he held tight to my hair. Footsteps were rapidly approaching, and I began to fight in earnest, praying that this wasn't backup for him, but was help for me instead. I looked over at the door hopefully, shocked to find that it was once again, back to its regular untouched state. Blinking rapidly in confusion, I was caught off guard when my captor was punched solidly in the face, by the second intruder, with the same green glow. Falling onto the floor in a heap, I looked up at them both pissed and confused.

"She is not for you," the second intruder said viciously. Grabbing his compatriot by the collar, he shook him for emphasis. "We must take her to him, so that the war can begin." Take me to him? That was not a preferred pronoun at the moment; trying to remain invisible from my perch on the floor, I glanced around the room for something to help me escape, when my eyes landed on the chakri at my wrist. In awe, I wondered how I'd avoided cutting myself. Running a finger gently across one, I realized the metal was smooth. Then my head was banged against the floor and things went sideways.

"Tell the others to circle back, we'll transport her from here." Even as I heard his words, my brain was attempting to adjust. The door was off its hinges again and that green light was growing brighter. Wait…what was wrong with his feet? My captor's feet were backwards, literally backwards. They faced his butt, how did he walk, what the? The world was slowing down, he was rearing back to kick me in the ribs, why the violence?

My body started acting of its own accord. Muscle memory I couldn't quite trace, I slid the Chakri on each of my wrists across each other and the sharpened blades popped out. In a fluid motion, I leaned forward and sliced the blades threw the achilles of my would-be captor. He let out a shriek of pain as I jumped up from the floor whirled and sliced my left wrist across his exposed torso dodged his friend, sidekicked, spun and sliced my right wrist up through his arm pit in a punching motion. The second of my captors let out the same shrill shriek and light seemed to gush out of them both, light that was rushing towards me, blinding me. The green light that glowed from them ebbed and dissipated, but a pure iridescent light raced towards me, and I felt the impact as seven different colored lights punched right into my torso filling me with an unnatural high. Stunned I froze, as even in the face of this danger euphoria and peace and washed over me! The back door crashed inward at the same time as new enemies filtered in through the front. The reinforcements must have heard the screams and came running. I didn't know how I pulled off that last little stunt and I wasn't sure I could duplicate it with this next set of guys. Four had filed in through the front and I'm not sure how many were coming through the kitchen now. Wait. Yes, I was; I heard the sound of six sets of footsteps. This wasn't good. How could I hear that? All my senses felt heightened. Each of these guys had that green glow and backwards feet. But all of them had pinpricks of iridescent light inside them. Whatever that light was it hadn't melded with their natural green glow.

While I was wool gathering, they were closing in. I guess I better go down fighting. Angling myself to see the troops from the kitchen and the one's at the front door, I let my arms hang loosely at my sides, tensed to defend. But they seemed hesitant, each glancing down at their disintegrating buddies on the floor, then at each other. They couldn't possibly be scared of little old me. That's when the picture window at the front of the house crashed in. Ki was a blur, but somehow my eyes were able to keep up with his movements this time. As he came through the window, he took the glowing green beast in fronts head with the curved sword in his left hand, whirled, caught the second in the gut with the sword in his right hand and then extending his arms took the heads of the other two in one clean motion. Light rushed out of each of his decapitated and maimed victims.

The other six were moving in, not even taking note of Aseema who'd come up behind them. Silent like an assassin, tensed on the balls of her feet, she'd taken out two with her throwing knives before they realized she was back there. Ki was headed that way and as much as I wanted to watch, I had problems of my own. A particularly large man, exceeding Kimoni in height and breadth, grabbed me by my arms, thinking to take me captive. I slumped in his arms as though in a faint, his grip tightened and I slumped even further, he let me slide low enough to slice my chakras up behind me and through the meat of his thigh. He growled in pain, pushing me forward, but I caught myself on the balls of my feet, turned and curved my arm, slicing my left wrist across his throat. The same thing happened again, the iridescent light flowed into me and the green ebbed away. Shaking with the sheer joy of that light it was a moment before I clued into what happened. While I was taking care of my single henchmen, Ki and Aseema had dispatched the rest. Light coalesced from the bodies they'd taken down, then it arced around racing right for me. Powerless to stop it, I braced myself for the impact as it punched into my torso. Why me? Why was it targeting me? It was a whirlwind of emotion and pleasure that caused me to stagger, almost falling to one knee when Kimoni and Aseema rushed to either side of me, helping me quickly out of the house.

Absently I heard them talking. "The Father must be truly ill if the light is targeting her as the source. Ki what haven't you told us?" There was a long pause before he answered, "There is no time to explain now. We will have to do it out of her hearing anyway. I know not what the Yamanu will do."

Aseema's attention then turned to me. "I can't believe you came here of all places Mali." Out of the corner of my eye, I caught Kimoni's confused look.

"Why? What is this place?" I shot Aseema a quelling look, but she only shrugged as they hustled me into the car. Auntie Rami was at the wheel and after helping me into the back, Aseema hopped into the front, leaving Ki and I alone in the spacious back seat. Oh, the possibilities. I think we had a little wiggle room for some fun back here. I caught myself before I giggled like a little schoolgirl. Or at least I thought I did. Ki looked down at me in question. My head was resting on his lap, God he smelled good. I'd have to ask him what that was later. His thigh flexed under my head. Mmm, yummy muscles. I clasped one of my hands around the top of his thigh and couldn't help but smile as I nestled in.

I felt him stiffen under me and opened my eyes to tell him to relax, I'd be gentle. But my eyes met Aseema's, as she peered into the backseat. I didn't know she was a voyeur. I guess she could watch, but Auntie was going to be a problem. Tilting her head to the side in thought, Aseema said with a smile, "She's drunk. Or high, whichever you think is a better way of describing it." I felt Kimoni shift beneath me again. "Is that what it is?" he asked wryly.

Drunk, I thought happily, maybe I was. But on what? Assessing myself momentarily, I considered it. This may be more adequately described as being sated, yet hungry at the same time. I felt the rosy glow that the aftereffects of sex usually produced (it's a wonder I remembered) but I was also intensely keyed up. I wanted more, I wanted more everything! At the moment, I just wanted to take a bite out of Kimoni and my body was agreeing loudly if the heartbeat that was thrumming between my legs was any indication.

Ki adjusted again, clearing his throat, and resting a hand on my hip. Yep, that wasn't helping. I just might be drunk. Aseema was still looking, privacy friend! I thought at her, hoping she'd get the hint. She only smiled at us. "It's surprising," she said to Kimoni. "That the light went to her and not you. Does that mean she is now strongest?" I had no idea what she was talking about, but I looked up past the beautiful expanse of muscled chest that was clearly defined in his fitted leathers. Feeling my gaze, he looked down and met my eyes. Removing his hand from my hip, he gently smoothed the stray strands of hair that had pulled loose from my ponytail. Closing my eyes, I reveled in the feel of his strong fingers sliding over my hair. I love having my hair rubbed, so soothing and…pleasurable.

"I feel what she feels," he said softly.

Aseema inhaled sharply and I opened my eyes looking at him in question.

"The light is shared," Auntie said, speaking quietly for the first time since I got in the car.

Kimoni held my gaze, steadily stroking my hair. My eyes were getting heavy all a sudden. Were these the aftereffects of the light? I didn't even get to play with him in the backseat, I thought sleepily. Kimoni smiled suddenly, then leaned closer to me, and I felt the muscles in his abdomen bunch. *Perhaps when we don't have an audience moto wangu. Sleep.* Had he read my mind? Wait, had he spoken into my mind? Lead weights were on my eyelids and before I could feel the slightest bit embarrassed or inquire about his knowledge of what I was thinking, his words worked like a command, and I fell asleep. I woke to sun streaming into my eyes, again! Only it was much more intense this time. Where was I? Kimoni's electric heat was absent and though the sun was shining I felt cold. Looking down at myself, I realized someone must have cleaned me off while I was sleeping. The green goo had been sliding down my leathers in thick droplets after that little encounter. I wondered why some of it turned into dust and other parts of it this viscous gook. With a start I realized that at some point I'd have to deal with the fact I'd killed or maimed three...well they weren't men. Beasts? Animals? Whatever they were. I'd ended the lives of sentient beings and though it was in self-defense, I knew it was going to take its toll. At the moment though, the lingering effects of the lights that had surged into me, kept me buoyant and guilt free.

Sitting up slowly, I looked around the large, clean range rover with its leather seats and then out the window to find that we'd parked at the beachfront. What happened to the Volvo? Where did the rover come from and what the heck were we doing at the beach? What would Steven think when he saw what we'd done in his home? And to his home for that matter? I paused, waiting for the sharp sting to my heart that occurred on the rare occasion I thought or said his name. After several seconds of feeling absolutely nothing, I allowed a small smile to spread. Whatever those lights were, I could get used to the effects, especially with Kimoni gone. The accompanying sexual heat was much less pressing now that we had some distance between us. Instead of being at the closest beach by Stevens' home, they'd made the trip to Rainbow Beach...why?

Swinging open the door, Aseema said, "Hey sleepy head, we've got to get a move on it. The sun is almost at its highest point and that's the optimal time to move. It'll give us some cover. You're a bit bright after ingesting all of that light."

She assessed me for a moment, then her eyes widened in a look of surprise. "Somethings happening. I shouldn't have been able

to say that much. Thank the Creator, we are making progress."
Smiling, she grabbed my hand and pulled me towards the door.
I took her hand and jumped out, landing lightly on the balls of
my feet. She flashed me another smile, then walked behind me,
strapping something to my back. I felt behind me to find that
she'd somehow anchored my Chakram between my shoulder
blades. "I see you learned how to use these," she said, placing my
Chakri back on my wrist. They were clean, no green gook, she
must have taken care of that for me. Giving her a grateful smile,
I studied them, feeling a great deal of comfort seeing them back
in place on my wrists. "For an added blessing," she said, tying the
starlight scarf at my hips.

She then helped me into my trench coat. It was gorgeous. The
sleeves of the supple leather had a thumb hook, which I promptly
put my hands through. Though fitted through the top, the coat
flared at the hips and flowed down to my ankles. Gold embroidery
reminiscent of the gentlemen's Mao suit in my vision circled the
buttons that traced down the length of the coat. I popped up
the hood and walked out, somehow making my way gracefully
across the sand. The knee-high lace up boots I was sporting had
me feeling like a dominatrix with all the leather, not to mention
out of place at the beach. But Aseema had on a variation of what
I was wearing, opting instead for a hooded leather jacket that
stopped at her hips in a peplum style.

"The coat and leathers will be added protection. They are
enchanted to shield our light," she explained. We were halfway
to Auntie and Ki when she stopped me, lacing her arm through
mine. "Sis, I don't know why you ran. I do know that this is all

overwhelming, so I won't ask too many questions now. But know this, you are safest with us, she met my eyes. I will protect you. No one will harm you on my watch. Please don't run from us again. We cannot lose you." Not giving me time to respond, she propelled us forward quickly.

Auntie who I'd have to have a little chitchat with later, was dressed in the supple leather as well. She was still built well for a woman of her age. Grudgingly I had to admit she looked fierce and capable. Kimoni had that heartbeat fluttering at the core of my body again. He stood with his back to us, clad in black with blue stitching running throughout. Instead of a coat, he was wearing a vest with a long-sleeved shirt underneath. He'd also donned a pair of gloves and the two Kotel blades rested between his shoulders. The positioning made me wonder if it were to accommodate his wings, then I noticed vents in his vest where his wings would rest.

Curious I reached a hand behind me to touch my own shoulder blades. "You've got them too," Aseema said absently, checking the numerous throwing knifes at her waist. There was a new addition at her hip though, a leather whip. Noticing my eyes on it, Aseema took it out. "It's a sjambok. But it is our own special leather, infused with…the stuff that takes out our enemy." She was being very careful. I guess she was concerned about the gag order again. I nodded, grateful for the small detail and I tested the whip she handed to me. It was light, but the tip was a bit heavier. Swung the right way, it would do some damage. After a few more fascinated swings, I handed it back to her reluctantly.

Smiling, Aseema gave me a pat on the shoulder. "I'll get you one, once we get back home."

Purposely I stood on the edge of the group, next to Aseema. Until Ramla and I had it out, I was keeping my distance. Oddly enough, my best friend, who'd thrown a dagger at me, was the safest of the three. Perceptive as always, Ramla looked over at me. "You will understand in time my lady. In the interim, I can only continue to protect you as has always been my mission. You'll do well to stay near one of us at all times in the Ardhi Iliyotengwa."

There was an unfamiliar coldness inside me, mixed in with the array of sensations the lingering aftereffects of the light continued to cause in me. Sidling closer to Aseema until we were shoulder to shoulder, I met Ramla's eyes and asked, "Are we going to do something or is the plan to continue standing here under the heat of the sun in leather?" Kimoni and Aseema made eye contact, she nodded and moved from my right side to my left. Taking my left hand in his, Ki began to countdown from five. I felt Aseema take my right hand in hers, but I kept my eyes on him as he gazed out over the lake. When Ki got to three, they began to walk, pulling me in step with them until we were in the water.

Before the chill could seep through, we were…elsewhere. I don't know how else to explain it, but we went from being in water up to our ankles, to being somewhere else completely. Sand covered the ground, but it was no normal sand. The range of colors in the grains was startling yet beautiful. There were shades of green, purple, blue, red…the Crayola box couldn't cover the assortment of colors that spread before me. But that was all there was. Multicolored sand and a burning hot sun, high in the sky. There was nothing else, at least that I could see, for miles.

"Where we must go is across the sand but hidden from natural eyes. Even we cannot see, but the mother will guide us once we are close. Stay vigilant. Remain by my side. I will keep you safe." Kimoni spoke softly, squeezing my hand gently before releasing it and drawing his twin Shotel's. They glistened in the light of the noonday sun, like my Chakram the hilt was onyx and gold, with a silver blade that seemed to be imbued with iridescent light. Unable to resist, I reached out and lightly caressed the flat of the blade. Fighting a smile, Kimoni looked at me out the corner of his eye, a smile spreading over his face. "Don't say it," I said quickly, fighting the blush rising up my cheeks. "Say what?" he asked innocently. I gave him a look. "You are free to touch my blade anytime you like," he said. That startled a nervous laugh out of me. Throwing knives in each hand, Aseema just rolled her eyes as we all started our trek through the Ardhi Iliyotengwa, the deserted land.

After what seemed like an hour of walking with no reprieve and the sun still shining high in the sky, I realized how apt a name the deserted land was for this barren place. Seeming to intuit my distress, Ki stopped and handed me a canteen. I floundered a moment, wondering where he'd gotten it from. Then thirst won out and I drank deeply, before realizing that perhaps I should save some for him. He simply smiled and lifted a hand. The weight of the canteen changed. I hefted it a moment before taking another sip. He'd somehow refilled it! Speechless, I just looked at the container in my hands, wondering how. After a few more moments of me just standing there, Ki took it from my hands and downed the entire thing. I watched droplets of water spill over the sides of his mouth and down his neck, fascinated by the way his Adams Apple bobbed with each gulp. Wiping his mouth with the back of his hand, he refilled the canteen again and handed it back to me. This time I tried to be more considerate, turning first to Aseema, but she was gulping down her own, then reluctantly to Rami. Couldn't have the old bird passing out in dehydration, but she also had her own. Shrugging I put the canteen back to my lips, hyperaware that Ki's mouth had been there before gulping down a few more mouthfuls. I wondered briefly why they'd not provided me with my own. There was a certain intimacy to sharing with this stranger who said we were once everything to one another.

Meeting his eyes as I handed back the canteen, I had another one of those out of body experiences. This time I was neither in the sky, nor on the mountaintop overlooking the beautiful starlit city. I was sitting in a garden on a rooftop surrounded by flowers in the most surreal colors. They brought me to mind of the many colors of the sand that my body should still be standing on. But there I was, surrounded by flowers, sitting in front of a beautiful fountain, that had a winged being spouting water from it. I'd transformed again. Long hair in rope like strands hung down around my shoulders and past my waist, in full sister locs. My clothes were flowing and so light weight, I almost felt naked. Wings settled comfortably around my shoulders and there was a peaceful feeling that surrounded me, sitting in this place that felt like home. Then Ki walked in, looking regal and strong. He was dressed in a suit similar to the strange man who warned me in my previous dream, only his looked to be more of a linen material, and his jacket was unbuttoned, revealing a beautiful smooth chest and those gorgeous abs. He came and sat next to me.

"Why is there never enough time with you Moto wangu?" He curved a hand gently around the nape of my neck and I smiled up at him affectionately. "You are always in motion. But I won't hold you back. I won't try to slow you down. I only desire to be where you are, and now…you are even taking that from me."

"Forgive me my love," I said. "I would not do this if I thought it not absolutely necessary." As I looked up at him, I realized suddenly, this wasn't a vision or dream like the others. This was a memory.

Then the memory me nestled in his arms, my head resting on his chest, and I gave myself entirely over to this remembered comfort. If it was a memory and not my imagination, it was a good one. He traced a finger around the pointed curve of my ear, and I shivered in delight. Somehow, I could feel his smile, where his chin rested on the top of my head. Wanting to see the gentle curve of his lips, I looked up into his eyes, loving the swirl of caramel that made up his irises.

Inhaling for courage, I asked, "Will you do something for me before I go?"

He frowned. "Need you ask? At this juncture I have acquiesced to all of your less than savory requests to the letter." Smiling at me to lighten his words, he nodded, urging me to ask. Yet I hesitated, unsure of how he would react. It was outside of our traditional way of doing things. But I wanted this, needed to remember this before I left. Taking a breath, I said-.

I pulled out of the memory, straining to do so, I back peddled out of it with a strong mental push. Turning away from Ki quickly, I paced out further on the sand, he did not follow, giving me space, but Aseema was right on my heels. Was he in that memory with me? Did he cause it? In the end, it didn't really matter. He knew what I'd asked, and he may have even…acquiesced as he said he did with my other requests. Rubbing a hand over my face in frustration, I gave myself a mental push. I needed to know but was afraid to find out how deep this rabbit hole went. Apparently, I'd been in love with this stranger. But now, aside from a clear attraction, all I felt toward him was curiosity, with a heavy dose of confusion. Who was I kidding? I didn't remember him, and I was already smitten. But first I needed to figure out who I was or rather, who I used to be. What I was being drawn to across these sands to do? To see? Before yesterday I could have answered the question of, who I am without hesitation. Now I wasn't so sure.

I felt Aseema at my back. "You are glowing Mali. The sun and your protective leathers can only do so much against your powers. You've ingested much light, please stay with us. We can and will protect you."

Turning to her abruptly, I said, "You keep saying that. I can't take much more of this. It's like everything I've known is a lie. Who finds out right before their 25th birthday that their whole life is not their whole life? Instead, I have all of these hidden memories, this life, this past I cannot remember. Except I keep getting glimpses of it and it is freaking me out!" I'd started pacing during my rant, but came up short, because suddenly it was so bright, I could barely see. Trying to make out what was around me, peering through the blinding light, it looked like the very sand was glowing.

Aseema was saying something I could barely make out and I was starting to panic. It was like I was standing in the middle of a lightbulb or a fire! It was suddenly so hot, the light engulfing me. Oh God, I can't breathe.

I felt myself hyperventilating.

Looking around me frantically for a way out, all I could see was the light. Feeling faint, I had sunk to the sand, when a familiar shape stepped into the ring of light, and right up to me. It was still so bright, I shielded my eyes, trying to see. Then I felt his hands at my waist pulling me up off the sand and his mouth at my ear. "Breathe. Be calm my love, I am here."

Immediately, the light began to dim, but it was still so bright. He repeated it again, in Swahili this time, "Tulia. Niko Hapa." The light dimmed even more, until I could make out his face, his eyes on mine. Moistening my lips nervously, I gazed at him, hoping to calm the fire that was boiling through my veins. His eyes followed my tongue across my lips and suddenly my mouth was dry. I inhaled as his lips met mine, barely brushing, sending a tingling sensation from my lips down to my stomach, when he deepened the kiss, applying more pressure, liquid pooled in my abdomen, and I melted into him.

Just as I parted my lips, inviting him deeper, his hands left my waist in a flurry of motion, grabbing his blades and extending outward. Lifting his head from mine, he looked left and right.

Dreamily I followed his gaze. He speared a green lit creature on either side of us, while over his shoulder I saw Aseema fighting another two off. That's when I heard Auntie behind me and whirled around in horror. She couldn't possibly be...

But she was. Rami stood calmly behind me with what looked like a dainty staff in her hand. It was a long thin number she held loosely at her side. She was intuiting their actions adeptly. One would step up and she would slice through the air with deadly precision, responding just a hair before they acted. Within minutes? Seconds? She had three laying at her feet. Bracing myself I waited for them to fly into me, but nothing happened.

"We're too close to home," Ki said at my back. "They will go straight up now." I turned to ask him what he meant, but he was dispatching another two creatures with his curved blades. Aseema swaggered over, having finished her battle she stabbed the last one Ki was either fighting or toying with (I was leaning towards toying with) in the back.

"Ki, don't play with your food," she said in a singsong voice. Flicking the goo off his blades, Ki rolled his eyes at her re-sheathing them.

Aseema ignored him, walking jauntily over to Rami. "Auntie how many did you get?" she asked with barely concealed excitement. Rami looked at her sharply. "This is not a time to rejoice daughter. It is something we must take on with sobriety. Our creation is twisted and dying." Looking chastened, Aseema gave a contrite nod and I tried to hold back my smile as she silently counted the bodies. Once she finished, she pointed to herself and held up five fingers, declaring herself the winner, with the most kills. Though I was convinced, that if Ki hadn't been distracted kissing me, he'd have won. He had four and she took his final kill. Auntie was still eyeballing Aseema, with an arched eyebrow, she glanced over to three additional outlines in the sand. They'd already started joining the piles of greenish dust all around us, but it looked like 3 additional kills for Rami, bringing her total to six. Auntie won. Aseema's jaw dropped briefly before she gave a respectful nod. Auntie looked over at me and winked, I smiled before catching myself.

Ki was still on high alert. "That was only the first wave. We must move." He looked at me and held out his hand. Without hesitation, I placed my hand in his large palm and we began our trek once again. This time we hurried through the sands at a light jog. In silence we journeyed for about twenty minutes more, before the questions started bubbling out of me. Seema, Rami, and Ki were all sweeping the terrain with their eyes as we walked. They'd created a type of triangle formation around me. Aseema was to my back, Auntie to my left and Ki holding my hand at my right. I was surprised he was hindering his sword hand to hold mine. "By holding your hand, I hope to help shield your light." Unspoken was that he was also attempting to keep me calm. He wasn't worried about his sword hand because he was fast and just as adept with his left hand as with his right. The man was an impressive swordsman. "Thank you," he said simply. I tossed him an annoyed look and his steps faltered just a bit. This time he didn't answer me aloud, but in my head.

The more we communicate in this way, the easier it will become. I was not lying to you when I said I could not read your thoughts. It requires a connection and your...permission.

I contemplated that for a moment. *So, because we kissed, you can read my thoughts? That's the connection?*

He hesitated, his grip tightening slightly on my hand as he surveyed our surroundings. *The kiss didn't hurt, but... you remembered something. You are starting to regain your memory. Perhaps it has something to do with our proximity to home. We are nearing our pathway there.*

I nodded, wondering if the gag order would prevent him sharing information with me here, in our minds. There was only one way to find out. He met my eyes then, raising a brow.

Ok, I thought. *Where should I start?* He patiently waited for me to decide on a question, not interrupting my thought process, but somehow, I could feel him hovering at the corners of my mind. It was an odd, but comforting feeling. Though I was working hard to tamp down certain thoughts that I didn't want him to see? Hear? What adjective did you use for someone listening in on your brain? Either I was doing a good job of hiding certain things or he was just that much of a gentleman.

Landing on a safe, but extremely pertinent question, I decided to force it to the forefront of mind.

Can you tell me what these things are that keep attacking us? Out of the corner of my eye, I spotted his nod of approval. I guess I was asking the right questions. Sweet!

I hate to answer a question with a question, but will you first tell me what you've noticed about them so far?

I pondered that a moment before answering. *Their feet are backwards. They face the backs of their bodies like some African folktale. I wouldn't have noticed except they seem to have an aversion to shoes and those feet are u-g-ly! They are covered in hair; the toenails are long and feral. I haven't been able to make out their true facial features yet, but they seem able to make themselves look normal…almost like how I can see your wings sometimes and sometimes I can't.* I squinted in thought for a moment. *Like a glamour.*

Yes. His tone was encouraging. *Keep going, my love.* He squeezed my hand, and I tried not to mull over the "my love" endearment. I knew we were in love once, I felt that much in the memory, but it was still a foreign concept. Forcing my mind back to the topic at hand, I continued mentally chewing over what I'd saw so Ki could listen and tell me whether I was on the right track.

So, we are glamoured, like our enemies…Their light also seems, rotten? Tainted? It glows green from low in their bodies. While your glow for example seems to shine from your abdomen. His gloriously muscled abdomen that I wanted to take my time and kiss each pec of… Dang it! Did he hear that? I mean read that, in my mind? I tried to glimpse his expression out the corner of my eye. His face was deceptively still and unreadable, but I forged on. Vowing not to think about kissing my way down his six-pack again. Behave, I reminded myself sharply.

Their light seems to come from the darkest places on their forms. Armpits? Butt? It's tainted. They have their own green hue that shines a sickly light, but there has been other light in them. Light without darkness. It seems to gather in them separate from their natural, or maybe distorted is the word, light. Oh, and there are stumps on their backs as though they once had wings…are they some fallen form of us? Us, I was saying us…it's official, I'm not human. But when I felt Kimoni's pride in what I'd deduced, tickle across my skin all thoughts fled. He was proud I'd remembered or figured so much out.

They are the Anguka, the fallen. Most similar to the African tales of the Asiman who emit phosphorescent light from their armpits and anus. It is not so much that they use glamour on themselves, but they can glamour other things. Those that walk around on Earth take on human flesh, cannibalizing their bodies as they do the light of the Azizafri. Our people. Their feasting on our spirits and eating of human bodies has distorted their light. Gradually, their wings fall from them, leaving stumps. Then their feet become backwards much like their minds. Their tainted light sours their blood which brings about that smell, turns their blood green and thickens it into the goo you saw earlier. After so long the goo goes back to the dust from which it was created, resulting in this sand like substance you see around you… He hesitated, as if holding something important back. I'd fallen into their ritual scans of the horizon, so I simply squeezed his hand in encouragement. It wasn't difficult to catch his deep intake of breath.

The Anguka become more powerful when they ingest our power, the power of the Azizafri. That is why they are so dangerous to us. The more of us they devour, the stronger they grow and… I waited while he worked through what he needed to say. Finally, as though he were whispering across my mind, he shared the true horror of our enemies. *Our light when they take it from us becomes trapped inside the Anguka. It's like we become a constant battery fueling their power, giving them strength to defeat more and more of us. This is why you felt such euphoria when the trapped lights entered you. They were happy to be free, so grateful that they offer you their last bit of strength before returning to the creator.*

I don't know at what point I'd stopped moving, but I'd come to a standstill on the multicolored sand. Looking up at Kimoni in horror, I watched the myriad of emotions cross his face: sadness, concern, and anger. Then looking down at the sand, I asked, *And these?* I swept my hand over the vastness around us.

From the dust we were created and to the dust we shall return, he said simply. Then seeing my look, he amended. *Their light returned to the creator from this place. But when the Anguka perish, they simply return to dust.* Pointing to a trail of green sand, he said, *That is Anguka.* Then pointing to a trail of orange, red, and yellow, he said, *And that is Azizafri. We leave the dust behind when we are ingested.*

My heart filled with sadness at the amount of lives lost here. The beautiful colors I had been admiring were the dust of a people I had no knowledge of but was descended from and the others from a cannibalistic race. Though the power of the light was heady and euphoric, I couldn't take this level of devastation. Without another word, Ki pulled the hand that he had yet to let go of and I went willingly into his arms. Resting my head on his chest, I inhaled deeply, taking in his comforting scent of patchouli, jojoba oil, and that sweet faint scent of cocoa mixed in with sweat. Momentarily the desire to bite him overrode the overwhelming sadness that encompassed this place.

Feeling his chest rumble in silent mirth, I pulled back quickly. His eyes were filled with laughter, and he fought to school his features. Leaning down close to my ear he whispered, "I'm going to have to teach you how to severe the connection for when you want your thoughts to be your own. In the meantime, where exactly were you thinking of biting?"

CHAPTER 7

Into the unknown...or at least what was once known and has now been hidden.

We'd been journeying for at least another hour when I had a sudden realization. It had only been an hour since our last stop, but we'd been walking for at least 3 hours total, while the sun looked to be at the same spot in the sky and we were by no means closer to anything but more sand...or should I say, evil and light dead ashes.

Kimoni grinned suddenly and I looked at him accusingly. He said calmly, "I told you that you are in charge of severing the connection. See it being cut off in your mind or blocked and I will be unable to hear you. In answer to your train of thought, this place is outside of time. Each phase of the sun and moon lasts much longer than the human 24-hour cycle. We are almost at our destination, so stay close. The enemies we have encountered thus far are nothing compared to that which we may face ahead. As you know they become stronger with each light they ingest. Those that we have met with have only supped on a few low-level Azizafri; we may encounter those who have supped on many, many more, with greater power levels, and they will not fall as easily as the rest."

Looking into his solemn face, I said just as solemnly, "Thank you most kindly for the encouraging pep talk." Kimoni opened his mouth to respond, when my Auntie, who had been uncharacteristically quiet except to give instruction here and there, responded, "He is correct. Your light and our proximity to the portal will draw them out. They cannot find it on their own, so we must kill anything that spots us nearing it to protect the safety of our kin."

"Who exactly are our kin?" I asked more sharply than I'd intended. Aseema and Kimoni gave each other wary looks, while Auntie only shook her head. "What Ki has shared with you through the connection, was only allowable because you'd deduced most of the information about our enemies through your direct contact with them. The gag order, as you call it, will not allow us to share much about our race. It is our hope that once we return, you will begin to remember, or at least deduce things that will loosen the orders hold." I nodded stiffly, still not quite able to forgive her, for that whole, "you may have to kill her" conversation she'd had with Ki. Can you blame me?

A little. I heard Ki's voice quietly respond in my mind. I gave him another sharp look. He only laughed and said aloud, "It's up to you to severe it." *Then again, perhaps you want me to stay inside your thoughts.*

Not likely, I thought back, casting him another sideways glance. He only smiled again…it was a really nice smile. Dang it! He can hear that, I chastised myself internally.

Suddenly something else occurred to me. I decided to ask him mind to mind, since he was listening anyway. *How did my aunt know what we discussed? Can she hear us when we talk this way? Can Aseema? Wait! Is she even my real Aunt?* I must have been thinking loud, because he winced slightly, with each of my panicked thoughts.

Not taking his eyes from his continual sweep of the horizon, he responded in our silent way. Absently I noticed that Auntie and Aseema were more alert. Auntie had her staff out to her side and Aseema had a blade in one hand, while the other held her whip loosely. I'd had to crane my head around to look at her and she only gave me a firm nod before going back to her continuous vigil of our surroundings.

It startled me when Ki began speaking into my mind, answering my stream of thought. *She cannot hear us here. No one can. It is very useful, especially in high-risk situations. Because I am used to doing such things I can open a different link in my mind with Ramla, while we talk through another link. I told her and Aseema through a separate link, what you'd figured out. We are all anxious to see your memory restored. Ramla is your true kin. She is your family.* He hesitated a moment, subconsciously I realized that he was testing the gag order, to see if this was off limits. Interesting that even they didn't seem to know what they could and could not share with me. The next group of thoughts came slowly as though he were carefully choosing or filtering through each word that he sent my way.

There is a block, he paused to point at his head. *There are even certain things that my mind will block you from due to this restriction. Mind to mind dialogue is only possible between two who already have a connection. It would not work with a stranger for example. Perhaps you would consider trying to open a new strand with Aseema?*

I'd really like to severe this one before opening another. You in my head is already a lot to deal with. His expression did something funny at my response, but I couldn't quite catch it. I tried a glance into his thoughts, but they were now closed off to me.

"Why is it that you can't close off our connection?" I clearly read the hesitancy on his face. Then he looked at me with a quick smile, sincerity pouring from his eyes, and said, "You're stronger than I." That one threw me for a loop. I looked him up and down, raising a brow in incredulity. "How Sway?" I asked aloud, giving him another once over. 6 '6, a trim waist, broad shoulders, muscular arms, calves, and thighs (yum) and a well-defined stomach that his layers didn't care to hide, and I was stronger. Hah! He only gave me another small smile and kept pushing forward.

I wanted to press more, but suddenly the air seemed to distort in front of us. Gazing intently ahead of me, I tried to make out what it was I was seeing. When my eyes went slightly out of focus, I saw… a rainbow? It was in an arch that spanned thousands of feet overhead, yet somehow my eyes focused in and were able to discern the top, where colors flowed through it, beautiful and iridescent. But when I tried to study it more closely, it seemed to disappear. Letting my eyes go out of focus, I saw it again. Mesmerized, I focused in and then let my eyes drift out of focus several times before realizing that the cross-eyed look probably wasn't the look I was going for standing next to this chocolate mocha dream. I glanced over at him and saw his mouth twitch slightly. With a concerted effort, I imagined slamming a book closed on our connection. Immediately I saw him wince. Then tugging me lightly by the hand so that our sides brushed, he whispered so quietly it could have been my imagination, "Gentle, my love...it's been a while."

I took in a sharp gasp of breath. What the...? I laughed. Yeah right, looking as good as he did there was a line outside his door of available women, men and whatever else he might want. Just to test the connection, making sure it really was closed for the moment, I imagined him in that towel he was wearing yesterday. Glancing at him from under my lashes, I saw no change in his facial expression. Either it was working, or he had a good poker face. So, I visualized us naked, together. Still no response (not from him anyway). These leathers were getting a little too hot on my already overheated skin. In this case, my imagination was a bit too vivid, so I quickly closed that train of thought. Surprisingly, the sun's rays hadn't had any effect on me in my many layers until I started thinking about a naked Ki and Mali. Quickly I backpedaled out of those appealing thoughts once again and decided to try my hand at reopening the connection. Putting my brain to work, I imagined opening a book, then I gently nudged him with my thoughts asking, *What's up with the arched rainbow doorway thingy?*

He looked over at me before going back to his study of the horizon. *You can see it then? This is where we enter or exit. However, you'd like to look at it. But we must be very careful, there are eyes all around us.* I nodded; though I couldn't see anyone or anything, I trusted that he knew what he was talking about.

Good job, by the way. Shutting, then reopening the connection. As you get better at it you can block certain thoughts as well. Though I'm not eager for you to learn that. I like that you're an open book when we talk in this way. Kimoni squeezed my hand and I felt warmth wash over me at the sincerity that colored his thoughts. *I need to learn that fast,* I replied teasingly. He only shook his head.

Then I felt it, there was immense power approaching quickly from our left and right. At least 20 fallen were coming and they were chock full of Azizafri light. They must have all felt it because our entire group stopped and fell into fighting stances. Kimoni, dropped my hand and pulled his swords, holding them loosely at his sides, Auntie Rami stood with her staff resting in front of her looking completely unbothered and Aseema graceful as always was in a deep crouch with a throwing knife in each hand. Feeling exposed and shaky, noticing how they all formed an arc of protection around me, I pulled my Chakram from the holster at my back. I'd protect them just as fiercely as they sought to protect me. Ki gave a slight nod of approval. Then our attackers appeared, as though they were simply popping into being out of beams of light.

Two leapt toward me immediately and Ki met them in the air, shooting up so high it was as though he was flying. Both feet connected with the chest of my first assailant and arching his back he reached over and sliced into the other with his curved Kotal blade. As soon as he could flick the gook from his blades, there were more to replace those who had fallen. Suddenly the battle was taking place in mid-air. The flurry of motion was hard to follow. Partly because they were moving so quickly and also because my eyes kept wanting to jump to Aseema and Rami where they fought just as fiercely.

How could the fallen fight in the air? I thought they'd lost their wings? But Kimoni's were spread wide and majestic. He looked like some beautiful avenging angel, though I'd never seen one with such beautiful multi-colored wings.

Then I was in the air, frozen in shock. Someone had grabbed me! What the what? I was about to start struggling when my eyes met Aseema's. She'd launched me up, and I looked down realizing why. I'd been so busy watching Kimoni's fight I'd almost lost my own to the two fallen below us who'd gotten past Aseema and Auntie to close in on me.

"You ready bestie?" she asked breathlessly. A wild excitement lit her eyes. I nodded quickly as she started to descend. "Put those weapons to use then. I'll fight at your back, but stay alert."

We landed gently on the ground and right back into action. Auntie was heading off those that came my way, while Seema fought at my back. But one got through and with heart thumping, I brought my Chakram up, blocking his first blow, ducking his second, then kicking out catching him in his stomach. My enemy snarled in protest, flying back much farther than I thought my little kick could ever accomplish. That's when his features became clear. His eyes were like a black pit, hair covered his face and most of his bare torso. The green light shining from his arms and bottom was almost blinding, and emitted a putrid, rotten smell. But the feet were the worst, cracked backward at what looked to be such a painful angle. His features were a mixture of human and beast, with long canines that hung past his lips and his nose pushed up like that of a pig. He was wrong, he was broken and then he was on me again, grasping for my neck.

Without thinking, I raised my left hand catching his grasping fingers with the blade of my Chakram, watching in horror as three of his fingertips flew into the air. The beast barely paused, reaching around with his other hand. In a knee jerk reaction, I brought up my left hand, grasped his head and shouted, "Ponya!" His reaction was immediate, he scrambled back, looking at me in horror. I stood frozen, hands still extended in the air. What had I done? Why did he react that way? I searched his face frantically as he crawled awkwardly backwards on his hands and distorted feet. It was apparent that he was trying to put distance between him and I, but after a few jerky movements backwards, he began to come undone. His light started to separate.

He'd eaten 25 Azizafri, five of them extremely powerful, and they began to escape right into me. How I'd come by this knowledge, I did not know. Though Ki had said that the lights would not escape into me in this place, I saw them as they came rushing at me, filling me with power and euphoria. The Anguka lay on the ground shaking and convulsing, the others around us frozen, as finally he stopped moving, his eyes that were once black had turned brown. Then, he looked at me with an expression that I had to be mistaken in reading…it looked like gratitude crossed his now normal looking face. Then, he disappeared in a cloud of colored dust. Not the green that they usually became, instead it was a long streak of red that mixed in with the vibrant colors of the sand. The fallen who'd still been fighting, began to flee as the rest of our small unit stared at me in awe.

I looked around for Ki and found him still hovering in the air, wings outstretched. Auntie had her staff in front of her again, her head tilted to the side in thought and Aseema who had been at my back, had turned to me fully and was gaping at me in wonder.

"Well, that was different," I said, before a giggle escaped. I sunk to my knees on the sand, and gave way to full throated laughter. Yep, I was drunk again. Those were some powerful Azizafri who'd lent their power to me this time. It was like I was flying...in fact. With a thought my wings snapped into place, and I soared upward giggling into the wind as it hit my face. Up and up I went! The wind in my hair and the feel of wings at my back was exhilarating. I flapped them a few more times before catching the current and soaring gracefully, gazing in the direction of the sun. Enjoying its rays. I was giggling like a loon. No wonder the fallen got addicted to the power of the Azizafri's light. It was heady and intoxicating. I arced around when my gaze met the ground. Wait! That was really far down. I would die if I fell! What am I doing? I can't fly! Just like that, my wings disappeared, and I began to fall, right to the...arms of Ki.

"Well, hello handsome," I said, nestling into his chest. "Come here often?"

Ki grinned, a look of wonder still gracing his strong features. "Anybody ever tell you that you make a sexy drunk?" I smiled at him as he began to descend, wrapping my arms around his neck and nuzzling his throat. "No, but do feel free to tell me more." Ki tightened his grip where his left hand rested at my back and his right under my legs. "Makini, moto wangu." He shivered lightly and I laughed. He wanted me to be careful? But I am his flame, why should I be careful. With him I should be very, very uninhibited. Opening the book I'd closed on our connection, I let him see a glimpse of what I'd like to do to him at that moment. His feet had just touched the ground, and his usually graceful movements faltered in response. Startled his eyes met mine, as he freed my legs, letting my body slide down his until my feet met the ground as well. He closed his eyes briefly, letting the visions I was sharing with him play out. My vivid imagination was having a field day today, as I gave him my full focus.

Aseema cleared her throat loudly. "Mwanamke wangu. Binamu." She said, addressing us individually. "My lady. Cousin. I hate to interrupt, but I must know." Hesitating, she waved her hand towards the red streak in the sand. "What did you do to him? I have never seen anything like that before. He started changing back to his original state, and…and…" she faltered. "You are able to absorb light." She waved a hand around her again. "In this place."

With an effort, fighting the euphoria clinging to me. I struggled to quiet my sensual thoughts and then pull back from Kimoni, but he tightened his hold, pulling me closer to him and giving me a meaningful look. *Oh, oh…I should probably give you a minute before I move hunh, I asked through our mental connection.* Ki gave me a sarcastic look. *I'd hate to scandalize my cousin or the prophetess for that matter…you did start this.* He gave me another look that clearly said, "you started something and didn't finish it." I tried to stifle a smile. He had no idea how badly I wanted to finish it. Again, he pulled me closer. Dang it. Concentration was difficult due to all the light I had just absorbed. His nearness was only making it worse.

Giving Ki another meaningful look, I decided to turn slowly in his arms, still covering him but now his pelvis was to my back. Very deliciously pressed against my back to be exact, I closed my eyes briefly. He was…impressive…everywhere. *That's not helping,* he growled into my thoughts, sending shivers up and down my spine. With an effort, I imagined gently closing that book that was open between our minds and made eye contact with Aseema, still fighting against my body's response to Ki's.

Clearing my throat, I said, "I truly don't know. We were fighting. I felt how strong he was, the many lights, the spirits in him. There were five strong and 20…normal level lights that he'd eaten. They wanted out. It was as though they were calling for release." I tried to gather my racing thoughts, still high, still euphoric, so I could adequately explain what had occurred in mere seconds. "I knew his strength; they didn't want to be used to harm me. The word 'heal' came to me. But in Swahili. So, as he rushed me, I laid my hand on his head and said it, 'ponya.'"

Aseema looked at me in disbelief, Auntie just seemed curious, I craned my head to look at Kimoni. He simply seemed interested, but I couldn't tell if that was because of the evidence of his desire still pressed against my back or because he was really interested in my story. I didn't want to chance where my mind would go if

I reopened our mental book, so I forged on. "He was something else, before he was fallen. My words were taking him back to that state. But he couldn't live through it. He'd ingested too many. Yet he was grateful. He was in pain." I spoke haltingly, thoughtfully as I pieced it all together. "Those he…killed. They were so grateful to be free, they forced through the desert plain and into me. Giving me their last vestiges of strength…in gratitude."

Everyone was quiet for several moments.

"We were right to bring her here," Auntie said, breaking the long silence. "Her power grows as we near home." She looked as though she were about to say more when her head jerked to the left as though listening. I felt Kimoni stiffen behind me at the same time; whatever they were hearing, or sensing, was eluding me. Then we were all moving so quickly the ground seemed to blur beneath my feet. For a moment I wondered if we'd somehow taken flight again when Auntie whispered a word that echoed around us musically before we were launched through the rainbow arch.

As we flew through, Ki wrapped his arms and wings around us in a protective cocoon. It had to hurt as we landed and rolled halfway down a mountainside before coming to a stop. But he didn't make a sound and though I was jostled around a bit, the steel of his arms didn't let up and the contrast of soft wings around us prevented me from much injury. Once we stopped our descent, he rolled from me, groaning in pain. Leaning up quickly, I laid a hand on his chest and asked, "Are you ok?" He sat up with another groan and said ruefully, "That's one alternative to a cold shower." I gave him a smile, before climbing slowly to my feet. His sense of humor was still intact, he'd live to fight another day.

"Halt! You are trespassing on these lands." Looked like that fight would be happening sooner than we thought. There were five guards around us, if their matching attire was any indication. I could sense there were more in the trees. They had us surrounded. Quickly I looked around, noting the numerous spears, swords and it looked like a few archers in the sky before my eyes landed on Aseema and Auntie. They were both rising carefully from the ground, hands out at their sides non-threateningly.

Auntie spoke first, in a clear voice, "Protectors of Mahali Pa Amani, permit us to remove our glamours. We are kin of the Second Father, King of Amani." Place of Peace, Auntie called it. This contingent of leather clad warriors didn't look particularly peaceful as far as welcome wagons go.

"The Second Father is not in rule. We are ruled by King Nyoka," the man with the spear nearest Kimoni's throat said. He hadn't allowed Ki to stand, and he had aggressive eyes trained on him. Assuming he was the greatest threat, I suppose. Rami's eyes narrowed on the guard, who I would guess was their leader, and said crisply, "Nyoka may rule in his stead, but the Second Father is our King until he returns to dust. That is our way. So, stand down now." With that, Rami pulled a hand over her head as though removing an invisible hood and my mouth dropped in awe. Her body began to glow, a glorious light gleaming from her midsection and illuminating a gorgeous face. She'd always been a looker, but the 50 plus years that she carried on Earth fell away, leaving a svelte woman who looked to be no more than 20 years old. Her eyes glowed and swirled with a beautiful amber light, her usually braided hair fell into a riot of gorgeous curls that coiled around her shoulders. Rami usually stood about 5'3 and had grown several inches, but the most beautiful change was her wings. They flowed behind her in every shade of purple one could imagine. They were mesmerizing.

Immediately the guards fell to their knees with heads bowed around her in obeisance. "Prophetess," several lips whispered in reverence. Ki finally stood gracefully to his feet and in a similar motion as Rami, removed his glamour. The man was already beautiful in his glamoured form, but good God. I was having a hard time looking away from him. He tossed me a sensual smile (or maybe my brain just interpreted it as sensual, it could have been his normal smile), before focusing hard eyes back on the guards. Oddly enough, Aseema kept her glamour on, moving closer to me on silent feet. It didn't escape my notice that she was being incredibly careful not to bring attention to herself. She gave me a conspiratorial look and edged slightly behind me.

One of the guard's in back of the group snapped his head up as though listening intently before rising to his feet, sweeping a bow in Aunties direction and inclining his head to Ki respectfully. "Forgive our ignorance. We have heard rumors of infiltration and the King, he said irreverently, has asked us to tighten up on security protocols." He gave Auntie an apologetic look, she only inclined her head in response. "King," he said again in a way that indicated he didn't honor this man as such. "Nyoka has communicated with me, asking that I bring you to the core. He sensed your presence once your glamour was removed."

"Lead the way Captain," my aunt said kindly.

"Your friends," the Captain said hesitantly, gesturing in the general direction of Aseema and I, "will have to wait in the city. Our new protocols do not allow us to bring guests into the heart of our kingdom." Though they did not give an outward indication of it, I felt something pass between Ki and Rami. Quickly Ki said, "I would see my mother and Father. Prophetess, I am sure that these capable guards of Mahali Pa Amani will be ample protection for you as you travel. If you would permit, I will leave you to escort our guests to my home in the city." The guards straightened their backs at Kimoni's commendation and Auntie gave him a knowing smile. "Thank you, my son, I will meet you there later."

Without hesitation, Kimoni had me in his arms and we were in the sky. "Interesting how I keep ending up in your arms," I said. Smiling broadly, he tightened his grip on me, "You could just pop your wings out and fly yourself. Shall I let you go so you can give it a try?" I tightened my arms around his neck, giving him a reproving look. He laughed and turned us in the air in a smooth motion. Aseema laughed joyously, twisting and turning gracefully in the sky. I smiled, watching her enjoy the flight. Then my eyes were everywhere, admiring the beautiful mountains in the strangest colors of violet, fuchsia and emerald. They looked so familiar…like the mountains I'd stood on in my dream. The city below us was all beautiful lights that flickered in various hues of color. This whole place was a gorgeous contrasting riot of dark and light hues of every color imaginable, some flowing in a monochrome of one shade and then going into the monochrome variation of another.

"It feels so good to be home," Aseema breathed, coasting through the air with her eyes closed in bliss. I looked up at Ki, only to find that he was gazing down at me, with a small smile on his face. Waves of joy rolled off him. Leaning his head closer to my ear he whispered, "Welcome home." A sense of peace washed over me at his words, and I beamed up at him happily. Now this felt like a place of peace, high in the sky, held in this beautiful man's capable arms.

It seemed that we reached our destination in only a matter of minutes, making the flight entirely too short for my liking. We landed at the base of a small hill when I said as much. "Well, Aseema said, practically dancing up the hill, turning every so often in a ballet like pirouette, time is much different here." I was about to ask how so, when halfway up the hill the front door burst open and what looked like a medium sized rocket flew straight at us. Ki set me aside quickly, braced his legs and spread his arms apart as the rocket barreled into him.

"You're home," a small voice squeaked in excitement. "I missed you so, so, so, so much!" Little arms wrapped around his neck in the tightest hug. He embraced her with just as much joy evident in his features. A woman was moving towards us in the child's wake at a much more leisurely pace. In confusion, I realized how much the three of them looked alike. The little child had Ki's eyes, that same caramel swirl captured in big innocent eyes, a small nose, and round cherubic cheeks. The pointed ears that were signifiers of the Azizafri were evident along with a tiny pair of wings in various hues of pink at her back. I looked over at the woman quickly, who was hugging and rocking Aseema with tears in her eyes. Was this…Ki's family? Did he have a wife and child? Oh God…how embarrassing …maybe here they were allowed multiple wives! No way in any planet or dimension was I going to be a sister wife! Besides, the child's mother was gorgeous. I had a great rack, but how could I compete with the grace and beauty headed my way? Jealousy and distrust burst hot over me, and I didn't realize I was glowing until Aseema and Ki crowded around me, blocking me from view, urging me not to allow my light to escape. Ki spoke quickly into my mind, *Moto wangu! What is wrong? Please calm down. We cannot yet allow them to know you are here.*

I took several deep breaths; Aseema was stroking my back, but my eyes were all for the mother who held the child that looked just like Ki tightly in her grasp. Shutting Ki out of my mind, I tried to calm myself. I felt his confusion at being shut out, but I couldn't let him hear these insecurities. Is it possible to have relationship PTSD? In all my memories and visions Ki loved me, but I thought Steven had loved me and look what happened there. Men could not be trusted.

Aseema waved Ki away gently, and he went reluctantly to hold his wife and child in a tight grasp that caused a sharp pain in my abdomen. Gasping for air, I rested my head against Aseema trying to get myself together.

"Best friend, I have to tell you something." I waited, but when she didn't answer I looked up reluctantly. If she was going to tell me about Ki's family, I really didn't want to hear it. Though I was pissed she knew and hadn't warned me. She knew what I'd been through! How could she withhold this from me? The hurt must have shown in my eyes because her expression softened in pity. "You know what, I'll just introduce you."

Grabbing my hand she led me over to Ki's beautiful family as I fought not to hyperventilate. They were standing there looking super adorable and at home. Ki had his arm slung around his wife's shoulder and his daughter balanced on his left hip. This would explain the sadness that always lingered in his eyes, whenever ours met. I'd asked him what we were to each other. Though he'd told me that we were everything, I couldn't help but realize that he's said it in the past tense. I'd been gone, I'd forgotten or so they told me. I couldn't blame him for moving on. Though he'd been extremely caring, sweet, and loving to me, perhaps he was remembering our past. I wouldn't rat him out to his wife, but he was a total jerk for being so familiar with me, while she waited patiently here for him. Suddenly, an anger on her behalf overrode my sense of loss at not being able to further explore the constant tug I felt between Kimoni and me.

Before I could further follow that train of thought, Aseema said brightly, "Binamu, I want you to meet a friend of mine from Earth. Bestie, this is my cousin, Kimoni's sister Lea and her daughter, Ki's niece, Issa." Relief flooded my body. Kimoni looked confused; Issa and Lea just looked at me oddly. Then, Aseema gave Ki a look and I knew instinctively that they were communicating mind to mind, so I elbowed her in the ribs. Or at least tried to. She dodged it gracefully, pulling out of my grasp and taking my hand to lead me the rest of the way.

Kimoni was looking at me with a mixture of affection and amusement, which I worked hard to ignore. Reaching out a hand to Lea, I waited for her to shake it. She simply stood there looking at me like I was some strange creature. Her brows furrowed as she looked me over, as if trying to see through me. Looking over her shoulder at Ki, her eyes filled with questions. Before I could try to figure out what was passing between them, Aseema smiled patiently and put my hand down. "We greet each other like this," she said quietly. Then she walked up to Lea, pulling her away from whatever silent conversation she was having with Ki, and touched her forehead to hers. They both said "peace" as if in greeting, but in Swahili, "Amani."

Now that I looked at them, there was a family resemblance between Ki and Lea. They both had the same full mouths that seemed to be both teasing and sensual no matter what the facial expression. Their noses were also similar, prominent and strong. While it sharpened the angles of Ki's face, it softened Lea's most beautifully. She was tall as well, her head hit at about his shoulder. Odd that her daughter had taken her uncle's eyes instead of her mother's beautiful violet flecked irises.

Tentatively Lea walked over to me and said, "Amani," then touched her head to mine. I leaned in and felt a sense of familiarity as our heads touched briefly. "There is something familiar about you. You are from Earth, but you are a halfling, yes?" Handing Issa off to Aseema, Ki moved smoothly over to my side. "Yes, my sister, she is. This is the secret mission the Queen asked of me." His sister nodded as if in understanding, then walking over to the other side of her brother, she asked softly, "Did you get to see her, my brother?"

See who, I wondered? And why would their queen want me? So, I was only Half Azizafri? Maybe that's why my memories were impaired. Then my thoughts stuttered and halted as Kimoni's face lit up in a warm, brilliant smile. "Yes, my sister, I did," he said. She put her hand around his waist, giving him a squeeze and as we started walking up to the house, he gave me a sly wink. It felt as though fingers slid down the spine of the book I'd closed between our minds. Without thinking, I opened immediately and felt his joy pour into my mind. I looked up at him in surprise. It was me his sister was asking about, but she did not recognize me. His joy was at seeing me again. I tried to stifle the blush that suffused my face, but there was no stopping it. Quietly whispering in my mind, he said, *My flame, my one and only flame.* The way he emphasized the word only. I knew that Aseema had ratted me out on my teeny tiny meltdown upon seeing him with his sister and niece. Apparently, I had some past issues I was still working through. The past two terrifying days hadn't helped.

CHAPTER 8

Learning to keep my hands to myself...then again,
maybe not.

The house was amazing. From the sky all I could see were thousands of lights twinkling below me. No buildings or structures, just the light and color that was this beautiful city? Planet? I had no idea what this place was, but it was straight out of a dream. A beautiful, detailed dream. As we walked up to the house, my jaw dropped in amazement. The grass was covered in flowers, flowers everywhere, in every color imaginable, like a huge Crayola box of buds. There were more flowers than grass beneath my feet and they seemed to move out of my way as I walked. As awed as I was by it, I was glad I didn't have to crush them beneath my feet. They were much too beautiful to be trampled by my size 8's. A path started halfway up the hill and I quickly moved to walk on it, in deference to the beauty of the ground beneath me. There was no real temperature. I was neither hot nor cold in my leathers, while Lea and Issa were dressed in flowing gowns of chiffon which they seemed completely comfortable in.

There was no sun in the sky, no stars, no moon, but the place was lit as though it were daylight, as though we stood in the center of the sun. The very ground effused light, but it didn't hurt my eyes or prevent me from seeing clearly. Then the house, my God. I am not an artist, but how I wish I could draw it. Kimoni told me quietly that all their homes were shaped like starbursts. The higher your home rose into the sky, the more influence and power you had. Their home was stories of stacked starbursts that boggled the mind. There were windows all over and it reached into the sky at points and peaks that made me wonder how they traversed the house without falling or consistently walking at a slanted angle. There must be thousands of steps inside.

I was used to houses of brick, wood or covered in siding, but their home shimmered in an unknown metal that glistened in the light pouring from the very ground. We walked through the double front doors into a large foyer. There were hallways branching off in every direction. New levels were separated by three to five steps before going up into the next long hallway and the next. This was nothing short of amazing…walking into the middle of the entryway I looked up, there was a circle right in the middle of the starburst that had to be 1,000's of square feet alone. Looking up at the vaulted ceilings, I noticed there must be several rooms above this. The house was decorated in beautiful hues of cream, teal and silver accents. Definitely not Ki's place then. If his home in the city was any indication, he leaned towards darker, more masculine colors over this lovely, bright home.

"Finally," Aseema said, heaving a huge sigh. Reaching up in the same motion that Auntie Rami and Kimoni had used earlier, she pulled her glamour off and rose to her full height. Stretching and extending her wings before tucking them away again, Aseema smiled and twirled happily. "Come on bestie," Aseema said, grabbing my arm. "Let me show you where you'll be staying for the night."

Nodding, I followed her up a set of stairs to the right. We went up five steps and came out onto a landing where three rooms branched out, all like long, wide tunnels, but decorated with furniture, books, beds, and the like. We didn't stop at any of them, instead we kept going until we'd reached about the fourth or fifth level, I'd lost count. "Seema?" I asked, as we walked down one of the corridors. She didn't respond; instead she kept hold of my arm moving briskly into a room at the middle of the structure. It was massive, decorated in gold and lilac, I just looked around for a moment taking in the enormous fireplace, four poster king sized bed with draping around it, the enormous library of books and a huge jacuzzi tub in the corner. Closing the door behind us, Aseema led me over to a sitting area beside the fireplace and with a wave of her hand it lit. Jumping back from her on the loveseat, I gasped in surprise. When did she learn how to do that?

Ignoring my obvious shock, Aseema clasped my hands in hers and began talking softly. "Something is wrong mwanamke wangu." At her tone, I snapped to attention, meeting her eyes, and inhaling sharply at the worried expression on her face.

Rushing on, she said, "You've heard already that Kimoni was sent to get you by the Queen, this is true. The gag order prevents us from saying much on that. But know that you are in danger. We thought it would be safer once we got you home, but there is a problem. Nyoka will not be pleased that we have returned. He will be looking for you and until we know what he wants, it is best that we stay hidden. Rami will delay as long as she can until we find a way to get you to the Mother. In the meantime, no one must know who you are. We cannot use your real name. That's why I introduced you to Lea as Bestie. She now thinks your name is Bessie."

Looking at her in horror I said, "The girl thinks I'm named after a cow!" Aseema stifled a smile and said, "I called you bestie, because I couldn't think of another cover-up and she thought it was Bessie, so...there you go." Crossing my arms and shaking my head in mutiny, I said, "You've got to do something about that." Putting her hands on my crossed arms with a smile, Aseema shook her head. "It's best not to create confusion. This is only temporary until we get you to the Mother. Please focus on trying to regain your memories." Curiously, I tried to create a connection with Aseema, opening the book that was my mind. Instantaneously, I flew back against the farthest end of the loveseat, gasping for air.

I looked up at Aseema in shock, "What was that?" Her eyes were wide, and she was holding her head. After several minutes of both of us attempting to get our bearings, she said quietly, "The gag order is in full effect."

Once we caught our breath, Aseema laid her hand over my head and reinforced the glamour that was keeping me hidden.

Or so she said. It mostly included a warmth on my head and her whispering in Swahili. "I am supposed to be on Earth protecting you. Lea knows I was with you, so I had to tell her I was part of the mission Ki was sent on and that someone else was sent to you in my stead. Stick with that story and you should be fine. Fewer details mean less to remember. She knows not to ask." With those words, she left to shower, suggesting I do the same. Apparently, the houses in this city were set-up so that each person could have their own floor in the starburst. The higher you went up the more lavish it became. I couldn't imagine what it was like on the tenth floor, given how amazing things were here on the fourth or fifth floor that I was on. I'd have to ask her what floor this was. Deciding I'd go hunt around in the rest of the rooms on my floor later, I went swimming in the giant jacuzzi.

Dozing with my head resting against the edge of the tub, filled to the brim with the excessive amount of bubbles I'd added from the canister near me, I was in bliss. I was just trying to work up the energy to open my eyes and wash, when I heard light footsteps scurrying across the floor. Allowing a small smile to slip across my features, I shrugged lightly as if not noticing anyone. Then I heard footsteps again. Unmoving from my position of repose, I asked casually, "Does Mommy know you're sneaking around my room?"

A startled intake of breath was the only response. Then leaning up in the tub, glancing down to make sure the bubbles still covered my important bits, I looked over by the writing desk where my little visitor was crouched. Realizing I had her in my sights, she straightened slowly. Issa had to be no more than seven or eight.

She was still in the cute, innocent phase. She'd changed and now wore a pair of hot pink linen pants and a loose-fitting tunic like shirt in a paler pink color. Her wings were tucked around her and tiny braids with beads on the end, hung down to her waist. She reminded me of my babies. I missed my third graders already.

"This isn't your room," she said solemnly. I smothered a smile, captivated by her eyes that reminded me so much of her handsome uncle. "Then whose room is it?" Tilting her head to the side, she considered my question briefly before responding. "Well, nobody's room, I guess. We just use it for visitors."

"Well, aren't I a visitor?" Again, she paused, before nodding reluctantly.

"I wonder how your mother would feel about you sneaking about her visitor's room. Especially while I'm bathing."

"Technically," she said carefully, "You weren't bathing, you were sleeping." I didn't try to hold back my laughter, and little Issa smiled triumphantly as though she'd won something. I wasn't sure what she thought she'd won, but I was most certain that it was my heart. Sobering quickly, feeling sadness wash over me, I realized I may never see my third graders again. Issa stepped closer. "I'm sorry, I didn't mean to make you sad."

Before I could reply, the door burst open, "Issa what are you…" I sunk down further in the tub upon seeing Kimoni barrel into the room. He halted immediately, eyes widening before quickly turning his back. Aww what a gentleman. Can't say I'd have turned my back if I caught him in a jacuzzi tub, I might've snuck a peek. "Issa, he said firmly, come. You should not interrupt our guest while she is bathing."

"I'm a Mother spirit," Issa said simply. "We have the same parts; except I don't have breasts yet." At that she cast me a sorrowful look, putting her little hands over her chest sadly. "One day though, I'll have big breasts like you, and I'll be so pretty." She did a little spin to accent her statement. I laughed as Kimoni went even more rigid if that were possible. Couldn't blame the kid, my breasts are quite amazing, glancing down surreptitiously I made sure they weren't peeking above the bubbles. Sighing I was relieved that they were still concealed for now. Didn't want to give the little lady false expectations, her mommy didn't look to be more than a B cup, which was fine, but it definitely wasn't the Double-D's the little peanut was hoping for.

"You should go Mjomba Ki, you don't have the same parts as us. It's in-a-pro-pri-ate," she said, taking her time to carefully pronounce 'inappropriate.'

"Issa, come here now," he said tightly. Looking chastened, Issa skipped over to her uncle and grabbed his hand, looking up at him sorrowfully. "Are you mad?" Though his back was to me, I could see the softening in the lines of his body as she gave him big, beautiful puppy dog eyes. "No, my niece, I love you too much to be angry. Though you both have the same parts it is still inappropriate and rude to interrupt her while she bathes. It is private"

"Like when Mommy and Daddy need to go talk in private?" Ki shook his head as he led her the rest of the way out of the room. I didn't envy him that conversation. But I thought absently, he was going to make a great father someday. At that I felt a rush of pleasure across my mind and then whispering quietly into my

thoughts he said, *Sustenance will be ready shortly. Enjoy your bath*.
I shivered in the water; each word was like a caress against the
nerve endings in my body. Ugh, I thought, sinking further into
the water, trying not to wet my hair, though it was in desperate
need of a wash. This whole mind talking thing was dangerous, I
was going to need more practice.

The closet was fully stocked and somehow everything was my
size. I wasn't overly shocked, given that my BFF was lighting
fireplaces with her hands and casting glamours. My Auntie Rami
was a fighting machine, barely moving, intuiting her attackers
moves and executing them with deadly force and Ki. Kimoni
Fayola was...intriguing, strong, confident, sexy and a complete
mystery. He'd been opting for brute force over displays of power,
but I had a feeling that he was more than capable of both.

Flipping through the various garments in the closet, I finally
settled on a pair of burnt orange palazzo pants, then pulled out a
cream and gold high low shirt with capped sleeves to go with it.
There was even an assortment of sandals in the massive walk-in
closet. It looked more like a small boutique. I slid on a pair of
gold mules, much like a pair I had at home and then turned in
the mirror, making a face of disgust. My natural hair was a frizzy
mess. I sighed in resignation considering how long it was going
to take me to detangle and bring this mess under subjection when
a collection of scarves to the right of the closet caught my eye.
With a triumphant smile, I grabbed a lovely orange scarf that
matched my pants and wrapped it deftly around my head. I was
twirling in the mirror, wishing I had some hoop earrings and
just a touch of foundation or concealer when Aseema walked in.

"You need some hoops with that look sis," she said thoughtfully before walking over to one of the smaller drawers where there was an array of jewelry laid out like a display. I looked at her in astonishment. "This is like a freaking store! They have this stuff just sitting here?" Glancing at me out of the corner of her eye, she hedged, "It was stocked, specially." I lifted an eyebrow at her and she only shrugged, handing me a pair of hoop earrings, and then fastening a chunky necklace around my neck. When I turned to the mirror again, I noticed she was dressed similarly in a pair of emerald palazzo pants with a flowing light tan top that left her torso bare. Aseema's ab's were to die for. She looked beautiful as always.

Meeting my gaze in the mirror, she smiled. "As you can see, we like color, lots of vibrant color. We are…creatures of light." I squinted at her as she made the halting statement. All too well I was coming to see the extent of the light these people were made from. As I looked at her now, the light from her abdomen seemed to brighten. The longer I was here the more I became accustomed to the light coming from everywhere and everyone, though at different levels of wattage. Those guards we encountered upon arriving, they'd been full of light as well.

Looking harder at Aseema I began to notice different textures and hues in her light. There were sharp pinpoints of an aqua color, then there were smooth bands of red light; I even saw some green. But not like the green of the Anguka, the fallen. This was more of an olive green. The Anguka were full of dark green and yellow green hues…what did the colors mean? Finally, meeting Aseema's eyes, I asked, "What do all the different hues in your light mean? There are about eight colors shining inside you." Touching a hand to her abdomen in surprise, Aseema tilted her head at me with a mixture of wonder and curiosity filling her gaze. "My sister," she said slowly. "You can separate the different colors in me?" I only nodded, still searching her features curiously. "Praise the Creator," she said breathlessly. "You are growing and perhaps even closer to regaining your true self."

"The gag order didn't catch you."

She nodded slowly, thinking before saying, "The more you see, the easier it will be to work around it. I can comment on that which you can see, but unfortunately adding new information to it will still prove to be...difficult."

We stood in the closet for another few minutes lost in our own thoughts. Then my stomach broke the silence with an angry growl. It startled us both, causing me to freeze in embarrassment and Aseema to jump lightly. I met her eyes and we fell into a fit of giggles at the absurdity of it all. We'd just dispatched several Anguka in the deserted land, the Ardhi Iliyotengwa, not to mention at the house and here we were frightened by my greedy tummy. Linking arms, we headed towards the food in companionable silence.

The first bite of food had my eyes drifting closed in ecstasy. Ki's sister was some type of wizard. She had Auntie Ramla-like skills and I did not say things like that lightly. There was a full spread of food, which was being served family style, bowls everywhere at a large round table that could seat ten. The meal was an eclectic one, with beef, seafood, the Haitian rice that I was orgasming on at the moment, mac and cheese...I couldn't even see or identify it all. Oh! Cornbread, I grabbed a piece as I shoveled another mouthful of rice in my mouth. Then I realized there were multiple pairs of eyes on me. Issa who'd claimed a chair next to me was giggling and imitating my movements, with a slice of cornbread in one hand and a mouthful of rice. Looking around at everyone, chewing as my gaze drifted, I finally made eye contact with Lea. With a loud swallow I said, "This is delicious!" Everyone laughed softly and Issa nudged me in the ribs, looking up at me with big round eyes, "Mama has the best cooking!" A few pieces of rice fell out as she spoke and I laughed, dabbing at her chin. She'd taken up a spot in between Ki and I, though her mother protested strongly, I was happy to be near a little one that so reminded me of my students. Aseema was on my right and Lea right across from me.

She thanked me with a humble nod of her head. I decided I liked her. Lea had a quiet strength about her that was welcoming. Squinting my eyes at her thoughtfully as I chewed, I tried to see if I could pick out the colors of her light, but Aseema nudged me gently giving me a small shake of her head. I didn't know why she wouldn't want me to look, but I acquiesced and struck up a conversation with little Issa about school and her friends. Sitting her cornbread down, happy to have an audience, she chatted with me excitedly. "Wait," I interrupted her at one point. "How old are you, love?" Her experiences were vast for a little girl of no more than 10. Issa only cocked her head, looking at me curiously.

Kimoni and Aseema had their heads down chewing, so Lea answered as though giving gentle instruction to a child. In this situation, I guess that was me.

"My brother says that you don't have much experience in the culture of the Azizafri. That as a halfling you are not versed in our ways. So please do not take Issa's silence for rudeness. Or..." she said, looking around. "That of my brother and cousin." They only continued to avert their eyes and chew, allowing only a small smile to slip through. Lea went on, "In your human Bible, it says that a thousand years is like a day that has just gone by to the Creator. Our time progresses in much of the same fashion. With humans it is day to day, there is a limit on your time, a beginning, and an end. There is no beginning or end for the Azizafri, time is limitless. One day a light is sparked, we are born, we are curious, we explore and learn. Our learning begins to build up our potential. As our potential is realized, we grow, we mature, we then begin to create. For some it takes minimal time to develop, for others much time, but it is at our own speed we grow and realize this potential."

I must have looked as shocked as I felt. They lived...outside of time? My mind couldn't quite grasp that concept. Aseema laid a hand on mine; I suppose she sensed my confusion. I felt Ki's eyes on me but refused to meet his gaze. Instead, I looked down at Issa as she kicked her legs, humming as she dug into her plate with the appetite of a growing girl. But how old was this growing girl? Was she telling me that Issa could be two million years old?

Lea smiled at me when I met her eyes again. "It is a lot to take in, I am sure. In human years, let's say that Issa has the mind frame of a seven-year-old as you thought. While in your time she has lived many millennia, it is but a blink of an eye to us. It is a blessing if you expend your light creating. If you do not, it is difficult to suffer through not producing when those around you continue to produce and reach for their next level. Physically, we stop aging at our prime, though for most of us as we continue to learn and grow, the ancientness of our intellect shines through. I am Ki's older sister. My potential has been enhanced by uniting with moto wangu, what we call 'my flame.'"

"When we unite with our flame, our creative potential accelerates, we heighten one another's abilities. Not only do we have creative power of our own, but those powers are boosted by the powers of our flame. It would be something like what humans think of as a 'soulmate.' The Azizafri Mother and Father spirit have a twin star or a twin flame, which causes us to meet our maximum potential upon uniting." Putting her head down for a moment and taking a bite of food, Lea let that marinate. I was shocked, but for reasons I'm sure she did not understand.

*Kimoni...*I felt his fingertips brush across the pages of my mind. Slowly, I cracked open the book I imagined in my mind's eye to both open and close my thoughts to him.

Do not be alarmed. I could feel the gentleness in that thought and for some reason, it immediately calmed me. *Go by your own thoughts and feelings, not by my own claims. You are new to this, and it is a lot to take in. You must decide for yourself. Either way, Niko Hapa.*

He'd repeated the words I'd said to him again, "I'm here," or "Niko Hapa" in Swahili. Before I could respond, with every intention to thank him for his gentleness with me, Lea began to speak again, softly but firmly.

"I believe it is the creator who selects our twin flame. He does this before we are even born. Some believe he separates the one light into two before placing them in each Mother. They can then rejoin once they've realized individual success. As creatures of light, it only makes sense for light to join to light and then burn ever brighter."

Her words were doing something to me; my mind was racing, and I didn't realize I was leaning towards her as she spoke. My breasts were almost on my plate when Aseema gently pushed me back, trying not to laugh. I only gave her a quick grateful smile before looking back to Lea and nodding at her to continue.

She smiled slowly and with a deep breath said, "I joined to my flame long ago, but I knew he was mine from the first time I saw him." She flashed Ki a rueful smile before continuing. "Not as soon as Kimoni did though. He was about Issa's age when he touched the Queen's belly, recognizing his twin flame."

Ki choked and coughed next to me, setting the drink he'd been sipping down with a solid thud. Aseema only peeked at me from the corner of her eye. As his coughing fit continued, Lea walked over with water and patted his back lightly as my mind raced. Queen's belly? Issa's age? That couldn't be. This was wrong. My parents were Angela and Roland Nichols, not some Azizafri royalty. I know who I am, I know where I came from. These people cannot change that, I chanted it over and over. Even though this would mean I am not Ki's flame, I would not give up who I am, who I'd been for the past 24, soon to be 25 years. I celebrated birthdays, I acknowledged time, I would not fall victim to this fantasy world.

Quickly, Aseema said, "Excuse us." She helped me up and began leading me back in the direction of what I assumed was my room. Kimoni rose to follow, but his sister stilled him with a hand. I caught his frantic look before we disappeared down the steps. Once we were back safely in the room, I practically dived onto the bed and melted into the soft covers. They looked like a silken fabric but felt soft and warm like a nice Sherpa blanket. Nestling in further, I buried my head in the pillows.

The bed sank in slightly as Aseema sat gingerly on the edge. "You don't need sleep here. As cousin Lea said there is no day or night, just…productivity. But since you are used to the cycles of humans, you may need to sleep in your normal patterns until you adjust. Others of our kind, rest in cycles, like the creator." My head shot up at that. Cycles? Like the creator? I was understanding that the Creator for them was like "God." So did they rest every seven days? Wait, no, that couldn't be right. They did not have nights and days. My headache was back. I let my head drop back to the pillow. "I will remain on this floor with you, so simply call out if you need me. Get some rest my friend. The answers are coming." With those words, Aseema left quietly. Leaving me to my thoughts.

Since I'm used to the cycles of humans? Up until a day ago, or however many years it had been in this warped concept of time they had, she had adhered to human cycles as well. What was the deal? I kept my head buried, not looking up as she exited the room. I didn't even bother to take my clothes off, I just snuggled deeper into the soft blankets and prayed I wouldn't dream or have another vision. I was sick of this madness. I just wanted to rest without any further revelations. Unfortunately, I wasn't destined to get my wish.

"I'm so very sorry to do this." She truly did look contrite, I could tell by the look in her eyes, they were filled with sadness and regret. I looked her over sullenly, she was dressed in a long gown and robe in an ivory color that shimmered with purples, pinks, and yellows. It was gorgeous and flowed around her like a frothy dream. Her hair was in gorgeous curls that hung to her waist, and she had the kindest eyes I'd ever seen; they were a soft honey color.

"I know that you are tired. If it were not of great import, I would not contact you in this way." She rushed forward and pulled me into a tight embrace. Without meaning to, I sunk into her arms and breathed her in. She smelled of peppermint and lavender. Pulling back from me, she held me at arms-length, stroking a hand through my hair gently. "You don't remember, beautiful girl, but you will in time. I believe in you. Be on your guard. There are those who would prevent you from taking what is rightfully yours. But the Creator's will, will be done, on Amani, as it is in heaven." She said it like a prayer, resting her head on mine, she braced one hand behind my neck, while the other rested on my cheek. "Be at peace. Open your mind to knowing and be free. It is your creative power that must meet the need. Kumbuka," she whispered. "Remember."

"Mama," I breathed, sitting up with a jolt. My heart was racing, tears were streaming down my face. I felt so much regret, so much pain and loss. But why? That beautiful, regal woman was not my mother. But she needed me, needed my help with something and everything in me wanted to assist her in whatever plight she faced. With a jolt, I realized I may be feeling her pain, her loss and regret. What was going on here? What was happening in this place of peace as they referred to it, Mahali Pa Amani?

My head was spinning. I'd been visited by different people competing for head space. The older gentlemen who tried to hand me the staff, Kimoni (but in a sexier way), the well-dressed man and the woman. I didn't have enough room in my brain for all this action. My own internal voices were loud enough without adding all these extra people into the mix.

Then I heard his voice. No, not God. The well-dressed man who'd aggressively addressed me while I spoke with Ki on the steps at his home in Chicago. "Trust no one. If they bring you to our land, then you must escape them and come to me at the core. I will protect you."

With a steely resolve I jumped out of bed, searched out a toothbrush and something to wash my face with. Quickly, I retied the scarf around my wild hair, tsk-ing at the nappy mess I'd have to face later. Once I was presentable and done mourning my less than restful nap, I opened the pages of the book that separated Ki's mind from mine and asked him to come to my room. When he knocked, I'd made myself comfortable on the loveseat in front of the fireplace, so I called for him to come in, hoping he could hear. I'd just been wishing the fire were a little higher. It wasn't that I was cold, this place had no real temperature I could identify, but I craved the feeling of warmth and the security that I seemed to associate with it. He must have heard me, because the fire flared higher as he walked in and sat down next to me, giving me ample space on the cozy couch.

With my bare feet tucked under me, I scooted around to face him. Giving me a wary, but concerned look, Ki threw his arm over the back of the couch and angled toward me. Taking a deep breath, I said, "I had another dream."

"Tell me," he said simply.

"You're not at all curious why I didn't call for Aseema or Auntie?"

Ki smiled and it turned my insides into goo. White teeth on a brown man were the sexiest thing. Also, the addition of the full, well-groomed beard was enough to turn me into a puddle on the floor. Absently, I checked my imaginary book and the lock I'd added. Soundly closed again, thank God.

"You are angry at your aunt and she is still at the core. I know you overheard her words, and it is difficult to associate those words with the woman you have known. So, you find it hard to confide in her. Aseema, your best friend is in the know about things that have been kept hidden from you. You two tell each other everything, this deception hurts more than you will acknowledge. It feels personal…" He paused. "To give me a knowing once over. At some point you will have to hash that out. I suppose I am the lesser of the three evils at this point. I am here to listen, please, unburden yourself, allow me to earn your trust."

Dropping my head for a moment, I had a quick inner conversation with my treacherous heart. Don't even think about falling for this man. This little crush you have is fine, I'll even deal with the healthy dose of lust mixed in, but do not, I repeat do not fall! We can't afford to be broken again. Get yourself together girl.

When I was finished, I looked up at Kimoni, he had a bemused expression on his face. I chose to ignore it, gave my wayward heart one more mental threat and dove into the details of my dream as well as the voice I heard afterwards. Throughout the entirety of my telling of the dream, he only watched me curiously, but at the mention of the man's voice at the end, he jolted upright on the couch.

"What does it mean?" I asked desperately.

He hesitated before saying, "I do not pause so that I can lie to you. I pause so that I am not caught by the gag order as you call it."

"What do you call it?" I interrupted anxiously.

"Yamanu," he said quickly before his vocal chords were choked off. I don't know that he'd gotten it all out before it just clicked in my brain.

I saw myself, laughing mischievously, "We'll call it Yamanu, the hidden one. Cause I'll be in hiding right? It's going to be great!" There I was, or the other version of me, wings rustling behind me in excitement as I looked at a sad Kimoni and Aseema. But their sadness did nothing to dispel the joy rolling off me in waves. This was going to be an adventure, this was the answer we were looking for, I just knew it!

Shaking myself out of the memory, like filtering through a heavy fog, I looked up to find Ki gazing at me in wonder. In fact, I thought with a start, he'd moved closer, our knees touching on the sofa seat and his hand rested on my leg.

Apologies, Ki said, removing his hand. No, not said, he was speaking into my mind; when had I opened the connection?

Looking up at him, I cocked my head in question. *It opened with that memory you just had. I lived it with you. Look down.* Looking down, I jumped; I'd transformed again, into the me I'd seen in the dream, still curvy but more toned and limber. Yep, I thought, moving my shoulders, the wings were back and tracing a finger over my left ear gently, I felt the point there. Ki reached out and traced his finger over my right ear, and I heard him whisper across our link, *Beautiful.* I smiled at him and traced a finger over his ear as well. *Is this how you are used to seeing me? This is what you like?*

He smiled. "I like you," he said lightly. Ugh, I hated blushing, I tried to duck my head, but he dipped his down to meet my gaze, until I gave in, lifting my eyes only, chin still tucked protectively. *Whatever version of you that you choose to appear in. Even this one that does not remember me.*

With that, he touched a fingertip to my forehead, and my glamour shifted back in place. I was back to the normal me. Looking down, I felt slightly saddened to see the sexy me leave. *Both are sexy, your heart is the same.* At his words, I felt heat lick at me, igniting me from the inside out. As if he felt it too, his body stiffened and I let my hand drop from where it had been resting on his shoulder, trying to breathe through the wave of emotion and ardor that swept over me. It wasn't working. I looked up at him and he seemed to be struggling as well.

You can feel that? He gave a slight nod and then his hands were at my waist as I leaned up on my knees wrapping my arms around his neck, allowing my body to mold into his. With molten intensity in his eyes, he looked at me and I allowed my eyes to drift shut, preparing for the brush of his lips. Instead, he rested his head on mine and I felt…everything. Each nerve ending in my body exploded into life, I felt tingles ripple down my spine, over my glutes and down my calves, tickling the sensitive soles of my feet before arcing up and over the tops of my legs. The sensation shivered up my knees over my thighs and left a heated trail over my hip bones before racing up my sides and across my neck. I moaned softly, too aroused to be embarrassed. The tingles lingered over my neck moving up and around my earlobes, ending in a heated burst against my scalp. Ki pulled back from me slightly, leaning down until he hovered a breath away from kissing me. Achingly slow, he brushed his lips across mine, causing my nerve endings to electrify as teasingly he brushed across my lips a second, then third time before fully resting lightly against me.

My body was tight and aching as he sent sensations racing faster, down my spine, over the backs of my thighs, legs and feet before racing over the front of my body in the same arc. The tingling sensation kept up a steady course, moving over my heated skin until my body began to tremble in Kimoni's arms. He held me gently by my waist, lips pressed against mine, while I drowned in the sensations running over and through me. I moaned into his mouth, and he took the invitation, sliding his tongue between my lips, melding us into a dance that had me close to the brink. The world was slipping away from me in a rosy haze as my body became one large, throbbing mass with a single, central focus. *More.*

A knock at the door jolted us out of our heated embrace. Ki's sensual circuit ceased, and he lifted his head slowly, focusing intense eyes on me. I fought the desire to force his head back down to mine, as my wayward body called for release. A few more minutes, and I would have had it. How had he been causing that electric trail that was caressing my body only moments before? He must have heard me, because I felt a warmth at the nape of my neck, which slid down my spine and ended at the base of it, tapering off in a sensuous sensation.

The knock on the door grew more persistent. "Mali? Are you ok? The door is locked," Aseema called out. I groaned. "Can you make her disappear or something? We're kind of busy here." He laughed aloud, sending a spark of that tingling electricity cascading slowly down my neck and between my breasts, over my belly before dispersing. I leaned into him, feeling weak. Our visitor knocked again and with a sigh, Ki said reluctantly, "She'll break the door down in a moment. Come in."

The lock clicked and Aseema rushed in, "I heard…" But her words cut off when she saw us on the sofa. "Oooh, word? I'm glad I knocked. Bye y'all." She turned on her heel and closed the door quickly. I don't know who started laughing first, but I enjoyed the sound of our shared mirth so much I almost didn't want it to end. Kimoni sobered first, resting a hand on my neck, and looking at me seriously. "I'm sorry. I shouldn't be so forward. You don't remember and I…shouldn't take advantage." He dropped his head and took a deep breath. I laughed, and he jerked his head up almost immediately.

"This is our second kiss. Well, in this version of me… shall we say, 2.0?"

"More like 1.0."

"Dang! You sweep me off my feet with the best kiss and now you trying to play me?" I slapped my hands over my mouth. Why did I say that? This whole mind communication thing had me being way too free.

He laughed and shook his head, giving me a sensual grin as he removed my hands from my mouth. "I apologize, I misspoke. Whether you are 1.0 or 2.0 depends on the scale we're using. The old-you gets higher points for remembering me. I might also add," he said thoughtfully. "That is the best kiss you can remember having." He grinned again and I wished I could bottle those smiles up and keep them for rainy days. They effused such light; I couldn't help but smile back happily.

"So…we never?" He gave me a saucy grin and whispered into my mind, *That is something you'd definitely remember.* This was a super blunt conversation, unlike any I'd ever had with a man and surprisingly, I liked it. Fighting fiercely not to compare him to Steven, I was about to ask him another question when he interrupted, brushing a thumb over my lips. "This Steven hurt you." I flinched at the mention of his name. "If I did not fight to preserve life as our Creator intended, I'd end his with extreme prejudice." Tension ebbed out of me and I laughed, happy to sit and talk to this amazing man.

"It wouldn't be extreme prejudice; he deserves every bit of a beat down. But it's ancient history."

"Not so ancient as you say," he said, searching my eyes as his brow furrowed in concern.

"Ok," I said, moving out of his grasp and regretting it instantly. He gave off an exquisite, electric heat. "It's kind of a sensitive subject." His only acknowledgement was a slight nod, as he settled himself back in a forward-facing position on the sofa. I wondered momentarily if I'd offended him. Looking over at me, he offered a smile, which had that tinge of sadness again and offered me his hand. Shifting to sit up, I looked at him as he sat with his legs crossed in front him, looking a combination of regal and relaxed, I put my hand in his. It felt natural.

"Your dream means that this place is helping to open up your memory, your...power. We hoped that this would be the case. Yet, there are those here, such as the Mother spirit you saw, who will help guide you to remembrance. As for the Father Spirit..."

He trailed off and I sat quietly, watching him carefully. I could feel that he had some sort of recognition when I mentioned the Mother Spirit as he called her. Just as much as he had a sense of unease wafting off him as he mentioned the demanding guy who had shown up twice now.

Smiling slightly, he continued. "The Father spirit you spoke to is correct. You should trust no one. Including him. The fact that he offers protection if you will come to him at the core is concerning, especially since that is currently where we find there is...trouble." Then he looked at me and it was hard to breathe. Okay, it was very hard. Those warm caramel eyes were filled with such tenderness, it caused my insides to ache. More than the drama that was brewing on this planet, remembering what we had was a huge incentive for getting my memories back. If it were stronger than this pull, we'd shared since I first laid eyes on him, it would be worth regaining those memories.

"Will you tell me about your time on Earth?"

I jolted, abruptly thrown off by the topic shift. Regaining my bearings, I tossed a teasing smile his way. "I don't know of a time I've spent on any other planets aside from my time here with you at your sister's beautiful home."

Shaking his head in amusement, he said, "True enough. Though this is not my sister's house, it is my parents.' Lea and Issa are only staying here while my brother, her husband, he said clarifying, is on official business at the core. My parents are off visiting friends, so we have the place all to ourselves it seems. Our parents' home is much closer to the core than where my sister usually lives. But not near enough for you to go noticed," he added quickly. "When Rashidi has time from his meetings, he can drop by to be with his wife and child without leaving the city." My mind caught on his name; how unusual, I'd heard Rashid and Rashad, but Rashidi was different. The history scholar in me wondered where it originated.

"It is of Egyptian origin, meaning wise," Ki replied to my thought casually, slumping down further on the loveseat and anchoring his free hand behind his head comfortably. "Lea is an Egyptian name as well, meaning bringer of good news." I nodded, fascinated, about to ask more questions about their people and name meanings, when he looked over at me, his eyes full of amusement. "It is good to see you have not lost your endless curiosity my lady, but I do believe I asked you a question first. Which, if I am not mistaken, you have yet to answer."

Rolling my eyes in exasperation, I started telling him my uneventful life story. From the passing of my parents, to being raised by the hood "seer" Auntie Rami, to the shenanigans that Aseema and I had gotten into from day one. He laughed, watching me, and taking in everything as I droned on and on about my no doubt boring life in comparison to his.

Squeezing my hand gently, he said into my mind, *You not only created while you were there, you molded young minds. You operated in your Creator given potential until you left.* I rested my head on my hand in thought, chewing over his words. He sat quietly, allowing his mind to blank as I thought it over. Then something else occurred to me. "Wait," I said. "How is it that you can read my every thought and I can only read some of yours?"

He looked up at me with such innocent eyes that I frowned in reproof. Grinning unabashedly, he said, "I can direct thoughts at you, because I am versed in shielding what I don't want to share and making clear that which I do." I tugged my hand from his and crossed my arms petulantly, raising my eyebrow at him in reproach. Spreading his hands in a guileless way he said, "I don't mean to lie or hide anything from you. But you are aware that Yamanu, he smiled brightly when the gag order neglected to catch him, prevents much. Aseema told me what happened when you tried mind speaking with her."

"Now that I know about Yamnu, this hidden one, it is odd that you can't speak of it freely."

He shrugged. "I neither made, nor can break this."

"But you are a key," I said with confidence. Turning to me in a blur of motion, he grabbed my shoulders. "How, how am I the key? Tell me." His eyes were locked on mine, with fierce intensity and…hope? Thinking rapidly of possible answers, I found none; sagging in disappointment, I looked up at him and shrugged. His hands slid off my shoulders and he looked just as dejected as I.

If I were truly being honest, I was afraid. My life had been great for a young woman, I'd traveled a great deal of the world, learning cultures, languages and history that had shaped me into the woman I am. My friends were great. Aseema, my Assistant Principal Kim, a few of the girls in my grade level team, not to mention the friends I had in Spain, Africa, and Korea. Then there were my students. Not just my third-grade class this year, but those who still wrote me letters and called from around the world. The students I'd taught in those exotic places and their parents, their families and communities had become a part of me. If I became this, this Azizafri, he remembered, I'd lose the one I'd become, and truth was I liked her. What if I didn't like the winged, pointy eared version of myself? No scratch that. The winged, pointy eared version of me had killer abs, arms and legs, her body was banging! I'd at least like that part. Turning my head, I noticed Kimoni regarding me with a mixture of sadness and amusement.

"What?" I asked self-consciously.

"I see now, why you cannot remember."

"You heard that hunh?"

He nodded solemnly. Then taking my hands into his again, he said, "No one will force you. I will not let them. Do what brings you joy, Mali Ali." At those words, he smiled, and it made me want to kiss him again. What did I do to deserve such support? It was apparent that they needed me to remember. There was some danger, which I wasn't quite sure I wanted to know full details about. But this man, he was willing to risk danger for me to stay ensconced in my safe memories of the only life I knew.

As I thought it all through, completely in his hearing, not bothering to block him from my mind, he simply watched with a neutral expression on his face. In my mind's usual ADD fashion, I jumped to another thought. It doused me like a bucket of cold water, and I shivered in dread under the weight of it. Unable to say it aloud, I spoke through our shared telepathic line. *I killed people.*

He dropped his head a moment before nodding in affirmation. *I wondered when it would hit you.*

I'm a terrible person. I haven't thought about it once. At Steven's house and then in the Ardhi, the deserted land. This is something that-that should have stayed with me...but...what kind of person am I?

Ki let me ramble on without giving away anything, no reproof or chastening in his expression, he just listened. But when I asked that question, he lifted a brow, as though asking if I really wanted an answer. Reluctantly, I nodded.

What is the value of your life mwanamke wangu?

My head snapped up in confusion. "And their lives mean less than mine?"

Looking at me with steel in his eyes, he nodded in utmost gravity. "Yes, that is exactly what I am saying." Before I could protest, he forged on, holding up a hand to halt me from speaking further. "Their lives lost meaning when they decided that their lives meant more than that of all those that they ended. Those Anguka would have killed you without a second thought. They would have ingested your essence, your light and siphoned off your power for an eternity. You would be cognizant during this. A hell of their making for you. They would do this again and again to any Azizafri they find. You were a hero in that desert. Not only did you overcome those who sought to not just kill you, but capture your very spirit, you released the spirits of those they have fed off for the Creator knows how many moons. You saved them, you set them free. I know that this will not take away your sorrow at having ended life by your own hands, even that of the Anguka, but it should comfort you to know that you restored much more than you took. The Creator is to be praised for your decisive action."

I fought the tears threatening to spill over as Kimoni pulled me into his embrace. Surrendering to his warmth I clasped him tightly, biting my lip to stave off the tears. I promised myself that when I was alone, I would mourn not just for the lives I took, but for the innocence I lost in taking them. But he wouldn't have it. *Cry now, my love. You don't have to endure this pain alone. Let me be your strength, I can bear it.* That did it; I let loose a sob and couldn't stop until I traded Kimoni's embrace for that of my dreams.

CHAPTER 9

"You want the truth? You can't handle the truth!"
- A Few Good Men
(Jack Nicholson as Col. Nathan Jessup)

*W*here *are you princess? I cannot see you. Are you here? It is not safe for you.* It was the well-dressed stranger again. *I am no stranger; I am your friend. You may call me Max. I will protect you and keep you safe, but you must tell me where you are. Trust no one, dearest.*

Realizing he'd somehow infiltrated my mind, I closed a steel door between his thoughts and mine. As they closed, I felt his surprise and then a mighty flare of anger. It burned across my consciousness, and I grasped my head in pain.

"Mali," Ki's voice drifted to my ears. "Mali," he said, shaking me lightly this time. Slitting my eyes open, I felt pain slice through my head again; what had he done? The door opened and I felt

Aseema at my side, along with some onlookers at the door. I bet it was Lea and Issa. Trying to pull it together for my rapt audience, I tried sitting up, but the pain shot through me again. Kimoni quickly gathered me in his arms, resting his hand on my forehead gingerly. I heard his thoughts as he whispered, *Ponya.*

Just as I spoke the word "heal" to the Anguka in the desert, Ki whispered it into my mind now. Instantaneously a cooling balm coursed through my head and seeped into my bones. I breathed a sigh of relief. Whatever that was, it was not Max being friendly.

Max? Ki asked sharply, reading my thoughts. I guess the steel door didn't work on him. *Steel?* Ki parroted. I looked up at him in derision, but he was too busy exploring the steel door I'd closed in my brain. It was weird, I could feel his hands on it, testing its strength. Maybe I needed to build a steel door for Kimoni. At that he stopped his perusal to give me a look. "I'm kidding," I said, rolling my eyes in afterthought.

"May I speak to you in private kaba?" Lea's tone was unusually sharp. Kimoni, Aseema, and I jerked our heads in her direction. Issa was looking between her mother and uncle solemnly. "You're in trouble Mjomba Ki and you ain't even been here that long." As she shook her head sorrowfully, Aseema and I looked at each other trying not to laugh. But Ki still looked confused. "You may speak freely here Dada." Lea tried again, looking pointedly at me and then back at her brother. He looked down at me with knee weakening tenderness, before easing me back onto the pillows. When had I ended up in the bed? Wait…this probably didn't look good to his sister.

Ki smiled down at me and looked pointedly at the chair next to my bed. *I was a complete gentleman.* Smirking at him I replied, *Except for that whole couch fiasco.* Caressing mental fingers down my spine, making me fight not to shiver and give us both away in his sister's presence, he asked aloud, "Fiasco? You started it."

Straightening, Ki looked at Issa first, "Mpenzi, will you go and play for a bit? I need to speak with Mommy and the ladies. I'll come and take you for a ride when we are done." Issa preened at her uncle calling her sweetheart but was still obviously disappointed at the request.

"After we eat," Lea interjected with a raised eyebrow. Ki nodded and Issa reluctantly agreed, pausing to give her Mjomba a big hug before she left. He swept her off her feet spinning in a circle until she giggled gleefully. Finally, he set her on her feet, and she skipped to the door, giving us all a wave and some parting words, "I hope Mama doesn't put you on punishment, then no ride." Giving her mom a pleading look, she finally disappeared down the hallway.

Lea smiled ruefully before turning back to Kimoni. "I would speak to you alone Kaba, umm, brother," she said with a small nod at me. "If you'd be so inclined." In response, Ki sat in the chair next to my bed and propped his feet up on the edge, nudging my thigh with his bare toes. A giggle escaped before I could stop it. Lea's lips pursed tight, and I knew she was at her limit. As if guessing the same, Aseema climbed into the bed and snuggled next me, resting her head on my shoulder. I smiled down at my sister- friend in affection. She gave me an exaggerated wink and settled down to watch the family drama unfold.

"You are promised to another, Kimoni Fayola. She is beautiful and I do see your interest in the halfling. But remember your mission, and your betrothed. I would not see you return to the child you were, playing with the affections of others, instead of embracing your Moto wa kweli." His sister had no idea. *I am his true flame*, I thought resolutely, then mentally kicked myself at the look Kimoni was flashing me. *She doesn't know, he said into my mind, if she did, she'd be ecstatic.* I started to close the book on our connection, but he gave me puppy dog eyes and I left it open, with another roll of my eyes.

Lea was looking between us in horror. "Ki, you didn't! Malika will be heartbroken to know that you were true for so long only to dash it away when you were so near her return." Her eyes watered in sorrow at what she thought was some tryst with another woman…a little girl in her eyes. Though we looked the same age, she must be ancient. Ki stifled a laugh and then, when his sister looked mortally wounded at his insincerity, he jumped up and went to her side.

She'd be mortified at you calling her ancient, my love.

Oops! I thought, is that like a cultural faux pas? You gotta tell me these things.

He only smirked at me over his sister's head, whom he held close to his chest. She clung to him with waves of sadness and disappointment rolling off her. After a moment, she pushed away from him and turned pleading eyes on me. "You must understand Bessie," I cringed at the cow name. "When my Kaba, my-my brother…"

"I know Swahili, you don't have to translate. Please continue."

Nodding with a small amount of relief, she continued, "When he was a very young Azizafri, not much older than Issa, he recognized his Moto wa kweli in the Queen Mother's stomach. The Queen was very early in her carrying of the Lady Heir's light, when on a visit to the core, Kimoni accompanied our mother and father. She came into their meeting for some reason no one remembers, and Kimoni immediately rose from his chair, where he sat building models at the King's desk, creating from a young age, and ran to the Queen. He asked her if he could touch her belly. She smiled and said yes. When he touched her stomach, he says it was like a jolt of electricity went through him and not even fully understanding the concept of a twin flame, he knew her at that very moment. Kimoni spoke the words 'Moto wa kweli' and the Queen laughed and said, 'Well, it seems you will be my son then Kimoni Fayola.' He was destined for Malika Alika, the most beautiful Queen, before her light fully entered Mahali Pa Amani. Do you understand? She is his completion. You cannot continue this liaison with him."

All I could do was gape at her. There was a war happening in my brain. On one hand that was the most beautiful story I'd ever heard. Kimoni had loved me since he was seven? Apparently, he was older than me, I'd explore that later. But it couldn't have been me. I was not the Queen's daughter; I did not know the Queen or King. Shaking my head in consternation I repeated the mantra I'd taken to since all of this began, I am Malika Alika Nichols, daughter of Angela and Roland Nichols. I was born at Little Company of Mary hospital in Chicago, Illinois on February 13th. I am a human woman. But for some reason, even with the additions of where I was born and when, I wasn't convinced. Lea was telling the truth. She'd even used my full name; how did she know my first and middle name? I had these memories of Kimoni and being here in Amani. Deep down inside, I knew this place. Perhaps I was a reincarnation of their Mali. I mean I'd never believed in reincarnation before, but a lot of unbelievable things had happened over the past few days. Pulling away from my thoughts, I asked Ki through our connection, *Am I a priestess?*

No...not that I know of. Any particular reason why you ask that?

One of my favorite anime shows...well never mind. You'll just have to watch Inuyasha *sometime. I just hope Kikyo doesn't show up.*

Um...ok.

My confusion was confusing him. Never mind, as far as I could see there was only one solution.

Is it too dangerous to tell her?

He tilted his head in thought.

Please tell her.

Yes ma'am, he responded casually.

I got the impression that he'd needed my permission to do that. Interesting. He gave me a sidelong look before leading his sister over to the chair by my bed and taking a spot by my feet. Honestly this bed was so huge, we could all four of us have a party in it. Wait...that came out kinkier than I intended. Kimoni snorted and turned to look at me incredulously. *I want you all to myself and never, never with my cousin and sister.* His disgust colored his thoughts, and I shook my head in amusement. Lea kept watching us with growing concern. She must have picked up that we were communicating telepathically, and it was deeply disturbing to her. Aseema wasn't helping, just looking at her contentedly, then she piped up, "Don't berate me binamu, she has earned my loyalty."

Before Lea could explode, Kimoni knelt beside her. "I must tell you something, my sister. I could not at first, but I can now."

In distress Lea covered her mouth. "Please, please do not tell me that Malika's light has gone to the creator. Or worse to the Anguka. Kaba…please." My features softened as I gazed at Lea, I really liked her. Maybe we were friends in my life before.

Kimoni sighed and shook his sister as she was bordering on hysteria. "You know what, this will be easier." Kimoni stood up and walked over to me. *May I?* he asked, with a hand hovering over my head. *May you what?* I asked suspiciously. *Remove…* He hesitated, my jaw dropped as he mischievously said, *Your glamour.* Narrowing my eyes at him with underlying threat, I said "Sure" aloud, closing the book between our minds soundly and latching it with a diary like lock and key for good measure. He ran fingertips in a seductive caress over the lock and then touching my head, he whispered, "Ubembe, ondoka." As soon as he asked the glamour to leave, it stripped away. Lea leapt to her feet.

I had to adjust a great deal to sit my wings more comfortably behind me and I was sitting on my long, thick locs as well. Aseema helped me adjust as Lea just gazed at me in shock. I was about to give up on the bed, when Seema touched a fingertip to it, causing the mattress to curve around my wings and body comfortably. I needed her to teach me how to do that. Giving her a grateful smile, I settled back on the pillows, and she snuggled into my shoulder again. Swirling an index finger in a circle, a tray of popcorn, Twizzlers, peppermint sticks, pickles and grape sodas appeared on the bed beside us. I craned my neck, gaping at her. It was the same spread we'd always lay out for movie nights when we were kids…okay, okay we'd had the same thing a week ago for movie night, but tradition was tradition.

"Stop showing off Seemie," Kimoni said, snatching the Twizzler I'd just picked up and popping it in his mouth with a wink. Aseema scowled at the nickname. "It's been so long since I've been able to." Aseema waggled her fingers in explanation before stretching to crack her knuckles in front of her. Lea cleared her throat, bringing our attention back to her. Apparently, she didn't suffer from the same lack of focus the three of us did.

"Malika?"

"You can call me Mali," I said with an amicable shrug.

"I should be saying mwanamke wangu. My lady! But where is your light?"

Ki walked over to her and touched his head to hers. They stayed that way for several minutes, so Aseema grabbed a remote and a screen dropped down from the ceiling. She turned on *Drunk History*, and I gave her a happy side hug. I love history, and mixing it with the comedy of drunken storytelling was so much fun. This one was one of my favorites with Lin Manuel Miranda doing the drunken storytelling. Dude is a freaking genius. We were all into the show when the siblings turned eyes back on us. Reluctantly, Aseema paused the show and we looked over at them. But before they could follow their train of thought, I unloaded the questions I'd been holding in.

"Aseema, can you teach me how to finger twirl items to me? And how to make the mattress adjust to me? Oh, and light the fireplace. Wait, where did my wings go? The glamour is back on already. Ugh my hair is a mess. How do you guys get *Drunk History* out here? Since y'all don't have, like, time does that mean you get all the episodes of every show before they were ever created on Earth?" Then turning to Lea, I asked, "Were we friends before?"

"Yep," Lea said, deadpan. "That's our Mali, alright."

I gave her a big smile, moving my peppermint stick over to the side.

With a wry chuckle, Ki sat back down on the bed and grabbed a pickle, sticking a peppermint stick in the middle before taking a bite. "You're supposed to let it soften some." I handed him mine and he took it, setting the other one down. Taking a thoughtful bite, he nodded gratefully, before taking a sip of grape soda.

Aseema, quite used to responding to my million questions answered in order, "I can't teach you what you already know how to do, boo. So, to those first three questions certain things will return with your memory."

Then Ki interrupted, perhaps he was just as used to my jumbled mind as my bestie. "I only removed the glamour temporarily. It took away the glamour over your look but not your light, that's much more deeply embedded. You look beautiful, your hair is fine." I beamed at him, the old me had great taste. The new me needed to get on board. Ki leaned in and whispered, "You still need convincing?" Checking the locks on my thoughts, I wondered how he'd gotten through, I was a closed book. "It's written all over your face, you don't have to say a word," Aseema sang, doing a light body roll with it. I laughed at her softly and went back to the food tray.

Lea finally pulled her chair closer and grabbed a handful of popcorn. "You can watch whatever you want here, food can appear here, but you can't make it from nothing, you need solid material to create from. Aseema used the raw material for the food from what we had in the kitchen. We have televisions here, though they are not used as often as on Earth. So, she had the raw material to create what she wanted to watch. To your final question, you have always been my friend and I will always be yours. More importantly, you will always have my fealty mwanamke wangu."

I blanched and started choking on the popcorn I'd been enthusiastically chewing. Aseema started patting my back and Kimoni placed a straw in one of the grape sodas before holding it to my lips. Wheezing for air, I took a long sip and started to intake a normal amount of oxygen. Why was she swearing fealty to me, what the heck?

"Wait! There is no gag order on you is there? Yamanu doesn't apply to you," I said, my throat rasping from the kernels still lodged there. Looking thoughtful Ki answered quietly, "Though the gag order may not be on Lea, anything she may say that you do not discern yourself, will not reach your hearing. This order is...intricate, with good reason. No one anticipated this current situation. There are many safeguards to bypass." My shoulders slumped in disappointment. Aseema draped an arm around me, giving my shoulders a squeeze, when Issa ran in.

"Hey! Is this privacy? A whole party without me!" Running across the wide expanse of the room, she swept past her mother and into Ki's waiting arms. He sat her between us on the bed and with a quick look at her mom to make certain it was ok, she dug into our tray of snacks. Giving her young cousin a loving smile, Aseema turned on *Moana* and we all snuggled in to watch. Lea stayed in her chair, occasionally looking at Ki, Issa, and I cuddled together with a smile. I guess we looked like one big happy family if you excluded Aseema's long limbs stretched across the bottom of the bed.

I felt surprisingly content and at home here. It was almost scary. Is this what it had been like before? Tapping on our telepathic connection I asked Kimoni and was met with a ready smile, *even better, he immediately responded.* Patting Issa on the back and leaning into Kimoni's shoulder I enjoyed this rare feeling of love and family. This was a step beyond the little family that had been Auntie and I back home.

Soon though, the peace was disrupted as Aseema swept Issa off the bed so they could loudly sing and dance to "You're Welcome." We all laughed as they put on their impromptu show, but I sobered quickly. The questions swirling through my mind were getting harder to hold at bay. Reading my mood quickly, Ki excused us and led me out of the room and into the hallway. We ended up in a dimly lit sitting room with soft music playing. It was decorated in soft pinks with silver accents. The sofa was gray with pink pillows, and I plopped onto it wondering where they'd found the most comfortable furniture in the world to place all over the house. Kimoni chuckled, finally taking a seat next to me. Did every room in this house have a fireplace?

"Most sitting, sleeping or resting areas have fireplaces. We like the light and warmth of the blaze. It's a thing," he said with a shrug. Then in afterthought, "We also enjoy comfortable furniture that molds to us, like…memory foam. It is best to accommodate our wings. You'll find that the poufs and sack chairs are super comfy as well." He pointed at the items around the room. There were multiple seats that looked like bean bag chairs and smaller ones that looked to be footrests. I moved around the room testing a few out and he was correct, you sunk right in. After I wiggled out of my second memory foam-like bean bag chair I sat in the bay window that served as a padded window seat. The view was breathtaking. Each house rose in various heights of the same starburst pattern, all in different but equally beautiful colors. The city glowed with light, but still gave off the impression of an evening sky above us.

I was lost in it for some time when the music that Kimoni had been fiddling with changed and caught my attention. Turning to him I smiled, "I love this song." I hummed along with Moonchild's "Cure" as our eyes locked. "So do I." He had his head resting on his hands, leaning on the armrest of the sofa. I yearned to touch him, but refused to give in. This draw he had on me was confusing and exhilarating all at the same time. I hadn't been this tangled up in knots over a man since…no, I couldn't compare this to my time with Steven. My thoughts colored with disappointment and disgust at every thought of his name. Kimoni was something different. There was something magnetic between us that made me want to remember my past, just so I could remember where this inexplicable draw originated. It would be quite amazing if I really was the girl he'd identified in my mother's womb. Wrong mother, wrong womb though. It couldn't be me.

Giving myself a mental and then physical shake, I refocused on Ki, where he waited quietly in the same patient way. He had to have heard that entire thought process. I directed a mental reprimand his way, by scraping my nails down his consciousness, but not digging so deep as to harm him. Ki shivered and then frowned at me. "I can block your thoughts as well. While you were thinking, I blocked you so you could have your privacy. I don't want to know what you are not comfortable sharing." He hesitated. "Though the odd thought is bound to leak through on occasion. Emotions are especially difficult as we get…closer."

"I know that you are a gentleman, you've proven that," I said, feeling more than a little ashamed. He continued to study me with a carefully neutral expression. Taking a deep breath, I continued, "I'd like to tell you about my dream, and ask some questions. I-I know you can't answer everything but…" I broke off, not quite knowing what to say. "Even if it causes you pain, can you try to answer my questions?" No, that wasn't right.

"I will answer what I can, my lady," he said. While I was vacillating over how to ask my question, he moved over to sit next to me in the window seat. "But I must tell you that…when I was sleeping, my-my defenses were down. I saw your dream." Speechless, I just froze for several moments. "You can do that?" Dropping his head and rubbing a hand over his beard he sighed before looking up and saying, "It has never happened to us before." How was this happening? It was hard to ask my old questions when new questions kept arising. Deciding resolutely not to focus on this query, I forged ahead with what I was going to dub, "the old questions."

"Did you hear what Max said to me?"

"Someone spoke to you?"

"Yes, he said his name was Max, he says he is my friend and to trust no one. He wants me to come to him, but he grew angry when I shut him out of my mind."

"That was the steel door you erected?" He asked briskly. "I knew there was an attack, but I thought you threw the door up on instinct, I didn't realize he'd been able to speak to you."

"He always says trust no one, but this time he added that he would keep me safe…though the whole mental/psychic attack or whatever you want to call it didn't endear me to him much. Do you know who this Max is?"

"No, I do not. You were right to shut him out. I did not question you about the attack because I wrongly assumed it was simply them searching for you. Trying to catch you off guard so your light would flare and alert them to your location." He was beating himself up and I couldn't have that; grabbing his hand, I added light pressure with my fingertips until he looked up.

"This isn't your fault," I said earnestly. Though he nodded, the concern in his eyes didn't fade. So, I decided to distract him with my barrage of questions. "What do you all do with all of this free time you have?" Thrown off by the sudden subject change, he just looked at me for a while before responding with a knowing smile tugging at his lips. "We create." He twined his fingers with mine. "Though right now we are relearning each other, this is a form of creating. We are building a relationship. I may go and compose music, develop new weaponry, write a book, or create something completely new. But we consistently exercise our creative gene because we have been charged to create like the divine Creator. As he created worlds and beings since the dawn of life itself, we've all been created with purpose, and it is our job to work until that purpose erupts from us. Each creation propels us from one level to the next. We operate in a never-ending cycle, from the high heights of new thoughts and ideas to the satisfaction of completion. It is a life filled with meaning."

Studying our joined hands, I let that marinate in my thoughts for a while. I chewed it over and decided that just might be a life I'd thoroughly enjoy. "In a world of such creativity and light, why do the Anguka hate your people so much?" Putting a hand over our clasped fingers he corrected, "We are far from people. *We*," he emphasized, "Are celestial beings. As with most created beings, the Anguka strive to be more than they are. They became thirsty for more and were granted a sinister way to satisfy those appetites. So, it was the Second Father's desire to protect the Azizafri that caused us to close the borders of Amani and hide us from those who would do us harm."

"So, you can't leave here?"

"We leave this place, but with the understanding that we do so with risks. Great precaution must be taken when leaving Amani. We cannot reveal the gate between our worlds to outsiders lest the Anguka find their way back in. You saw what our last war did to the Ardhi Iliyotengwa."

"Then... Why is the gate hidden in a place where the Anguka linger?"

"Good question," he said smiling. "The gate is not always in the same place."

I looked at him, puzzled by this.

Relinquishing his hold on our hands, Kimoni lifted his free hand, leaving the other clasped in mine. With a wave of his fingers an orb appeared between us that looked much like the view of Earth from a distance. Pointing at the floating orb, Kimoni said, "Earth rotates every 23 hours 56 minutes and about four seconds. It spins at an average of 1,000 miles per hour." Waving his hand again, Kimoni produced a starburst similar to the shape of their homes, only it wasn't stacked. It just sat above his makeshift Earth hologram twinkling brightly. "Mahali Pa Amani, the Place of Peace, where we are now, spins at a much slower rate. Everything in the universe spins, but we do so much less than the planets around us. To put it in the simplest terms, while it takes Earth 365 days to fully rotate around the sun, it may take Amani 9,125 days or 25 years according to Earth's standard of calculating. Therefore, we have no day or night here. It is always light because we are the light. It is also why it is almost impossible to line up the gate between here and other planets. Most of the places we orbit among are moving too quickly to line up with us for more than mere human minutes or even seconds."

The floating solar system showed rapidly spinning planets and ours turning so slowly, that its line up with the other planets was barely visible. There was something else strange happening though. "What are these lines?"

Kimoni smiled broadly. "Very observant, Mali. We are created from the dust of the stars, when we tire of this corporeal flesh we go back to the sky. Amani is connected to every single star in the sky. We can teleport to any one at will."

System failure, brain overload…I don't know why my inner thoughts were coming out in a robot voice, but I went with it. *Cannot compute, failure to understand. Flatline, beeeeeeeeeeeeeeeeeep.* I guess Ki was no longer blocking because he waved away his little illustration, trying not to let me see his shoulders shaking in mirth. I'd have feigned anger at his amusement if I weren't so blown away by this abundance of information. Be careful what you wish for; no that wasn't right. This was more of a careful what you ask for type of situation. Asking for the truth had been infinitely mind-boggling in this instance.

"Wait," I said, grabbing his arm, "So, I've been away from this planet for 25 years? How can that be? Was I here as a baby? Did they send me to Earth as a child? Is that how I was in the Queen's belly and then in my…." I fell silent, stunned. With melancholy darkening his features, Kimoni carefully tugged on a loose curl on the nape of my neck. I'd hastily thrown it into a pineapple ponytail on top of my head this morning. Afternoon? There was no way of knowing what time it was here.

"Time is irrelevant here. It is never-ending. We have an immortal's concept of time. No need to mark day to day. But if I were to attempt to quantify it for you, it's more like you've been gone for millennia. It's been an eternity. Yet depending on which gate you exited back to Earth through you could come out after the Creator's return or at the very minute or even second that you left." Either I'd become an empath overnight or my emotions were entirely too tied to his because I felt such a wave of sadness wash over me that it made my chest ache. *My apologies,* he said into my mind. *How thoughtless of me.* Instantly, my emotions were my own again and my brain whirled with the implication. Our connection was telepathic, but it was also empathic? Whoa. Somehow it came out sounding like Keanu in my head and that made me feel lighter. Who isn't made happier by thoughts of Keanu?

The music changed, and Ki pulled me up from the window seat and into his arms. It was a slow sensual dance step that required more hip swaying than anything else. Pulling me close and leaning in, he whispered, "Happy Msimu wa mwanga." I looked up at him in surprise, still swaying to the rhythm. "What?" With a gentle smile, he said, "On Earth, your birthday has passed, but in Amani we celebrate an entire season of light. It is more like, a season of birth. First you sit in reflection on what you have accomplished and created during that season of your life. Then, there is a great celebration as your light grows and you begin to enter your next creative cycle. Though we do not calculate time, we recognize and rejoice in these consistent cycles."

"See-moo, wA-wan-goo," I said, attempting to pronounce it phonetically. Msimu wa mwanga. Not a term I'd come across during my time in Africa, but I liked it. Then I was distracted as Bob Marley sang to us asking if this was love. Following Kimoni's supple, masculine, yet sensual hip movements, I got lost in the music... and in him. We danced for what seemed like hours, staring into each other's eyes, my honey irises focused on his swirling caramel orbs. We gave ourselves over to the rhythm.

....

185

Once we finished our dance, hungry and ready to hit the showers, a realization hit me. "How were you able to share so much information without the Yamanu stopping you?" We walked side by side, not touching, but still in our own intimate bubble, headed back to my borrowed rooms. "I've been thinking about that," he said. "My conclusion is that because you are back in Amani it has loosened the grip some. There are certain things you must discover on your own, but the makeup of our world, because you are here, in it, should no longer fall under the Yamanu." Looking down at me for a moment, he shrugged and said, "Hopefully it is an indication that a release will be forthcoming." He said it as though the gag order was a type of prison for him.

"I wonder why," I said, thinking it through, "the Yamanu was put on you. With my being on Earth and you being here…why would it have been necessary?" We were at my bedroom door, and Kimoni turned to look at me. "Unfortunately, that is not something I can answer for you mwanamke wangu. It falls under those things which you must remember. You will remember Mali; I have no doubt." The conviction in his eyes warmed my heart, but I couldn't get around the little seed of doubt that existed deep inside. I still didn't quite believe any of this was real.

"Listen, Lea has prepared a lovely meal for you. Why don't you get cleaned up and then we'll eat?" My mind told me that it was lunchtime, but Kimoni simply smiled and said, "Call it whatever you like, we will eat." He'd explained to me that they nourished themselves at their leisure, slept if they so desired, but didn't really need it. That would explain why Lea was fine with

Issa eating pickles and Twizzlers with us at what I thought of as breakfast time.

"We are Roho, spirits in control of celestial bodies. We are eternal, even once returned to the creator we live on. It is in our power to eat what we like when we like." With a gentle poke in my side he added, "There is no weight gain once you take on your celestial body, unless you will it." Now that was cool. All the healthy eating and calorie counting I'd done back home would mean absolutely nothing here.

At my borrowed bedroom door, he brushed a soft kiss to my forehead, and I really wished that a cold shower would work for me. But I knew from experience that it didn't, so I resigned myself to quelling my heated blood while I dressed for our meal.

When I came out of the massive bathroom, I almost had a handle on my libido, but I asked Aseema who was once again sprawled across the bed, "Do we get cycles here?"

"Why? You two boning already?" I threw a brush from the vanity at her, which she caught and casually started brushing through her curls with. Cocky wretch, I thought venomously. "It's possible that you could since your body is flickering between its celestial and human state. But you haven't had it this long, so you should be fine."

"What do you mean this long? It's been what, two days? I should be due." Aseema shook her head at me. "It's going to take a while to get used to the concepts of eternity and immortality. It's like we are simultaneously moving faster and slower. Seeing the future, present and past in one endless breathtaking stream.

Speaking of which, it's your Season of Light. Do you want your gift now or later?"

"So basically, I've been here for years already? This is nuts. I'm losing what's left of my mind. Wait! I still get a gift? Gimme, gimme, gimme!" I jumped up from the vanity stool and ran to her then bounced on the bed where she sat, shaking her like an eager child. Laughing, she held up a palm and a box appeared in her hand. "Ooh, aaah," I crooned as though she'd done a particularly neat magic trick, which for me she had.

"Open it," she urged, tossing me a smirk. The box was a flat rectangle about the size of her palm. I studied it, trying to guess what it was before taking it from her hand. Aseema was an unpredictable gift giver. She loved gag gifts, but occasionally she'd surprise me with something meaningful. Mostly though she liked to embarrass me with random sex toys or odd trinkets that I'd have to research the meaning of. Seriously, one time she gave me a fertility statue. I was not amused.

She did her little Jedi mind trick, and the box was in my hand. It was heavy. Taking a deep breath and giving her a wary side-eye, I opened the box. It was empty. Confused, I turned it upside down. Nothing. I gave it a shake; it was still so heavy. With a loud exasperated sigh, I tried to bodily shove Aseema on the floor. With catlike reflexes she escaped before I could even lay a hand on her. But her laughter pushed me to try another sneak attack. Jumping off the bed I ran for her as she knelt at the waist, enjoying a good belly laugh. When I was one step away, she whirled out of my reach again. Game on, I thought with determination and moved to grab her again. Aseema deftly, sidestepped each of my attempts to mete out vengeance.

After several failed attempts, I slumped my shoulders and made to walk back over to the vanity in defeat. Behind me I felt her hesitate before saying, "Girl your face is priceless! The disappointment, almost as good as when I gave you that vib-" her words cut off into a light buzzing in my ears as I whirled and lunged at her, feeling the wind in my hair as before she could even react, I tackled her to the ground. Sitting up into a crouch over her body, I began pummeling the meat of her thighs in triumph. But quick as lightning, her hands gripped my arms. "No fair, I protested, I caught you so I should get my licks!" Meeting my eyes in utter seriousness, Aseema said, "How did you do that?" In confusion I asked, "Do what? Tackle your scrawny butt?"

Letting go of my arms and sitting up on her elbows she said, "No sis, how did you move that fast?' I wondered if this was another trick to distract me from bruising up her legs in punishment, but Aseema had her serious face on, so I thought back. I'd whirled, she was still talking while following behind me slowly, distracted. I launched myself at her, jumping higher than I'd expected and landed with precision. She was right. I must have been moving fast, she was still mid-word when I'd taken her to the ground. It had happened in all of three seconds.

I stood up and then offered Aseema a hand, pulling her to her feet. "You're coming into it," she said softly. Her gaze was filled with wonder, but I turned away quickly, busying myself with getting dressed for our impending meal. I'd conjecture that "coming into it" had something to do with my memories or power, or both. But I dared not ask, the gag order was most stringent on her. Before I made it all the way to the closet, she stopped me with a hand on my shoulder. Turning slowly, I was about to tell her I didn't want to talk about it. For her sake. I hated that look of pain and frustration on her face when the gag order did its magic on her. The Yamanu, as I found out it was referred to, "the hidden one."

My eyes widened when I saw the long box in her hands. Excitement welled up in me, before I tamped it down. This could be another trick; I wouldn't put it past her. "It's not a trick," Aseema said with a roll of her eyes. "I've already had my fun, please open it." Giving her a look that promised retribution if this was another joke, I took the box and went to sit on the bed with it. As she joined me on the bed, I pulled back the lid. My eyes widened and I looked up at my best friend, full of gratitude. "How did you get it so quickly?' Breathless with excitement, I pulled the long sjambok from its place in the box and examined it carefully.

A bit shyly, Aseema said, "It is the first thing I've created since returning home. While you and my cousin rekindled, she said with a wink, I made it in the shop." Unable to answer as I studied the intricate work, I nodded, studying the leather whip closely. It was about 50 inches long. Like hers, it had a handle at the end, with a weave pattern where you would hold the sjambok. I hefted it and found it was quite heavy. Studying the end of the whip, I realized she'd inlaid the leather with onyx, no doubt to increase the level of injury upon impact. It was beautiful, with sincerity in my heart, I told her so and she glowed with pleasure at the compliment.

"I had something different for you, for your birthday on Earth. But now that we are here, things are different; priorities are different, my sister." I nodded, not completely understanding, but pleased, nonetheless. That's when it hit me. Images of her whip striking Anguka down in the desert. Of those that I struck down. Feeling slightly faint, I closed my eyes and struggled to breathe through my nose. Don't faint, I chided myself. It was kill or be killed. *You saved the spirits of the fallen Azizafri with your actions,* I repeated Kimoni's arguments to myself. Eyes still closed, I felt the sjambok being removed from my hands and snapped back into the present. "I'm sorry Aseema," I said, afraid I'd hurt her feelings. "I love it. I'm just trying to deal with…everything, still." Pulling me into a hug, she silently lent me her strength, before releasing me so that we could get ready to eat.

Lea had set up a feast for my Season of Light, or Msimu wa mwanga. Aseema made me dress up, pinning my hair into a braided crown around my head. This evening I'd opted for a coral dress with thin straps that cinched in at my waist and flowed past my hips into my favorite A-line style, stopping just above my knees. I'd paired it with gold strappy heels and a chunky necklace that Aseema had retrieved from that special drawer again. When I left, I sure was going to miss this magical closet. Taking my time, since there was no time, I added some light make-up, feeling quite pretty as we made our way to the formal eating area. Apparently, we'd been in the family area last night? Yesterday? 10 years ago? This time thing was still escaping me, either way, despite the journey here and the drama we'd encountered in Chicago I was having a great time. Like a vacation on another planet. Why I allowed myself to think that, I don't know. I should have known it forebode trouble.

Once Aseema and I arrived at the formal eating area, which required going higher up into the beautiful castle? Mansion? Whatever you wanted to call it, it was ginormous, everyone was present, including Auntie Rami, posted by the large window. She looked gorgeous, like a young woman in her prime. She'd changed into loose white linen pants and a matching ankle length linen duster over a shimmering gold top. As we walked through the doorway, she turned with staff in hand. It looked less beat up today. Inlaid with gold and silver, shimmering next to her at about the height of her chin, it looked less like a fighting implement and more like a gorgeous walking stick.

"Mwanamke wangu," she said with a deep nod of her head. "I hear that Lea now knows of your secret. We must talk quickly, there is trouble brewing." The happy glow I'd been sporting since dancing with Ki, receiving an amazing gift from my best friend and getting all dolled up for what I considered to be a birthday dinner, seemed to fizzle and die. It must have shown on my face because Ki started to walk over to me, when Ramla raised her hand in the universal sign for stop. With the same hand, she motioned Aseema away from me and ventured closer to where I stood at the door. Everyone obeyed her without question, so I just stood quietly waiting for the bad news.

Ramla searched my face, seeming to consider me and her words carefully. "You look lovely, my niece." I nodded my thanks, while peeking at Kimoni from the corner of my eye. If his heated gaze was any indication, he agreed with Auntie's statement. Inhaling for strength, I said, "Thank you. Please tell me what you came to say." With a confidence that I was far from feeling, I moved around her and walked over to the beautiful marble table filled with food, then sat down to wait. Everyone in the room had been standing, but at Auntie's nod they followed my lead. Looking around I knew that they must have sent Issa away. Poor little lady was going to really hate "privacy." For her it usually meant being left out.

Kimoni sat at the head of the table this time, I was sitting to his right, Lea to his left and Aseema to my right. Auntie took the seat across from me next to Lea. Though the table looked long enough to seat 20 people, we were all somehow close enough to speak. Absently I wondered why Auntie Ramla hadn't taken the head of the table. Without looking at me, Ki responded through our connection, *Technically, Lea is the head of my parents dwelling in their absence. Though I am the younger brother, she often cedes the leadership position to me. Mama Ramla is our prophetess, but she is a guest in our familial home.* I nodded again, turning to my aunt impatiently. "Let's have it out, shall we? You said we must talk quickly, yet you are taking your time Auntie." I don't know why I was speaking to her so formally, I guess I was still angry. Well, angrier with her than I'd like to admit.

She nodded, a look of respect passing over her features before she concealed it. "Mwanamke wangu, Happy Msimu wa mwanga to you. I hate to bring you grave news in this season of happiness, but I see your light has grown in my absence and the more it grows the harder it will be for the glamour to conceal. Praise to the Creator that the shields around this place are strong and sound, so I could not see your light from the core. I fear even this will not help for much longer." She paused to take a deep breath, I had a feeling she'd given me the light news first and that I was about to hear the truly unsavory details now.. "Your..." She paused. "The Second Father is gravely ill. The Mother is unable to leave his side. She fears there is a plot on his life. His light has been gradually being siphoned away from him. If this does not end soon, he will be forced to leave us and return to the Creator. The Second Father has been in a healing sleep for a great many rotations of Amani. Nyoka has been leading in the Second Father's place, while the Mother tends to the Father."

I couldn't explain why if I tried but my heart ached upon hearing this. I did not know their so-called Second Father, but the man who had been visiting my dream for months, appeared in my mind's eye. I saw him smiling. Trying to hand me his staff. Suddenly, I realized the sadness and weariness I'd seen in his eyes had been due to his light being siphoned off these past months. But what or who had caused this illness which was draining him of his light? Kimoni reached over to where my hand rested on my lap and squeezed gently. Without thinking I turned my hand over and clasped his fingers desperately. He didn't flinch back, but only tightened his grip. Perhaps he'd sensed my sadness, or maybe it was written all over my face, but something in me did not want this man to die.

"What can I do to help the S-s-second, F-f-father?" Again, Rami studied me briefly before answering, "The Mother asks that

I bring you to him, in the core." There were audible gasps at the table. Why? What was so scary about the core? Why did I have to stay hidden? Max kept telling me I should come to the core, but his mental assault wasn't exactly persuasive. Perhaps it had been an accident. Due to his surprise at my shutting him out? There were always more questions than answers lately. It took me a minute to realize that Aseema was talking angrily.

"You can't be serious? That was not a part of the plan. How can we take her there without her memories restored? This is ludicrous! I will not put her in that type of danger. The Mother did not ask this. She couldn't have. I would hear her say this myself. She would not endanger her…" She broke off. "She would not needlessly endanger Mali." Her teeth were clenched, so hard, I could hear them grinding. Reaching over I grasped her hand tightly.

Looking completely unbothered, Auntie grabbed a roll off one of the many platters on the table that we'd all seemed to have completely forgotten about, cut it open and placed meat and a few other items on it for a sandwich. Taking a bite, she chewed thoughtfully before turning her attention to Ki. "His attempts have not proven successful thus far. There is no other way." Aseema's head whipped to look at Kimoni; he gave her an apologetic look before saying, "We must take her."

When she started to object again, Auntie held up a hand. "If we do not move quickly, we could lose everything. He does not have much longer in this form and we cannot allow the alternative. It will mean loss all around." Lea sat in stunned silence, looking between the three of them as they spoke, eyes wide, lips parted in shock. I wondered if the two of us were mirror images right now, because I felt the shock evident on my own face. Aseema seemed to consider this, and I was just plain confused. Ramla scooped a few different items onto her plate and ate quietly for a moment before saying, "I have a plan to get her safely in and out of the core."

That got everyone's attention. Their eyes lit up as she detailed her plan; Aseema even said aloud a few times, "It could work." Thus, they plotted how to put me into certain danger (from whom, I did not know) to save a man (how, I did not know) that I'd only ever met in my dreams at the request of the Mother, who I also didn't know. This was going to be fun, I thought sarcastically, finally helping myself to my birthday, or Season of Light, meal. *Oooh! I hope they have cake*, I thought excitedly.

CHAPTER 10

"Maybe I should have rethought wishing for
superpowers as a young girl. It seems to have
backfired." - Malika

There was cake, and it was delicious. My very favorite, German Chocolate…yum! I was happily stuffed, avoiding thoughts of my impending mission impossible to the core to meet the Second Father, ruler of Mahali Pa Amani, and his wife, the Mother of the Azizafri. Though they were King and Queen of this land, they were more commonly known as Mother and Second Father. The King was known as the Second Father, because apparently, the Creator was and is the First Father. It seemed as though the Second Father was sort of crowned as a Father Abraham of the Azizafri. Or at least that's how I interpreted it. The entirety of the people here are royal. There is no class system or race, though so far, I'd only seen people of color. It was a utopia of sorts, one that good old planet Earth would do well to duplicate. Everyone here owned something, created something and families worked together to maintain it. No person in this place was useless to the cause, there was an understanding that they needed one another to survive. Each Azizafri had some special gift from the Creator to contribute to the good of Mahali Pa Amani and all its inhabitants.

Once Auntie had finished dropping her bombshells and game plan, we were able to enjoy the meal. Aseema tried to lighten the mood with stories about Kimoni and Lea as kids. It helped, but then I dived in with 21 questions, which is how I got my new tidbits about the Father, Mother, and their creation. I was soon to meet these ancient beings, though the Second Father was in some type of coma from what I understood. Perhaps as a halfling, I had some way to wake him. I don't rightly know; Rami wasn't very forthcoming with that information.

We'd all gone back to our rooms after eating for a little siesta. Lea had sadly told me she'd had a tour of the city planned for me and wanted to take me to see her home where she and her husband usually stayed but was vetoed. We were to rest and then head to a ball of sorts. It seemed I wasn't the only one in my season of light. There was a ball at the core celebrating someone's Msimu wa mwanga. It was then that we'd sneak in with the party goers and I'd get my audience with the rulers of Amani.

When I asked how they knew what time they needed to be places if there was no time, they laughed and said, "we just know. The spirit guides us." *I'd never get used to this*, I thought sadly, too keyed up to sleep. I'd just changed into a silky shorts and tank ensemble and settled in to try to figure out how the tv worked when there was a light knock at the door. Jumping up, I walked over and swung the door open about to ask Aseema to come work the TV, but it wasn't her at the door. It was Ki. Suddenly I was conscious of how tiny my shorts were and the fact that I was not wearing a bra. My breasts must have realized it at the same time as me because they tightened beneath my shirt.

Ki was giving me a once over that had my cheeks growing warm and that heartbeat thing that happens between your legs when you are really attracted to a handsome man. Yeah, that. When he finished his perusal, he looked into my eyes, and I thought I'd drown in his gaze. It was as though his irises moved, hypnotizing me with their light. "I brought you something," he said softly. I cocked my head to the side in question. "A season of light gift if you will. I do not want to disturb your siesta, so I'll leave it with you and go." Frowning at him, I took the box from him and grabbed his arm with my other hand, tugging him into the room, all the while wondering whether this was the best idea.

I'd already done it, so I kept propelling him in, taking his hand and leading him to the loveseat. Plopping down sitting criss-cross applesauce I patted the seat next to me in a sit-down gesture and he acquiesced. Looking down at the box in my hands, I realized that my top wasn't leaving much to the imagination. My breasts were straining against it, as if reaching for Ki; looking up at him under my lashes, I noticed his gaze where mine had been. I smirked before moving to open the small pink box. But first I shook it and examined it as was my usual process. With a heavy sigh, he refocused on me, took the box from my hand, removed the ribbon and lid then handed it to me. "Hey," I protested. Ignoring me, he looked pointedly at the box I'd yet to look at the contents of. Finally, I looked down. Nestled in what looked like ivory silk was a rose quartz necklace. Fascinated, I twisted the box this way and that. The piece of rose quartz had been chiseled into the shape of a budding rose about one inch in size. Golden leaves sprouted from the sides and as I picked it up, I noticed it was threaded onto a lovely gold chain. I looked up at Ki, feeling a little teary. "Thank you, it's beautiful."

This was the first time a man had ever bought me anything. Steven had said... *No Mali, don't go there,* I chastised myself. *Screw Steven.* Looking at me sadly, Kimoni said, "I will be glad when the shadow that he cast over your light passes from you. I would see you healed from the scars of his love." When I started to deny it, he only leaned forward and took the necklace from my hands. Leaning into him, I filled my senses with his strong masculine scent, he fastened the necklace around my neck. It nestled comfortably, right below my collar bone. Leaning back, he looked at it and smiled. "Do you know the significance of rose quartz moto wangu?" I shook my head no. Well, I did know she was a crystal gem, but that was about it.

"This particular gem," he said pointing to where it rested on my chest, "represents love. Not just romantic love, but universal love, trust, harmony, it is a symbol of agape love. Love that is unconditional." I smiled at him, touching my fingertips to it. "The rose quartz, he continued, is also said to open your heart to self-love, peace and inner healing."

"That's a lot for one little gem," I said with a smile.

"I hope that it does all of that for you and more Malika," he said, brushing a hand lightly over the stone. I clasped his hand to where it rested on my chest. Enjoying the warmth of his hand on my skin, his eyes widened momentarily. He then moved in one of those sinuous, predatory moves that I'd seen him use during a fight, clasped the back of my neck and pressed his lips to mine. Immediately my nervous system responded with a rush of heat and pleasure, shooting through my lips and down to the heartbeat pounding all the more furious between my legs.

He pushed into me further until my back met the couch cushions and he hovered over me, one knee bent at the right side of my hip and the other leg resting on the floor. I inhaled sharply, running out of air and his tongue pushed expertly between my lips in a dance that had me trembling with excitement. My hands developed a mind of their own, tracing down his sides, pausing at the dip at his hip bones, caressing, loving the feel of him. Then his weight was resting on me, breasts flattening against his chest and the impressive length of him nudging between my spread legs. His beautiful, iridescent wings spread around us, giving a greater air of intimacy, cocooning us in. Without a second thought, I wrapped my left leg around his waist and pressed his buttocks into me with both hands.

Momentarily, he froze, and I thought, *Crap, crap, crap! Don't come to your senses now,* but he deepened the kiss with the hand resting on my neck and then began tracing fingers from collar bone and down around the curve of my breasts. Involuntarily my body arched further into him, and my hips jerked in excitement when he ground into me once.

Distantly I heard him groan and moan, "Mpenzi wangu." He ground into me again and I cried out; his lips were on mine as he spoke, "You make it so hard to stop." Then he did, he stopped. But my body wasn't quite ready yet. I angled my head and nipped his neck, grinding my hips into his and he shuddered so hard that I thought I'd climax from the sheer pleasure of doing anything that turned this sensual man on. Fully intent on repeating the action that had yielded me results, I was stunned when I felt cool air hit my body and my hands empty. Looking around quickly, I realized that somehow he'd moved and was now standing at the fireplace with his back to me, wings once again tucked into his back.

Sitting up quickly, I grabbed the blanket from the back of the couch. Suddenly I felt naked and vulnerable. What changed? He probably thought I was a tramp; we'd only know each other a few days and here I was throwing myself at him. Though in his mind we'd known each other longer. He called me mpenzi wangu, my love. I knew he felt strongly for me, so what was the problem?

Then he turned to me where I was huddled under a blanket on the couch. He'd been unsuccessfully trying to calm himself; it was apparent. I tried valiantly not to look down, but *DANG*! He was quite an improvement. I hated to compare, but no wonder I'd never had an orgasm. I was sure that the man I was looking at would never fail me in that department. Right now, though he was looking both guilty and uncomfortable. The discomfort I got, I was feeling it myself, but guilty?

"Tell me," I said softly.

He looked at me a moment before answering, "It may sound silly to you." I started to protest, but he waved a hand and went to sit in one of the armchairs to the left of the loveseat. He was purposefully keeping his distance. Again my eyes drifted down when he sat. Though he was putting on the breaks, his body was still straining towards me. Licking my lips, I forced my eyes back to his face. "It's hard to concentrate when you're looking at me like you want to eat me," he said roughly. My eyes widened and I bit my lip to keep from saying anything raunchy. He wanted to stop, I needed to respect that. Dang, when did I become the dude? *Whore,* I chastised myself.

Kimoni had closed his eyes and rested his head against the back of the chair. "You are not a whore," he said, eyes still closed. Narrowing my eyes at him, I said, "Stay out of my thoughts, uninvited Kimoni." Opening his eyes, he looked at me thoughtfully, "Our...mutual affection opens up that connection all on its own. If it were not for Yamanu, you'd be hearing my very inappropriate thoughts right now," he said with a smirk. Unable to help myself, I preened a bit. Laughing, he continued, "I used to be...rebellious. I did not want you to remember that part, but it is why I am attempting to be respectful in this." I looked at him quizzically. Unbidden, I thought, I wouldn't mind you doing some disrespectful things to my body right now. "You're projecting mpenzi wangu, I can only take so much."

"Sorry," I said quickly.

"During your season of light, it is natural for you to desire to create, especially when your moto wa kweli, your true flame, is present. We are...drawn closer to one another during this time.

But, you do not remember everything. There are things hidden that you should know before we join. I would not deceive you in this or in anything. You must understand how badly I want you and I am not in my season of light," he added absently. Turning his full gaze on me, I saw clearly the desire in his eyes. Point taken. "I will not allow this until the Yamanu is completely gone and your memory has returned." With that assertion, he stood up, touched a fingertip to the necklace he'd placed on my neck and walked out the room.

After he left, I sat several minutes snuggled in the pink blanket I'd been huddled under. My mind raced through the events of the past few days. I certainly had been more sexually attracted to him than any other man I'd ever met. We'd gone from the 'hello, nice to meet you' phase to 'making out' fairly quickly. It was out of character for me, and I took some comfort in knowing that part of it was attributed to my being in this place. I felt a little better about my wanton behavior. That made me giggle. Wanton reminded me of a Harlequin Romance, "The Duke's Desire." Oh, "The Deviant Duchess" or "The Bare Baroness." After a few more random titles to cheer myself, I decided that resting was out of the question. Aseema said she'd come get me when it was time to prepare for the ball. I'd gotten the idea that we had some time before we needed to leave, since I was told that while we wait I should "rest, reflect or create." *Whatever that means,* I thought with a roll of my eyes. Remembering I'd seen a workout area on this floor, I decided to find some appropriate gear and go work off some "light induced," sexual tension in the gym.

Each room had a vibrant color scheme. The workout room (once I found it) was enormous and done in shades of army green, black, and bronze. It was surprisingly fitting. Though I'd only got a short glance at it before, I had underestimated how large it was. The center of the room was a sparring ring, fitted with forest green mats. Surrounding the sparring area were various fighting implements, easily identifiable workout equipment such as an exercise bike and punching bag, but there were other items that had me totally confused.

Walking further back, I spotted a swimming pool and my jaw dropped. The dimensions of this room were mind boggling. How had they fit this Olympic sized pool here? Shaking my head before another barrage of questions pushed me into another headache, I walked over to a practice dummy with my sjambok in hand wishing I had some music. Before my wishful thought could complete, music began blaring loudly throughout the room. I looked around quickly. No one was here but me. I searched around for speakers or a sound system and saw none, but sure enough, the steady thrum of Beyonce's "My Power," filled the room. Smiling brightly, I sat the leather whip down and began stretching. Once my muscles were nice and fluid, I started throwing a few punches at the practice dummy, remembering a few classes I'd taken in undergrad. The well-stocked closet had provided me with a pair of gray leggings, a white tank and some running shoes that molded perfectly to my feet. It was like walking barefoot on pillows! After a few more punches and kicks to the practice dummy, I jogged around the outlined track that traced the perimeter of the room, keeping a steady pace, enjoying the blood flow through my body and the slight mist of sweat starting to glaze my skin. After four laps around the track, I went back to the test dummy, grabbing my sjambok, testing its weight in my hand. Alternating between upward, downward, and sideways flicks of my wrist with the weapon I fell into a rhythm. Whip up across the face, down across the torso, roundhouse kick, whip across the chest, activate chakras and up across the throat. My body had taken over as it had in the battles I'd fought over the past days. Throwing me into a mindless rhythm that came somewhere from the depths of my memory.

My breathing was even, my focus unwavering and perhaps that's why I reacted the way I did when I heard someone clear their throat behind me. Still in my rhythm, I whirled, flicking the whip out and across, then snapping my leg up into a kick that came so closely behind the arc of the sjambok, I was surprised I hadn't accidently hit myself in the leg. Ramla only moved smoothly out of my way and gave me a look of interest. She was still dressed in her white ensemble and carrying her staff. "Again," she said simply. Without thought, my body sprung into motion. I flicked the whip out, following it with an upward thrust of my left hand, Chakras out to cut and tear. Ramla sidestepped me easily and I whirled fluidly kicking out and she retreated, dodging my thrusts, making no move to counter, strictly on the defensive. I hadn't laid a finger on her yet, she didn't seem out of breath either as she continued to sidestep my moves easily. Kicking it up a notch, I switched my pattern moving left, then right, kicking out first and whirling around to strike out with the whip. This time she didn't have time to sidestep, she caught it with her staff. "Nicely done," she said, and for some reason that made me angry. With a burst of speed, I threw a combo of punches, jab-jab- uppercut and forward kick out at her knees. She smirked easily evading me and my brain clicked into high gear, jumping up, much higher than I intended, I flipped over her head, simultaneously striking out with my sjambok, knocking her staff to the floor, landed behind her and had my left wrist, with chakri exposed wrapped around her throat.

Somewhere during the leap I'd shed my glamour, allowing my wings to take me up a bit higher. Auntie was up on her tiptoes attempting to avoid the blade. My chin reached the top of her head, and her eyes were rolled back trying to look at my face. With a hand resting on my arm she said, "Well done, niece. Perhaps we should talk before your anger gets the best of you." I hesitated, looking down. She looked perfectly calm even standing on her tiptoes, straining away from the blade exposed at her neck. I hadn't noticed the hand holding my whip was pressing into her ribcage. Body had taken over for mind. Those few self-defense classes couldn't have caused me to do all that. Very slowly, I let go, surprised at my own actions, but somehow, I wasn't at all regretful. Stepping back away from her, I held my sjambok out loosely in my left hand and my right arm in front of me, on guard still. Some part of me felt that this was odd, I was acting strangely, but I persisted in my actions.

"Stand down," Ramla said firmly. For a moment I contemplated attacking again. But gradually I realized I'd regret it. I was still angry with her. She had told Ki, he needed to be prepared to kill me if he needed to. In fact, she didn't seem averse to doing the job herself. But I couldn't just off my aunt, no matter how angry I was. I did have some questions though. Easing out of my fighting stance, I sat my sjambok down lightly and slid my wrists together to sheathe my chakri, showing her that I was calm.

"I will not be as easy to kill as you thought Shangazi. Why are you so set on taking me to the core? Aseema says that it is dangerous. How can I trust that you are not leading us into a trap?" Ramla sighed and waved her hand causing the pounding rhythm of the music to lower to a quiet thrum. Then she flicked her hand, and I felt the tug on my natural form, to be covered again by the glamour. But for reasons I couldn't explain, I resisted. With a surge of will, I held my form in place, flaring out my wings in displeasure. Ramla raised her brow in a combination of query and reproof. "It is not safe for you to be this way," she said. I didn't like conceding to her, but with a sigh, I let go of my natural form, feeling a wave of disappointment as I lost those valuable inches of height and that lovely hair.

"Answer my question," I said firmly, notching my chin up higher to make up for the lost height.

"I would never unnecessarily harm you, child."

"So, you would harm me if it were necessary?" I asked more calmly than I actually felt.

"There are extenuating circumstances playing out that you do not understand my dear."

I couldn't answer at first. It took several deep breaths for me to tamp down the swell of rage in me before I could answer. "Calm yourself," Ramla reminded. That did it, I felt the rage begin to blaze and my glamour dissolved again. My breathing was coming out labored and shallow, I don't think I'd ever been this angry in my life. Reaching out her hand towards her staff, Ramla didn't take her eyes off me. The staff flew into her hand and as she moved to point it at me, I reacted off instinct, letting lose the sjambok in a flurry of motion I knocked it out of her hand so hard, it flew into the far left wall, stepping into her, and leaning down until we were nose to nose, eye to eye, I bit out, "Don't. You. Dare."

"Malika!" Despite hearing Kimoni call my name, I kept my eyes locked on Ramla, knowing that Aseema was there as well. Ramla held up a hand to both of them as though she were still in control, halting them so they wouldn't help her. The tension in my shoulders started to ebb and I backed away from her slowly, eyes still locked with hers. Then my anger seemed to pop, and I deflated like a balloon, sinking to the practice mat, head and heart full of hurt, anger, and confusion.

For a while, no one moved. Kimoni and Aseema seemed confused as to what to do now that they were here. Finally, the cousins looked at one another briefly, before walking over to me. Kimoni reached down to help me up off the floor, while Aseema crossed her arms, standing guard at my right. I allowed Kimoni to help me up. I gazed blindly down at the mat, confused by my own behavior, and trying not to cry. "Don't beat yourself up," Auntie Ramla said. "You deserve to be angry, my lady niece, but you cannot take chances with outbursts of your light like the one that just occurred."

"She's right," Aseema said, giving me an apologetic look.

"It's what brought us into the room," Kimoni chimed in. "Your light called to me."

"There is no time for self-recrimination. We have a job to do. It is only natural during your season and with all the light you've taken in, that you would be very emotionally sensitive. It will pass."

Still unable to look up at her or anyone else, I just stood there wishing I could exit this emotional roller coaster. I crossed my arms in front of me and simultaneously, Aseema and Kimoni wrapped me into a group embrace. Tears began escaping my eyes and then Aseema started singing "Me and You, Us Never Part, Makidada." I laughed beside myself, finally uncrossing my arms from my chest and wrapping one around each cousin. I felt peace wash over me. It was like they'd built a safe haven around me with their arms.

"Ain't no ocean, ain't no sea," Aseema continued.

"What are you singing?" Kimoni asked. In unison, Aseema and I looked up at Kimoni in incredulity.

"You've never seen *The Color Purple*?" I held my breath waiting for his answer. If he'd never seen the movie or read the book for that matter, this just wouldn't work out. He'd never understand me if he hadn't watched one of my favorite films.

Face stretching into a grin, he said, "Yeah, I've seen it. I just haven't watched it a thousand times like the two of you." I heaved a sigh of relief and Aseema corrected him, "One thousand and two, Binamu. We've seen it at least a thousand and two times. Right, sis?" I nodded absently, pulling slowly out of the cousin sandwich, grateful for their lingering warmth by my side. "I am sorry Auntie, I-I can't believe I did that. My anger should have never taken me that far."

Waving my words away dismissively, Ramla said, "You are beginning to see and come into your own. Though Yamanu prevents full disclosure, know that I love you with all my light and would never let anyone harm you. What Kimoni and I discussed was not your demise, but the salvation of our created beings."

Malika! Where are you?

I rocked back on my heels as the voice roared through my head. Had Kimoni not caught my arms, I would have fallen to the mat. It was Max's voice again.

I felt your light. WHERE ARE YOU?

Carefully building up steel walls against any thoughts besides the one I directed at him, I replied softly.

Light? What light?

I felt his relief filter through my thoughts. That was sloppy of him, to let that emotion carry through. He was giving me creep vibes. Distantly I understood that Ki was a ghost of a shadow in my mind. Hopefully, he could hear the exchange.

What were you just doing my dear? Max asked calmly.

Ki nudged a thought in my direction, and I answered in kind. *I was sleeping. There was a strange dream, someone was…after me.* With a small effort of will, I infused fear into my thoughts, letting my uncertainty color my mind. It wasn't hard after what I'd been facing these past few…well however long it had been. Kimoni squeezed my upper arms where his hands rested, in approval. But I couldn't focus on him, I kept my mind sluggish as though I'd just woken. Every time my light burst through it became easier to control my thoughts and communication through them.

Suspiciously, Max asked, *How did you shut me out last time my la- halfing?* He'd almost called me lady and midway through changed it to halfing, saying it with a certain amount of disdain. What was that about?

Shut you out? I asked in confusion. *Shut you out from where? Last time we spoke I was so confused, and you-you hurt me.* I should've been an actress.

Immediately an image of him was projected into my mind. He was dressed casually this time in a pair of loose-fitting pants and a V-neck shirt. Still, he stood erect, tall, and imposing, chin held high. Somehow, I got the impression he was overcompensating. I started to project myself as well, but Ki squeezed me in warning. He was right, I couldn't let Max know I could do that. Something was wrong here. I had a feeling that even the clothes were to ease my mind. It wasn't working.

He waved a hand and I appeared before him in my night shirt and shorts like before. I looked around warily. Then crossed my hands defensively over my incorporeal breasts.

Have you seen the old man again?

No, I replied instantly. *Who is he? Why does he come to me? Why do you?*

He grimaced. *Still inquisitive I see.*

You, know me?

Studying his nails, he said haughtily, *I know all Azizafri. Even halflings such as yourself.*

Immediately, I heard Kimoni on the other side of my steel wall. *Lie.*

I tensed, wondering if Max had heard it, but he continued as if uninterrupted. *I am the King of the Azizafri.*

Lie, Ki said again, anger lacing his tone. Focusing to do so, I leaned into Kimoni in the physical room where we sat, while remaining still in Max's projection of me. Though I very carefully executed the action, I was surprised at how easy it was.

There is a war coming. You are safest on Earth, where you are. If you come here, you could die. Be careful of anyone who comes to you in this way aside from me. Remember there is no one that you can trust. Do not take the staff that the old man offers you. It is dangerous.

How did he know about the staff? Or about the Second Father offering it to me? This guy, this King, had to know who the Second Father was. He must think me very foolish. I wouldn't dissuade him of that notion…for now.

Thank you for warning me, I said humbly. *I have no interest in war. I'm just a teacher and I don't understand what your people even are. I just thought I was going crazy with these dreams. Why do they want to usurp you? You seem like a good king.* I lowered my lashes; my eyes tend to give things away.

Max seemed to buy it, if his puffed-out chest and arrogant smirk meant anything. *Even good kings find themselves with foes. It's nothing I cannot handle. I simply want to keep my subjects safe, even you halfling.*

I gave him a smile that was meant to show gratitude and awe at his graciousness. He continued silkily, *Your Aunt though. She is back here. In my land. Do you know why?*

I widened my eyes at him. *Auntie Rami? She is…she is…where you are? She is what you are?*

Kimoni was laughing. Maybe I was laying the innocence on a bit thick. *You think?* Ki asked sarcastically. But the pretty boy King was buying it, so I kept it coming. Kimoni seemed to bristle at the pretty boy comment, and I tried not to smirk in either of my forms.

She is not what I am, but a halfling like you. Without Ki's resounding assertion that that was a lie, I knew my Auntie had to be the real deal. No doubt I was part Azizafri on my mother's side. Auntie was entirely to "light" to be a mere halfling like me.

Auntie left for vacation. She said she'd be gone for two months to visit her friends in Jamaica. I had no idea, I paused for effect looking down. Then as if it had just dawned on me, I looked up, filling my expression with surprise and hurt. *She lied to me.* Covering my mouth as though appalled I dropped my head again.

I am sorry you had to find out in this way, he said solemnly. I managed a slight nod, my head still down as though attempting to process. Clearing his throat, he went for the jugular. *One last warning before we are out of time. There are other things she has not been honest about. Should the prophetess ever try to bring you here, you must run far from her. She allies with the man from your dream. I would not have you hurt. Perhaps someday when the war has died down, you may see your homeland. Until then halfling, continue to immerse yourself in your humanity.*

This time he left my thoughts much more delicately; my eyes sprang open as his image evaporated and I looked right up at Ki. The concern he felt was evident on his face. Without breaking eye contact with me, he said to Aseema and Rami. "She was talking with Max. He felt her light, but he does not know where it came from."

"Max," Aseema said, stepping away from Ramla. "Who is Max?"

Ki's expression hardened and he finally broke eye contact with me, looking toward Ramla, "Max is Nyoka." Aseema inhaled sharply and craning my head around I saw Auntie's face harden. "I wondered if he was keeping tabs on her," Ramla said softly.

"This is not his first time contacting her," Ki said, dropping his hands from where they'd been gripping my arms for the past several minutes. Whenever he stopped touching me, I felt its absence much stronger than I'd like to admit. Looking disappointed in himself he turned away from me, rubbing a hand over his head before turning back. "I didn't know. I should have known it was him. But why the ruse? Why is he trying to keep her away from the core? I know that he could not have told her who he truly is due to the Yamanu, but...." A look of displeasure passed over Kimoni's face as he began to pace the floor.

"Max, I didn't catch it. He has been trying to keep her away. Whatever his connection is, he can only feel her surges of light, he uses them to warn her away. Thank the Creator he cannot track where she is. Auntie, do you think?" Kimoni and Ramla looked at one another having a wordless conversation.

Aseema stepped over to me and gingerly took my hand, giving it a squeeze. "Nyoka has wanted to rule all his life. We all grew up together. It has been his desire to be King. Now that the Second Father is in a healing stasis with...no, no heir." She stumbled over the words. "He is in charge and reluctant to give that up."

"Nyoka, as in snake?" I asked wryly. Aseema gave me a grim smile and nod. "As in viper. I know not what his parents were thinking." I studied Ramla and Kimoni as they finished their silent conversation. "I understand that he is King. I am also getting the vibe he got the job by nefarious means. But, he wants me to stay away from the core, you want me to go to it, I said looking pointedly at Ramla. I am conflicted as to which option will be in my best interest, though off principle I don't trust a guy named viper." I rolled my eyes before continuing. "What threat do I make to his rule? How can I help? I do want to assist, but as I am currently in the dark and continue to be so, I don't know *HOW*!"

Walking over to me, Ramla took my hands and looked me in my eyes. "Your memory is slowly coming back. Taking on the spirits of the Azizafri who were released from the Anguka has assisted with that, as well as," she looked over at Kimoni briefly before saying, "being back home. But it seems your muscle memory and light are leading more so than your mind." She tapped my head soundly with two surprisingly strong fingers, but I remained still, hoping for clarity. "My hope is that our journey to the core will unlock more of your memories, if not all of them. We pray the Creator will grant us assistance in getting you back so that you can fulfill your purpose here. It is hard to answer much, we are still tightly chained by the Yamanu, but what keeps us from speaking is the same thing which continues to keep you hidden, for when your memory returns…" She trailed off. I waited for her to give me more than that half-revealed tidbit, but I was sorely disappointed when she said no more.

"Oh, well you should have said that before. That clears *EVERYTHING* up." Dropping my Auntie's hand's I walked briskly out of the training room, feeling only partially guilty for my sarcasm, but mostly exasperation. I'd gone to the gym to work off my frustrations, not pick up additional angst!

Instead of going back to my borrowed bedroom, I headed for the room with the spectacular view of the city, where Ki and I had danced. Unfortunately, being alone was not in the cards for me. Lea intercepted me two steps from the doorway I was seeking. Instead of stopping me she fell in step with me and entered the room beside me. Heading straight for the window seat, I turned my eyes towards the city, hoping she'd get the hint. Instead, dressed in another flowing garment in a peach color today, she sank down into one of the softest bean bag shaped chairs I'd ever sat in. They reminded me of the *love sac* chairs in the mall because they were more like memory foam than beans.

My brain wouldn't tolerate the distraction for too long. It was like a vacuum sucking me down into a dark place, killing the Anguka in Steven's house. What would he think when he and his wife returned? There were broken doors, windows, and the dusts of the fallen had to be all over his home. Actually, screw him, I hoped he was allergic to dust and stepped barefoot on glass. But the vacuum continued to suck me down, to the desert where I'd killed the Anguka, to grabbing Mrs. Reisner in front of my students, the light escaping me and all of these-these voices in my head! Clasping my hands over my ears, I pulled my knees to my chest in the window alcove, feeling as though I was splitting apart. I was afraid, angry, confused, and almost certain

I was losing my mind! But mostly, I was at war with whether I wanted to remember my past or forget everything I'd learned since Ki showed up at my school. My heart stuttered over his name. I never wanted to forget him, who was I kidding?

Then there were hands around me, not Ki, but his sister and she smelled of cinnamon and clove. Wrapping her arms around the literal ball of confusion I'd bunched myself into, she whispered, "Kuwa na utulivu, dada yangu." Be calm my sister. I melted into her. Were we once like sisters? Was she as close to me as Aseema? Wait. Were Kimoni and I...? I searched my memory, but even through my closed lids the light was intense. Opening them quickly to find the source, I looked down at Lea in surprise. Somewhere during my tumultuous thoughts, I must have started doing my glow worm thing again. Lea had molded herself to my side and released her light so that it covered mine completely. Somehow, I knew that the brightness of her light had hidden mine before anyone could detect me again. I imagined that another outburst from me may have sent Nyoka our way.

Finally, pulling my eyes away from our joined light, I glanced up at Lea, who was smiling at me gently, with her arms still wrapped gently around me. "Are you better now? Can we turn down the wattage?" Her smile widened as I looked down slightly embarrassed and willed my wayward light back under its cover. Giving me a gentle squeeze, she stepped back and then sank into the chair closest to me.

"You have questions? I will try to answer what I can."

"Were we very close?"

She startled as if surprised by my query. Then with a soft smile she said, "Not at first." My eyebrow quirked at that. "You were always full of questions, very curious and as someone who has always accepted things for what they are. I did not like you constantly challenging and questioning everything and everyone around you." I hated to tell her that hadn't changed very much. Instead, I nodded, encouraging her to continue. "Eventually I came to the understanding that I should not hold these qualities in contempt, but that instead I should be learning from you. I owe you a great debt. It is because of you that I was able to truly begin walking in my creative potential."

She'd lost me again. It must have shown on my face because she laughed softly before clarifying. "I can't go into much detail because I am sure it will be filtered out through the Yamanu. Though my light came into being much before yours, it was your spontaneity and organic approach to creation that inspired me. I've always been so careful, so meticulous and you opened my mind. You challenged me. It is not because of Ki that we became friends, but your precocious spirit and determination. I did not know what your plan was, I would have tried to stop you and…" She hesitated. "I guess that's why you did not share it with me." Smiling to herself for a moment, she seemed to be contemplating that. After a comfortable silence, in which I was certain she was reflecting, her attention returned to me. "I'm just glad to have you back mwanamke wangu."

"Why does everyone call me that? I thought it was something that Aseema just made up being funny, but you all use it as well." Lea thought for a moment before responding, "Do you know what your name means?" I nodded immediately, "Malika means Queen and Alika means most beautiful." My middle name always came out in such a self-depreciating way, to me it was a bit of an overkill on my parents' part. Lea didn't seem to notice, she only nodded thoughtfully before saying, "Names have great meaning here. Parents name their children in the hopes that they will live up to that name. It's like...the Bible on Earth says that the power of life and death is in the tongue, that you can speak those things that are not into being. When we name our children, we speak their destiny into being. My name means 'bringer of good news,' so the thought was that I was good news to my parents and that I would always bring, well, good news. News of blessings and not sorrow. Your parents named you believing you'd be a beautiful Queen, so to speak."

Laughing at her softly I said, "But my parents are not Azizafri, they just thought it was a pretty name. What does it have to do with all this my lady business?"

"We believe in the power of a name," she said simply. But her eyes gave her away, she was staring at me hard. They thought I was a queen? Is that what it was? A laugh bubbled up in me, but her look quelled it. Was I to overthrow their current monarchy? Impossible, I was a freaking third-grade teacher who had a love for history. Hostile takeovers were interesting and good historical reading, but they weren't something a 25-year-old "halfling" like myself undertook in a country, wait planet, I knew nothing about.

"Is this a planet?" I asked suddenly.

Lea didn't look disturbed by the change in subject, she just smiled and replied carefully, "Amani, is much like what you would think of as a planet because beings live, thrive, work, and grow here. Traditionally you think of planets needing things such as oxygen, gravity, water, day, and night. We do not. Mahali Pa Amani is technically a cluster of stars."

Why did I bother to ask questions? It only led to more questions! I fell back into the alcove, letting my head thud against the glass of the window. There was a traffic jam in my head again. How could there be no gravity, I was sitting here, able to touch the ground? We'd had water with our food, right? I was breathing right now, wasn't I? Then Lea was near me again, with a hand resting on my head, "Utulivu, calm sister. This is my fault, I've said too much, please forgive me." I only shook my head, still trying to slow my thoughts down. Focusing on keeping my light from springing forth again, I inhaled and exhaled slowly, wondering if there was no oxygen, what in the Creator's name was I breathing?

Once I'd gotten myself under control, Lea walked with me back to my room so I could get some rest. I confided in her that I hadn't been sleeping well. Beings I didn't know kept interrupting my dreams with covert meetings about things I had no way of understanding. This sparked a response that I wasn't quite expecting. She was excited and began talking rapidly. "One of the things I've been able to create is a protective veil! It-it goes around your dreams actually. That way no one can project into your dreams and have covert meetings as you say. It allows your body to sleep uninterrupted and wake into consciousness on its own internal clock. There are those who have slept away quite a while because it protects against any disturbance."

"That's pretty cool actually. What happens if I sleep through the ball though?"

Lea smiled brightly; producing crinkles at the corners of her eyes that only made her more beautiful. "After a few people overslept, so to speak, I installed an internal alarm system. As you know around here there are no clocks or time constraints. So, when you should begin to prepare for the ball, you'll hear the call within the veil for you to rise."

Now that I understood, I shared her excitement and told her how much of a genius she was. Gushing over her invention until she fanned me away, blushing a becoming red over her smooth caramel skin. With her violet eyes dancing in delight, she further explained that the veil helped in muting one's light. Giving her a huge hug of gratitude, I went to get ready for what I hoped was my first peaceful sleep in forever! Waiting patiently, while I showered and changed, Lea told me to snuggle in bed before she spread a shimmery silver veil over me. Instantly it molded to the front of my body from head to foot. It was so soft, woven together with such thin threads they looked like they'd break with the lightest touch. Once she'd tested all the edges of it, she explained, "It is molded to you so even if you toss and turn in your sleep, it will stay covering you until you wake up and remove it." I gave her a grateful smile, which she returned before whispering, "Enlightened sleep, sister." Almost immediately, I fell into a deep, dreamless slumber.

CHAPTER 11

"A ball of confusion at the ball...that's a lot of balls."
- Malika

I was floating on light. A sea of luminescence twinkling all around me. It was like being captured inside a rainbow, except there was no shape or form to it. I was a part of this brilliant radiance, endless and consuming. My body hummed with joy and peace as my spirit, my light became one with this vast universe. There I spun in bliss, full of beauty and purpose. Because I felt it. I was beautiful, I felt it through and through, with no pride, only an awareness that it was fact. I was this beautiful light. But... I wasn't alone. There was a supernova next to me, an explosion of such amazing color that if I had eyes in this state, I was sure they'd fall out of their sockets from the sheer brilliance of it. Studying the mass of light, I sorted through an assortment of royal blues, reds, greens, and even tinges of brown? It was breathtaking and everything about it made me want to venture closer, to join with this magnificent light, so that we could enjoy bliss together. The supernova was calling to me, urgently. I hesitated for only a moment, before my desire overrode thought and I rushed to meet this glorious light, filled with a surety that this was right, this would make me whole. I'd gladly race across space and time just to get to it. With a frisson of pure elation, I noticed that the supernova was racing towards me just as quickly. From afar we most assuredly must look like shooting stars on a direct collision course with one another.

My speed picked up, wind gusting all around and I laughed in delight, hearing the tinkling sound, and wondering how with no ears or lips that was even possible. But those thoughts quickly drowned away in my joy as I neared my flame. It was him! My Moto wa kweli, Kimoni Fayola. We crashed right into one another with an explosion of brilliance! Astonished and elated, I couldn't tell where his light began and mine ended. Churning in waves of our own essence, united we shone brighter than the sun's rays. My entire being seized in delight as I marveled at the completeness I felt, the rapture of our joined light! Ripples of pleasure flowed through me as I felt the echoes of his joy. I sent mine right back until we both vibrated with this shared feeling. Our emotions now joined, the same euphoria I felt took him over and we blazed brighter and brighter until I could barely contain it.

My eyes popped open. The silken veil resting over my face and conforming to my body. Gently I removed it and reacquainted myself with the feel of my own body. Wiggling my fingers and toes, adjusting to accommodate my wings and lengthened limbs.

It was time for the ball. Removing the spider silk from my legs, I got up from the bed in a lithe motion that should have startled me. Stretching as euphoria rolled over my body in waves. For several moments I just stood, letting those waves of pleasure play with my senses, before heaving a regretful sigh and touching a fingertip to my torso.

"Umbembe," I said softly, putting my glamour back in place. As a creator I could have said anything to restore it, but that was simple enough. Somehow, I knew I was strong enough to conceal or create as much as I wanted. There were several things that joining with Kimoni's light had revealed to me. Auntie was right. He was a key of sorts, but I wasn't completely back to my normal self. A safety precaution I'd guess in situations such as this. It was taking all my strength not to run to him, to be near moto wangu. Suddenly my heart ached with it. But I knew something else as strongly as I knew that Ki was my flame. I had to free the Second Father, and I knew exactly how.

Determination flooding through me, I took a step towards the closet; it was time to prepare. But after a few steps, I was stopped in my tracks. Soft strains of music filled the air, it was entrancing. There must be speakers installed throughout the house. The melody was so familiar, so hypnotic, but I couldn't grasp where I'd heard it before. It was like something out of a dream.... With a start, I realized I'd been standing there, swaying, eyes closed, lost in the notes. It was as though they'd been drawing me somewhere...but, where? Instantly, it came to me, Home. The melody was calling me home, home to, the core. Perhaps this was my guide to the King...I needed to dress quickly. There was work to do.

Lea must have told everyone that she'd given me the veil because no one disturbed me as I dressed. It was decided I'd go disguised as Kimoni's halfling date, with not much light, but a great desire to increase it and learn about my heritage. Apparently, halflings were very rare, coming from those who left Amani to visit other planets. Azizafri married other Azizafri because no other race could survive in our light. The birth of a half Azizafri to a mortal was a special occurrence indeed, an unsanctioned, frowned upon one at that. I'd garner some interest, but most would try to ignore the truth of my heritage. The people were welcoming, but curious about newcomers. They'd tried to explain some of this, but my dream, uniting with Ki was giving a whole new meaning to many things that were difficult to understand before this very moment.

Once I was satisfied with my appearance, adding additional glamour to my hair and nails (what? I didn't have time to do them) I headed out to join the group. We were to meet on the first floor of the house, but when I came down the last set of steps, I saw only Aseema standing there, and she wasn't dressed. Walking over to me in her leather fighting ensemble, equipped with several weapons including her sjambok, her forehead was creased with worry.

"What's going on, sis? Why aren't you dressed?"

"Girl, you look gorgeous. Ki is going to freak."

"Thanks," I said, doing a slow spin and then peeking over my shoulder. "Now what's up, why aren't you dressed?"

"I'm not supposed to be here," she replied grimly.

"Hunh," I said in confusion.

"I'm supposed to be on Earth, where you are, so I can't be seen at the ball."

"But…Auntie is here."

She nodded, "Yes, she has an alibi. It is only right that she would return home for the celebration of Nyoka's Msimu wa mwanga, especially with the bridge being aligned. I on the other hand would be left on Earth to care for you in her absence."

"You couldn't have just worn a glamour?" I asked sullenly. She smiled at me fondly and straightened my necklace, lingering at it for a moment, no doubt wondering where it had come from. "Birthday slash Msimu wa mwanga gift from Ki. Hey, why does Nyoka's season of light coincide with mine?"

Stepping back, Aseema lifted an eyebrow. "It doesn't." I started to ask another question, but she held up her hand. "I can't say more, otherwise I would. Now I will not be at the ball as a guest, but I will be in the vicinity in case something goes down. I am your sworn protector after all."

"Ahhh," I said, finally getting it. They would understand why someone of Auntie's station would travel back for such an event, but Aseema was my protector and expected to remain with me. Something else that was revealed to me when Ki and I joined. Aseema was a born protector and had been assigned to me from birth. There was no way they'd buy both Aseema and Ramla being gone, leaving me alone and showing up with some strange, "unknown" halfling. Very suspicious indeed. Ki and Lea came down the steps arm in arm. His eyes met mine and he stopped short, causing Lea's arm to be jerked back comically, she gave him an inquiring look before her eyes landed on me.

I was told to try to fly under the radar, but I still had to at least look like I was going to a formal ball. After my dream of Kimoni and I connecting in the light, I'd chosen a yellow and royal blue Ankara dress, representing the prominent colors we sparked when united. That magic closet had simply spit out what I'd envisioned. The dress was off the shoulder and fitted through the bust and waist then flared out below my hips in a ruffle of fabric that flowed around my feet into a modest train. My hair was fanned about my head in an abundance of thick brown and honey blonde curls. I wore the rose quartz necklace he'd gifted me, dangling earrings that brushed the top of my neck and the chakri at each wrist. A gal could never be too careful. I watched Ki take in my hair, modest makeup, pausing at the necklace and then drifting down the length of my body. With a small smile I pointed a toe so he could get a peek at my royal blue heels that sported yellow fringe.

I glanced over at Aseema; she winked at me and smirked as Lea made her way across the room and gave me a sisterly peck on the cheek. "While my brother stares in awe, I would ask how you slept with the veil?" Giving her a gentle hug so as not to wrinkle either of us, I said, "Better than I ever have. Thank you dada yangu." Her eyes lit up as I whispered the words my sister, "dada yangu." Then with a knowing smile she backed away, picking up the skirts of her flowing lavender dress. It was a true ball gown, with a sweetheart neckline and flaring out into a bell-shaped bottom where the lavender fell into deeper shades of purple, causing a beautiful cascading effect. She'd pinned her hair up into a complicated braided style and she looked gorgeous.

"Alika, mwanamke wangu," Ki bent over my hand in a formal bow. The way he said my middle name, I knew he was calling on its meaning, most beautiful and I blushed, finally giving him a once over. I was startled to realize he was wearing the same colors as I, though much more subtle. The suit was well tailored and fit him in such a way that I could still see traces of muscle through the lines of it. He'd opted for a double-breasted jacket in royal blue, with matching slacks. His shirt and oxfords were black, but he'd opted for a tie with yellow starbursts on a blue background. Standing up from his graceful bow, he touched a hand to my waist and leaned down to whisper in my ear, "I thought perhaps it was a dream. Otherwise, I would have come to you immediately after I woke."

Startled, I looked up at him. *Your secret is safe with me Alika.* He knew I didn't want anyone to know how much I remembered just yet, so he spoke directly into my mind. Somehow, I knew the more I acknowledged what I remembered, the harder it would be to hide my light. Now more than ever, I realized how numerous my enemies were. I could not keep them completely at bay until I came into the fullness of my power. In the meantime, I had to use wisdom and stealth. *Thank you,* I said into his mind. The heated look he gave me, promised that we would explore this newfound memory later. Dropping my head, I blushed again as he took my left arm and offered his other to Lea. Aseema looked slightly melancholy as we left her behind and momentarily, I wondered how she would get to the ball. *She'll fly,* Kimoni spoke through our mind connection again and I realized something.

There were no barriers between us. Had our minds become one just as our light had?

Not quite, he corrected. *Yamanu has not been completely removed. While you can see all things present, the past will still prove to be a bit hazy.* Fear lanced through me. I didn't know how comfortable I was with us having zero barriers between us. Clearly in my mind, Ki showed me the book closing, the same one I'd used to open and close our thoughts previously. His mind was cut off to me. Then he opened it and I could see clearly again. *Anytime you want your thoughts to yourself,* he said solemnly. *Good to know,* I thought back at him, closing the book.

A wave of disappointment wafted from him, and I realized that though we could close off our thoughts, his emotions would never be closed off to me. Which also meant he'd have full access to my emotions as well. This was a definite recipe for some awkwardness down the line. I glanced at him out of the corner of my eye and he looked completely at peace now, even his thoughts had become placid. Maybe I'd imagined it. Or maybe he just had a good poker face. Poker mind? Poker emotions? Kimoni winked at me, then helped Lea into the car first, before assisting me.

It was the strangest car I'd ever seen. There were no wheels, it was a pearlescent colored, domed vessel with windows and butterfly doors. I had no idea how this thing would move or if it were possible. Would we just float? Once I was inside my consternation increased as I studied the contraption further. It diverged further from what I'd expect of a car on Earth. It could seat maybe six people, but there was no driver seat, it was as though we only had the back half of a limo. Three seats sat across from one another, and the entire roof was transparent.

I was looking around in awe when we took off on a beam of light. Grabbing for the door handle and whatever I could find (which ended up being Lea), I looked around in shock as lights flashed all around us. She laughed, patting my hand to loosen my grip. "I see my modest brother did not tell you about his latest creation." My eyes widened as I looked across the moving vehicle at him. He held something small and black in his hand, but he wasn't looking at me, instead he was giving his sister a hard expression. Shrugging, obviously unaffected by his stony look, Lea took my chin which had been alternating between the window, ceiling and Ki's face and turned it towards her. "Your moto wa kweli has been creating vigorously while you were gone. He has increased our productivity with his ingenuity. Hopefully once all is settled, he can rest with you awhile. I fear he has not paid much attention to the cycles of creation which includes rest." The siblings glared at one another for a few moments while I wrapped my head around my "true flame" as Lea referred to him, creating furiously in my absence. That was a lot of creating, especially since my 25 years on Earth was much longer in Amani.

"How did you engineer this mpenzi wangu? It's like something out of a movie!" I was looking up at the flashing lights through the ceiling, so I didn't catch his facial expression, but his sharp intake of breath caused me to drop my head abruptly. By then he seemed completely at ease; maybe I'd imagined the spike in his adrenaline. *My love,* he inquired through our connection. I blushed realizing what I'd just said. It had come out so casually. This was going to be harder than I anticipated.

He didn't further taunt me , instead he began explaining. "The Second Father did not begin with wings. When we were created, we flitted from place to place, traveling on waves of light. With our creative energies we developed wings, much like the celestial beings known as angels. But as you can see," he said, indicating his back, free of Mabawa, "we can make them appear and disappear at will." He demonstrated by shrugging, causing his beautiful feathers to flare out behind him, then he shrugged again, and they were gone. "Aside from flying, flitting, or walking we had no other modes of transportation. Horses and cars like you have on Earth were of no use to us given how fast we can flit or fly. But for longer distances, this could grow tiresome, expending a great deal of energy."

"Yes!" Lea interrupted excitedly. "So my genius brother took the human vehicle and modified into a more meaningful way of travel in the cosmos by combining it with similar components to a-a spaceship!" Kimoni smiled fondly at his sister. She was full of pride and excitement at his accomplishment. He waited patiently for her to try to explain before fanning at him, telling him to continue. Ki tossed me a small smile.

"Many things were invented before mine. Other Azizafri have constructed acceptable modes of transport, but I've modified two for longer distance travel. This one is most like a car. It takes the light energies from the place it leaves, to propel it to the next point of light." He held up a device the size of a cell phone. "I enter coordinates here and it's like a large magnet, the vehicle is propelled from one wave of light to the destination, entered here." He pointed to the phone-like device.

Looking around me at the swirl of lights, I was still completely flummoxed by what he'd created, but it was, "Amazing," I said simply. "Have you given it a name?" Pausing for a moment, looking down at his hands, Kimoni said, "Mpanda Farasi, or light rider."

I started laughing. He looked up at me in surprise and that made me laugh harder. Soon Lea joined me and eventually Ki reluctantly joined in. "So does this light rider talk then?" Again, that sheepish grin appeared on his handsome features. "LR, do you have our invitations for the ball?"

"Yes sir," a pleasant voice responded. Then three tickets popped out of a side panel. My mouth dropped. Looking at Kimoni, I gave him his props. "You are a genius. But is LR really like the Knight rider car? Will she help you solve complex problems?" Giving me a smug smile, Kimoni said, "LR, please answer the lady's question."

"I would be happy to sir," the car responded. You are seated in the Mpanda Farasi Series X. I am a fully equipped transportation vehicle fitted with artificial intelligence. My capabilities are extensive and would take more time than you have, as we are fast approaching your destination. In brief, I am far superior to the Knight Rider vehicle Father Kimoni so loved. Not only do I act as personal assistant, but I can assist him outside the vehicle, enact evasive maneuvers when I sense danger and provide medical assistance should there be a need."

"Impressive," I said.

"Thank you miss," the LR responded.

"How do you sense danger?"

"I am fitted with sensors to detect physical danger, but AI allows me to respond to any other imminent threats as well."

"Were you designed with the Bugatti Veyron model in mind? You actually resemble it but without wheels."

Kimoni looked stunned and then mildly impressed. I just smiled. Girls like cars as well. "Why yes, my lady, I am. You are quite quick in your assessments. I would be more than happy to talk more with you about my construction when time permits."

"Thank you LR, I would love that."

Taking in the leather seats that could recline on top of being super comfy. I wondered if they'd let me take some Azizafri chairs back home when I left, because never had I ever sat on more comfortable furniture. There was even a compartment on each door with snacks (I know because I checked). Sexy and smart. *I'm a lucky girl,* I said through our connection. Kimoni smiled broadly and replied, *I am the one who is blessed.* This was the coolest thing ever. My beautiful Tesla had nothing on this. Boy did I miss Tessy I thought, momentarily sad that I wouldn't see my car for quite some time. One of my favorite things to do was just drive and listen to music. As soon as it entered my mind, music popped on, filtering through speakers located in each of the four corners of the vehicle.

Looking up at Ki in question I asked, "How does that keep happening?" He smiled, "I can converse with LR without speaking, much like a telepathic connection. She's…linked into your wishes as well. It was the system responding to your internal request." Lea smiled over at me, beaming with pride at her Kaba's genius.

"Would LR protect me if I were in danger?" Kimoni gazed at me quietly, and LR responded, "I protect all Azizafri, but my priority is Malika and all immediate kin of my creator." My protection came first? The siblings just smiled at me as I sat quietly, stunned? Flummoxed?

Returning their smiles and thanking LR again, I continued to study my surroundings. We all sat in a comfortable silence, listening to the soft strums of music filtering through the superior speaker system. Next thing I knew, my eyes had drifted shut and I was swaying. The music seemed to distort and meld into that haunting melody I'd heard in the house. The entrancing, dreamlike strains were louder this time, but no less intoxicating. It seemed to be pulling at me and I wanted nothing more than to wrap up in the canorous tune and just rest there. A feeling of safety and security washed over me with each note. We were nearing the core. This sweet refrain would lead me directly to the King and I'd use what I'd discovered after joining with Kimoni in the cosmos.

The lights around us changed abruptly, startlingly bright against my closed lids. Opening my eyes slowly, feeling sluggish, I peered around. Lea was staring peacefully out the window. Ki was looking at me strangely, "We're entering the core," he said quietly, a hint of apprehension in his voice. I was about to ask him if he could hear the music as well, but a hint of unease washed over me at the thought. I'd keep it to myself for now.

There were beautiful gates in front of us, intertwined with gold, silver, onyx, and various jewels. They seemed to be checking guests at the entrance. Not everyone was in a vehicle such as ours. Some flew on wings, others had rides that looked more like planes or spaceships, but each halted obediently at the gate dead ahead. For some reason I couldn't get the image of Dorothy and her crew waiting outside to meet the *Great and Powerful Oz* out of my head. I realized Ki was listening when he smiled, I didn't close the book. At that moment, I didn't mind. Our connection would make it easier to ask my numerous questions during the ball. Playfully I felt him start slowly closing the book. I gave him a mental shove, laughing softly. One of my hands was still in Lea's and she gave me a gentle squeeze, looking back and forth between the two of us. "I'm sorry, we're being rude," I said.

"Not at all," she responded quickly. "I'm just glad to see you two back together. He truly missed you while you were away. And…" Suddenly, Lea's words were lost in a buzzing sound that filled my ears. Her lips were moving, and she was still smiling, but I couldn't even decipher the shape the words were making coming from her mouth. Ki lifted a hand and she halted. "She didn't hear anything you just said," Ki said grimly. Looking startled Lea's head jerked over to stare at me, as if asking for confirmation. "I don't know what happened. There was a buzzing in my ears. Even your lips blurred. I'm usually a good lip reader," I said in wonder.

"It's the Yamanu. She was saying things she should not, things that you'll have to find out on your own my lady." He shot his sister a warning look and she dropped her head. Putting a protective arm around her shoulder, I shot Ki a dark look. "It's ok Lele you didn't know. You weren't there when the Yamanu was laid, you aren't expected to know such things. Chin up friend, though we're on mission impossible you'll see Rashidi, there'll be some fun to be had." Lea looked at me and a tear fell from her eye. I pulled back in shock, searching for a tissue. Ki held a few out to me solemnly. But he wasn't looking at his sister, he was staring at me with a strange look on his face. Patting at the tears on her cheeks, so as not to mess up her makeup, Lea tried to get herself together. I continued to hold her in the crook of my arm, and focused on Ki, giving her some privacy.

What's wrong?

You haven't called her LeLe since we were kids. She knows you're starting to remember. They are…happy tears.

I pulled Lea closer to me. She'd always been my big sister, even before Ki finally realized he could date all the girls on Amani, but he'd still end up with little old me. At that thought he gave me a guarded look.

Yes, I remember you and all the pretty girls.

I added a dash of reprimand to that thought, though it was all water under the bridge. At one time, I'd cried to Lea, wondering why Kimoni didn't want me. Why he had rebelled so strongly against our joining together. Why could I remember that, but so much else was a blur?

The younger me couldn't wrap my head around my… He hesitated. *Future wife being chosen for me at such a young age. I was foolish and it was a total waste of time. The regret will ever be mine for taking what we have for granted.*

I shook my head at him, only teasing really. *Everyone has been young and foolish at some point, even Kimoni Fayola. But you now walk in what your parents spoke over you at birth, A great Father Roho who walks with honor. You cannot continue to blame the sins of the child on the being you've become.*

Pleasure emanated from his thoughts in waves; he tried to tamp it down, but I sent him responding feelings of comfort and peace. I could see remnants of my dream as our individual lights became one brilliant whole, floating around the edges of my vision.

Lea drew my attention back to her as she moved out from my arm, tears finally dried. "We are nearing the gate. Two people away from our turn. They are moving quickly. Listen kids, I'm the big sis here. Remember to keep that connection of yours on the low or others will know something is up. Kimoni, you are playing a rogue who found a halfling to make your plaything while Mali is away. That should be easy for you to do." Kimoni nodded, giving his sister his full attention. I wanted to come to his defense again, but he gave me a look that quelled that instinct.

No need, she is being matter of fact my love, he said resolutely.

I only nodded as Lea continued. "You will be besotted with Kimoni, also easy, she said with a roll of her eyes. You'll entreat me for a tour of the Father's home. This is normal, the first floor is like a museum. But there are passages all throughout the palace for us to traverse through and look for the King and Queen. Hopefully, you will be drawn to their light." Ki nodded in agreement with his sister's words. "I'll stay behind to make sure you two aren't missed. The best time to go will be during the presentation of gifts to Nyoka." We'd been through this information already, so I only nodded in agreement as apprehension started to bloom in my belly. Looking down quickly to make sure I wasn't emitting light, I heaved a sigh of relief, realizing I still had it under wraps.

Again, I could hear the strains of the melody playing in the background of my mind, calling me closer. It felt wrong not to share with Kimoni and Lea what I was hearing, but there was something holding me back. I just couldn't get the words out. When the time was right, Lea and I would go find the King and Queen, my parents, then I could free the Father and go back home. Home. My thoughts splintered. A large part of me wanted to return to Earth, to my third graders, my position as a team leader and my doctorate studies. I hadn't even gotten a chance to finish my third degree. There was so much I had planned, a life I had mapped out with goal lists and vision boards. My studies of ancient African history and my plan to travel to write my first book, all on hold? Gone forever? I had a life and friends to get back to. Yet the thought of leaving Ki behind or Lele or even little Issa was painful. Would Aseema or Auntie Rami even want to go back? I got the impression that both were much happier here.

No! I chastised myself; I could think about that later. Right now, I needed to focus. Focus on my mission and following the beautiful melody that continued to draw me. This was the key to finding the King and restoring his light. I was sure of it. A thought passed through my brain so quickly, I barely caught it. Why couldn't Ki see the melody in my thoughts? Then the thought was gone, and I was looking at the well-dressed guards walking up to us.

Our invitation was quickly taken, and we were dropped at the steps of the palace, or the core as everyone referred to it. Kimoni pressed a button on his device and the car zoomed off on another beam of light. When I asked him where it went, he simply pointed above his head. I flinched, seeing hundreds or more transport vehicles hovering above us, just sitting in the sky.

He laughed at my startled expression and said softly, "Welcome back home," he gestured towards the beautiful structure.

This was the most guarded place in the city. The gates that rose around it surrounded the entirety of a starburst structure so vast it seemed to be a city of its own. With my new memories I realized that the structure was just as deep as it was high. It reached so high up into the sky, I couldn't make out the top of it. While the homes in the parts of Amani I'd seen had one central color, the core represented every color and was reinforced beyond any other defense in the land. The core was large enough to house every citizen of this place, the Second Father wanted all his children to find shelter in his gates should they ever need it. But this starburst was different, right in the middle of it was a cylinder like structure that only a select few knew about. I had a feeling that knowledge would aid me soon.

Several glamours were laid over me at the moment. The Yamanu, Auntie Ramla's additional coverings and protections, along with a few of my own. Then Ki had added some to make my features indistinguishable. For the first time I could remember, I felt the many layers laying snugly against my skin. I had the strangest sensation that with a thought I could shrug them all away simultaneously. That probably wouldn't be the best idea at the moment, but the thought of it was exhilarating. Kimoni had also added glamours to both Lea and himself so that when they spoke my name, it came out as Angela, my Mother's name. I was honored to carry that name, if only for a night.

Though the steps coming up had been endless, most just flitted to the top. Some moved so quickly that it was as though they simply were at the bottom one minute and appeared at the top in the next. I wasn't supposed to know how to flit, but with my newfound memories I was sure I could. Just as much as I was sure that while we could flit on the steps, the inside of the core would be off limits to the use of Azizafri power, unless you were one of the first family. Kimoni stood at my left and Lea at my right. Before I could protest, they flitted me to the top of the stairs in a gentle movement. Once we were inside Lea was to distance herself from me, because she would not approve of her brother's dalliances, and everyone knew that. But she'd also never be outright rude to anyone, so they'd understand her riding with us and giving me the staged tour later.

No sooner had we stepped into the ballroom than my mouth fell open in breathless astonishment. This place was a riot of color, amazing sound, and strategically placed art. My favorite home renovators could never! From the full orchestra in the corner, to the longest table of delicacies I'd ever seen, the magnificent chandeliers and the Azizafri all around! Each one of them looked straight from a magazine. Beautiful in all shapes, sizes, and variances of color. Only paired Azizafri mates seemed to wear the same colors, other than that there were no repeats. There was no way of knowing for sure, but I would guess that every color on the spectrum was represented in this room, including some new hues I'd never seen. This was a who's-who of proud, Azizafri beauty. These were the colors, styles and culture of the continent, and the light, oh my Creator! The light. The room was so brilliant I was amazed that everyone didn't have sunglasses or protective eyewear! Each person emanated bright luminescence from their solar plexus. All gorgeous and unique, emitting radiant shades of; purple, pink, blue, red, green, yellow and orange. Variations of color I could neither name nor identify adorned the room in a riotous rainbow of stunning brilliance. If you had asked me previously I would say my favorite color was sky blue, but now I just didn't know! There was a woman who sported folds of coral and ivory that I couldn't tear my eyes from, but then my eye caught onto a shade of emerald that took my breath away. Who could choose amidst this assortment?

I was sure that my jaw was dragging along on the floor and was made certain when Kimoni gently put a fingertip to my chin, pushing my mouth closed. He laughed huskily when I shot daggers his way. But my eyes veered back to their exploration of the melanated parade happening all around me. My chest swelled with pride at the beauty that filled this room.

I didn't realize I'd begun turning in tiny circles, so intent was I on taking every little detail in; that when Ki stepped in front of me and twirled me into his arms, humming into my ear, "As the World Falls Down," in a rich tenor, all I could do was laugh at myself. "Am I to be Sarah, oh great Goblin King?" I asked. Humming as he swayed me side to side a few more steps, he finally answered, "No, though you were doing a good job of parroting her. She leaves the Goblin King in the end…"

There was a pained look on his face that leeched all the humor out of mine. A few of the partygoers were looking at us strangely. We'd created our own little dance space in the middle of several groups of quietly talking couples. I blushed and Kimoni tucked my arm in his elbow, nodding to a few who dared meet his eye.

Lea gave us both a look from where she'd been watching us. "Good job blending, guys," she murmured.

"I didn't even pull out the good moves yet," Ki said good naturedly. She gave him a wry grin, kissed him on the cheek, winked at me and headed off to find her husband.

I didn't know how to reassure Kimoni about my leaving. Things were still too uncertain; I had more questions than answers. I couldn't promise him I'd stay when I didn't know what this was. He pulled me to a stop again and looked down at me intently, *I will not ask you to stay. But I will NOT be coerced into not following YOU wherever you choose to be.*

Gazing up into his swirling caramel eyes, I believed him. I also believed I wasn't quite ready for this conversation either. So, my ADD kicked in, it was the beautiful chandeliers hanging up above his head. They were adorned with millions of diamonds, rubies, emeralds, and other precious jewels. You'd think all of that would be gaudy, but it was spaced in such a way that it had an elegant beauty that caught the eye. My recovering memory clicked, these jewels were real, not fake and the brilliant kaleidoscope of color that each of the jewels reflected only added to the brilliance of the room. The floors beneath our feet, picked up the shine of the numerous lights in their marble swirl of cream and gold. I was afraid I'd snap my own neck as I craned around admiring the ceilings that were impossibly high and the murals on the wall.

Kimoni heaved a sigh of resignation and began leading me through the crowd again. We stopped to talk to a few guests here and there. Well, he stopped to talk, I was mostly introduced and then promptly ignored. He was introducing me as "Angela," his halfling friend whom he'd met on a journey to the southern tip of the stars. They all seemed to accept it for face value, nodding politely and then engaging him in conversation about some of his newest inventions. It seemed that Mpanda Farasi or LR was a major hit and many of the Azizafri in attendance wanted to own a model of their own.

Everyone here knew that Kimoni was promised to me…well tonight I was Angela, and he was promised to Malika, the real me (this was already confusing). So, his selection of colors like mine and appearance with me would shine attention on him and only send sympathetic glances my way. Which, unfortunately, was already happening. Colors like those that we wore together, were usually only for Azizafri houses who had joined together. It seemed they were willing to talk with him extensively about his product but avoiding me was a must. At the same time, they were curious, so they couldn't help but continue throwing sidelong glances my way. Unbothered, I smiled, while looking towards the long table of hors d'oeuvres stretched down the length of the room, so long was the table that I couldn't tell where it began and the room ended.

As I continued my perusal of the room, I felt rather dull in comparison, no light illuminated my dress. Some women had opted for cutouts in the sides or bare torsos to let their light take center stage. Dresses hung to the floor in translucent monochromatic folds in every shade imaginable. Lea fit right in with her gown, mine wasn't quite the norm.

"You look exquisite. No one can tell me that you aren't the most gorgeous Azizafri in this room." Smiling up at Kimoni,

I was about to thank him when another woman interrupted. Wait…No, not a woman. There was no man and no woman in Azizafri. There were Mother and Father Spirits here, Mama and Baba Roho. Though they walked and lived within celestial bodies, it was their spirit with the strength to hold the body together, they could shred or transform it at will. My thoughts stuttered over that remembered tidbit. This was surreal. The Mother Spirit who'd interrupted us was speaking, but I couldn't quite hear her as I studied her light. It was tainted, a grayish black. There was so much gray to her light, I felt the weight of it. Looking around the room, I noticed she was the only one with this dominant color. *Malika, do not stare. Your gift to decipher the colors is…not common. I can see a swirl of colors in her, but only those she pushes to the forefront. You see her true light. Gray is affiliated with depression, a loss of hope. The black is…something else entirely. She doesn't want that seen so don't make it known that you can.* I forced myself not to react to his words urgently whispered into my mind, instead squeezing his arm lightly in understanding.

"But she is not Azizafri. She is more of a woman than Roho, yes?" Immediately I felt the disdain dripping off of her. Usually people didn't dislike me automatically, but there was a first time for everything. "Vivienne," Kimoni said, bowing over her hand and planting a soft kiss on her wrist. "You look lovely as always." She pouted prettily, making a striking figure in a dress that hugged every curve of her impressive body before flaring out at her ankles in a lovely froth of deeper reds. The top was a light pink that darkened as it went down, ending in a bloody red train. She'd opted to straighten her hair and it fell artfully over her bare brown shoulders "But not the most gorgeous apparently. That title is reserved for your halfling guest." She gave me a derisive look before turning her gaze back to Kimoni. Smoothly straightening and tucking my arm back into his he said, "I can appreciate the beauty of all Mother Roho. A compliment to one does not void those I've made to others. And if I remember correctly, I've paid you quite a few unforgettable one's on more than one occasion." He ran strong fingertips gently down her bare arm, causing Vivienne to shiver delicately. The implied intimacy was enough to make me bristle with anger, but I played the part of besotted and unknowing halfling, pretending disinterest in the conversation. I occupied myself examining the room and its inhabitants like an especially excited child.

Gazing off into the crowd, feigning indifference, I began to hear the hypnotic melody again, calling me to it, promising safety, and warmth if I'd just surrender. I caught myself swaying side to side when Ki's hand tightened gently where it rested on my arm. It took all my willpower not to dash off to find its source. With everything in me I wanted to follow it. This entrancing song was blocking out the strains of the full orchestra as they played their own otherworldly melody. They were situated high in a balcony where they could take the best advantage of the room's acoustics. But I couldn't hear them anymore. Only this melody…it was important somehow and it was much closer than it'd previously been.

I was starting to feel woozy when Vivienne's preening and over the top flirtations drew me out of my trance. Leaning in closer to my date, she seemed to have forgotten I was standing there and was effectively invading my space as well as his. "You've been in solitude for so long…I've forgotten all of the things you used to say…and do," she added coyly. "I thought you'd never get over Malika, only creating, never…loving anymore." With a smirk, he only shrugged the comment off, so the heaux continued. I felt the pressure of Ki's fingertips on my arm again and closed the book between our minds. Decisively, I added a padlock to that closed connection. "I thought when you came out of your little depression that you'd come to find me. As a lonely widow, I'd have appreciated the company. But here you are. With this, child." She looked at him from beneath her lashes, giving him her full-on seductive routine right in my presence. I ground my teeth at the child insult and barely stopped myself from rolling my eyes. "I'll keep that in mind, mpenzi. Save me a dance, yes", Ki asked casually. She gave him another seductive look, "I'll save you more than that once you rid yourself of the halfling." At that, I looked back at her and bared my teeth in a cruel smile. She startled a moment, visibly surprised at my response, before composing herself and sauntering away. I watched the sway of her hips as she strutted in her impossibly high heels.

"Angela," Kimoni said, calling me by my code name for the night. He brushed mental fingertips down the spine of the book that separated our minds and I fought not to shiver. That shouldn't happen when I was angry at him. But his mental caress was just as effective as his capable hands. "Can we get some snacks?" I asked brightly, eyeing the snack table. Facing my issues head on, that was me! He gave me a wary look and I smiled up at him like the empty headed halfling I was playing tonight. See, I was so smitten with the Azizafri Father next to me that I couldn't possibly care about Vivienne approaching him. On to the snack table I thought with a grim determination not to analyze the fact that he'd obviously slept with Vivienne. When had that happened? She'd never liked me, even when her husband was alive. I wonder what happened to Roderick? Grudgingly I cracked open our mental communication, and asked Kimoni. His relief at me opening back up to him was suddenly tinged with regret. *We lost him in a battle with the Anguka. He was ingested, so his soul is…in captivity until that Anguka is killed or devours him completely,* he murmured into my mind.

Roderick had been a kind, gentle soul, completely at odds with his flame Vivienne. I liked him a great deal, we'd learned and played together long ago. It's odd the things I suddenly remember. Mostly insignificant things. But the important stuff, when I try to reach for it, there is still this thick fog. Ki only gave me a sad look. He knew more than anyone how I struggled to remember. He could see the battle in my mind. *Something is still holding you back my darling. When you release completely, the memories will come.* I was at a loss. Instead of trying to muddle through my fog ridden brain, I turned my attention to the assortment of delicacies laid out on the portion of the ridiculously overladen table that was nearest me. I'd started stacking my plate when something dawned on me. *This food isn't going to make it so that I can't leave here or that I'm in servitude to the Azizafri forever is it?*

Ki didn't miss a beat. He'd opted for one of the colorful beverages being carried around on trays, taking a sip, then nodding to a knot of pretty ladies eyeing him. *We aren't the fae. We don't indulge in such trickery. Though we have been mistaken for the Tuatha De' Danaan as well as other such deities on occasion.*

He said it in such a casual tone that I almost didn't catch it. *Wait, what? There are other deities? Oh! Are the Tuatha De' real?* That was a scary thought if I'd ever had one. Kind of exciting as well; fae males were supposed to be HOT.

Kimoni didn't answer; rather, he gave me a lazy shrug that could have meant, "yes, all the scary beings you've read about are real and waiting for you to slip up so you can make a deal that you can't get out of." Or the shrug could have simply meant he chose not to answer such a stupid question. I looked over at him again, the champagne flute was at his lips, but he wasn't drinking. Then I clued into his thoughts, he was laughing at me.

Creating a clear vision in my mind, I projected a crude gesture his way. His beautiful caramel eyes widened and a flash of white, straight teeth through the sensual upturn of his lips had me feeling a little gooey on the inside. As if sensing it, he caressed my bare shoulder with his fingertips, causing the women across the room to give me dirty looks. I cringed slightly, aware that he'd just done the same with Vivienne. Reading my expression he looked as though he were about to apologize, when pretending to be besotted, I leaned into him, taking one of the slices of mango off my plate, I rubbed the ripe piece of fruit across my lips, sticking out my tongue to lick off the juice before taking it from my lips and placing it at his. His eyes were lit with mischief as he took the mango in his mouth, making sure that his tongue and teeth brushed across my fingertips gently.

Things were getting hazy; I'd meant to toy with him while pissing off his fan club, but I'd only succeeded in getting myself hot and bothered. *You're not alone*, he said through our connection. I dropped my gaze shyly, taking another mango from my plate and popping it in my mouth. It was the most succulent I'd ever tasted.

I froze, mid chew. *HURRY. We are waiting, my dear. We need you to come quickly.* I would have dropped the plate if it weren't for Ki's reflexes. He steadied my hand, looking at me inquisitively. "You didn't hear that?" Shaking his head with a worried look on his face, Ki studied me intensely. *I heard someone calling me, telling me to hurry. To come quickly.* Kimoni looked around sharply, then quickly schooled his features back into the charming playboy. He took my plate and sat it on the edge of the table. I was sad to see it go, there was so much appetizing food I hadn't tasted yet. He set his glass next to it and slid one hand around my waist, then gripping the nape of my neck with the other he leaned down and brushed a kiss across my lips. For a moment, I stiffened in surprise.

Play along, I'm creating a reason for us to sneak off somewhere so I can get you to the Queen. It had to be her who called you.

I relaxed into his arms, going pliant. *Change of plans?* He only brushed his lips across mine again, before nuzzling my neck. I giggled a little louder than I normally would, not having to force it too much, my neck was a definite erogenous zone. "I'll have to keep that in mind," he murmured into my ear. Then he took my hand, giving me a little twirl before leading me out of the consistently increasing crowd in the ballroom. We were stopped several times along the way, but Ki brusquely told everyone he had a dark corner to find and kept moving. I was blushing profusely by the time we made it into an area empty of Azizafri. It was filled with gorgeous paintings and statues, and the ceilings were like looking up into a gorgeous skyscape.

"This portion is blocked off for the evening," a Father in uniform informed us firmly. Ki's back was to him, but when he turned the Azizafri smiled broadly. "Father Kimoni, he said with a formal bow, forgive me." Walking towards him, Ki waved away the formal greeting and they touched foreheads briefly, saying, "Amani," or "peace," in the traditional greeting. This one was not like the guard's we'd encountered when entering the edges of Amani. They were new, he'd been working the core since before I was born. Once they finished exchanging pleasantries, Ki introduced me to General Tau. He was a tall, muscular, imposing man with piercing eyes and large dark blue-black wings that he wore out proudly against his standard leathers. I'd known him all my life, he used to perform tricks for me as a young girl, entertaining me until Mama told me to leave him be. Aseema had been in love with him for as far back as I could remember. It was a silly crush then, but I think she was still smitten with the general…and there went my memory with random, unimportant tidbits that did nothing to help me in this situation.

Tau greeted me with a cool nod, speaking the words of greeting, from a distance without the contact that showed respect. He obviously did not agree with Ki being here with me, he knew that Ki was promised to me, Mali. I smiled to myself; his loyalty was admirable. After a few pleasantries, Tau did not linger, but left us to our liaison, tossing one last disapproving look our way.

Daughter! Hurry! I startled into action at the Mother's voice, tossing a quick glance over my shoulder to make sure that the general was out of sight, I raced over to the imposing statue of my father in the center of the room. He'd always hated it, said that it was the height of vanity, that the Creator's form should be at the center. But for the Azizafri, my father, the Second Father was honored as the first creation and thereby the center of their universe. Shaking out of the tidbits of memory that continued to flow back, all these minor details, I pulled at the statues pinky and started towards the entrance that swung out right below our feet. Gathering my skirts in my hands I hurried down the winding staircase, not bothering to check if my companion was behind me. The Second Father was in danger, his light was fading and when I joined with the light of my moto wangu in that dream, I realized I knew how to save him.

Kimoni kept close behind me as I raced down the endless staircase. "Close it," I reminded him as we continued down. I realized belatedly that he may not know how but kept moving when I heard it swing back into place above us. Were it not for Ki releasing his light, we would have been plunged into complete darkness. A rich wave of warm blue was emanating from behind me and illuminating the way in front of me. If we weren't in such a hurry, I'd have liked to explore the variances in his light. Time just to explore him. I'd forgotten we still had an open line of telepathic communication, so I jumped a little when he said, *we have an eternity mpenzi wangu.* He said it with such certainty and longing that I shivered at the thought. *Focus,* I chided myself. *Save dear old dad first and then jump Ki's bones! Priorities Mali.*

The glow of Ki's humor tickled through my mind, and I was too focused to be embarrassed…or so I told myself. The steps finally ended and the tunnel at the bottom branched off in two different directions. I looked back at Ki, and he only gazed back at me, waiting. Then I heard it, the strains of that enchanting melody again, walking to my left I followed the strains until the tunnel split again, this time in four directions that all looked the same. We were in a glittering stone passageway that had a purple hue to the rock. Everything was smoothed out around us as though perfectly rounded out for passage through the tunnels.

I made off down the third tunnel to my right, sure that Ki would follow as the music pulled me as though we were attached by a cord, a cord leading from my light to it. This had to be the Second Father and Mother calling me. Absently I realized I could no longer see Ki's blue light in front of me. The glittering purple stone that made the cavern around me illuminated my way. Running as quickly as I could in my four-inch heels, with my skirts balled in each hand, I made my way through the rough stone tunnel, surprised I had yet to twist an ankle. The speed of my movements blew my curls back and the walls around me began to blur as the melody pulled on me harder, making me feel slightly weak, while increasing the sense of urgency. I stumbled slightly as the melody seemed to grasp and claw at me feverishly. Righting myself quickly, I continued, powerless to deny the beckoning force.

Part of me knew that these tunnels branched out wider and wider, going by twos, into mind blowing options until anyone who stumbled upon them would find themselves lost. But these tunnels recognized me. I played here as a child, and I knew my way.

Moving faster and faster, breathing even, yet heart racing, I made my way into a hollowed-out cavern that had a gorgeous waterfall at its center, pouring down from overhead, yet no droplets splashed on me as I carefully walked around the edge. It fell straight into the enormous pond beneath it, causing lovely ripples in glowing depths. The music was so deafening here, I couldn't even hear the waterfall. Spinning in circles I looked for that which I sought and found nothing. I stood still for a moment. Then my body began swaying to the captivating strains of the haunting melody, eyes closed, and arms lifted in rapture. My movements felt sluggish, but that didn't stop me. This refrain was all there was.

When strong fingers wrapped around my waist, it barely registered. Those hands turned me slowly into a tall, lean body, but my eyes were so heavy, I couldn't work up the strength to look. My hands fell uselessly to his biceps as we continued to sway. Drowsily, I tried again to open my eyes and could only crack them the tiniest bit. My dance partner was out of focus. He felt familiar but I could not pick one defining characteristic if I tried. It was all unimportant, nothing mattered but the notes drifting on the air as we swayed, wrapped in one another's embrace.

It felt as though hours passed in this fashion. My head resting against his lean chest, rocking side to side, body to body. This was so peaceful…but I felt-I felt so weak. Leaning into my partner, letting my weight rest on him, I felt my knees start to quake. Lifting my head with difficulty, I looked up at him, wanting to tell him I needed to rest. But he took the brunt of my weight against his body and whirled us in a smooth movement, effectively cutting off my words. "You're not tired yet, are you Malika?" he asked in a husky baritone voice, filled with challenge. There was something familiar and playful in his tone. "I like you like this, he said softly. Pliant, beautiful and…demure. So…human." He laughed as though my humanity was some great joke. That laugh was so familiar, I knew it from somewhere, but my brain was entrenched in the melody. It was hard to get a thought past its mellow strains. I slumped into him further. In a nonchalant move, he lifted me into his arms, murmuring, "Relax my darling." Then he danced with me in his arms, and I felt my head loll back. If I could just close my eyes for a moment, I'd be fine. I was so tired. I just needed to rest…

Wait…darling? No, no, this was not Ki. This is not moto wangu. I struggled for consciousness, finding my limbs slow to cooperate. Then I heard it. A ferocious command slicing through my haze-filled mind: *Malika, fight!* My eyelids flew open, and I began clawing through the mental fog. Looking up from where my head hung over my dance partner's arms, I saw a thick greenish smoke filling the cavern. But wait, there was a glimmer of movement. Kimoni was…fighting? We were still inside the gorgeous, glowing cavern, with the walls sparkling like purple crystals. But we were surrounded by a concealing haze, from which enemies kept dashing out and back in again, taking advantage of the low visibility to surprise attack Ki. Still, he fought fiercely. Whirling and slashing as soon as one popped out, he fought them back with his twin blades moving in a whirl of light and motion too hard for my addled brain to follow. He whirled to meet each challenger, moving at unbelievable speeds that only increased the dizzy sensation I was feeling.

Slowly, I looked up at the man who held me in his arms, I couldn't bring his features into focus, but those eyes…they glittered dangerously. "I am here my darling. We can stay like this forever," he crooned, as he swayed me gently. Then I heard another voice. It was the Queen, yelling from a distance, *Daughter! Your light!*

Jolting in his arms, I looked down at my midsection and jerked in surprise. My dance partner had been siphoning my light out of me and into himself. He was slowly stealing my life force and I'd been letting him. I'd been dancing with an Anguka. Eyes widening in disbelief, I looked up at him and then threw my hands forward, aiming for his chest, while simultaneously throwing my body backwards and out of his arms.

Anticipating me, he turned, releasing me, so that I went careening towards the cavern floor. "Kurejesha! Restore," I yelled and hit the cavern floor with a thud that shook me to my bones. Curling into a ball, I shook violently as my light began to flow back into me rapidly, eagerly! It was like what I'd imagine gripping a lightning bolt with both of my bare hands would resemble. My skin began to tighten as it filled with power, my power. The Anguka looked down in disbelief. But wait… he wasn't distorted like the others of his kind. In fact, he looked familiar; maybe it was a glamour? I reached up to rip it away, but as if sensing my intent, he instantly blinked out of existence. Or should I say I just couldn't see him anymore? He had to be around, because my power was still surging back into me, causing tremors to rack my body. It was never like this before. But then I'd never had to take in my own power. As I got to the end of my own light, I realized that with a simple word I could keep pulling until I devoured his light. I could kill him with a thought. Kneeling on the floor, trembling, I was filled with indecision. Then the choice was gone. He fled the room, and I could no longer feel him.

How had he done that? Who was he? Euphoria cleared my head, and it was a good thing, because a circle of three gorgeous Azizafri surrounded me with blades aimed. With a heavy sigh, I held up my hands innocently, "I come in peace guys." They looked less than amused. "You are in a restricted area. You will be taken into custody to be dealt with by our ruler at his discretion." Hanging my head in frustration, I thought quickly as they prodded me to my feet. Glancing over I saw that Kimoni was whirling his blade in graceful arcs as he battled, the now seven attackers surrounding him. It occurred to me that he would have defeated them by now if he were truly aiming to hurt them. He was simply defending himself without inflicting any true blows to his opponents. Finally, on my feet I tried to reason with the… ooh these guys were hot. *Wait, focus, Mali.*

"I am here to help the King. I am not a threat. Please stop attacking my friend." They only angled their weapons at me, apparently on the brink of violence should I resist. Wryly I thought, none of my dreams that included three attractive males ever included swords. Well…not the sharp kind. Today was apparently not my day. "Oh well," I said with a shrug and then flitting behind the gray eyed male on my left (the cutest of the three if you asked me) hit him in the temple with my Chakri. He crumpled and I glanced down sadly as the two males standing in front of me with blades pointed, shared a twin expression of shock. "Only the King can teleport in the core. How did you…"

he broke off in confusion and I took that stunned moment to teleport behind him and his friend, bang their heads together viciously and appear at Ki's back. I laughed triumphantly; I'd always wanted to do that.

"Took you long enough, darling," Kimoni said quietly. But not quietly enough apparently. "Blasphemy," one of our attackers yelled. I was blocking with my Chakri as Ki kept blocking and moving with his Kotel blades whirling. We moved in harmony clockwise then counterclockwise. Barely keeping our seven captors at bay as they were slowly circling us towards the waterfall. I felt Ki, brushing gently against the pages of the book between our minds, trying not to startle me, as I dodged and ducked the blades coming my way. Strangely they weren't using any other powers. Kimoni, now linked to my thoughts, said, *No powers can be used in the core to protect the First Family. Though there are certain exceptions. Do you trust me?* I sent him a resounding *yes* as a blade nearly clipped my shoulder. Then I felt him tug on my light. Out of reflex I almost pulled back but stopped myself. I truly did trust him.

The cavern was suddenly filled with gorgeous yellow light, it took me a moment before finding the source. Kimoni was shooting light, my light, from his fingertips and into the Azizafri crowded around us. Immediately they began dropping as though paralyzed. "Now that's just awesome," I exclaimed in awe. Kimoni threw me a smirk. "Yep, now we run." With the hand that wasn't shooting light from its tips, Ki grabbed my arm. With a joyful laugh that bubbled up from my very depths, I laced my fingers with his, focused on our combined light and teleported us. Unfortunately, my aim was off, and we ended up in the hallway where 10 more guards were gathered, waiting for the light to fade to enter the cavern.

Ki gave me a wry look. "My bad," I said sheepishly looking around at the guards that lined the hallway. They'd frozen in shock. *You're not supposed to be able to do that in the core,* Ki reminded me telepathically. I looked up at him and he swung his Kotel out to block a blade coming for my throat. *Do it again!* Trying to focus while blocking blows in the tight space, I teleported us again.

The next landing space was cramped. Kimoni and I were pressed flush against one another inside a narrow passageway. *Good job, Mali.* The compliment combined with an interested look in his eyes made my cheeks suffuse with color. Before I could thank him, he leaned down and pressed his lips against mine briefly, then pulled back gently, resting his forehead on mine. Though his face was placid, I could feel his heart beating fast and loud. I pressed a hand to it, *Are you alright?* Closing his eyes and inhaling deeply, he said, "I could not bear to lose you Malika. Back there, I-I couldn't see you…but I could feel your pain, your light being stripped from you, but I couldn't get to you. There was a barrier…I thought…" He grasped my shoulders for a moment before pulling back, quickly checking himself. "You saved us back there." I smiled up at him and responded in kind, "So did you." "Where are your blades? Where did you get them?" Looking grim he studied our surroundings. I left them with their owner. There was a long narrow hallway to the left and to the right, we were right in the middle, where the passageway curved in. "Do you know where we are?" He asked it without any inflection or admonition.

Malika, come to us. The Queen's voice drifted to me again. I broke eye contact with him, looking to my right. Her voice seemed to come from that direction. "What did you hear?" Ki asked softly. I frowned; the last time I followed my instincts, I'd led us into a trap. What if this was another? I couldn't keep leading Kimoni into danger. Raising one finger in the small space that existed between us, he met my eyes and spoke directly into my mind.

I would follow you anywhere. Though you do not always allow it. I started to interrupt, wanting to ask where I'd told him not to follow me, but he shook his head with a small smile playing on his lips. Then he lifted another finger and spoke aloud. "If you are in danger, so am I. We are connected. Raising a third finger he said, "In the book of creation, it says that the Creator's sheep will hear his voice and a stranger they will not follow."

My eyebrows knitted together; I was with him until we got to number three. What did that mean? "You know the Queen Mother's voice as you know the Father's. So, tell me, who calls to you?" I looked up at him a moment longer, mesmerized by his light. It was pouring from his abdomen and suffusing his face with an ethereal glow that made him look angelic. Then I forced my eyes closed, blocking out the gorgeous man in front of me and concentrating on that voice. It was like a beacon. Though it did not speak, its location, its light called out to mine. We were connected. That voice had sung to me, whispered to me words of love and encouragement. It never hurt me or led me astray... this voice was home. That melody had been tainted. It had drawn me feverishly, unconcerned for safety or stealth. This voice was a gentle plea…Opening my eyes, I looked up at Ki again. He only nodded.

I began walking towards the curved hallway, barely able to walk straight, turning just a bit to fit. I looked behind me to find that Ki was shuffling through the passages sideways. Somehow, he was still able to look graceful, I sighed, unable to contain my jealousy.

"Hey, why didn't the guards recognize you? You're like a powerful, important guy around here, right? Why would they attack you without question?" Ki was silent a moment, still shuffling behind me, before finally answering. I noticed that he was slow to speak. A man of careful thought. I liked that about him. "Thank you mwanamke wangu. This is a good question that you ask. My thought is that your captor, the one who was attempting to take your light, had a glamour over the cavern that prevented them from ascertaining my true face. Did your captor's face seem hazy to you? Did you recognize him?"

"No," I said, shaking my head. "There was something familiar about him, but I did not recognize him, nor could I discern any features." I glanced behind me to see Ki nod, his face scrunched up in thought. "The fog made for low visibility, I believe he had the cavern and entryway covered in a strong glamour. They could not have known me. To attack me, even breaching our betrothal as I was, would have been punished as treason."

"Oh, you have clout-clout. Ok," I said with an impressed nod of my head.

"Mali…what does that mean?"

"It's an Earthly way of saying you have plug, influence, power. You know that type of thing."

"If I have this clout, it is only because I am promised to you."

Shaking my head, not believing that for a second, I focused completely on the pull of the Queen. Her light was incredibly weak for some reason. If the Second Father was ill, had he somehow infected her as well? *If I may, my lady*, Ki said into my thoughts, in such a formal tone, it made me pause. *Yes*, I responded cautiously. My back was to him, yet I felt his nod. *When we pulled on one another's light it strengthened our connection. Moto wa kweli, true flame, such as the Second Father and the Mother are, become one so completely that their separate lights become almost indistinguishable unless one is gifted to see.* He said "see" in such a way that I was certain he wasn't referring to just regular sight.

Before I could ask, the trail of my fingertips along the smooth walls of the inner core pulled me into another memory. The soothing, cultured cadences of the Second Father's voice layered the memory making me feel as though I were in two bubbles of time at once.

The palace, like all the structures in Amani, is shaped much like a starburst. To protect us further, we created an inner sanctum, it is the core of the core. The Second Father pointed to the cylinder shaped, narrow passage we were walking through. I could see a version of me no taller than Issa, holding the Second Father's hand and trailing her fingertips along the smooth amber walls. *This inner cylinder winds all the way up to the top. We have created a fortress within the fortress, protected from enemies of our own making.* I knew he meant the Anguka, but why were they enemies of our own making?

My mother's faint voice came to me again, telling me I was close and to hurry. With a jolt I let go of the memory. There would be time for that later, I began to move faster through the tight space, glad that my wings were hidden away behind glamour. They would have made for an uncomfortable journey through these inner walls. Ki was shuffling faster, his broad shoulders suffered in the tight space. "There that's the door," I said, seeing the light ahead.

Urgency bubbled up in me and I shuffled towards it as fast as I could in my skirt and heels, until I reached the door. Then, I hesitated, my hand hovering near the knob. It took Ki a few additional moments to make it to me, moving carefully along as he was. Looking back at him, I knew the same fears that filled my head were present in my eyes. Touching fingertips to my jaw gently he said, "Let go, Mali." Allowing myself a few more seconds to gain strength from the warm caramel depths of his eyes, I nodded then placed my hand on the knob, it was warm. It pulsed beneath my hand, once, twice, three times and then faded away completely.

Then we were in a cozy room, quite at odds with the rest of the castle and even what I'd seen of Ki's parents' home. It was a wide half-moon shape. Decorated in all shades of gold and cream, the ceiling sported a mural of the night sky, in direct contrast to the colors of the room itself. The fireplace was so big I could stand in it, upright, stretching my arms out. The entire room was lit by it, along with candles scattered here and there. In the center of the room was a four poster bed with curtains all around. Next to it, a chaise with a lovely woman draped across it, fully clothed in loose fitting cream pants and a lovely mauve sweater that left one shoulder bare.

Her eyes were on the figure in the bed. As Kimoni stepped forward, the door clicked back in place, causing the woman to look up sharply. Then her expression morphed into one of wonder. Gingerly standing up from the chaise she looked me over, eyes widening in wonder. "Malika," she said in a breathy whisper, pronouncing my name carefully, Ma-LI-kA. I could only stare back at her, watching beautiful brown eyes fill with tears. My heart was thumping a dangerous rhythm in my chest and all I could do was stare.

The trance was broken when the figure on the bed began shaking violently. Then I heard it. The melody. It was playing in this room. The same one that had drawn me through the tunnels below the castle. Looking around me at Ki, the Queen and King, I noticed they didn't seem to hear it. The Queen Mother...my mother whirled to her ailing husband, laying a calming hand on his brow as the shudders began to abate. Speaking softly over her shoulder, she said, "He has been peacefully in stasis for some time now. Only recently has he been afflicted with violent tremors. Still, he does not wake, and his light grows dimmer by the day. I fear he will have nothing left to take his place in the heavens."

Queen Mother, Roselia Fari, was gorgeous. She could pass for my sister before passing for my mother. Her gentle curves stood out in her simple outfit and her hair hung down to her waist in honey brown curls that seemed heavy just looking at them. Maybe about 5'10 and regal, she stood tall by her husband's bed, full of concern, but unbreakable as ever.

I walked over slowly, taking a place by her side. She stood holding the Second Father's hand, but with my approach, she looked up and gave me a sad smile. "When you truly love, even an eternity seems to short a time." Laying a hand gently atop my head, she stripped away my glamour until she was no longer looking down at me, we were eye to eye. Touching my face gently she said, "There is my daughter." I touched her hand where it rested on my cheek and then gently pushed in closer to my father. The strains of the haunting melody were loudest here, near the bed. They didn't pull and tug at me the way they had before I broke out of the Anguka's spell. If my suspicions were correct, it had been playing for so long that neither the King nor Queen took notice of it any longer. I checked behind me on Kimoni; he seemed unaffected, and I heaved a sigh of relief.

The King looked to be sleeping. He was a handsome man, with pepper gray flecks at his temples and in his beard. But his light. His beautiful light was barely there. It was thin and wispy like the candles around the room. I remembered what it should be, what it once was. An inferno, blazing brighter than the fireplace across the room, brighter than the sun. He was the Second Father, and his light was usually a glorious thing to behold; it encompassed every color imaginable. The Second Father was the first of the Azizafri people, he carried the light of the Creator. No wonder Mama couldn't heal him, their lights were connected. As his true flame, his moto wa kweli, their flames, their lights had been joined. She'd been expending her own to keep him in his stasis. Looking over at her, I realized how dim the blaze from her midsection had become. There was no shame or regret in her expression. I'd almost lost both of my parents. Grief tried to strangle me as I thought of losing yet another set of parents that I'd never really gotten to know. The Queen Mother rested a hand on my arm, then gave me a nod of encouragement, as if giving me the go ahead to do what I'd come here to do. I gave her a small smile, her faith in me strengthening my resolve.

Kimoni stepped up and took my mother's hand, I smiled gratefully at him before returning my attention to the Second Father. My Father. I watched the light flow out of him on the currents of the music. His essence, so intertwined with that of the Queen's that I couldn't tell where their individual light ended. I wondered briefly if I could follow those strains to the culprit, before resolutely laying the fingertips of my left hand on the King's head and my palm flat on his belly. "Kurudi kwa nuru na kupona!" Light return and heal! As the words left my lips, I felt a surge of power flow into the Father. His back arched off the bed as light flowed into him in a steady current, as though the music had reversed course. I kept my hands on him, willing the light back from wherever it had been siphoned off to and felt the resistance. Someone was fighting to hold onto it. "Kurudi kwa nuru na kupona! Light return and heal!" The haunting melody was playing, but softer and softer. It didn't have the same draw now that I heard it for what it was. This was a song of destruction.

Focusing on the hypnotic tune, I envisioned claws in my mind's eye, then with a burst of will, shredded the chords until all I heard were discordant notes and a shriek of pain echoed through my mind. Tightening my grasp on the Father, I resisted the urge to clasp my hands to my ears. Faster and faster the light flowed, eager to return to its rightful owner, the thief had lost his grip. Queen Mother weakened behind me as her light began to return as well. Kimoni eased her back onto the chaise as she mirrored Fathers position, back arched as light flowed back into their bodies, eager to return to its true owners. It wasn't affecting me as greatly. I was just a conduit, pulling it from the thief and returning it back to the King and Queen's bodies.

As I pulled, I tried to trace the stream back to the Anguka who'd stolen it, this was what they specialized in. The consumption of light that did not belong to them. I don't know how they got to the Second Father, but there would be hell to pay if I could trace their identity. We needed to know who created this song of destruction and how. Unfortunately, they were expending a great deal of their energy keeping themselves hidden, which made it easier to reclaim the lost light, but harder to track them. As we neared the end of that which had been stolen, two options presented themselves to me once again. I could stop at the end of the King and Queens stolen light. Somehow, I could see exactly where their light ended and this thief's light began. Or, I could suck the dirty Anguka dry and either bestow his light on the King or I could devour it whole myself.

A rage welled in me, one I hadn't felt at my own attack. They'd come for my parents, our Second Father and Mother. Trembling with anger, I began to siphon the power faster, feeling the resolve. I'd suck this Anguka dry for this attempt on the King and Queens' lives. They would not see these cosmos much longer. I wanted to blast them out of existence for this offense. They would deprive our people of their King, their Father. An eerie calm washed over me at the thought of this divine retribution. The Father's light was much more than my own, especially combined with the mother and it took time to recall each and every bit of it. It was almost time to make that Anguka pay dearly.

Then, I felt eyes on me. Opening my lid's, I found the king staring at me with a mixture of love, pride and…concern. Trying to puzzle out what that meant, I felt the end of the King's light coming back to him and the tug of the Anguka's. There was a great deal of it. This Anguka's personal light was strong, and he had also stolen much. But the Father's eyes warned me to quell my rage and I closed the stream as the very last of the Kings light seeped in. A surety washed over me that neither I nor my father needed the light of a tainted Anguka. We would find the thief and make him return all the light he had stolen from the Azizafri.

I lifted my hands and was immediately pulled down into a hug, "Binti Yangu." Tears raced down my cheeks unbidden as I sank into his embrace, half laying across his chest. It was apparent that he'd been ill, the usual solid frame of my father was much leaner, but the strength in his arms had not changed. Arms that had held me and lifted me high up to the heavens while I squealed in delight. My mind struggled with the concept. I still remembered Roland Nichols holding me and playing with me, my life on Earth warred with the snippets of memory I had from my time here. But it was real. The Second Father was just as much my father as Roland Nichols. Somehow, I had two sets of parents. I felt Mother's hand resting on my back atop Father's and just basked in having a family, a mother, and a father, for a few moments. After some time cocooned in my father's warm embrace, he loosened his grip and my mother pulled me into hers. Our tears mingled together as we held each other cheek to cheek.

Kimoni stood behind my mother, and I looked up at him with a tear-stained face and smiled gratefully. He only bowed his head in a solemn show of respect. Once Mother and I were done holding one another, she looked at me a long moment before covering my entire face with butterfly kisses. My memory showed me a vision of her doing this every day before I slept. "I am so glad to have you home binti yangu." They both called me binti yangu, "my daughter," and the words warmed me beyond reason. Then she looked over at her husband and in a lightning-fast movement, she climbed into the bed straddling him and covering his face with kisses. These were much more passionate than those she'd bestowed on me. Embarrassed, Ki and I turned away, giving them privacy.

"Kids," he said wryly, reaching over and entwining his fingers with mine. I gave him a big smile, hoping I hadn't ruined my makeup. "Your makeup is fine but"…he looked meaningfully down at my dress. I looked down quickly and gaped at myself. Mama had shredded my glamour, I was taller, but I was also more toned, curvier and my dress wasn't accommodating those changes well. Wresting my hand from his, I crossed my arms over my chest protectively. Laughing, Ki put his hands on my waist and turned me to face him, quite easily despite my resistance. After assessing me briefly he waved a hand over my gown. Automatically it cinched in at the waist, accommodated my full bosom and lengthened back to the floor so that the train hung behind me as it was supposed to.

Smiling, Ki took the hand I'd wrested from him to cover my breasts and twined our fingers once more. Looking down at myself again, I thought, *I could really grow to love this guy.* "That would be nice," he said softly, giving me an innocent smile. "Then again, maybe not," I said playfully. Feigning a wounded expression, Ki placed his free hand over his heart in pain. I rolled my eyes at him. "Wait, how did you do that?" I indicated myself, wondering how he'd been able to use his gifts inside the core walls. Briefly he just looked at me before answering, "We are connected. You can create here, so I can create here. In the cave, you lent me your power and strengthened our link." I had so many more questions, but Father called.

"Kimoni my son, come." At my father's summons, Ki straightened immediately and turned to go to the bedside once more, pulling me along with him. "My Father," he said with a bow. The King took Ki's free hand and looked up at him gratefully. Mother still nestled in the crook of his arm smiling happily. "Thank you for bringing our daughter back to us." Ki started to protest, but the King simply waved his protests away. "I know that you love Malika and wanted her back anyway, but I am still grateful." Ki gave another humble nod of his head, bowing deeper this time.

"There is much to be done. But sit for a moment." He waved a hand at the chaise the Queen Mother had been sitting on when we entered, and it transformed into two chairs. I looked at him in surprise and awe. The King only smiled as we took our seats. Kimoni allowed me to take the chair closest to the bed, where my father reached out his free hand. I took it shyly and the Queen Mother laid her delicate fingertips atop ours. "Daughter, tell me. What has been causing the Anguka's increased strength?" I started; how did he know that I knew? I'd only just figured it out while my hands were drawing his light back.

"It-well, I believe it is the melody, Si-si-sire," I said humbly, stumbling over the words. I wasn't quite ready to call him my father aloud yet. That would make all of this too real. So, I'd opted for something respectful when addressing a King. He looked disappointed and my heart twinged with guilt. Sitting quietly in the chair next to me, Ki took my hand without a word. Waves of peace seemed to flow from him, and I tossed him a grateful look.

"Please, explain binti," the King requested. So, I told him how I'd been hearing the melody quietly in my mind at Kimoni's parents' home. They all seemed surprised that the melody had gotten through the protections surrounding the house. Then I explained how the song called to me here in the core and through the underground tunnels of the Core. How the stranger had danced with me and glamoured me while sucking the life force out of me slowly, with each strain of the melody. "It was because of you," I said, looking up at the Queen Mother, "that I was able to break free."

She gave me a knowing look. "Not just me." I blushed; how did she know? "Well, yes, it was Kimoni as well, who helped me pull out of the trance." He looked at me inquisitively. I averted my gaze, not willing to go into it. But the Queen Mother smiled. "The heart recognizes what is true. Very rarely do we listen to it, allowing logic and principle to override the simplest truth of all."

Sure, that I didn't want to know where she was going with this, I refused to ask what that "simple truth" was. Kimoni had no such reservations. "What truth is that Mother?" I cast him a derisive look, but his eyes were all for the Queen's response.

She wasn't looking at him though, she met my eyes as she said, "The heart knows what it wants and recognizes its missing piece, even when the mind does not. Your heart will not accept a counterfeit when it's already recognized it's Moto wa kweli." Unable to endure this whole, bringing a guy home to meet my parents, I looked over at the Second Father with pleading eyes.

"We have much to discuss, my children, but first," he said with a twinkle in his eyes, "We must prepare for a ball." I looked at my father in wonder. How could he think of going down there when he'd just regained his strength? Though I appreciated the diversion, I was concerned for his health. He looked at the Queen who sat up immediately. They both climbed off the bed limber and graceful as though they hadn't been locked away, the Creator knew how long.

"Shall we?" The Second Father asked Queen Mother, holding out his hand to her. She took it and immediately began twirling from his lifted fingertips. As if we were in some fairytale, her clothes, hair, and makeup changed. No longer was she wearing the cream slacks and mauve top, but she also wore a gown fit for a queen. It wasn't the monochrome ball gown that the ladies downstairs were sporting, but she'd opted for something more lavish. She glimmered in golden sparkles on a cream ball gown that cinched at the waist and trailed behind her in folds that looked to be light as air. She sported a high neckline and her hair had been swept up in the front, leaving the back down so that her curls hung in gorgeous waves down her back. Mama was a fox.

She gave me a wink as the King spun around her back in a smooth, graceful dance-like move and came out dressed in a black tux. The jacket was the eye catcher, flecked with the same gold sparkle as mom's dress. His hair and beard had even been trimmed; they made a stunning pair. Atop his head sat a crown that was a simple starburst fitted to his head, laced with silver and gold all the way through. Snapping his fingers, a delicate onyx walking stick appeared in his hand with a ruby twinkling atop it. "Shall we?" he asked with an upward tick of his brow. Shaking my head in wonder, I started to take Ki's arm when the Second Father held up a hand to halt us. "I almost forgot." He beckoned with the hand that held his walking stick, for me to come closer. I stepped over to him slowly, timidly. "Daughter, you look lovely." I found myself immensely pleased by the compliment. "But, there is one thing missing." I stiffened momentarily, but he only smiled and touched his fingertip to my head. There was a slight weight there and I suddenly wished there was a mirror nearby, when just like that one popped up to my left. Both of my parents glanced at each other before smiling broadly at me in approval. I caught sight of my reflection and my mouth had formed into a little "O" of wonder.

While my father's crown laid flat against his head, mine was a starburst that curved out and around my head glimmering in varying lengths of gold and silver, twinkling at the tips with jewels I couldn't even name. It was breathtaking and extravagant. Dare I say it, I was breathtaking. The yellow in my dress had taken on more of a golden tinge, the train was longer, my long locks were in a long braid across my shoulder that hit my waist. But my eyes, they practically glittered with life. I didn't recognize myself. My eyes locked with Kimoni's in the mirror, for a moment I got lost there. He was looking at me like I was the most beautiful, precious thing on the planet. For the first time in my life, I felt cherished, and all he was doing was looking at me. He opened his mind to me and instead of words, filled my thoughts with his love and awe.

The King cleared his throat, jolting us out of our private moment. I looked up to find the Queen Mother smiling at us broadly, while the Second Father looked slightly uncomfortable. "We have much to do children. Let us handle business first..." He gave my mother a small smile. "And matters of the heart later." Blushing, I nodded, and took the arm that the King offered me, glancing back at Kimoni who only inclined his head and followed behind us.

CHAPTER 12

Party crashers.

The door I'd walked through had vanished. Mother informed me that only I could have opened it. The door recognized my light and once my light joined with my parents it dissolved into another smooth portion of the wall. They'd created this room for times of danger and only my parents, myself and now Kimoni knew about it. So, Father created an exit with a simple thought. Walking through the inner core, I admired the marble floors, the crystal chandeliers overhead. Dad really did like his chandeliers. The walls were in that same amber color and sparkled as though inlaid with even more crystals. I noticed the odd lack of doors or exits. Though I was grateful that this passage was wide enough for the three of us to walk side by side with Kimoni trailing us; I was slightly perturbed at the lack of ways to escape. *You are safe here. No attacks will come in this place.* Kimoni assured me through our connection and instantly I relaxed.

As we headed down to the ball, which was to honor Nyoka's season of light, my parents filled us in. Well, they filled me in, Ki was pretty versed in what had been going on in Amani. Shortly after my departure to Earth (I still wasn't sure why I'd gone), the Second Father realized he was losing light. He was unsure how, but he felt it being siphoned from him in small doses as he'd hear little snippets of the melody off and on. He knew there was a traitor in their midst. Being the Father of the Azizafri people, his light was so great, no one could take it in one sitting, not even the most powerful of the Anguka. It would have to be ingested slowly, over many rotations of Amani. Stealthily he tried to find out who the culprit was, enlisting the help of trusted advisors. No one was able to pinpoint it and no one in the core was showing signs of having taken in his power, not that he recognized. The King asked Nyoka to take over leadership while he went into a healing stasis to preserve what was left of his light. Nyoka didn't want to see this happen, he wanted to find the offender and bring them to justice, but the King made him promise to begin the search after he went into hiding and he reluctantly obliged. The King and Queen then departed to their cozy sanctum, telling no one of what their plan was or where they were going.

The King expended the last of his energies putting a protective veil around them, and the Queen kept it reinforced while he slept so that no one would find them. The only person who could open the door or get past the barrier was me, and by default Ki now that our lights had joined. "Whoever it is must know that you have your power back now," I said worriedly.

"Yes," the King agreed, nodding solemnly. "I felt the rage as the power was siphoned from him." I'd felt it as well, the Anguka had resisted the return of power. Thinking aloud I said, "This does not explain why Nyoka did not want me to return to the core."

"What do you mean, daughter? When did you speak to your brother? What did he say?" Queen Mother asked with concern, filling her eyes. Quickly I filled them in on the interactions I'd had with Nyoka who went as Max to me. "His bedside manner has not always been the best, but I would imagine he was afraid that if you returned whoever was siphoning my power would turn on you and try to ingest your power as well. No doubt he wanted to keep you safe."

"Wait, did you call him my brother?" Both the King and Queen eyed me strangely. Kimoni chimed in to clarify. "Look closer Mama, Baba, the Yamanu is still covering much more than you can imagine." They both halted, pulling me to a stop with them. We were still in the inner cylinder of the core, hidden, they both gave me a once over. Startled, I realized that the Second Father was where I'd gotten my strange eye color from. He had the same honey-colored eyes with green flecks. Even the shape of his eyes, slightly slanted upward, were like mine. As I looked at him in wonder, the Second Father placed a hand on my abdomen, causing my light to brighten visibly. He looked at me as if finally understanding, while Queen Mother looked at Kimoni sadly.

"Fear not," Father said with confidence, "She will be restored." He then gave Kimoni a meaningful look. "Faith, my son."

With a determined jut to his chin, Kimoni only nodded in acknowledgement.

"Baba mwenye heshima, honored father," Kimoni began formally. "You must be made aware that your heir and binti mwenye heshima has been repeatedly attacked." I wondered for a moment why he was being so formal, referring to us as honored father and daughter. The whole heir thing was pretty mind boggling as well.

I craned around to toss him a questioning look, when my father stopped me, turning my face to his. "What happened binti yangu?" My eyes met his and I felt suddenly full of an odd combination of joy and sorrow. "Baba," I began, stopping as my voice cracked. Without hesitation, he pulled me into a warm hug, which my Mother quickly added her slender arms to. I was cocooned in their love and light. For a few moments, I inhaled and exhaled slowly letting it sink in. Ki gently urged me to open my mind to them and share our journey with them in that way. So, I skipped to the good parts, promising I'd go back and give them the full story later. I showed them the multiple attacks on Earth and then in the cave for a clearer picture, the music that called to me and enticed me. Unable to hold it back, I even showed them the sadness I'd felt having to take life. Though they were fallen creatures they were sentient beings, and it was against all I stood for to harm another living creature. Several moments seemed to pass before the Father pulled back wiping tears from my cheeks.

"You are a creator daughter. Of course it hurts you to destroy. It is at odds with what your light was created to do. The Anguka have found a way to use this melody to siphon away our light.

I heard the melody for so long, I cast it off as perhaps a song I was destined to create but hadn't fully formulated. It soothed and lulled me into a place of comfort. When I realized my light was being stolen, I still didn't intuit that the music was connected…" He broke off looking up quickly. "We must go, we will finish this later, Malika." The Second Father looked over his shoulder and Ki walked up quickly, placing a hand on his arm. Before I could ask what was going on, we were outside the hidden cylinder and standing on a dais at the apex of the long ballroom. We'd appeared right behind a throne where gifts were being given to Max aka Nyoka.

For several moments I wondered why no one noticed the four of us standing right behind the very person they were looking at. Glancing over at the Second Father inquisitively, I realized he had yet to remove the glamour that had kept us hidden. It was solidly in place now that his light had been fully restored. I gazed around the room at the great mass of at least 10,000 Azizafri, yet the room did not seem crowded, no one appeared pressed for space. Nyoka lounged in the massive golden and emerald tufted throne as gifts were brought forward and laid at his feet. Some of the faces around the dais I recognized, Lea and her husband Rashidi were near the front. She leaned against him happily and he had his arm wrapped around her waist casually. Next to them were Ki's parents, they made a stunning pair, regal and bright. Their colors were so familiar to me, I got the feeling that they were very much like family to me.

I felt Ki's mind brush against mine gently as if affirming the thought. Then I saw my Auntie Ramla standing off to the side, looking absolutely gorgeous in a surprisingly stunning gray dress that shimmered under the chandeliers. It startled me when she made direct eye contact with me and winked, before giving each of my parents a slight incline of her head. My father nodded back, while my mother blew a kiss to her beloved sister. Rami smiled softly before diverting her attention so as not to alert anyone else to our presence. How had she seen us? Kimoni's thoughts whispered across mine, *your father allowed it.*

The King's eyes were on me, and I looked up questioningly; he whispered into my thoughts as Ki had. *Can you feel where the power was siphoned from, my dear?* The question startled me. Did I have the power to figure that out? An assurance washed over me. I did. Closing my eyes instinctively, I focused, feeling for the energies that were responsible for pushing the King into hiding and stealing his life force. There was a slight tug to my left and my eyes popped open, searching the colors in the lights in that area, zeroing in on the wrongness I felt there. Shock shot through me as I noticed there was more than one Anguka in the room; in fact there were many. Not only were they here but so was the melody wafting gently on the breeze, so faint I had to strain to hear it. But it was there. With this many Azizafri in the room, only siphoning off a portion of their light, would make the Anguka powerful enough to infiltrate and perhaps take the core. At least it would have been if the Second Father were not awake. I felt their sense of urgency. They had to know that something had gone wrong. If they had any hope of standing against us, they'd have to strike fast. The pull was coming from the back of the room, pushing my senses outward, I focused there. The Azizafri at the rear of the ballroom were losing the most light; as the melody increased in volume, traveling forward like a wave, light was flowing out of the people present in a constant flow. Suddenly, I knew exactly how many of my kin were in that room, I'd been way off. 50, 602 Azizafri of high creative power were in the room and 10, 308 mid to low level creators were there guarding, serving, playing music, or fulfilling some other creative duty. Though, if I was sensing correctly, some of the guards attributed to the group of higher creative powers present.

I looked at my father, blown away by what I was just able to discern. He gave me a knowing look. *Yes, my child,* he said into my thoughts. *Now focus. We can see all our children, all their power levels. But only you can decipher the colors. Find the Anguka who betrays our creation before it is too late.*

I wanted to ask him why only I could see the colors, but his sense of urgency filtered into my thoughts. Thinking about how difficult it had been to fight those Anguka who'd feasted on 100's of souls I thought of fighting one who'd feasted on over 60,000. With a mental push I wrapped my light around myself, feeling Kimoni with me. I looked down. My essence was thinly layered in his. I felt his fingers twine into mine as I closed my eyes and focused my mental eye on the colors in the room, looking for that telltale hue that differentiated Anguka from Azizafri. One of them had to be the one siphoning off the light of our people with the sound waves that formed this haunting melody. After several moments, I felt frustration surge through me, along with a healthy dose of fear. The lower creative powers, all 10,308 had fallen to the ground and been covered with a glamour. They were not dead, but their light was slipping from them quickly, much faster than they'd been pulling at my father's light, and soon their physical bodies would return to stardust.

Tamping down the fear, I set my jaw, thrusting out a hand and sending my consciousness flying through the crowd searching, seeking the culprit. I started pinpointing the Anguka in the room; their lights were hidden from me, I'd only been searching for Azizafri. There were hundreds of Anguka in the room. They thought to share the power and take the core, with… a group of 300. *How poetic of them,* I thought wryly. Acting on instincts that had to be part of my former self, I sent mental messages to Aseema, Ramla, and Kimoni to go and begin picking off the Anguka I'd pinpointed.

Father assisted by surrounding each of them with a circle of his own light that shot out like a lasso and holding each Anguka I identified. His light froze them in place and Father stood next to me tall and proud not even breaking a sweat as the light from his abdomen held the 100 I'd identified so far. Aseema and Ramla immediately dispersed throughout the room, killing the Anguka where they stood. Mother threw a glamour over them so that none of the partygoers were the wiser as they moved smoothly through the crowd, slicing, and cutting down our enemies. Kimoni hesitated for several moments, reluctant to leave my side. I squeezed his hand in reassurance and he was off, grabbing his brother-in-law Rashidi and several guards to assist him. Queen Mother quickly glamoured them as well.

Nyoka sat on his borrowed throne oblivious, smiling and nodding gratefully as gifts were placed at his feet. Each gift a creation especially for their interim rulers "supposed" season of light. He looked different from the way in which he projected himself in my dream. In person he was harder. Sitting with back rigid and legs crossed in a regal manner, he stroked his beard, nodding pleasantly with each gift presented. He looked every bit the ruler, dressed in black, so deep it looked blue or purple contingent on the reflection of the swirl of color in his abdomen. I looked deeper into his light but couldn't find anything off there.

Squinting, I tried to look deeper when my father placed a hand gently on my arm. Our eyes met. *Focus my child, the song is still doing its dirty work. I have picked up all 300 of the Anguka, but the song still plays. It seems that only we are immune.* He'd emphasized we, causing my eyes to dart to my mother and unerringly to Kimoni across the room, moving deftly. But it seemed that most of the rest of the room was swaying to the strains. They didn't seem to even realize that they were doing it.

Then inspiration struck. *Father, remove the glamour from the frozen Anguka and from us. The person guiding the song must know that they are found out. It may spark a reaction which will lead me to them. The glamour on them is quite strong.*

My father gave me a proud smile, tightened his light around those he held captive, who were still attempting to fight back. I glanced out at my friends, family, and the guards as they fought underneath the glamour. They were sending the light the Anguka had ingested back into the bodies on the floor, and they were beginning to wake and assist in the fight. Father looked at Queen Mother and with an absent wave of her hand she stripped away all the glamour she'd set. Immediately the crowd stopped swaying and an audible gasp filled the room. Nyoka straightened on his throne and the melody that had gotten decidedly louder stuttered before continuing to play at half its volume. It wasn't calling to me anymore. *You defeated it already,* Father said to me proudly. My mother looked around my father to meet my eyes and gave me her own grin of pride.

The room had devolved into stunned gasps and even tears streaming down many faces as they whispered, "He lives." The Anguka around the room had been subdued for the most part, so the vast majority of the crowd was able to nod, bow or show some other form of obeisance to their King. Even Nyoka turned abruptly and fell on his face before his King Father.

There was only one who dared remain standing. He was glamoured, but I knew him for what he was, Anguka. I studied him as he glared at my Father, a gift in his hand which it seemed he'd been about to present to Nyoka. The gift was wrong. As wrong as its owner. I couldn't tell what it was, but it was not good. Moving faster than I ever had, I made my way over to the perpetrator, mildly shocked that no one in my group had stopped me. Things blurred slightly as I slid my wrists together, unsheathing my chakri and stepped in behind my old friend, holding one wrist at his throat and the other right under his ribcage, leaning him back until his head almost rested on my bosom. "You will not make it out of this room alive," I whispered in a tone that surprised even me. Half growl, half whisper, full of deadly promise. Kicking my foot up and angling it towards his hands, I knocked the gift he held to the floor, looked up at the King and immediately the package exploded into tiny pieces. I couldn't even discern what it had previously been. The melody cut off abruptly and I felt the abundance of power and light that rested on the air waiting to go...somewhere. It hadn't been going into the man in front of me, a man who had served in my father's court since I was a child, one I'd called friend. The light was being siphoned out of the room and into someone or something else.

Nyoka straightened from where he knelt before my father. "Malika, my kin, what are you doing here? Are you alright? I told you it was dangerous for you to be here." I only stared at him, feeling slightly off kilter. Something still wasn't right. Then the Second Father stole my attention as he and the queen began descending from their spot behind Nyoka's chair to the front. Slowly Nyoka turned; if I didn't know any better, I'd say fear had passed over his features, but it fled quickly and was replaced with joy. Falling at the King's feet, he began to weep.

With a hand to Nyoka's bowed head, the Second Father continued to where I stood with blades at the deathly still Anguka's throat. As the King drew nearer, he started to move, but I dug the Chakri into his ribs and felt his sharp intake of breath. "You know not what you've gotten yourself into, girl. It would have been best if you'd stayed on Earth." The King's fingers curved into a claw, and he made a slicing motion, ripping the glamour from the Anguka. The pleasant looking gentlemen in a suit fell away, revealing the Anguka with his backwards feet, hair covered body, green glow, and stench of rot. I fought not to loosen my hold on him to cover my nose. A grin slid across his face, revealing sharp, pointed teeth, as though he realized I struggled with his smell. Baring my own teeth in a grimace, I sliced ever so slightly into his ribcage, green goo began to dribble out and his eyes widened momentarily.

"Look at me, fallen son," the King commanded. The Anguka's eyes veered to the King and he sneered in disgust, "Fallen son? I am no son of yours," he spat venomously. "What then do I address you as, child," the King asked, with a tinge of sadness to his voice. The Anguka went to straighten his spine but was held fast by my blades at his throat, "A puppet who broke from his puppet master's strings. A free ROHO. I would see your power devoured by my allies. We will take Amani and there is nothing you can do. We've already done the unthinkable and infiltrated your most protected core. Proof positive that you have weakened. Now everyone knows it and you will fall." The Anguka had a gravelly voice that grated across my ears with each word. Add to that the fact that he spoke each word with venom and disdain. I searched my father's face; he only looked on with pity.

Then Kimoni was beside me; our eyes met, I nodded in assent and at the edge of his Kotel he forced the Anguka to kneel. Suddenly my Chakram was in my hand; I split it and pointed it at the kneeling form in front of me, right over his back where his heart would be, while Kimoni rested his blade on the fallen's neck. I assumed Kimoni had willed my Chakram into my hand and wondered why he hadn't done it earlier. *I still can't use much power within these walls, only small things. You did that all on your own, love.* Looking up at him with startled eyes, I inhaled sharply, but he only nodded, keeping his full attention on our captive.

Perhaps I could heal this Anguka as I had the one in the Arhdi Iliyotengwa. Forcing myself to focus on his light, I realized I was now able to see the Azizafri he'd eaten, there were hundreds. Gasping, I was astounded at the amount of life he'd been willing to take, just for power. This wasn't right. Tears sprung to my eyes, feeling the pain of these trapped spirits. Mother and Father Roho who did nothing to deserve such torment and anguish. My Father turned sad eyes on me and then shot out another lasso of light winding it around the Anguka until he hung suspended in the air. Looking around the room I noticed that only about 50 of the 300 that had been spotted in the room were alive. Focusing in, I saw piles of green dust all around us. Our little contingent of fighters had had the element of surprise. The stealthy invaders had not ever expected to be seen or challenged in this attack. Undoubtedly, they'd intended to siphon off as much power as they could. But how had they gotten in?

The remaining Anguka were pulled forward by King Father's lassos of light and hung suspended in the air before the dais. Nyoka hadn't gotten up from his position at my father's feet and was staring, not at those suspended in the air, but rather at my father with a mixture of awe and…something else I couldn't quite place. There was a nagging sensation at my consciousness, but I couldn't quite put my finger on what exactly was bothering me. Feeling the brush of Kimoni's concern against my mind, I gave him a small smile letting him know I was alright. The Azizafri congregated in the ballroom were looking around at the Anguka suspended in the air. It was like the Second Father had unerringly grabbed them from every corner of the room like a heat seeking missile and now they were all bound above us. He was eyeing each one with a mixture of sadness, concern, and resolve. Then it dawned on me. He would have to kill them. His creation would expect no less, these fallen had snuck into the safest place in the city. How?

My Father did not relish killing these fallen creatures; I saw the warring emotions on his face. Then there was that tugging sensation on the back of my mind again. I could heal them…or I could try. Kimoni grabbed my hand and squeezed it. I looked up at him to see if it was a squeeze of approval or to negate my train of thought. He gave me a sharp nod, so I let go of his hand and started walking towards the dais. Once I reached the bottom of the steps I knelt. "King Father, may I provide an alternative?" My head was down, and I felt a gust of wind that made me jump. Looking around warily, I found that the father had come to stand in front of me, leaving Queen Mother and Nyoka on the dais. He knelt in front of me and cupped my face in his hands, "Binti yangu, you do not kneel in front of me. We only bend our knees for the Creator. You are the heir of Mahali Pa Amani and first King Mother of the Azizafri." Shock raced through me, "I-I didn't know women could be King."

Whispers rose from the crowd, shocked at my words or at the fact that the King had moved so quickly to my side, while still keeping a hold on his captives. "You are not a wombed man, you are Roho; you are Mother Spirit and you will be King." Behind my father I saw my mother's eyes dancing with joy, but Nyoka was stiff and very carefully controlling his features. I gave him a tilt of my head and he only bowed slightly, fixing his face into a small encouraging smile.

Tentatively, I touched the crown atop my head; my father smiled again. "Yes daughter, it is so. You will rule." Looking at my mother something struck me as odd, perhaps I was focusing on mundane things, because I didn't want to think about having to rule the creatures standing just behind me. "Why does the Queen not wear a crown? Yet you have given me one?"

"We are not a patriarchal line. When the creator molded me, I was but spirit and light. It was my choice as I began to explore and create, to take on a form much like the angels of heaven. Azizafri inherited wings due to this. When I took my spirit and more dust from the stars to create your mother, she took on a form much different than the angels, for there are no female angels, she shaped herself, quite beautifully I might add." He tossed a warm smile over his shoulder, and my mother preened. "Spirits are neither male nor female, they just are. We chose these shapes of our own accord and can shed them at will. The rulers of the Azizafri are crowned. Queen Mother is Mother of all Azizafri, nurturer, counselor, but she is not ruler. I am the ruler and father of the people. You are my heir and you alone. But..." he said, turning his gaze toward the Queen. "Rosie doesn't particularly care for the crown, it messes her hair, otherwise...." A modest crown appeared on the Queen Mother's head. It looked like a more feminine twin to his own. Rolling her eyes, she dropped into a saucy curtsy, winked at me, and waved the crown away again, fluffing her hair as if to make sure it wasn't mussed.

Grinning at her brightly, even as my head whirled with this new information, I hoped we'd get to spend more time together. She made me want to curl up in her lap and pour out my heart.

Pulling me back into the present moment, the King said, "We will discuss more of this later binti yangu, what is this alternate solution you speak of?" I glanced at Nyoka again. For some reason, my would-be brother made me uneasy. As though reading my thoughts, he gave me a warm, reassuring smile. It didn't work. I felt neither reassured nor warmth, dude was majorly oily.

Tearing my gaze from the enigma that was Nyoka, I looked back at my father. "I'm not sure, I said slowly, but I think I can heal the fallen." The King tilted his head at me, processing my words. Then with fluid grace he rose to his feet, pulling me up with him. "Create, daughter," he said simply.

Looking up at each Anguka, suspended in the air, some of them struggling in their bonds, I assessed them. Father had the foresight to bind their mouths as well. Pulling on that part of me that could decipher the nuances of each Azizafri's light, I began delving into the light of each of the suspended invaders. I could see their green, tainted light and the lights of the many Azizafri they'd eaten, which had refused to meld with the rotten diseased Anguka. I saw how their light was abused, misshapen and distorted, going against their created purpose. The fallen had turned their backs on the mandate to create. Instead, they became destroyers. We Azizafri created to fill needs and fill our world with more beauty, more light. The Anguka were our polar opposite, destructive spirits. Their specialty was complete devastation; they were led by pride and lust. I saw all of this in their light and still I felt pity for them. They did not know or even understand the joy of creation. My eyes met the Anguka I'd been holding captive. For some reason I couldn't explain, I didn't want to say aloud that

I recognized Roderick. Kimoni said his light had been ingested by an Anguka, but no. He'd become Anguka. My sweet, gentle friend Roderick who laughed with me and played in the gardens with me, creating. The Father Spirit who was so gentle that his unity with Vivienne had been so foreign to me.

Wait, Vivienne! I looked around for her in the crowd. Without a single doubt, I knew she had to be a part of this. I looked at Kimoni, showed him my thoughts and he disappeared into the crowd to find her. Lending him some of my light, familiar to the core as being of the First Family, it would allow him to pull on his speed.

Then I looked back at Roderick. "Will you uncover his mouth, Second Father?" Though he obeyed, he gave me a look that I read clearly as, "Baba or Dad will do." Tossing him a shy smile, I turned back to my old friend, sadness filling my eyes as they met his. Though he'd once had gorgeous hazel eyes, the ingesting of spirits, the destructive power had turned them black as coal and it was unnerving.

"Ro-" I began before he cut me off, practically spitting with distaste. "Do not refer to me as that name of light. I am no longer an Azizafri slave; I am Anguka, reborn, stronger, faster, better. I am known as Haribu now, because my purpose is no longer to create, he said with a sneer, it is to destroy." His green light glowed brighter with his speech. The Azizafri whose powers he had ingested and used to destroy others mourned inside him. He excelled at stealth attacks and had approached many of them in glamour, using the song to seduce and devour them. It all played out for me in his swirl of light. Unlike the Anguka I'd healed in the desert place, he did not want to be healed, he liked what he was.

Fighting waves of sadness and acting on pure instinct, which seemed to be my norm these days, I opened my fingers directing my light towards the many Anguka in the air. Immediately, I accessed their light and knew them all by name. I even knew the names of the 1,042 Azizafri they'd killed and siphoned light from. Bands made of light lashed out from my fingertips banding around the ones that my father had bound them in. The only reason we'd been able to subdue them so easily is that they hadn't seen us coming. Well, that and father's ropes of light. Other than that, we'd have had quite a different battle on our hands. Once my bands of light were nice and tight, I clapped my hands together. Roderick, now known as Haribu, shot me a cruel look as I said in a loud voice, "Kurudi kwa nuru na kupona," Instead of repeating it as I had over my father, I layered my voice so that the words echoed around the enormous chamber, bouncing off the walls. "Kurudi kwa nuru na kupona, Kurudi kwa nuru na kupona, Kurudi kwa nuru na kupona."

With each echoing repetition the Anguka began to shake harder, their eyes wide and focused on me, as the light they ingested began to scatter. Instead of taking the stolen light back into myself, I commanded it to return to molded flesh. Still, they shot at me, lending bits of their strength. Then the room seemed to stretch with the added bodies. Except for one. One had gone to the wrong place. But my attention was divided; I couldn't track it as distantly I heard Azizafri yelling names of loved ones. Excitement filled the room as light materialized and then coalesced into the form of Azizafri Mother and Father spirits. As the echo subsided, and I felt the last of the stolen light restored, I whispered one last time, in English, "Light return and heal."

I'd been looking at the faces of the Anguka as they trembled, weakening with each light that left them, but just as the end was nearing, I looked at Roderick one last time. He wasn't looking at me, but at Vivienne, Kimoni had found her and was now holding her at the point of his Kotel. She'd shed her seductress look and was staring up at Roderick, who now called himself Haribu, with tears rolling down her cheeks. The built-up pressure between my palms was starting to become too much and losing my grip, I let go. Green dust exploded before my eyes, there were shrieks all around us and I covered my eyes quickly to guard against the cloud of destroyed Anguka falling from the sky. My father's arm went around me, thinking he was protecting me from the flying dust, I nestled into the crook of his arm. He squeezed for a minute before saying softly, "Look." So, I did. Astonished, I looked between him and the cloud of dust as it trailed overhead and out of the balcony doors behind us. Though I couldn't see it, my slowly returning memory filled in for me what was over the railing. It was a beautiful waterfall with a grotto. There were gorgeous waters I used to sneak out and swim in. They'd once been blue, but I loved pink, so my father had added swirls of pink into the falls to appease me.

Shaking myself from the memory of Aseema and I diving into the falls and swimming in the grotto, laughing and giggling until Mother demanded we return to our studies, I focused back on my father. His arm was still wrapped around me, but he'd looked back at my Mother, reaching out a hand for her. She came to his side quickly nestling into his right arm and touching a hand to my cheek lovingly. My heart soared at the joy and pride in her eyes as she looked at me. I'd never really had this. Not that I could remember, and I felt… at home. I was completely at peace with these people who were my Azizafri parents. But, I couldn't let go of the small memories of Roland and Angela. They would always be my parents as well. From being a girl with no parents, I was now blessed with two sets, even if one pair had left. I could grow to like this.

Squeezing me lightly and straightening, the King began to speak, "My children." Every head in the room shot up, even those who'd had loved one's returned and were crying and hugging, stopped to give their King Father their full attention.

"We rejoice and we mourn," the King continued, speaking slowly. "We rejoice in seeing the return of our loved ones. Many of my children have returned today. He glanced down at me and smiled. Including my only begotten daughter. Though Nyoka has ruled admirably in my absence…" He paused to incline his head towards Nyoka. He was standing slightly behind us, looking shell shocked.

When I turned my eyes back to the crowded room, I began searching for Kimoni. My eyes met Lea and then her husband Rashidi. He bowed dramatically before grinning at me roguishly, amusement twinkling in his eyes. While Lea was staid and true, Rashidi was laid back and playful. After giving him a small smile I turned my eyes back to Lea and mouthed Kimoni's name, hoping she could read lips. With a small shake of her head, she glanced around, indicating she didn't know where he was.

Last I'd checked he had Vivienne at the end of his blade, but she was gone and so was he. My heart dropped. Attempting to breathe normally, I called to him through our telepathic connection.

Ki?

Kimoni?

Moto wangu! Where are you?

There was no answer and I started to pray to the Creator. *Please, please, please, please let him be alright.* Lea was watching me; I shook my head, to let her know I hadn't been able to connect to Ki's thoughts. Her head whipped to Rashidi, and I knew they were speaking telepathically. After a few moments, he swept another bow in my direction before jetting off at human speed to find Ki. This caught the attention of Lea's parents who came over, the three of them whispering furiously.

"We have a traitor in our midst," the King continued. "Someone has allowed the Anguka into our innermost place of peace. They have plotted against my life and that of the Queen Mother. But," he paused, looking around the room at his numerous children. "My daughter, future King Mother of Mahali Pa Amani, has rescued us as it was…" Then his words became static in my ears. Why did this keep happening? Why wouldn't the Yamanu just go away? Where was Ki?

I am here my love, he said softly, and another frisson of panic went through me. His voice was entirely too weak, he sounded hurt. *Do not worry. I am tired. Vivienne escaped and left me a small gift.*

I couldn't see him; I didn't know where he was, but I knew he was hurt and trying to downplay it. Pain colored his thoughts, and I could feel him trying to block me from it. Glancing at my parents as they focused on the concerned room full of Azizafri and then Lea as she spoke worriedly with her mother. I was guessing her father had joined Rashidi in the search for Kimoni. My resolve strengthened; I knew what I had to do. What only I could do. As if sensing my gaze, Lea looked up. Sending my thoughts to her, I said, *I'll bring him back.* She stepped forward as though to protest, but I'd already made up my mind and willed myself to Ki's side. Belatedly I thought it probably wasn't a good look to leave while the King was speaking, or to leave without saying anything for that matter…I'd explain later, he'd understand.

Blinking my eyes rapidly, I tried to adjust to the change in lighting. From the brightness of the ball room to this dim grotto. But it was familiar to me, we were right below the balcony where my father had allowed the Anguka dust to flow. So, I walked through the dim cavern, using my memory as my guide, footing sure from traversing it throughout most of my childhood and until I'd left for Earth. It was as though Kimoni's light was tugging at mine, leading me directly to him, leading me to its other half. That thought startled me, causing me to pause. Whoever I was in this former life, he was the center of it somehow. Forcing my brain out of its frozen state, so that my feet would begin moving again, I continued through the grotto, stopping again only to remove my heels. I knew that nothing hazardous would injure my sensitive soles. The feel of the smooth rock beneath my feet felt like coming home. A home that wasn't complete without moto wangu. Picking up my skirts and moving swiftly through the twists and turns, I finally found him, wondering absently why I'd not been able to will myself closer to him. He lay on the smooth stone, curled in upon himself. Without thinking I ran towards him, his eyes cracked open at the sound of my light footsteps. *Mali? No! Don't!* He whispered urgently into my mind, but I ignored him; I had dropped to my knees, searching for his injuries so I could heal him, when everything went dark.

CHAPTER 13

Playing kickball with Mali's head and other vital
body parts.

Something wet had slid into my eyes, causing my lashes to
stick together in the most annoying manner. At first, I didn't
feel the pain, as I was so distracted trying to pry my sticky lids
apart. But once I won that battle, I groaned in agony. I'd bumped
my head before, but this was a whole different level. What had
I been hit with? It felt like she'd cracked my skull. I wanted to
grasp both hands to my head to prevent my brain from sliding
out of the crevice in my cranium, but they were tied tight behind
me. Looking down, I realized that my legs were equally bound
against the grotto floor. My no doubt limp body had been propped
up against one of the stone walls. Gasping in pain with every
tiny movement, I attempted to get my bearings together. If only
the room would stop spinning quite so quickly, I could focus, I

could plan. Gingerly, I tried to move my bound legs, but it jolted my upper half and the shock of pain sent me reeling. Then I was retching, giving back what little I'd eaten to the stone floor beside me. I felt incredibly dizzy as consciousness tried to leave me again. Grasping for it with all my might, I searched through the haze for any sign of Kimoni.

I'm here. I heard him weakly through our connection. I slumped in relief even as my eyes darted around the dimness trying to find his face. What I'd give to see his face one last time.

You are NOT going to die. No thoughts of "one last time." He chastised me, and I would have smiled at that stern tone echoing through my mind, but I was certain that any movement of my face would just launch me into a greater level of pain than I was currently experiencing.

You, he had said. *You are not going to die.* What about him? I'd tried my best to direct that last thought at him, but my head was aching so forcefully that I didn't know if I'd aimed my thoughts at him correctly or if he was just ignoring me.

You are all that matters mpenzi wangu. You will survive this.

This time I ignored him. We were both going to get out of this. I would not lose him, I refused to lose him. Trying to focus, I glanced around the dim grotto again. We'd been taken deeper into the depths of the place. I was surprised that not only was Vivienne able to get the drop on me, but that she'd been able to move Kimoni a second time. She had to have had help. If I could just see straight, I could work us a way out of this thing. The grinding of Kimoni's teeth was audible, though I still couldn't see him from where I was seated against the wall.

I will distract her so that you can escape. I will be fine. She will not kill me. It would be an error on her part, to increase your power in such a way. You must be ready to flee from here when the time is right. Focus upon the Second Father so that you may get to him and bring back help.

He was right, I thought grumpily. Just as I'd willed myself here, I could will myself to my Father. But...I couldn't bring myself to leave Ki here. The thought of abandoning him made me sick to my stomach. He growled in frustration and under different circumstances I may have laughed, but my head was killing me, and we were both trussed up like pigs. The waves of frustration coming off him and into our connection were tinted with love as well as concern. There may have also been a bit of disbelief. Something to explore later. Focusing with a great deal of effort, I called out telepathically for my father. Immediately, it seemed as though there were a wall around my thoughts. *Interesting,* I thought. Focusing again I tried to teleport to Ki's side. Just like that, I was lying next to him where he slumped on the floor bleeding. I panicked.

"Ki! Ki? Where are you bleeding from? What did she do to you?" I spoke urgently in a whisper that was more focused on not causing my cranium any additional pain than alerting our kidnappers. Ki only stared at me in shock. "Mali...how?" I looked at him in confusion when his thoughts filled it in for me. He'd felt the block when I'd tried to reach out to my father, but for some reason, when I thought of being by his side, as though yanked by an invisible thread, I was there in an instant.

His face was contorting into an unreadable expression. I tried to ascertain his thoughts, but they were moving too quickly to follow. Instead of trying to figure out the man's mind, I focused all my energy on his wounds. He was tied in much the same way I was, but there was a knife in his abdomen, still wedged in. No wonder he'd sounded so breathless and weak. The knife was pulling Ki's light into itself. Startled, I looked up into his eyes. "How?" Frustration contorted his features again.

"You like?" a silky voice filtered through the darkness and into our hearing. Suddenly the grotto was filled with light. We were on the east side, where it was dry and smooth, casting a soft blue glow. This place was beautiful. As little girls, Aseema and I used to go to the small water filled area and swim in our underwear, giggling and feeling scandalous. How dare Vivienne taint this place. I narrowed my eyes at her. She glowed brilliantly in the dim cavern, now her true color shone a sickly green. But she wasn't full Anguka yet, meaning she hadn't ingested much, if any light. Perhaps she was just allied with them. I wondered how she'd hid it from me before.

"You aren't the only one skilled at glamour, princess," she sneered. At some point she'd changed into a halter top and matching pants that hugged her curves. She'd left her torso bare, and her hair hung around her shoulders in an effortless, tousled look. Right now, Vivienne was in her zone, and she was ready to milk it. I began thinking rapidly, willing my brain to be healed. Then it clicked, Vivienne's vice was a love of self. I had to get her talking about her favorite subject. I felt Kimoni affirm my thoughts through our connection and pushed for an outraged tone. It wasn't too hard. "What have you done to him Vivienne? He's hurt!" Her features slid into a slow, feline grin.

"An eye for an eye, a tooth for a tooth…is that not what the Creator says?"

"I don't understand Vivienne. I did not kill Roderick."

"Didn't you," she sneered, moving so quickly she was a blur one minute and right in my face the next. Her eyes were going the same black as her husbands. But she was wrong. He was not dead. Did she not know? Unease flooded my senses. Roderick was not dead. His light had not turned into dust like his comrades. Narrowing my eyes, I tried to stare into Vivienne's light, to find it. They were just as connected as Ki and me. He had to be there. But how could she not know? Not feel him?

"I will take Kimoni from you. I will end his corporeal body, devour his light, keeping him as my prisoner, fueling my power. You will be left alive and alone to mourn him. You will have no one, for the false Father will die as well." Her words fell short of the mark. I knew without a shadow of a doubt she'd wanted me to feel the fear she'd felt watching her husband return to dust. Somehow all I felt was pity. It must have shown in my eyes. Big mistake, out of nowhere I was struck in the chest with a blow that had me gasping desperately for air. My pain-addled brain took a moment to wonder why? Why the freaking chest? Of all places to kick a person. That shocked thought was overridden by loss of oxygen and the feeling that she'd shattered my breastbone. Distantly, I heard Ki talking to her soothingly, the strain evident in his voice. I couldn't decipher the words, but I wondered at him having the breath to speak around the knife lodged in his torso, still siphoning off his light.

As I curled in upon myself, without air enough to even groan, she reared back and kicked me in the head, rocking me back and away from Kimoni again. The world began to fade around the edges. She was knocking loose all my years of education. I still hadn't even paid off those degrees and she was stomping all that knowledge into oblivion.

This losing consciousness thing was for the birds. I was over it and I planned to tell Vivienne as soon as I woke up. But I was out in the stars again, surrounded by light and gorgeous sky. So caught up in the beauty, I couldn't stop twirling in a slow circle, taking in everything around me. I was in awe at the vastness of the heavens. Was I...dead? It was beautiful enough to be some type of afterlife. The sky was every shade of blue imaginable moving from deepest blue back to the lightest blue of a bright sunlit day. All around me lights twinkled merrily in an endless array of colors that spun slowly, seemingly in their own individual space. Fascinating. I twirled with them, slowly, feeling peace invade my senses and push out the pain that had previously consumed me.

I can't get to you. You are blocked from me. It must be you who overcomes this.

Confused beyond belief, I stopped mid-twirl searching for where this voice came from. I knew whose voice it was, but I couldn't find where it was coming from. My eyes searched the vast sky, trying to find the owner of said voice, but to no avail.

You cannot see me, but I am always with you. Just as when you were bound to Earth.

How could he have watched me on Earth? What was he talking about? *Help us. Moto wangu is gravely injured.* It came out in a rush as I gave the thoughts an extra mental boost, hoping they'd reach their intended hearer. I hoped to give a full picture of how much we needed help.

And you, my dear? Are you injured?

Frustrated, I didn't know how to respond, though I couldn't feel my body now, should I survive this night I would be broken and in pain.

A disapproving sigh seemed to bounce around my brain in a soft echo of sound. *You love him, he loves you. The Yamanu should be broken by now. I grow weary of this lack of understanding of your POWER.* His words weren't directed towards me; it was as though he were thinking aloud, and I got the distinct impression that were his body visible to me, he'd be pacing in frustration. *You acted so impulsively; we did not have time to follow you. But you are so well hidden, you must still be in the core.* I opened my mouth to tell him where I was but suddenly it was all a haze. Just a few minutes ago I remembered! How could I forget where I was that quickly? *You will have to come to us,* he said matter of factly.

This wasn't quite the response I was hoping for. What did Yamanu have to do with my current situation? Yes, I had some power, but how could being able to heal Anguka help me now? Why couldn't I remember where I was? Love…No I didn't love Ki; I didn't know him well enough to love him. I mean given time I could, he was a great guy, and we apparently had a long history, but…Wait? Heal?

Yessssss! A triumphant echo of excitement filled me. Though I could not see him, I knew he was smiling. *Wake, my daughter, heal. Bring us the one who captured you and we will deal with them directly.*

My eyes snapped open, and I jolted with a start, groaning with the impact of the pain radiating throughout my body. Vivienne was still standing there, taunting Kimoni as she wiped specks of my blood from her boot. She wasn't looking at me, so I acted quickly, priorities first.

I needed to be healed and my bonds needed to be loosed. Focusing, I reminded myself, I am of the Creator, a daughter of the Azizafri. We see a need and we meet it. So, I concentrated on my head mending together, then my chest and finally my ribs. My body began mending itself and I willed it to work quickly. Once that was done, I concentrated on my bound wrists and legs. She'd used spider silk and threaded her own light into it to hold us fast. If it wouldn't have alerted her to my growing strength, I would have laughed. Instead, I worked hard to suppress the smile that was tugging at my lips. No wonder the bonds were so strong. The thing is, on her best day Vivienne had nothing on me. Now that I realized it and I was healed that is. Pushing a small amount of my light from my fingertips, I touched the bonds and they fell away without another thought. Ki must have felt it because his thoughts flooded mine with warmth. Looking at his face, I couldn't see anything of that, he was laying on the floor, keeping Vivienne talking about how she was such a poor mistreated wretch. Cry me a river! Healed and finally free, I lay still, looking at Vivienne through slitted eyes, before focusing on

Kimoni. Still laying in a position of repose, as though the blow had knocked me completely unconscious, I sent strands of my light into Kimoni. The knife in his stomach was strong. It was sucking at his light; he was nearly depleted.

Glamour the knife, remove it, and then heal him.

My brows scrunched up in confusion at my Father's words. Glamour the knife? I didn't know how. A soft chuckle filled my mind. *You said it yourself, we see a need and we meet it. Meet the need, binti yangu.* He made it all sound so simple; just do it. I was improvising here. None of this was normal or commonplace to me. I'd only recently realized I had these powers.

Doubt is of the enemy. Doubt is not of the Creator. You must cast it off. Have faith in that which courses through your blood, your DNA, and your light. You are a celestial being, not to be trifled with. You can do all things through the Creator on the inside of you.

Immediately my light responded to the Second Fathers words of strength and encouragement. I had to focus on keeping it hidden, lest its sudden brightness alert Vivienne to the fact I was quietly plotting against her. Blinking tears back from my eyes, touched by how much faith the Second Father had in me, I mentally shrugged off those feelings of doubt and incompetence. I could do this because I had to do this. There was no other choice. They couldn't get to me. I had to save Kimoni, I had to save myself.

Assessing the dagger, zeroing in on it with laser focus, allowing my Azizafri senses to enhance my sight in the dimness of the grotto, I studied the details of the blade. Then I placed an identical version of it on top, lining it up perfectly. "Move," I whispered, or so I thought. But Vivienne's head jerked my way as though she'd heard me. Immediately Ki groaned loudly, trying to curl further around the blade with his arms still bound behind his back. Her head moved slowly back to him. She couldn't see much in the dim light; a wicked smile curled her lips at his pain.

"You will die, and your light will not rejoin with your love. Just as I lost mine…she will lose you." The sadness in her voice pulled at me, even as she threatened to take Ki from me. Vivienne was in a great deal of pain. I wished there was something I could do for her. But first. With a concerted effort, I slowly began to inch the dagger out of Kimoni's stomach, all while focusing not to disturb the glamour. He was already curled in on himself in pain, so the sharp intake of breath and arching of his back didn't surprise his bitter captor. My eyes watered as I continued to inch the knife out. It was deep and the way his lips pressed together in agony, trying not to cry out was breaking my heart. *Almost there, my love.* His back was rigid, and his eyes clenched shut as I finally got the dagger out. It was a curved blade, at least five inches in length and it glowed faintly with a yellowish light.

To me, I willed it and it raced across the room and into my upraised hand. Bouncing up off the ground in a limber movement that belied what I'd just endured, I sank into a crouch, ready. Vivienne's head whipped around, eyes widened in a mixture of shock and confusion before her face hardened into an unforgiving mask of hatred. With a growl, she began moving toward me with unbelievable speed. Whispering to the knife softly, "Kurudi kwa guru na kupona, light return and heal."

I had just a second or two to see light begin to fly out of it and back into Kimoni where he lay on the floor. Then Vivienne was up close. She apparently liked to fight with her feet, probably too afraid to break a nail. As soon as she neared me, she snapped out a front kick with perfect precision, aiming for my chin. I spun away quickly, sliding my wrists together to unsheathe my Chakri as I did, then ducking to avoid the side kick she flung out directly after. For several minutes, I ducked and dodged her fierce kicks in razor sharp stiletto boots no less, before realizing I could end this. A left hook was coming my way, I guess she'd realized the kicks weren't working, when I flitted behind her and jabbed the blade into her right side. Immediately her body stiffened, and I laced my left arm around her throat, holding the Chakri there. Unable to force back the memory of doing the same to her husband in the ballroom just a handful of hours? Minutes ago?

"Perhaps you could escape the blade in your side, but my Chakri will slit your throat if you dare move another step," I warned in a low growl. Before I could blink, her hands went up in surrender. I wondered why Kimoni hadn't joined us yet, when he appeared in front of me with an Anguka tossed over his shoulder. "You picking up strays?" I asked him with a quirked brow. Tossing me a huge grin that made me glow with happiness, Ki said, "Nah, I just wanted to grab him before he escaped the party. Seems he's been helping our girl Viv here. I think he was arranging transport out back when I made him go night-night." Glancing down at the prone figure over Ki's shoulder, I wondered how he was able to balance the large creature. He had to be near Ki's size. Reading my face, his smile brightened. "He is not light, Mali. Will you do the honors and lead the way out? You know this place much better than I, yes?"

I really wanted to just stand there and soak in that smile of his, but I had to keep an eye on the prisoner in my arms and the one over his shoulder. Thinking for a moment, I finally said, "One second." Then, with a twist of the knife, I had plunged into Vivienne's side, I whispered, "Ondoka." I braced myself as she went limp in my arms, and then I eased her to the ground. "Ondoka? Leave? What did you just do to her mwanamke wangu?"

"I save your life and I'm back to 'my lady' again huh?"

Stepping forward as though there weren't an unconscious being hanging over his shoulder, Ki gently laid his hand on my cheek, meeting my eyes fully. "You are many things to me Malika. My eyes drifted closed at the sound of my name on his lips. But you will always be my lady first." I cocked my head, leaning into his hand, while looking at him quizzically. There was some hidden meaning to what he'd just said, but I didn't have a clue what that could be. Before I could ask, he said, "We must go." I looked down at Vivienne, knowing I couldn't carry her and wondering what to do. "Leave her, we will send someone back." I nodded, still hesitating. Should I take the knife with me? It was too powerful to leave here unattended, but if I took it out, she could very well die. I'd taken all of her light, her life force out of her and put it into the knife. The link of the dagger with her body was possibly the only thing keeping her from permanently leaving this realm.

Daughter, the words whispered across my mind.

Yes Father, I responded and was rewarded with a loving glow from his thoughts to mine.

Concentrate on the dagger. Zoning in on the knife, I followed his directive. *Now, see it hidden beneath her skin, a part of her.*

It will be hidden in her flesh, unable to be extracted until you send someone for her. I know what you know, but still cannot ascertain your location. The glamour is strong wherever you are. This will be a security measure if someone happens upon her before you return. After following my father's instructions, my eyes went to Ki; he was watching me patiently, with the mystery Anguka still draped over his broad shoulders.

"Okay, we'll send someone back for her. The dagger is hidden." Then I took Kimoni by his free hand and began to flit. We made it to the mouth of the grotto in minutes, though without our ability to flit, it would have taken at least an hour, we were so deep into the cavern. How had Vivienne and her companion done this all alone? She couldn't flit inside the core. I could only because of the Second Father's light in me. Once we were outside the cave, I could feel my ability to teleport return, so I focused on my father and went directly to him.

CHAPTER 14

It was the butler in the pantry with the candelabra!
– A game of Clue

As soon as Ki and I appeared by my father's side, I was pulled into my mother's arms. Relief and left-over worry rolled off her in staggering waves, the Second Father looked on with affection as she covered my face with kisses. The guards quickly came in to assist Kimoni with the prisoner, binding him and taking him into custody. He told them where to find Vivienne, with a sharp reminder to bring her to us immediately. I knew he was concerned about extracting the dagger as soon as possible. He would have taken her as well if he could, but I knew his thoughts. Worried that the Anguka he'd carried in was one of the masterminds of this infiltration he couldn't leave him. Both of us knew that Vivienne wouldn't have constructed this plan on her own. My assumption was that she'd joined the fray after her husband was harmed. But at this juncture, finding out the origin of the melody was most important, and Vivienne didn't know its author.

The King wrapped my mother and I in his embrace. It was quite some time before I realized that we'd popped into the study and not the ballroom. They told me that the party ended immediately after my disappearing act. According to Nyoka the celebration had all been a ruse to try to root out whoever was attacking the King. He'd covered up the fact that it wasn't yet his season of light with the simple explanation that the people were down due to the King's absence and needed a "pick me up." It all still sounded odd to me, and I chewed it over as I took turns hugging everyone, Aseema was there, no longer needing to hide away. Nyoka pulled me into an awkward hug of his own after I was filled in on his sketchy reasoning. Then Auntie Rami, walked over hesitantly, looking me over, her brow furrowed in concern. I rushed into her arms. She made a soft sigh of surprise before returning my embrace, holding me just as fiercely as my mother had. We'd still have to talk through her mentioning to Ki that he may have to "kill me" later, but for now I was just glad to be alive and have my family all here with me.

Absently, I noticed that Ki's parents, sister, and brother-in-law had entered the room. They were much more subdued than my group, touching foreheads in the Azizafri way and talking quietly. After my aunt released me, Lea rushed over and squeezed me tight, thanking me for saving her Kaba's life. "Why thank her?" Rashidi asked teasingly, "We were almost rid of your perfect little brother before she stepped in." Lea gave him a scathing look and Rashidi only grinned at her before bowing over my hand formally. "Welcome back mwanamke wangu, looks like Earth was good to you, pinching my arm lightly he said, looks like the food was good." Lightly slapping his hand away, I smiled, I liked him already, he was a character. "Afraid I can beat you in the sparring circle now Kaba? Keep up that incendiary speech and I'll show you how these added pounds increase my combat skill, not diminish it." Rashidi's face lit up with mirth, while Lea and Kimoni's jaws hit the floor in unison.

I heard my father groan, "That you remember, but the important things," he threw up his hands, "Bless the Creator for the day the Yamanu fades completely." Kimoni and Lea looked disappointed at those words; I suppose my banter with Rashidi had made them believe my memory was more intact than it was. "Bring it on little princess," Rashidi threw in mockingly before his Mother-in-law gently moved him out of the way to kiss me lightly on each cheek. A petite woman, her head hit just below my chin, so I had to lean down to receive her kisses. Tiny braids were pinned up at the top of her head in a complicated knot. Her dress accented curves that one didn't quite associate with a "Mother," not on Earth anyway, but Ki's Mother was stunning. She smiled up at me. "It is good to see you again, my dear. I know that no heart rejoices like that of your Mama and Baba at your return, but I find myself doubly glad to find you here. You are already so loved by us, but you have also rescued my son. Though I know his life means much to you as well, I would be a thoughtless Mother if I did not thank you for seeing his safe return. We are truly grateful." Humbled, I only nodded and returned her second embrace. Then her husband stepped forward, and he was the spitting image of Kimoni, or vice versa I should say. As some of our people are prone to do, he'd allowed gray to pepper his beard and hair, signaling his longer existence in Amani. Though nothing else denoted age about his person, he was fit and toned, tall and handsome like his son. When his eyes met mine, I saw age, intellect, and joy twinkling in their depths. Kissing me on each cheek as his wife had done, he simply said, "Thank you mwanamke wangu. Welcome home."

Once all the hugs and greetings were done, we took seats around the room. I ended up right in front of the fireplace on a beautiful, lush Chesterfield sofa in a lovely royal blue, seated between my parents. As if in a practiced motion, my father grabbed my right hand, and my mother took my left. The love I felt ebbing from these two people was so overwhelming that I felt near tears. My Father looked down at me, as though feeling my struggle to hold back the flood of emotion. He smiled kindly at me, cupped my cheek with his free hand and kissed me gently on the top of my head. Then he rested his forehead against mine for a few moments, before speaking quietly into my thoughts.

We will have time to catch up, my daughter. But do not doubt the joy we feel at having you back. Though it has not been under the circumstances we thought, my heart is now at ease with you home in Amani.

The love and acceptance brimming from his thoughts sent me over the edge; tears flowed freely down my cheeks, and I rested my head against his shoulder with a shuddering sigh. He stroked my hair and it brought me such comfort. Then I felt my mother lean into my shoulder gently and my heart swelled.

Though the couch was big enough to fit at least six people, it seemed as though everyone in the room was giving us space to reunite as Mother, Father and Daughter. Kimoni's parents and Lea took a loveseat to our left, all fitting comfortably, with Rashidi taking up a position behind them, Auntie Ramla took a wing back chair to the left and Kimoni sat in one next to her. Aseema took up a guard position, standing directly behind my parents and I, while Nyoka had chosen to stand next to the fireplace, resting an arm on the mantle with glass in hand. It struck me as odd with the assortment of places to sit, that the three of them chose to stand.

After a moment though I realized that it was in Aseema and Rashidi's nature to guard the royal family. They would not be comfortable sitting with the danger that was just averted. Nyoka, on the other hand, likes to pretend he runs things. I smirked at that. Nyoka stood with an air of importance surveying the room. After being urged by our families, we rushed into the story of how we came to be in Vivienne's grasp. Kimoni started and his part was most interesting to me because I had no idea how she'd captured him. "I captured Vivienne attempting to flee the ballroom and brought her back. She came undone, unglued when Roderick was destroyed. She fell to her knees in agony as though her own light was being ripped from her and I couldn't help but think…." I knew without opening my mind to him that he was thinking of what it would do to him if it had been me.

A cold shudder went through my body, and my mother leaned up from where her head rested on my shoulder to wrap an arm around me, pulling me into her warmth. My Father went a step further, causing a soft pink sherpa blanket to appear in his hands and tucking it around me absently. My cheeks warmed. Never had I ever been so catered to; it was a foreign feeling for me. Was this what it was like before? In this life that I still could not completely recall? But then my attention was riveted again as Kimoni continued, eyes on me.

"Her pain was so real to me… I tried to console her. Vivienne looked up at me with tear filled eyes and asked if I would take her outside for air." Ki shook his head in shame, obviously thinking of how he'd so easily fallen for her duplicitous ploy. With a sigh he continued, "Once we were outside of the palace, she jammed that dagger into my abdomen. It began siphoning off my light, sucking it into the blade and draining me immediately. I was paralyzed with the pain of my very energy, my life force being sucked out of me. The hatred in her eyes was unreal. Still, I could have escaped her, but her friend, the one I carried in, blindsided me with a boot to the head. Next thing I knew, I was waking up bound completely in the grotto." Shaking his head in disbelief, he continued, "When I woke, I-I felt Malika's concern. I tried to assure her I was fine…King Father I would not have put her in danger. He looked at the King earnestly. I would not have asked her to come to me, to risk herself. But she did not believe my claims; she came anyway."

Kimoni tore his pleading gaze from the King, to look at me with a mixture of disapproval, admiration, and love. Suddenly, I wanted with all that was in me, to earn that love, to be worthy of it for who I was now. *Not the Malika he remembered.* I must have projected that thought, because his head cocked, and his brow furrowed in concerned confusion. With a subtle shake of my head, I stopped him from saying anything either through our mental communication or aloud. We didn't have time to address my hang-ups. His eyes hardened, and I heard him whisper into my thoughts, *later*. I gave the slightest of nods. "Kimoni," my father said, startling me. "You could not have stopped Malika. She has not changed as much as you think, my son. Though her time on Earth has wrought some alterations, it will never be in her nature to leave those whom she loves in need." He looked as if he wanted to say more, but he shared a look with my mother, they both nodded and then the Queen spoke. "We do not hold you responsible for Mali rushing into danger. We would be more surprised had she not gone to save you. Do not continue to carry this guilt dearest. You are both safe, by the grace of the Creator and that is all that matters."

Kimoni held himself stiffly, but gave a nod of acceptance, though I know he was still beating himself up about it. It was hard not to disentangle myself from the loving cocoon of my parents and go to him. "I make my own decisions; it wasn't even an option to leave you there. Admittedly, I could have brought back up," I acquiesced quietly, trying my best to ignore the nods and murmurs of agreement. Aseema squeezed my shoulder briefly, hard enough for it to be a reproof, but gentle enough for me to know she was relieved I was okay. With a deep breath, I launched into my portion of the story. My words did what I'd hoped, they softened Kimoni's face into a wry smile. I was strangely aware of Nyoka's smooth, yet subtle movements by the fireplace. It struck me that he was very carefully controlled in his every action.

When I finished my portion of the story, my Father sat forward, rubbing his hand across his beard, deep in thought. Mother's arms were still around me and I was suddenly feeling the drain of the adrenaline rush I'd experienced. Resting my head on her shoulder this time, I watched as my father mulled things over. With his piercing eyes, he finally looked at me. "What did the dagger look like, my love?"

Leaning up from my mother's embrace to think it through clearly, I described the blade. "I don't remember much but it had a pearlescent hilt that was about four inches long, enough for a good grip. There was a pommel on it that swirled and moved with iridescent colors. The blade was near translucent and curved to…rip out innards, or in this case…light and was about five inches in length." I guess I remembered more than I'd thought. My eyes met Ki's again, his blazed into mine and I held his gaze several moments before Father spoke again. Absently I realized Ki's eyes weren't the only ones on me. Nyoka had been giving me an unnerving amount of attention. I was trying my best to ignore it. Something about my kin caused me a great deal of unease.

"It is a celestial blade, which explains much about how I was blocked from you binti yangu." All eyes in the room shifted to the King in shock. I wondered if I was the only one confused. "What does that mean?" It had been surprisingly quiet, until this point; no one had really spoken aside from us. But it was Auntie Ramla that finally answered. "Celestial blades are used by the angels of heaven. They were created to battle against the fallen angels led by the Destroyer, Samael. These blades can completely destroy a celestial being, but because we are the first creation, of the Second Father, the blade slowly weakens us, siphoning off our light, clouding our gifting. The blade can store our light, making it a more powerful weapon to utilize against those such as us or the light can be absorbed by another being. Filled with Kimoni's light it could severely deplete an Azizafri and kill an Anguka almost instantly. It was empty, otherwise Ki would be dead."

The callousness with which she said it, had me bristling with indignation. How could she so casually speak of Ki's death? "My dear sister, the Queen said rushing in and giving her sister a warning look, does not mean to be so cavalier about it. Simply put, she is saying the level of the blade's power is based on the light it siphons. Had she stabbed you my dear, the blade would be capable of destroying countless Azizafri in a heartbeat." My jaw almost hit the floor with this revelation. How? Why? My brain exploded with questions I couldn't even formulate at the moment. Before I could get around to coherent thought, there was a brisk knock at the door.

"Enter," Nyoka called out in a commanding voice. Ramla gave him a sharp look and he began apologizing quickly. "Apologies King Father, Queen Mother, Sister Heir…I forget myself." He accompanied his apologies with a bow brimming with sincerity. I wasn't convinced. I looked up at Aseema and she was giving me a look that said she was thinking the same. Before I could get to the "Sister Heir" part, three of the Core security guards including our head of security General Tau walked in. I felt Aseema stiffen behind me and was about to ask what was up, when in an act that startled everyone in the room, the general fell at the King's feet and his two companions joined him on the floor. "What is it, my son?" the King asked gently, resting a hand on Tau's shoulder. "The woman is gone, my father," he said in a rush. The whole room went still. For some reason I found myself looking at Nyoka. There was an odd gleam in his eyes.

"If I may," Nyoka interjected, waiting for the King to incline his head before continuing, "we need to put the entire core on lockdown. This is a dangerous woman with a dangerous weapon that has gone missing. I can personally go down with a team to check for it and her. But we need all our best detail here in the core, protecting you Father, Mother and the Lady Heir." Again, the King gave a nod of his head, regal, yet apparent that he wasn't fully focused on Nyoka. The eager would-be prince I suppose, ran with it, walking toward the door to give orders. The General gave my father a look of question, as if affirming that this is what he wanted. Slowly, the King nodded, and General Tau stood. Without thinking I jumped up, "I'd like to join the search detail for Vivienne."

The resounding "no" that came from every voice in the room was deafening in its intensity. I looked around, shocked. My own desire to find Vivienne and the dagger was surprising to me, but their reaction was even more so. Glancing around me in confusion, I watched as Ki made his way over to me quickly kneeling in front of me. Taking my hand he said gently, "Please allow me to go in your stead, mwanamke wangu."

"No," I said fiercely, gripping his hand. Out of the corner of my eye, I saw his mother and sister slump in relief. They'd all been rather quiet throughout all of this. A bit softer, though I knew everyone could still hear me, I added, "I just got you back." The blush that flushed my cheeks couldn't be helped, but I gave him a stern look. No way was he going back out there. Nyoka was at the door with the guards, giving both of us a hard look that I couldn't quite understand. Kimoni only continued to kneel in front of me, holding my hand, warring emotions of pleasure at my wanting him to stay and displeasure at not being able to make up for his error rolling off him. Aseema touched my shoulder again, I turned slightly to look at her, keeping Kimoni's hand in mine, lest he rush out the door. She leaned in touching her forehead to my temple.

My sister, she whispered into my thoughts. *My sister I know why you want to go. But I also know it is much safer for you to stay. My cousin needs to be here with you so he can regroup from this ordeal. The two of you are too connected to be separated at this time. I will go and fulfill my duty to you. Quietly, I will spy and bring you back information. Trust me in this as you have entrusted me with your life.*

There was some other unspoken reason that was pushing her to go on this hunt for Vivienne. I glanced over at General Tau, his face was set in grim determination, his eyes fierce and focused. Then I looked back at Aseema, my sister and closest playmate growing up had been bred to be my protection detail. It did nothing to diminish our sisterhood or friendship. I trusted her implicitly. She would carry out what I needed, and she understood my selfish need to keep Ki near. But perhaps she wanted to keep someone near as well, a certain Azizafri whom she had a lot in common with.

Be safe. If you were hurt... Leaning back and meeting my eyes, she gave me a huge grin that said it all. She was the most elite of warriors. So much so that she was my chief security, aside from Ramla, while I was on Earth all these years. Yes, she would be fine, she'd come back in one piece. With a jolt, I realized joining with Ki allowed me to speak with Aseema telepathically. Something to mull over later.

Kimoni would take this to mean I did not have faith in his abilities. He was already beating himself up about falling for Vivienne's tricks. I'd talk with him later; time was of the essence. Squeezing my shoulders gently, Aseema gave me a kiss on the cheek and walked to meet the guards and Nyoka at the door. General Tau looked at Aseema and nodded in approval, but Nyoka stiffened imperceptibly. Aseema ignored it, fighting not to flush under the General's approval, but I saw it. We'd have to talk about that little connection later. Then Nyoka's face hardened when Rashidi walked quietly over. Lea held still in her chair, so I assume they'd been quietly discussing it while we were all distracted. Smiling and bowing toward the couch, where I sat with my parents, Rashidi said lightly, "It's been some time since I've had any excitement. I think I'll go and keep Nyoka and Aseema safe." He tossed Nyoka a self-assured smile as with each step towards the door, his ball clothes were replaced with battle leathers, until he reached the door fully clothed in battle gear.

With a gracious smile, my odd brother bowed. "Mwanamke wangu, there is no need to send your personal guard or…the Counselor with us. We will fare well enough on our own. The Kingdom was well taken care of in your absence." I paused, picking up the underlying nuances in his statement. He was offended. The King stood up, walking towards the group at the door. I sat still, feeling apprehensive for reasons I couldn't explain. Ki, finally rising from the floor, kept my hand in his, squeezing it reassuringly.

"You performed admirably and served your kingdom well, my son. My heir is only acting as a true ruler would, moving to put her own life at risk in order to protect her creation. You should not take offense to this instinct. I would not go against her, were it not for her need to rest after the energy she expended in the ballroom and then to save her betrothed. You will take Lady Protector, Aseema, and Lord Counselor, Rashidi on Malika and Kimoni's behalf. Report back when your mission is complete. Take the utmost care my son, I would not want to lose you." Placing a hand on Nyoka's shoulder, the King rested his head against his, before leaning back and giving him a nod of assent, releasing them to complete their mission.

"Apologies King Father," he said bowing. "Queen Mother, Sister Heir, I will be on my way." Without a backwards look, he led the way out. Aseema and Rashidi trailed behind, she blew me a kiss, and he winked at me before putting a hand over his heart, bowing in his wife's direction, and sauntering out.

At some point I'd dozed off on the couch. My Azizafri family did not need sleep. When they rested it was because they desired to, not out of necessity. Unfortunately for me, my human time clock had not yet adjusted to the Azizafri way. I did find out before sleep stole me away, that there were three mysteries on the table:

Who created the melody that could steal Azizafri light?

How could we stop the melody that stole Azizafri light? Though we were immune (the King and I), it didn't stop other Azizafri from being targeted.

Where had Vivienne gone and where (this question was a two for one) had she procured the celestial dagger?

Apparently, the dagger had clouded everything around her and the grotto. The only way I could get to Kimoni was because one cannot hide another's Moto wa kweli from them. Apparently, our connection was a lifelong homing beacon. I couldn't tell whether that was cool or extremely intrusive. In this case, since it saved Kimoni's life, I'd take it as a win. For Father, trying to get to me was like navigating through a heavy fog, much like the one that clouded my brain just being close to the dagger. Our telepathic communication was not as seamless, but as a creation of his own light, there was no way to block him completely. When I was knocked unconscious, he was able to navigate to me and assist me in getting Ki and I free. It was all a lot to take in. I guess that's how I ended up with my cheek smashed into the Chesterfield with a tiny bit of drool leaking from the corner of my mouth.

It was the drool that started dragging me back to consciousness, then I heard my name. "Kimoni, you must help Malika to remember. If we are to win this impending war, we will need her in her full faculties." It was Auntie Rami's voice. I bet she wouldn't say that crap about killing me in front of my parents. Then I heard Ki's voice, he sounded so sad. "I cannot make her remember that which she does not choose to remember. She holds onto her identity on Earth like a life line. I fear that, he hesitated, I may not be enough." I warred with wanting to get up and comfort him; and not wanting him to know I'd heard him sound so vulnerable.

So soft, I almost missed it, my father whispered, "Kuwa na imani, my son." Have faith, he'd told him. What did that even mean? Sleep was still tugging at my consciousness, and I was on the verge of giving over completely again when I felt strong arms lift me. Without opening my eyes, I knew that it was Moto wangu. His smell was unmistakable. I inhaled slowly and nestled my head into the hard planes of his chest. Soft, yet firm lips pressed to my temple, and I felt as though I were floating. I hoped he was taking me to a nice, soft bed and that he'd stay in it with me. *If you insist*, he said gently into my thoughts. I guess I was too groggy to be embarrassed because I must have fallen asleep again.

When I woke, my prayers had been answered. I was laying on the softest mattress in the world. It curved into my body as I lay snuggled under the blankets. Without thinking I tightened my hands on Kimoni's arms. "Stay," I whispered groggily. My eyes were still closed, but I heard the smile in his voice. "I would like nothing more mpenzi wangu, but it would be...unseemly for me to stay in your chambers like this." Groaning petulantly, I frowned up at him, eyes still tightly closed. "Are we really that old fashioned in Amani? You came to my chambers often enough at your parents' house." I heard a delicate cough, but still couldn't get my eyes to budge open.

Your mother is here in the room with us. That didn't sound quite gentlemanly of me the way you put it, he mentally chastised. At "your mother" my eyes had flown open to meet the amused face of Queen Mother. Suppressing a smile, Queen Mother said politely, "I could leave you two alone. I don't want to intrude." Too mortified to speak, I only looked between her and Ki, finally fully awake and wishing I'd stayed asleep. I'd just met her and here I was looking like a total whore in front of my mother. No, I preferred the term "wanton hussy" to whore. It was like elevated "hoedom." Honestly, I'd only wanted to fall asleep in his arms, Kimoni made me feel so at ease.

Putting me out of my misery, Ki leaned down and kissed me on my forehead, whispering into my mind, *I'll come back after your mother leaves, when no one is around. Wouldn't want to sully the reputation of the King's Heir.* I gave him a scathing look as he turned to leave the room. Then, staring at his backside, I decided I liked to see him go almost as much as I liked to see him coming. Who had that type of muscle in his buttocks? I had the sudden urge to take a bite out of him…then Ki threw me a look over his shoulder that told me I was projecting again. Sighing, I realized I was bound to continue to embarrass myself in front of this man. He left with a final thought that had me pink all the way down to my toes. *Tit for tat Mali. You bite me and I bite you back.*

My mind was in the depths of wanton "hussydom" (yes, I made that word up) when my mother nimbly perched on the edge of the bed. "I will not keep you daughter; I know that you are tired. Before you rest, I am sure you want to bathe. This is your room; it is fully equipped. But…may I finish healing you before you tend to your needs?" I gave her a surprised glance; how did she know I wasn't healed all the way? With a smile, she said, "I know how you walk and move. Your body has been curved in since you've returned as though your chest was paining you. Then touching my ankle, you favored your left ankle when you stood. So much has been going on, I'd imagine you weren't really focusing on it until I brought it up just now." Yep, I was feeling a little bruised and beaten. Looking into her eyes, I knew I loved this woman with an unconditional love that I couldn't quite explain. It was much easier to say that about her than… never mind that was food for later thought. She smiled at me kindly, placing one hand on my shoulder and the other across my forehead. Speaking rapidly in Swahili, I couldn't catch her words, but the sensation was immediate, light and strength swept over me in smooth waves. It left me feeling warm and at peace as she removed her hands a few moments later.

"Are you ok?" I asked her softly. "It seems a little soon for you to be lending me energy that you just regained." Again, that kind smile of hers was unleashed on me. "There is no time here. My full power has been restored and then some. That room you found us in was long ago. I am myself now. Especially with you here safe at home, binti yangu." My daughter. I don't know how long it would take me to get over that phrase. These people seemed to enjoy possessive titles; my lady, my flame, my daughter, my love… but my daughter, binti yangu filled me with the most profound joy. My Earth parents had died so long ago that I'd not known for some time what it was like to be someone's daughter. It felt right.

Patting me gently on the cheek, the Queen stood. "I'll leave you to rest." She leaned in and kissed me on the forehead. "It is your season of light, I see. Though it is almost at an end, you will still feel emotionally sensitive. Makini, careful she warned.

Kimoni is very in love with you. It took him a long time to accept, but once he did, there was no going back. Make sure that you are fully restored before giving in to your desire for him. There are things you must remember first."

Would the freaking blushing never end? I knew what my face looked like at this moment. My fair skin was suffused with a red hue I could not deny. How embarrassing that the Queen Mother whom I'd just met should know that I was basically "in heat." Kill me now. As if sensing my unease, she bid me good night and left quietly.

I soaked in the swimming pool for some time. The tub was big enough to fit six people. I wasn't quite sure you could call it a tub, but I loved it. It made me happy just to be in it and the healing I'd received from my mother gave me a little boost of energy. After I finished enjoying the most luxurious bathtub (if you could call that monstrosity that), I donned a comfortable pair of loose fitting pale pink pajama pants, with a matching V-neck shirt, I trailed out of the beautiful marble bathroom and back towards the four-poster bed that looked straight out of a fairytale. The sheer white curtains were hanging down, and the fireplace that was a staple of every room here blazed bright and beautiful.

As I neared the bed, I was startled to find Kimoni rocking gently in a chair placed near the bed, much like the one he'd pulled over to my bed at his parents' home. He'd washed and changed as well. My eyes slid over him slowly. His pajamas were in much the same fashion as my own, lounge wear, loose fitting pants, and a basic t-shirt, both in a pale blue. For some reason I was momentarily fascinated by his bare feet, for a male they were surprisingly well groomed. While I assessed him, he rocked in the chair peacefully, hands behind his head, one long leg thrown casually across the other. He was studying me under heavy lids, and I was suddenly very aware of my body, in a way that only a handsome man could make you feel. The soft light from his abdomen suffused the room and I felt my own light brighten in response. Suddenly eager to cuddle into his body, I walked over, tugging him from the chair and urging him to climb into the enormous bed with me. We curled into one another, eye to eye, in mirror positions. He had one hand curled under his head and the other resting on my waist. I curved one arm under my own head and rested the other hand on his bicep.

"I'm sorry," I said softly. My statement caused him to stiffen momentarily before he began rubbing soothing circles on my back, making my eyes feel heavy.

"For what Malika?" I closed my eyes for a second, letting his enunciation of my name in that tantalizing accent wash over me, sending tingles down my spine. Taking a deep breath, I said, "For seeming as though I doubted your abilities by denying you the opportunity to go after Vivienne." I knew his eyes were on me, but I didn't want to meet them just yet. He overrode me, stopping his circles on my back to lift my chin, waiting until I opened my lids, so that we were eye to eye again. "You were worried about me. I am happy that you care. Though I wanted to prove myself by going after her and not failing this time, I cannot be angry at you for wanting me near you. It would pain me to be away from you as well."

"Thank you for understanding," I said, snuggling into his chest and inhaling that unique combination of cocoa, jojoba oil and patchouli. "You smell wonderful." I felt his chest move with his laughter and I let my eyes drift shut. "Thank you. But, tell me, why are you thanking me? It is you who saved my life and restored my light. I owe you thanks, and my life." I made a soft tsking sound between my teeth. "You owe me nothing. You have saved my life many times over. Thank you for staying with me Kimoni."

Always. He whispered into my thoughts as I molded myself into him and sank into oblivion.

CHAPTER 15

Dreamwalking, and other dangerous pastimes.

"Malika, you should not be here. It is dangerous."

"I sent you because I know that you know the grotto better than all in that search party. You will find that which needs to be found. But you'll need my connection to it to locate it"

"That begs the point again, you should not be here, it is dangerous."

Her eyes met mine, glittering with silent promise and worry. I smiled at my dearest friend, my sister and personal protector. Look at me! How long had I been in Amani? Already I was on board with all the possessive "my's" these Roho liked to use.

"You are correct. I know the increased danger for someone such as I. That is why I did not follow you here."

Aseema looked at me, her exasperation evident. "Mali this is no time to joke! Go back to the core. Concentrate on Kimoni and you will appear next to him." I only gave her a lazy smile and started walking through the passages of the grotto, feeling the tug of the blade. "I am with Kimoni now; he talks in his sleep you know."

"Yeah, I know, but none of it is coherent. Wait! What do you mean you're with him now? Mali!" She reached for my arm and when her hand passed right through, I smirked in triumph. "Sis, what in the Creator's name is going on?"

"Honestly, I don't know," I said cheerfully. "One minute I was sleeping soundly in Ki's arms. Nothing happened between us! Then I was here in the grotto with you."

For a moment, Aseema was quiet, just staring at me in thought. "Where are the others, Seemie?" Shrugging with zero concern as she said it, "I ditched them. I don't trust Nyoka to scratch him. He always was an oily one. No wonder you're speaking so formally. In your dream state you sound more like yourself." She gave me a side long look and then added, "Of course nothing happened, you're a prude." More like my normal self? Who did I usually sound like?

"That is too bad, my Kaba is one Azizafri that needs to get laid." I jolted at the sound of Rashidi's voice. He stepped forward out of the shadows. I gave him a wary look and Aseema just rolled her eyes. "I knew you were following me binamu, you needn't do so, and watch your mouth with the future leader of Amani." With a noncommittal shrug, Rashidi looked at me, "Hey little princess. Perhaps you should have dressed more appropriately." He covered his eyes in shock. Had I come in my pajamas? I looked down with a start. No. The dream me was in leathers. With a disparaging look in Rashidi's direction I turned my back on him and resumed my conversation with Aseema. "You are tapping into your creative powers without trying. Not to sound full of myself here, but you were apparently worried about me, you knew you should not follow me here, so you created another alternative." Interest peaked, I asked, "What alternative was that?"

Aseema smiled at me fondly. "You sent your mind here and left your body in bed. It's like sending your consciousness into another place. I'd say right now you are dreamwalking, only this is reality, and you are not really here." Waving another hand through my incorporeal person, she tilted her head, studying me approvingly. With a hand in the air, Rashidi interrupted, "How do you know it was you she was worried about? Perhaps it was her favorite Kaba she was concerned about?"

"Favorite?" Aseema asked dubiously.

"Well, it most certainly isn't Nyoka," he said matter of factly. They gave each other a look that was in total agreement. Shaking my head at the absurdity of it all, I focused on what I could understand. The dagger was tugging at my light, pulling me towards it. Somehow the dagger piercing Kimoni's flesh had created a link with his light, thereby creating a link with mine. I wasn't sure how I knew that was the case, but I was as sure that I could find the dagger, as I had been that I could heal the Second Father and then those Anguka in the ballroom. My gut had yet to steer me wrong. Still, how had it been taken while it was hidden inside of Vivienne was the true question? Was she hiding here with the knife? Somehow, I didn't think that was the case. I could feel the dagger, but not her. Why would she remove it from herself, only to leave it here? None of it added up, but following my instincts, had been my saving grace thus far. Well… except for that whole fiasco when I'd run to Steven's house, only to end up being attacked. Never mind, no need to rehash. Focusing intently on the insistent pull, I prayed to their Creator that this luck would hold. "How do you think crazy Vivienne escaped? Her light had been absorbed by the dagger and the dagger into her flesh. How is it that it is still hidden here in this place?"

Rashidi frowned, "I wonder the same. She had the help of the leader Kimoni captured, I'd wager there were more of their numbers hidden here, else why glamour it so well? They had to know a bit because they knew this place was close enough to the core for a base of operations, but far enough away not to be included in the power limits the core holds."

"Agreed," Aseema said, casting Rashidi an approving glance. "Someone could have moved her and stowed her somewhere when they heard our little group enter here. They would be able to use some of their powers here, but not enough to teleport or flit this close to the Core."

"The real question is, why can the little princess now feel the pull of the blade?"

Startled by his words, I stopped in my tracks. "How do you…"

"Well, you are leading us to it, yes?" Rashidi asked softly.

With a sigh I shared my theory. "Kimoni was stabbed with the blade. It formed a connection to his light somehow, and…"

"His light is connected to your light," Rashidi finished cutting me off again. Aseema gave him a look of reproof which I mirrored less severely. "You've forgotten how irritating that can be?" He laughed, full throated and carefree. "I am sorry my dear, you know how fast my brain works, I cannot help but rush people along to the truth I've already established." I met Aseema's eyes and we rolled them in unison before I refocused on the pull of the dagger. We could solve this mystery after we had that dangerous weapon in hand.

So intent was my renewed focus that I didn't even see the blade coming towards me until it had passed fully through my incorporeal flesh and right towards Aseema. My scream of alarm was unwarranted, Aseema deftly sidestepped the swipe of the blade, and Rashidi brought up what looked like a khopesh sword in an arc so rapid that I barely saw the blade before the Anguka fell to the ground. I stared at him in shock and awe, Rashidi was smiling at Aseema smugly. If I knew her, she was pissed about him taking her kill.

"Lead the way mwanamke wangu, looks like Viv sent friends." Rashidi whirled his obsidian blade, flicking the goo from it with a fluid movement and gestured for me to lead the way. Shaking out of my stupor, I moved quickly in front of Aseema, when her hand shot through my incorporeal form and sliced up and out. The Anguka's eyes widened as he slid to the ground, and I swear I could smell the stench and feel the spatter of goo even in my dream walking state.

Stifling a gag of disgust, I tried to lighten the tense situation. "Should I call you Bond? Aseema Bond?" I teased her, picking up my pace as I felt us nearing the location of the item we sought. "I'd take Bond out blindfolded." She said it without inflection as if it were a bygone conclusion that she could easily take James

Bond down. I didn't know I could argue with her there. Maybe she was more of a Wonder Woman? Captain Marvel? I'd have to think about that later. Rashidi chuckled quietly behind us; he'd always been extremely good natured and despite his playful banter, he was exceptionally wise.

"Here," I said pointing. I was filled with a sense of excitement. We were standing in front of a wall of rock similar to all the rest that we'd passed, but I could feel the blade pulsing behind it. I thought Aseema would argue with the apparent roadblock in front of us, but without hesitation, she backed up, spun and kicked out at the rock in a seamless movement. The wall cracked right at the center where I'd felt the item. Rashidi put a hand where my torso would be and mimed pushing me back, then the three of us watched as the rock shards began falling away. Once the dust cleared, she stepped forward with a smile and I said, "James Bond definitely has nothing on you sis." Tossing me a cocky grin, she stepped forward and knelt down to brush away some of the debris, Rashidi joined her. Standing up after a few, she smiled at me with the knife held casually in front of her.

"We always made a good team, Mali." Twirling the knife in a showy manner, Aseema stuck the shining blade in her belt and gave me a head nod. "Go to sleep now, my friend. I'll head back to the castle, give the Father this weapon and we'll decide what to do once you've rested." No, no this wasn't right. That blade should still be inside Vivienne's body. Who would have been able to separate my glamour and take the blade out? Why would they hide it here? Something wasn't right.

Rashidi and Aseema were studying me with twin expressions of impatience. When I met my sister-friend's eyes, not speaking, not even mind to mind, just looking at her, letting her feel my unease she froze in place momentarily. As though we shared a moment of perfect harmony, she moved towards me and stepped into me hugging me lightly, instantly I hugged her back, before stiffening in shock. How did she-? I wasn't really here! Yet her toned arms were around me and I felt the knife slide discreetly, hidden even from Rashidi's view into the back of my waistband. My surprise and suspicion grew as she drew back.

Aseema only smiled and stepped back casually. Looking down at her waistband I noticed she'd glamoured another one of her knives to look like the one she'd hidden on my person. Stockstill, trying to overcome my shock, I watched as she made eye contact with Rashidi and they both turned, making their way through the grotto. For a moment I stood motionless trying to figure out if there was a way to wake myself up, will myself to her side and then teleport us back to the core. By the time I realized that may be outside my current level of power, Aseema was far ahead of me, making her way gracefully through the rocky passageway. It was easy to teleport Kimoni, our lights were connected, other beings may prove to be a challenge. Trailing behind her, Rashidi gave a subtle shake of his head, telling me without words that I needed to leave. Concentrating, I willed myself back to them. Aseema was traveling adeptly through the dark, only pausing to give me a reproving glare. I'd made sure my leathers were adjusted properly to hide the dagger; she needn't worry.

Obviously though, she was irritated that I hadn't left when she asked. I was about to tell them I had a weird feeling when she stopped short and looked around oddly. Rashidi drew his blade again and before I could ask what was wrong, Aseema whispered "Go." Her voice came out in a pained whisper, and I froze in distress. "Seemie?" I reached for her, but she was gone. Right before my eyes. We were talking one minute and the next she was gone. Terror washed over me, looking around frantically for Rashidi, I could see no sign of him or anyone else for that matter. There was no evidence that either one of them had ever been there, I had to wake up!

A thought was all it took, and I was abruptly sitting up in bed. Kimoni immediately sat up next to me. *What's happening?* His eyes were filled with concern as he searched my face. For a moment I couldn't voice what just occurred. I adjusted on the bed, moving to grab whatever was stabbing me in my back. My hands gripped the knife! The blade was in my hand, I looked down at the glowing implement in shock. Ki's eyes followed mine, then widened in alarm. "Mali! How did you-? Where did you-? What happened?" His thoughts came out in a string of questions I couldn't quite keep up with. All I could focus on was the fact that my best friend and Rashidi had gone missing in front of my very eyes. "Kimoni, we have to find Aseema. She's in danger, I know it! We must find her!" With shame in my voice, I said, "Rashidi too…oh, I'm so sorry Lea." He grabbed my shoulders firmly and shook me gently, until my eyes met his. He was half turned toward me in the bed, and I knew I must sound hysterical. I felt slightly hysterical. "Start from the beginning."

"That's just it," I said, fighting the tears that threatened to overcome me. "She didn't have a chance to fight, she was there one minute and gone the next. Then, I-I looked for Rashidi. They were together and then, they were, they were both just gone!" Nodding slowly, Kimoni gently pulled me into his arms. My hands stayed folded in front me, clutching the knife as I laid my head on his chest and fought tears. I couldn't lose her. We'd been through too much. Losing Aseema would be like losing a part of myself. If someone hurt her...no I couldn't think like that. What would I say to Lea though? What would happen if poor, sweet Issa lost her Daddy because of me? No-no I couldn't let that happen, I wouldn't! Focusing my mind on the anger, on the mission, to find my friend and return Rashdi to his wife, I pushed thoughts of panic away. I couldn't afford to break down, they needed me.

Then I felt it. A subtle vibration in the blade. Pulling back from Ki, I glanced down at it, mesmerized by the swirling light flowing through it. My eyes widened...there, it was there! Come on instincts, don't fail me now.

I didn't realize Ki had been speaking until he whispered gently into my thoughts. *We will find Aseema. You must know that she is extremely capable, and we have the dagger. They will be unable to hold her for long if they even have her still. Rashidi, if he is with her, is exceedingly wise and resourceful. They will protect each other.*

Taking a deep breath, as realization dawned, driving through me like a lightning bolt, I leaned away from him and met his eyes. "Will you go with me to find them?" Putting his lips to my ear, he said softly, "Now that I have you back, there is no more letting you go it alone. I am with you always." As heavy as my heart felt in this moment, those words lightened it just the slightest bit. Taking a deep breath, I moved from the circle of his arms. "We better get going then." Moving to get out of the bed and dress, I was surprised, when Ki stopped me with a hand on my arm. "I hate to say this to you, but we cannot leave without letting the King know. He will not be happy about you endangering yourself. I'm sure he'll want to send a contingent of Azizafri with us as well as Nyoka. Not to mention my love, we don't know where they are." I grimaced at the mention of my brother's name. Aseema did not trust him; therefore, I had no interest in allowing him to go on this rescue mission. But Kimoni was right. The King and Queen had the right to know. Though they would not stop me from saving my friend. Especially since I was one of the only people who could save her. Before I'd woken up, I heard a piece of what had made her pause. It was the melody that had stolen my father's light. Only the King and I were immune to it and Aseema was my protector. It was time for me to return the favor. I didn't know how I'd find her; I couldn't even feel her essence anymore but...

COME NOW OR SHE DIES, COME ALONE OR SHE DIES, TELL NO ONE OR SHE DIES! The voice rasped abrasively through my thoughts, causing me to go still and then shiver in derision. Hoping he was lying, I looked down at the blade again, it couldn't fall into their hands. There was no time to explain to anyone; I had to go now. Suddenly I could feel Aseema's light again, very faint, and even fainter than hers, Rashidi. *This must mean that they're hurt.*

The voice came again, less forceful this time, more cunning. They will both be dead if you do not decide quickly, First Daughter. I am allowing you to sense them. Once I block it off again, you will never find them. Not even when your light returns to the skies. Trembling all over, I knew that this disembodied voice spoke the truth. He'd thrown me a glimpse of Aseema and Rashidi, unconscious and bound. This was getting old, I thought as anger began to heat my blood.

Sliding out of the bed and standing with my back to him, mind full of steely resolve, I knew I had to do this, but…With a sad look I turned to Ki, then I created that which I needed. My leathers and weapons covered my body even as I began to will myself to my sister's side.

"Malika, NO," Kimoni roared, lunging for me. But he was too late, and as my body teleported to Aseema's side; my mind, my ears rang with the echo of his anguished words. I prayed to the creator that Aseema, Rashidi, and I would make it back so I could apologize for causing that stark look of fear to pass over his beautiful features. So, I could tell him how much I cared for him. But I couldn't focus on that now; before allowing myself to fully materialize, I sent thoughts to my father, quickly giving him the rundown, hoping he'd send help. Then I willed the dagger to him; it would be safest with the Second Father.

Usually when I thought of being next to someone, I found myself immediately there, but as my light moved toward my captured kin, things suddenly slowed down. Fearing for a moment that somehow my father had stopped me from teleporting, I layered my will with strength, refusing to be deterred. In answer, light slammed into me fiercely. Doubling over as it filled my gut with its beauty and wholeness I crouched over my midsection, arms wrapped around myself as though trying to hold it in. The beautiful colors surging into me were easily identifiable for what they were giving me. Purple light flowed into me, imbuing me with wisdom, black hues filled me with power, strength, and authority. Then an orange color that had me straightening my spine with the bravery it doused me with, lastly blue spread all over me, in shades that had me longingly thinking of Kimoni. The blue simultaneously filled me with a sense of peace and a feeling that I wasn't alone. The light that was all these colors together spread from my abdomen and out through my body, strengthening my limbs and making me feel…invincible.

Not quite what I had in mind, but thanks Dad! I sent the thought quickly and felt his smile. I guess I'd never called him Dad. When in my last-ditch effort, I sent my frantic thoughts to him, I thought he'd wait a bit and send reinforcements. Instead, there was that unbelievable surge of light, power, and peace. Had he sent me some of his power? Trying to direct my thoughts to him to ask, I met a brick wall. I couldn't feel him anymore. Then I tried to direct my thoughts at Kimoni. Nothing.

Materializing at my destination, I looked around absorbing my dark, and deserted surroundings. Standing tall and proud, arms braced at my sides, I readied myself for battle. Unfortunately, there was no one around to battle and I mean no one. I couldn't even feel Aseema or Rashidi anymore…something was terribly wrong.

EPILOGUE

What a lovely way to burn...

"**L**ord Prince, I have returned."

Vivienne gave a shallow bow in his direction, feeling the effects of his incubus spirit tremble through her, even as she grieved her fallen husband. She would not rest until Malika paid for Rodericks's death. Though she was responsible for his captivity, she would not have wanted for his death…in fact she'd held onto hope that he'd come over to her way of seeing things. Still, with all of that plaguing her mind, the draw of the Incubus Prince of Hell standing before her was causing her body to speak up in ways her mind could not abate.

"You've done well." Vivienne's head popped up from its submissive bow in surprise. Done well? They'd failed. She had all but made her peace with the fact that returning here, she would die and be reunited with Roderick.

"You seem surprised. Things did not go according to your plan, but they are going perfectly according to mine." He turned, smiling at her in a way that both weakened her knees in lust and caused her to tremble in fear. It was a heady mix and part of her wanted to just succumb to it to stop feeling the grief threatening to drown her.

"Ahhh, my deceptive little vixen is in pain. Come, let your Prince comfort you." Without thought her feet started leading her to his side. One moment they'd been in his office, the next in a lush bedroom in dark, bold tones. Suddenly her skin felt hot and flushed. Part of her struggled with this pull and the other part of her just didn't care.

"The need for vengeance wafting from you is intoxicating my dear. Mix that with your fear and hunger…" He paused, licking his lips sensually, "It makes me want to feast on your flesh." Walking a tight circle around her, he ran impossibly hot fingertips over her bare shoulders, assessing her lush curves. Stopping behind her, his body a hair's breadth away from hers, he leaned down, whispering into her ear, "I can make your pain go away. Would you like that?" Unable to stop herself, Vivienne nodded. "Of course, you would. Shall I make you…forget?" His tongue shot out tracing over her earlobe and down to the tender flesh at her neck.

Shivering, she knew without a shadow of a doubt that this dark being could never, ever make her forget her Moto wa kweli. But he could lead her to her vengeance. Malika had slipped through her grasp once. She probably thought she'd won, not knowing what deadly gifts Vivienne had left behind. Smiling, she reveled in the knowledge that there would be no rest until her appetite for vengeance was filled. She would not rest until the Heir was dead.

Splaying a hand over her abdomen and pulling her in tight to his pelvis, the Prince snuggled into her neck, a shiver running over him as he inhaled her deeply. "Oooh that is rich. Your need to kill the Heir is so pungent and tantalizing. Tell me, how will you do it? How will you end her light?"

Vivienne leaned back into him, pressing her buttocks against his hard body and rested her head against him. Letting her eyes drift closed, she spoke softly. "I'll take a knife and cut that celestial body of hers. Carve her up like some morbid piece of artwork. I want her lover to watch as I slice her pretty face into ribbons, take her beauty before I destroy her celestial body and ingest her light."

The Dark Prince groaned, one hand sliding up to her throat and the other sliding down to her core. Vivienne arched into him, moaning softly, surrendering to the lure of vengeance, focusing on her impending release. Deep down she knew that in the end she'd only feel shame and regret, but it was worth it for the few moments of respite this liaison would lend her. Continuing to stroke her gently with those fiery fingertips, he whispered, "I'll need more than moments I'm afraid. The passions of an Incubus run deep, and I haven't had an Azizafri in my bed in ages. I think I'd like to take my time with you. Your deviant tendencies are... mouthwatering."

Vivienne blinked and her body was on silken sheets; completely naked, her eyes widened in alarm. Then he appeared over her, and all thought fled. Coherent thought was nigh impossible with the heat of his bare body against hers. Trying anyway, she asked breathlessly, "I thought we were going to discuss the next phase of the plan first. My next assignment?" He smirked at her, as if sensing her hesitation. Grinding into her and scattering her thoughts, he said laughingly, "I have never been of the mind that one should not mix business with pleasure. In fact, around these parts, we are very firm on the policy, business and pleasure go hand in hand." He was punctuating his words with flicks of his fingers, well placed strokes of tongue and hip movements that had Vivienne rapidly losing any desire to speak further. But it seemed that the Prince was as adept at mixing business with pleasure as he said, because he continued to speak while working his dark magic.

"Your adversary is currently being held captive along with her friends. My ally will have first crack at her. If he is unable to break the Lady Heir, then it will be my turn to tempt her in the fires of the pit. She will break. When she does, it will devastate the Second Father, opening our way for attack. He will be to stricken with grief to overcome us. As my gift to you…you can be the one who finally ends her light."

Vivienne came undone, loving and hating how her body had responded and given in to his. Even at the height of her passion, she felt the grief and remorse of what she'd done and what she would do. Fighting back tears, she knew he would scorn, she tightened her grip around him, urging him on. As he had his fill, she focused on her ultimate goal. The death of Malika and the fall of Mahali Pa Amani. If she could have no peace, neither would any of them.

"That's it," he urged, as though hearing her thoughts. "Surrender to the call for chaos, no peace for the Azizafri. You are a destroyer now, my pet, *yesssss*." He reminded Vivienne of a serpent. But she was unable to give in to that thought for too long. The skill of the incubus was undeniable, and she went tumbling down that pit which was a combination of pleasure and despair over and over again. After an eternity in his heated embrace, she called out his name hoarsely, both horrified and awed as the voices of the pit raised up in praise of their Dark Prince, responding in joy to the sound of his name, cried out from her lips. If one was to succumb to the darkness, then this was a lovely wretched way to burn.